THE
RED ROOM

PRAISE FOR MARK DAWSON

"A literary sensation."

—*The Daily Telegraph*

"Absolutely brilliant."

—*The Daily Mail*

"Atticus Priest will be the star of many future novels."

—*Richard Madeley*

"Nerve-shreddingly tense. Utterly addictive."

— *MJ Arlidge*

"Dawson writes the kind of thrillers I love. Non-stop, grab-you-by-the-throat tales of doing the right thing no matter the odds. Simply excellent."

—*Brett Battles*

"A terrific, fast-paced read. Mark Dawson knows how to tell a great story."

—*Scott Mariani*

"Mark Dawson has all the skills. A great thriller writer on the top of his game."

—*Steve Cavanagh*

MORE THAN 18,000 FIVE STAR AMAZON REVIEWS

"Fast paced and a wonderful read."

"Brilliantly written - Dawson's best yet."

"Totally hooked now."

"Unbelievable!"

"Made me fall in love with reading again."

"Cannot get enough of these books."

"Wow - what a read."

"Brilliant, brilliant, brilliant!"

MARK DAWSON
THE RED ROOM

First published in 2023 by Unputdownable Limite

Copyright © Unputdownable Limited, 2020

Mark Dawson has asserted his moral right to be
identified as the author of this Work in accordance with
the Copyright Designs and Patents Act 1988.

This book is a work of fiction. Names, characters, businesses,
organisations, events, and incidents are either the product of the author's
imagination or are used in a fictitious manner. Any resemblance to actual
persons, living or dead, or to actual events, is entirely coincidental. While
real places may be mentioned or described for purposes of creating
a realistic setting, their inclusion is intended purely to enhance the
narrative and should not be interpreted as factual or as representing
actual events, individuals, or entities associated with those locations.

The author and publisher have made every effort to ensure
that this book does not contain defamatory material or invade
the privacy of any individual, living or deceased. Any errors
or unintended similarities to real persons, organisations,
or events are purely coincidental and unintentional.

The views and opinions expressed in this book are those
of fictional characters and do not reflect the views,
opinions, or beliefs of the author or publisher.

All rights reserved. No part of this publication may be reproduced,
stored in a retrieval system, or transmitted in any form, or by any means,
electronically, mechanical, photocopying, recording, or otherwise,
without the prior permission of the copyright owners and the publishers.

A CIP catalogue of record for this book is
available from the British Library.

Paperback ISBN: 978-1-0687754-3-7

Typeset by Riverside Publishing Solutions Ltd (UK)
Printed and bound by CPI Group (UK), Ltd., Croydon, CR0 4YY.

ALSO BY MARK DAWSON

In The Atticus Priest Series

The House in the Woods
A Place to Bury Strangers
The Red Room
All the Devils are Here
The Inheritance

In The John Milton Series

The Cleaner
Saint Death
The Driver
Ghosts
The Sword of God
Salvation Row
Headhunters
The Ninth Step
The Jungle
Blackout
The Alamo
Redeemer
Sleepers
Twelve Days
Bright Lights
The Man Who Never Was
Killa City
Ronin
Never Let Me Down Again
Bulletproof
Uppercut
Bloodlands
The Vulture
The Butcher

In The Beatrix Rose Series

In Cold Blood
Blood Moon Rising
Blood and Roses
The Dragon and the Ghost
Tempest
Phoenix

In The Isabella Rose Series

The Angel
The Asset
The Agent
The Assassin
The Avenger
Pretty Face

In The Charlie Cooper Series

Sandstorm
The Chameleon
Blood Brothers
Dead of Winter
Code Blue
North Star
Collateral
Leverage
Burnout

PART 1

Monday

CHAPTER 1

The glass roof of the refectory reverberated with the drumming of the rain as the clouds opened and thunder boomed overhead. Clive Mouton paid for his breakfast and took his tray to the table in the corner he preferred. He removed his green and yellow sash and folded it neatly, leaving it on the seat next to him. He had a bacon bloomer, and the last thing he wanted to do was to spill ketchup onto the sash; also, it marked him out as a guide, and it wasn't unheard of for visitors to ask him questions while he was eating. He was an enthusiastic member of the volunteer team at the cathedral, but he liked to spend the half hour he took before he started by checking his social media accounts to see the updates from his daughter and grandchildren. He was distracted from his phone today by the storm. A skein of lightning split across the sky, thunder boomed, and the rain kept thudding down, a deluge that raced down the slope of the glass. The gutters had quickly overflowed, and now they spilled the water down the windows in a sudden wash. The southwest of the country had seen an enormous amount of rain since Christmas with the result that several of the five rivers that converged on Salisbury—including the Avon—

had burst their banks. The water meadows were full, and some of the lower-lying villages had flooded.

The refectory served the cathedral and had been built in the space between the nave and the cloisters, replacing the unsightly 1970s prefabricated buildings that had once stood here. Mouton had been head of history at the nearby Chafyn Grove school and had always had a keen interest in his subject. He had studied the cathedral and taught his students about it; volunteering to show tourists around the building was an obvious way for him to fill the spare hours of his retirement. He always finished his tours by taking his guests to the refectory, explaining how it stood on the site of the old plumbery the cathedral's masons would once have used to repair the leadwork on the roof. Mouton would show them how the design had incorporated the ancient buttresses of the cloisters, and then he would point up, through the modern glass and steel roof, to the glorious view of the tower and spire. He was one of the handful of guides who was allowed to conduct tours of the tower itself, and showing visitors the spectacle from the ground just after they had descended the three hundred and thirty-two steps from the top was an excellent way to bring the tour to a close.

He looked up now and noted how the pale stone contrasted against the dark grey clouds. The forecast had been for more storms today, and it hadn't been wrong; dawn had broken with the sky an angry purple, and it had quickly grown gloomier and more ominous. The spire stood proud against the fast-moving clouds like the prow of a ship cutting through furious waves.

"Morning, Clive."

Mouton looked up and saw that the dean had stopped at his table. "Morning."

"What a start to the day."

"It's supposed to rain all week," Mouton said. "I was listening to the radio in the car."

"They're saying it's what's left of Hurricane Louise."

"As if we haven't had enough. You know the Avon's burst its banks? Britford's flooded. I've got friends there. The river's going right through the middle of it."

"Same with the Ebble. Berwick St. John and Bowerchalke look like they might flood. Stoke Farthing, too."

Mouton nodded. The Met Office was saying that a jet stream strengthened by the warm tropical air pushed northwards by Louise would push low pressure across the country, and that it wasn't likely to move for days.

The dean pointed up at the tower. "You know who I feel sorry for? Apart from anyone in those villages? David."

"No. Seriously? He'll still do it today?"

"Just saw him. He's only got another week to go, and then he's done. And he's stubborn as a goat."

Mouton looked up again at the tower. David Campbell—the cathedral's clerk of works—was a keen amateur photographer and had been undertaking a fundraising project where he took a photograph from the same parapet of the cathedral tower every day for a year. An exhibition was planned for when the project was completed. A lot of money had been raised—over fifty thousand pounds—and it had been earmarked for the restoration of the statuary of the West Front of the cathedral. Campbell had been blogging about it, too, posting daily pictures and his reflections as he looked out over the city from the same vantage point. Mouton had been following the blog and knew the dean was right; Campbell's stubbornness was legendary. He had continued with the project through autumn winds that registered at more than a hundred miles an hour on the anemometer atop the spire, and then again through the snows in February; he wouldn't let today's rain stop him and would probably see the storm as a perfect opportunity to take a particularly striking image.

They both looked up to the parapet. "He's going to get soaked," Mouton said.

"Rather him than me."

The dean wished Mouton a good day and took his coffee into the gift shop. Mouton tucked a napkin into his collar. He looked up again as another clap of thunder rumbled overhead. Rainwater swept down the camber of the glass, a ripple that passed through his view of the tower and the spire. Another fork of lightning spread out across the sky as he noticed something up at the juncture where the tower ended and the spire began.

Movement.

A dark blur against the stone.

It took him a moment to realise what it was.

A person.

Arms and legs flailing.

Falling down the side of the tower.

He watched for a second and then another.

The body caught against the stone, flipped into a spin and then bounced off a buttress. It spun again, head over heels, limbs flailing, and then disappeared.

Mouton heard the muffled thud of impact as it hit the ground.

He froze, slacked-jawed with confusion and not sure what he was supposed to do. The café was quiet for a moment, the silence interrupted by the sound of a dropped tray and then, finally, the first scream.

CHAPTER 2

"Come on," Mackenzie Jones said. "We need to get in the car or we're going to be late."

She was trying as hard as she could to keep a sunny temperament despite the challenges that two tired and irritable children were presenting. It had been her weekend to have the two of them and, despite the occasional argument, they had been on their best behaviour and a pleasure to be with. Mack had taken them to enjoy the rides at Paulton's Park on Saturday and then to the cinema to see the latest Pixar movie, followed by a visit to the city and lunch at Nando's on Sunday. They had gone to bed much later than would have been the case had they been staying with Mack's estranged husband, Andy, but now—after allowing them to stay up until ten for a midnight feast—she was paying the price. It had been difficult to get them out of bed, and their truculence looked like it was permanent, despite Mack's threats of a trip to the headmaster's study should they be late.

"Daddy never shouts at us," pouted Daisy.

Mack was about to retort that perhaps they should stay with Daddy, then, but bit her tongue. Andy's constant exhortations that she needed to be more patient with them hadn't helped their relationship as it entered its terminal phase, and she couldn't help but imagine his version of the morning routine—beatific smiles and "pleases" and "thank yous," whereas all she received were exasperated frowns and grunts, and that was if she was lucky.

Thinking of Andy brought her back to what he had said on Friday night, just after dropping the kids off. He had admitted he was in a relationship with a woman from work and that the two of them were thinking about moving in together. Mack had long since suspected that they had been more than just colleagues, and, keeping her voice down for fear of upsetting the children, had asked him how long it had been going on. Andy had confessed that he had been seeing her for six months, their relationship starting when he and Mack had still been together. It would have been the height of hypocrisy for Mack to criticise him for that given her own dalliance with Atticus Priest, but, as she had lain in bed that night thinking about what he had said, she found that it made her feel a little better about what had happened. She had convinced herself that the end of the marriage was all her fault, but that wasn't fair. They had both been miserable. Perhaps, if they had been more honest with each other, they might have been able to emerge from the wreckage of their union with a better chance of staying on good terms. That seemed like a lost cause now.

Mack knelt and helped Sebastian as he struggled to tie his laces. "All right," she said with a smile. "Let's get into the car and off we go."

***

Mack navigated the knot of traffic as parents deposited their kids at school, waited until Sebastian and Daisy were safely in the playground, and then repeated the feat as she drove slowly and carefully back toward town. She hadn't had time for her morning coffee and decided to stop and try the café that had opened at Parkwood gym on the London Road. She left the car outside the gym, and, sheltering from the rain beneath Daisy's Peppa Pig umbrella, she hurried inside. She bought a coffee and a pastry to go and was making her way back to the car when she felt the vibration of her phone in her pocket. She climbed back into the driver's seat, rested the coffee on the dashboard, wiped her sugary fingers against her trousers, and took out the phone.

It was Robbie Best. "Good morning."

"You might want to hold on before you say that, boss."

She sipped her coffee. "What's happened?"

"We've got a death. A bad one."

She put the cup back on the dashboard. "Go on."

"It's at the cathedral. The clerk of the works was up in the tower, and he fell off."

"Jesus." She paused, allowing that to sink in. "*Jesus.*"

"I'm there now. He fell into the space at the side of the refectory. I'll be honest—he's made a right mess. I think you'd better get down here."

Best was right: a death *that* macabre had the makings of a story that could get picked up nationally, and was something that she would need to supervise herself.

"Secure the scene," she said. "I'm on my way."

CHAPTER 3

"Bandit!" Atticus yelled. "*Bandit!*"

The dog raced away, ignoring Atticus's forlorn attempt to call him to heel. The two of them had gone up to Old Sarum, the ancient settlement that had once been the site of Salisbury itself. It had been defended by way of a motte-and-bailey castle, and the large mound of earthworks remained. It was one of their favourite spots for a walk. Bandit had sprinted away, and Atticus watched as he launched himself down into what was left of the old cathedral. Atticus jumped down into the foundations and jogged over to where the dog was standing over what looked like a rabbit hole.

"What was it, boy? You see a rabbit?"

The dog stood in the classic pose of the breed: one foreleg raised, snout pointing down. Atticus scrubbed the back of his head, clipped the lead to the ring on his collar and gave him a biscuit. He munched it happily and then looked up for another.

"I don't think so," Atticus said. "You only get two biscuits when you listen."

The dog stared up at him plaintively and, his resolve melting, Atticus tossed him a second treat. Bandit caught it in his mouth and wagged his tail happily as he crunched down on it.

Atticus led the way out of the foundations and back toward the monument. The rain was still lashing down, but Atticus was wearing his waterproofs, and Bandit didn't care. Atticus didn't care, either; it had been a good few weeks, and he had been happier than he could remember for months.

His professional reputation had been rehabilitated by two cases that had both received national attention. The first had involved his piercing of the veil surrounding the death of the Mallender family at their house in Grovely Woods. The second, trumping even the first, had seen him solve the mystery of the bodies that had been found in the graveyard of a church in Imber, the village in the middle of Salisbury Plain that had been abandoned to the army. Atticus had been mentioned on the television and radio and had been interviewed in national newspapers. He had been shrewd in anticipating the publicity and had made sure that he was able to take advantage of it; there had been a flood of enquiries for his assistance and, after quickly filling his own diary, he had cultivated relationships with ex-police officers who were striking out on their own as private investigators in Andover and Devizes. Atticus passed them the cases for which he had no interest in return for healthy finder's fees.

The Imber investigation had had other consequences, too. Atticus's time had also been taken up by working with the police in trying to solve the murder of Richard Miller, the sitting MP for Salisbury. Miller had been released pending his trial for an incident that took place while he was an officer in the army forty years ago. Miller had been in Londonderry and had been implicated in the deaths of two Irish locals. That case had also involved Alfred Burns—the paedophile who had returned to Salisbury and whom Atticus had been pursuing for months—and James York. Miller had admitted that he had stolen from the Irish, but pleaded ignorance as to the murders and said that Burns and York had been responsible. The Crown Prosecution Service had determined that there was insufficient evidence to charge Miller for murder and had limited their prosecution of him to the thefts to which he had confessed.

But the crimes of York and Burns went deeper than that. York had been questioned about the bodies of five teenage girls found at the Methodist chapel at Imber and had admitted that he and Burns had been involved in their deaths. York had confessed that the two of them had been guilty of kidnapping, abusing and then murdering teenagers that Burns had selected from those he worked with as part of a council scheme for disadvantaged youngsters.

Burns—chased out of the country by Atticus's investigation of him—had then blackmailed both York and Miller for the money he needed to maintain his lifestyle. York admitted that he had killed Burns when he realised that the blackmail would never end. York made his confession and then took his own life in his cell. It was discovered later that he had been suffering from terminal cancer.

Miller had been questioned and reported that Burns had been blackmailing him about the Londonderry incident. Atticus had doubted then that the thefts were the extent of his involvement, and his suspicions had been confirmed by Miller's subsequent murder. Atticus had found his body in the back of a car outside his office after a tip-off by someone he knew only as Jack_of_Hearts, his opponent in games of online chess who knew more about Atticus than ought to have been possible.

The affair was complicated, and, while Atticus had made progress in untangling some of it, he knew that Miller and York had lied to him about the extent of their culpability. All three men were dead, but that wasn't good enough for Atticus. His certainty that there were depths to their conspiracy that had yet to be plumbed irritated him beyond measure. He had never been able to leave a puzzle unsolved, and that—together with fear that there were more victims to discover—had seen him working long into the nights to try to discover new angles that might help him understand how deep things *really* went.

Bandit cocked his head to one side, his tongue lolling out of his mouth.

"What?"

The dog picked up a stick and dropped it at Atticus's feet.

"No time for that. We need to get back to the office."

Atticus had a busy day ahead of him. He had an appointment to see the senior officer who had been sent down from London to review the stalled investigation into Miller's death, and then a potential new client had arranged to come into the office to discuss the work that she was interested in giving him.

Atticus tried to set off, but the dog pulled against him.

"Come on, mutt."

Bandit growled at him.

Atticus reached into his pocket and took out another biscuit. "I'll make it worth your while."

The dog eyed the biscuit, licked his lips, and then relented. Atticus set off to the car before he could change his mind.

CHAPTER 4

Mack drove slowly through the High Street Gate and into the Cathedral Close. It was just before nine, and the narrow road beyond the gate was empty, yet to be choked by the tourists who would arrive in their tour buses later. The rain ran along the gutters and pooled around drains that had long since taken all the water they could manage. An inch of water spread across the stone from one side to the other. Mack rolled through the flood to the hut where the attendants checked the credentials of those who wanted to continue deeper into the Close. The guard stayed in the shelter of the hut and indicated that she should lower the window.

"Morning," she called out. "DCI Jones."

She took the leather wallet that held her warrant card and let it fall open so that the man could see it.

"Bloody awful start to the day," the man called back.

"You see anything?"

"I was in here, reading the paper. Only found out when the ambulance came, but a fat lot of good that would've done him."

"You know him?"

The man nodded. "David Campbell—the clerk of works. Been here for years—almost as long as me. Nice bloke."

"Thank you. Where should I park?"

The man pointed to a row of empty spaces to the right of the hut. "Anywhere over there."

Mack backed into the space and killed the engine. The rain hadn't let up at all, but all she had to shelter herself from it was the bright pink umbrella. She certainly couldn't use that, so she grabbed a copy of the *Times* from last week that she had chucked on the back seat and used that as a makeshift shield. She hurried across the grounds toward the cathedral's main door. She had been here with Atticus last week to exercise Bandit before they went back to his place. She hadn't seen him over the weekend—she wasn't quite ready to introduce him to her kids—but he had never been far from her thoughts.

Vernon Edwards, one of the uniformed constables who worked at Bourne Hill station, was standing in the doorway at the side of the cathedral that opened onto the cloisters.

He was pale. "Ma'am."

"You all right?"

"It's not pleasant. I was close to bringing up my breakfast."

"Where's Robbie?"

He pointed into the foyer beyond the main entrance to the cathedral. Mack saw that Best was waiting next to the cashier's desk.

"Keep everyone out until we've got a handle on it."

"Will do."

She stepped around Edwards and went into the foyer. Best was speaking to a member of the cathedral staff. He saw Mack and turned as she approached.

"Morning, boss."

She looked at the man to whom Best had been speaking. "I'm DCI Mackenzie Jones."

"Kingsley Lamb," he said. "I'm the dean."

Mack put out her hand and shook Lamb's.

"It's a dreadful morning," Lamb said. "Absolutely dreadful."

"The dean has closed the cathedral," Best said.

Lamb nodded. "We can't possibly open today."

"No," Mack said. "We'll need to have a good look around, too."

"Of course. It'll be obvious, though, surely? What happened, I mean?"

"Hard to say until we've been able to examine everything. The man who fell—the clerk of the works?"

"David Campbell."

"What can you tell me about him?"

"I've been here for ten years, but he's worked here for longer. More than thirty. Incredibly helpful to me when I was settling in. *Incredibly*. He knew everything about the cathedral. If I ever had a problem with the building, he was always the one to go to. Just a really good man. I can't *begin* to tell you how devastating this will be for everyone who works here. He was very popular. And goodness knows how awful this'll be for his family."

"Thank you. I'd better take a look." She turned to Best. "Where do we need to go?"

Best pointed. "There's a space between the refectory and the tower. He landed in there."

"Any witnesses?"

"Three. I've got them in the Chapter House."

"I was in the gift shop when it happened," the dean said. "I didn't see anything, but I heard the sound when… when…"

"Of course," Mack said. "Thank you. Do you think you could go to the Chapter House with the others? I'll want to talk to you once I've seen the body."

"Of course."

Mack turned to Best and indicated that he should lead on. They went through the gift shop, passed between the racks of trinkets and knick-knacks that the cathedral flogged to tourists with more money than sense, and went into the refectory. The glass ceiling overhead offered a spectacular view of the spire and the storm.

There was a door at the end of the café. They went through it and emerged on the narrow grassy margin that separated the walls of the cathedral from the refectory. The body of a man was sprawled face down across the ground, his head propped up at an unnatural angle against the stone and with his arms and legs spread wide. He was facing away from them. The rain streamed down onto them, living and dead alike, and a steady curtain fell down the wall from where a blocked gutter had overflowed. Mack abandoned the sodden newspaper and knelt next to the body. She saw that Campbell's right leg had been bent backwards beneath him, both arms were broken and that the hair on the back of his head was matted with blood.

"You weren't kidding," she said.

"Fyfe is on the way, but… well, cause of death is pretty bloody obvious."

She looked up and blinked through the rain at the tower and the spire and felt an emptiness in her gut. She had never been great with heights, and, as a child, she had found it difficult to stop imagining what it would feel like to fall off something tall.

She stepped back from the body. "What do we know about him?"

"Sixty-three years old, father of three, lived in Winterslow. Worked here all his professional life—stonemason out of college and then climbed the ladder." He paused, thinking about what he had just said. "Pun not intended. He's raised thousands for the cathedral over the years. This project was on course to make six figures."

"What project?"

"He was taking photos from the same parapet every day for a year. He called it 'A Year in the Life.' There was supposed to be an exhibition once he was done. He was raising money for the cathedral. The dean told me about it."

"I remember. I read about it in the *Journal*."

"There's a blog on the cathedral's website."

"Which parapet was it?"

"East."

"Was he up there on his own?"

"Think so."

"CCTV?"

"Plenty in the cathedral but nothing up there."

"Is it secured?"

"Yes. Yaxley's up there."

She looked down at the mangled body one more time and was grateful that she hadn't had time to finish the pastry. She had seen plenty of dead bodies over the course of her career in the police, but this one was near the top of the list when it came to gruesomeness.

"I'd better go and have a word with the witnesses."

CHAPTER 5

Atticus had been sitting in the waiting area for twenty minutes. Mack had told him that he needed to be on time, that his usual lackadaisical approach to punctuality would be unwise for this particular appointment, and that he should be on his best behaviour.

And for once, he had listened to her.

Detective Chief Superintendent Lee Murphy had been sent by the Metropolitan Police to oversee the investigation into Richard Miller's murder. Murphy worked in counterterrorism and, given that Miller had been an MP, he had been tasked with ruling out terrorism as a motive. Atticus knew that politics had nothing to do with why Miller had been killed, but realised there would be all manner of boxes that needed to be ticked when the victim was this high profile.

DCS Murphy had asked to see Atticus at nine thirty and, with Mack's advice fresh in his mind, he had arrived five minutes early. He was wearing his suit and shirt, freshly laundered at the dry-cleaner's in Waitrose, and drummed into himself the advice that Mack had given him: be polite, don't show off, don't let Murphy know what you really think of him.

All those things would be difficult, but he was going to do his best.

Atticus had just looked at his watch when the door to the interview room opened. A man stepped out into the corridor, saw Atticus and made his way over to him.

"Mr. Priest?"

"That's right."

"I'm DCS Lee Murphy."

Murphy put out his hand, and Atticus shook it. He was dressed in a navy-blue suit with a white shirt and a blue and white striped tie. He was bald, with a fuzz of hair to each side of his head that had evidently just been trimmed. He wore glasses with rectangular frames, his eyes were small, his nose was large, and his top lip curled up just a little in such a way as to give him an unfortunate and permanent sneer.

"Sorry for keeping you. Appreciate you coming over. Shall we get cracking?"

He gestured to the open door.

Atticus stood. "How long will you need?"

"Depends on what you have to say. I've spoken to everyone else, but I thought I'd save you until last. Miller's body was found outside your office, after all. You'll definitely have the most interesting perspective on all this, and I don't want to hurry. Please—come inside, and we can get started."

CHAPTER 6

Best led the way to the east walk of the cloisters and then into the Chapter House. John Fulbright, a uniformed constable from the station, had been posted in the vestibule to keep an eye on the witnesses. He nodded to Mack and Best and then held the door open for them. The octagonal building beyond was used to display the cathedral's copy of the Magna Carta; Mack had brought the kids here and had tried—and failed— to interest them in the document that was protected behind thick Perspex. Today, though, her attention was taken by the three people who were sitting and standing inside: one woman, who was dressed in the black uniform of the refectory waiting staff, and two men, one of whom wore chef's whites, while the other wore the green and yellow sash of a cathedral guide.

"Where's the dean?" she asked Fulbright.

"He said he had to take a call."

Mack nodded and turned her attention back to the two men and the woman.

"Who got the best look?"

Best pointed to the man with the green sash. "Him."

"I've seen him before," Mack said. "What's his name?"

Best opened his notebook. "Clive Mouton."

The name was familiar, too, and, as Mack looked over at the old man, she realised why: he had been a teacher at the school that she and Andy had been considering when they were looking for somewhere to send the kids.

She made her way across the room to where he was standing. "Mr. Mouton," she said. "I'm DCI Mackenzie Jones." She offered her hand, and he took it. "Do you remember me?"

"Have we met?"

"I came for a visit to the school."

He smiled. "Just before I retired. I remember. You had two children? Daisy and…"

"Daisy and Sebastian. That's right. You've got an excellent memory."

"You didn't put them with us, did you?"

"We decided we couldn't really afford it."

"Shame. Where did you send them?"

"Greentrees."

"Good school," he said. "Are they doing well?"

"Very, thanks." She indicated behind her in the direction of the refectory. "DI Best said you saw what happened?"

"I'm not sure I'd go that far."

"Tell me what you saw."

"I was having my breakfast. The rain was coming down hard, and it was hard to see much through it. I caught a glimpse of him falling and heard the noise when he hit the ground." He paused. "It's horrible. Poor man."

"Did you know him?"

"Of course. Everyone did. He *lived* for the cathedral. He told me once that he decided he was going to work here when he was a boy. Do you live in Salisbury?"

"I do."

"So you know what it's like—you look up and see the spire twenty times a day, the same as everyone else. I remember he told me once how his lifetime ambition was to climb to the top. He did it, too. Look on YouTube—he videoed himself going up to change the anemometer last year."

"That wouldn't be for me."

"Me neither. It's bloody high. I'm one of the guides who take people up the tower. That's more than high enough for me."

"What was he like as a person?"

"Larger than life. I don't know anyone who'd have a bad word to say about him."

"Could he have been depressed?"

"Why?" He frowned, and then, as he realised what Mack was implying, he shook his head vigorously. "Oh. You think he might've jumped." He shook his head again. "I can't see that at all."

"We have to look at all the possibilities. An accident is possible, but I think it's unlikely if all he was doing was taking photographs. I've been up to the tower, and the walls up there are quite high, aren't they?"

"The railings come up to here," he said, holding his hand up to the top of his chest.

"So it would be difficult to fall."

He nodded. "I see what you mean. Yes—you're right. He'd have to climb on top of them."

"Anything to make you think he might have done that?"

"I haven't spoken to him for a while. I'm probably not the person to ask."

Mack smiled. "Thank you, Mr. Mouton. You've been very helpful."

Mack asked Best to introduce her to the others, and she spoke to them in turn. The woman worked behind the counter and said that she had been looking down at the till when she heard Campbell hitting the ground. The man was a chef and explained that he had been preparing one of the soups for the lunchtime serving; he had been looking up and saw something fall, but, like it had with Mouton, the rain on the glass roof had made it impossible to make out any detail. He was pale and seemed to have taken what had happened worse than either of the other two; Mack had finished her gentle questions when he held up a hand, swallowed and stumbled for the door. He had only just made it into the cloisters when she heard him retching and then the splatter of vomit on the ground.

Mack went back to where Best was waiting for her.

"I'd better go up and have a look."

"I'll come up with you," he said. "I know the way."

CHAPTER 7

Murphy led the way into the room and indicated that Atticus should take one of the two chairs on the side of the desk. He did, undoing the button of his jacket and sitting down.

Murphy pointed to a jug and two cups that sat on the desk. "Coffee?"

"Please."

He looked around as Murphy busied himself with the drinks. Murphy had evidently taken this room as his base. The shelves to the right of the desk had been filled with ring binders arranged alphabetically; the names on the sides referred to people who had been involved in the twin investigations: the murders at Imber and the murder of Miller. He saw ring binders for Alfred Burns and James York and two labelled with Richard Miller's name. Others were labelled with the names of witnesses who had been interviewed during the investigations. Another—to Atticus's surprise and discomfort—bore his name. The desk was neat and tidy, with a notebook next to a closed laptop and a pen laid on top of it. Atticus noticed that everything had been lined up in perfect geometrical symmetry: the laptop, the notebook and the pen were all parallel to one another. It spoke to a punctiliousness that Atticus would bear in mind during the interview.

Murphy handed Atticus one of the two mugs of coffee and took the second around to the other side of the desk. He pulled out his chair and sat down. "Thank you for coming in, Mr. Priest."

Atticus manufactured an easy smile. "Happy to help."

"I'm glad to hear that. Like I said—you're of special interest to this review. You're the only person who's had any contact with the suspect in Mr. Miller's death."

"It seems so."

Murphy sipped his coffee. "Do you know how long I've been in Salisbury?"

"A month?"

"Just over. Chief Constable Beckton called my guv'nor three days after Miller's body was found. The two of them decided that they'd give Wiltshire a free run at it for the first week to see what they could turn up and, depending on progress, I'd bring my team down to see if we could lend a hand. You know what they found in the first week?"

"I don't know," Atticus said.

"Jack shit, Mr. Priest. They didn't find anything. Between you, me and the gatepost, I wanted to get down here straight away. You know how it is—the first day or two of any investigation is always the most important. The golden hours. The longer you leave it, the trickier it gets. Evidence is destroyed. Recollections fade. The trail goes cold. That's what's happened here—you had the murder of an MP, they wasted time, the trail went *very* cold very fast, and any advantage we might have had by getting off our arses and acting quickly was lost."

"I think that's a little unfair."

"Do you?"

"I do. They got a team on it quickly and did everything that you'd expect."

"What are you basing that on?"

"Sorry?"

"Your impression that the investigation went as it should—I'm just curious what information you're using to make that assumption. You don't work here anymore."

"No. But I was consulting on the bodies at Imber."

He stroked his chin. "That's true, you were. And I have to say—I found that all a little odd. But we'll get into that later." He reached down, opened one of the drawers in the desk, and took out a portable recording device. He laid it on the table and gestured down to it. "Do you mind?"

"Not at all."

"Super." Murphy pressed a button on the side of the device; it gave a bleep to indicate that it was recording. "This is DCS Murphy with Mr. Atticus Priest, previously a DC at Bourne Hill in Salisbury." He gave the time and the date and then reached over for the ring binder that bore Atticus's name. He opened it and flipped to a page that had been marked with a yellow Post-it note. "Now then, Mr. Priest—I'm particularly interested in the circumstances of your discovery of the body of Richard Miller. Do you think you could tell me what happened that night?"

"Of course. What would you like to know?"

"How about Jack_of_Hearts. Start there—tell me about him. How did you meet?"

"Jack? I've never met him in person. I play online chess, and he was someone I played against."

"Random, then?"

"From my point of view—yes."

"But not his."

"No. Clearly not."

"You think he picked you out?"

"I'm sure he did."

"But you don't know who he is?"

"No."

"Or where he is?"

"No. And I don't know if he's male or female, either."

"Noted—but we'll assume he's a man. Tell me about your first interactions with him."

"He'd leave me comments in the chat box while we played. Nothing out of the ordinary to start with, but then he started to say things that made it obvious that he knew more about me than he should've."

"Like what?"

"My name, for one. The game's anonymous, and he shouldn't have been able to find that out. I still don't know how he did it."

"What else?"

"Things about my personal life."

Murphy eyed him across the table. "He knew about you and DCI Jones?"

"Yes."

"I want to come back to that, too." Murphy scribbled in his notebook. "Tell me what happened the night you found Miller's body."

"Jack messaged me. He said he wanted to meet me in the Cathedral Close. He wasn't there, but he'd left a phone for me in one of the bins."

"And he called you on it?"

"Yes."

"What did he sound like?"

"He didn't want me to recognise his voice, so he used software to mask it."

"Software?"

"An app. There are loads of them. Look on the app store."

"What did he say?"

"That he knew Miller was involved with what York and Burns had been doing. He said they were abusing kids. He said he was looking for the names of the customers York and Burns were serving."

"'Customers'?"

"That's what he said."

"He said he was involved, too."

"Yes."

"What do you think he meant by that?"

"I don't know. He said he was hoping I could help him."

"But you couldn't?"

"I didn't—I *don't*—know anything about that. Customers? It was the first I'd heard of it. I asked if he had proof that Miller was involved in whatever York and Burns were doing, and he told me not to worry about it. He said it didn't matter. He said Miller had already been taken care of."

Murphy flicked through the ring binder. "You said he told you that Miller wouldn't be able to hurt anyone anymore."

"Exactly. He said he was giving him to me. I went back to my office, and there was a car on the street outside. I opened the boot and, well… I found Miller."

Murphy looked at the ring binder. "You said Jack quoted the Bible?"

"Psalm one hundred and six, verse three. 'Blessed are they who observe justice, who do righteousness at all times.' He left me a number of other passages, too. 'Vengeance is mine, and recompense, for the time when their foot shall slip; for the day of their calamity is at hand, and their doom comes swiftly.'"

Murphy looked down and read. "'Eye for eye, tooth for tooth, hand for hand, foot for foot, burn for burn, wound for wound, stripe for stripe.'"

Atticus nodded. "Exodus twenty-one."

"I read all the passages he left for you. None of them actually condone revenge."

"He has a selective understanding of scripture."

Murphy tapped his pen against the edge of the desk. "You said that you thought someone might have been watching when you found the body?"

"They were, for sure. My office is on New Street, opposite the multi-storey. There was someone down by the junction with Catherine Street."

"And they waved at you?"

"They raised an arm. I ran down to try to catch them up, but they'd gone."

"That's a shame."

Atticus nodded.

"You think it was him?"

"That'd be my guess."

"And any contact with him since?"

"None."

"No more chess?"

"There's an open game between us, but he hasn't made a move for weeks."

"You'll let us know if he does get back in touch, won't you?"

"Of course."

Murphy scribbled in his notebook again. Atticus tried to see what it was, but it was upside down, and Murphy was obscuring it with his hand.

"Can I help you with anything else?"

Murphy drew a line and looked up. "Yes," he said. "The second thing I wanted to discuss was the nature of your engagement with the police. A consultancy like the one you negotiated is unusual. More than unusual, actually—unprecedented. I've been police for twenty years, and I don't think I've ever seen anything like it before."

Atticus's condition meant that he had never been good at reading people when it came to what they thought of him, but even he could see that Murphy was not approaching the conversation in an even-handed manner. He had an agenda that was dangerous for him and *especially* for Mack. He knew where the discussion was headed and reminded himself to keep a civil tongue. "What would you like to know about it?"

"Who arranged it?"

"DCI Jones."

"And the two of you are in a relationship."

"We are, but I don't see how that's relevant—"

"Seriously? You don't?" The smile stayed on Murphy's face, but his eyes didn't mirror it. "Why did she think it was a good idea?"

"You'd have to ask her that."

"I will, but I'm asking *you* now—why do you think she wanted your help?"

"Because I'm very good at what I do." The tethers that had restrained Atticus's temper were starting to fray. "You know the murders in Grovely Woods?"

"Yes. You were able to cast some light on them."

"And the bodies at Imber?"

"That was you, too. I know. No one is doubting you've been able to get results. My question is more about DCI Jones's judgement in bringing you back. You failed a drug test—didn't you?"

"No," Atticus said. "I passed a drug test after someone grassed me up."

Atticus knew who had reported him—Mack's estranged husband, Andy—but there was no point in telling Murphy that.

"Semantics," Murphy said. "The urine test showed evidence of cannabis, but you were under the limit. You were asked to take a hair strand test—which you knew you would fail—so you resigned before the board could fire you. The thing I couldn't understand is how you were allowed back in the building without your clearance. So I checked. I called the vetting unit, and it appears that no one thought to tell them what had happened. You still have your clearance."

"I'm not sure how this is relevant to what happened to Miller."

"I'm looking at how the investigation was conducted. The DCI's judgement is relevant to that, and she put that in question when she put someone with whom she was in a relationship back on the payroll, especially when that someone—*you*, Mr. Priest—has what might charitably be described as a questionable disciplinary record. It's a classic conflict of interest."

Atticus started to stand. "Are we finished?"

"No," Murphy said. "We're not. You know the next thing that I didn't understand? Surely, I thought to myself, *surely* someone in accounts would've reported that you were being paid." He opened the ring binder, opened the rings and took out a sheaf of paper. He took one from the top and turned it around so that Atticus could see what it was: one of his invoices. "You set up a new company and invoiced through it. Wiltshire Police pays the company, and I presume it pays you—no one in admin knows any better."

"Come on," Atticus said. "Is that the best you can do? There's nothing wrong with that. It's normal."

"Yes, it is. But when you add it to the fact that you shouldn't have had clearance, it looks to me that we have a pattern of deceptive behaviour."

"DCI Jones cleared everything with the chief constable."

"So I understand. And I'm sure there'll be a conversation about that in due course."

Atticus rose and slid the chair back under the table. "We're definitely done."

"We are," Murphy said. "But it's a pause, Mr. Priest, not the end of my interest in you. I'm going back to London for a few days, but I'd like to see you again when I'm back."

CHAPTER 8

Mack followed Robbie Best into the cathedral. The door that was used to take visitors up the tower was at the western end of the nave. There was a diorama nearby that showed what the cathedral might have looked like when it was being built, together with silken Regimental Colours that were, according to custom, being allowed to disintegrate into nothingness, at which point the Colour and its pike would be cremated and interred.

Their footsteps echoed against the flagstones as they made their way to the door. Best opened it and gestured that Mack should go through. There was a small vestibule inside with a bank of lockers along one wall that were used by guests who wanted to leave their bags rather than carrying them all the way up the tower. Best took Mack up a narrow flight of stone steps and then along a passage that traced the wall of the nave, looking down on the dean and a group of volunteers who had gathered below. They continued, climbing another flight of stairs and then passing through the roof space above the nave. She could see the gentle curvature of the walls that held up the tower, as well as the buttresses that had been installed to strengthen the pillars when the spire was added.

A third flight took them into the tower itself. They saw the mechanism of the cathedral's clock and then, on the level above that, the bells. They continued, taking the narrowest stairway yet and emerging in a large square chamber with four doors that led onto the parapets outside. She looked up into the spire and saw the wooden scaffolding that had been used by the builders who had erected it nearly a thousand years before.

Another constable—Ryan Yaxley—was standing guard by one of the doors.

"Morning, boss."

"Morning, Ryan. Which one did he fall from?"

"South door," Yaxley said. "This one."

The doorway was low, and Mack had to duck her head to get through it. The parapet was narrow, and the door had to be closed again to get to the other side. The rain was still falling heavily, and puddles had gathered around the holes in the wall that had been drilled to allow the run-off to drain. The stone flags were soaked, too, sheeted with standing water. Sodden feathers had floated into the corners, and she saw the half-eaten carcass of a pigeon. A tripod had been set up at one end of the parapet.

She pointed down to the dead bird. "The peregrines did that?"

Best nodded. "They nest on the other parapet, but they leave dead birds and feathers everywhere."

Mack went up to the edge and looked down. The top of the tower was more than two hundred feet above the ground. The refectory was directly below them. She could see Campbell's body. An iron railing had been fixed to the wall, high enough to reach the top of her chest. Her first suspicions had been right: it would have been impossible for anyone to fall from the parapet unless they had purposefully climbed the wall.

The rain was still lashing down, and Mack's hair was quickly plastered to her forehead. Thunder boomed and, for a moment, she wondered what would happen if the spire was struck by lightning.

"Let's get back inside."

They went back through the door and closed it. Mack noticed a case for the tripod and a camera bag on the floor.

"Campbell's?"

"That's what I was told," Best said. "He must have put the tripod up first before he got his camera."

"Probably didn't want to get it wet."

"So why would he put up his tripod and then jump?"

Best shrugged. "People do weird things."

The wind picked up and rattled the doors against their frames. "It's getting worse," Yaxley said.

Beneath them, the bells sounded for the hour, and Mack shivered a little in the cold. She put a hand on Best's arm. "Can I leave you to deal with the follow-up?"

"Of course," he said. "What about you?"

"Better go and see the widow."

CHAPTER 9

Atticus concentrated on calming down as he walked back to the office. Murphy was the kind of man for whom he had no respect whatsoever: an overinflated opinion of his own ability contributed to a sneering sense of superiority that would have been hilarious if he didn't have the authority of rank and the potential to make things very difficult for him and—*especially*—for Mack. Atticus knew that he himself could be guilty of arrogance—Mack told him that regularly—but at least he could walk the walk as well as talk the talk. Murphy obviously could not, and having a man like that in a position to tell him what to do had been intolerable. Atticus had just about managed to keep a lid on his temper, but much more of his sarcasm today and things might have been different.

The rain was still coming down hard as Atticus cut through the Brown Street car park and continued along New Street to his office. He had given some thought to moving to a more impressive address, but, after talking it through with Mack, he'd decided that there was no point in going to the expense. The two rooms that he rented were adequate for what he needed, especially now that he was spending several nights every week with her at the house she was renting in Harnham. She had, however, exhorted him to get a cleaner to keep things neat and tidy and, after finding it more difficult than he had expected to secure the services of someone who was prepared to put up with his mess, he had finally found a woman looking for a handful of hours a week for extra money while her children were at school. Her name was Felicity, and she had already made a significant improvement to the accommodation. She had encouraged Atticus to ensure that there was a clear divide between the smaller room at the rear of the property that he used as his bedroom and the larger room that overlooked New Street where he worked and met his clients. Atticus had cleared out everything from each room that had no reason to be there, had filled three large bin bags with unwanted junk and had given several pieces of unwanted furniture to the Trussell Trust.

He climbed the exterior staircase at the back of the building to the door that opened into his bedroom. Bandit was waiting for him, his tail wagging so much that it beat out a rhythm against the wall.

"Move," Atticus said, giving the dog's head a pat and slipping inside.

The bedroom was much more presentable now. Mack had taken him to John Lewis and had picked out new bedding and other soft furnishings that made a difference to how the room looked. Atticus still slept on a mattress on the floor, but now, at least until he got around to buying a proper bed, it didn't look quite so much like a student squat.

He went to the tiny kitchen that was hidden under the stairs to the flat on the third floor, took out a tin of dog food, opened it and then spooned it into Bandit's bowl. He changed his water and put both bowls in the corner of the bedroom for him to enjoy. He scrubbed the dog behind the ears and told him to be quiet; Bandit wolfed his food, then curled up on the bed and closed his eyes.

Atticus went through into the office. This room had been transformed, too. He still had the small two-seat sofa in the bay that extended out over the pavement below, but he had exchanged the crate that he had used as a coffee table for a proper one with a glass surface and chrome legs. He had the same large desk with his laptop and two monitors, but had added two new filing cabinets for his case files and had commissioned a local carpenter to build a bespoke bookshelf upon which he could arrange his extensive collection of textbooks. Tomes on criminology, psychology, forensic science and a host of more ephemeral subjects were on show, with one of Felicity's tasks being to ensure that they were put back in the right place once he was done with them rather than being strewn around the room, as had been the case before.

He opened his diary and checked the entry that he had made when he had set up the appointment for this morning. The woman's name was Nina Parsons, and the email that she had sent had simply asked whether it would be possible to make an appointment. Atticus had searched online to see if he could find anything that would give him an idea about what she wanted to discuss, but 'Nina Parsons' was far from an original name, and there had been dozens of hits. He had replied and asked her to tell him what she wanted to talk to him about, but had been politely rebuffed. The matter was delicate, she said, and she would much rather discuss it face to face. There was intrigue in her secrecy, and, finding it impossible to say no, he had agreed to the appointment. If the case was not of interest, he would send it to one of the agencies to whom he had been referring work, and pocket the commission.

The bell rang. Atticus went outside, diverted quickly into the bathroom to check that he looked presentable and, happy enough that he did, descended the stairs to the door. He opened it; a woman was standing in the passageway with her back to him, shaking the rain from a large golfing umbrella.

"Nina?"

She turned and smiled. "Yes, that's right. Atticus Priest?"

"That's me."

"And we *did* say eleven, didn't we?"

"We did."

"Thank goodness. I had a blonde moment and thought it might have been twelve."

She was of medium height and build, with short dark hair and dark eyes. She wore no make-up and could, had she been of a mind to put any effort into it, have been strikingly attractive. She was slender, and her fine cheekbones and nose had a pixie-ish quality to them. She put out her hand, and Atticus shook it; her fingers were calloused, and her skin was cold to the touch.

Atticus led the way up the stairs and into the office. Nina followed and, at Atticus's suggestion, handed him her coat and umbrella. He guessed that she was in her mid-thirties, and her clothes—a bulky sweater with a T-shirt and jeans—looked like they might have been pulled together in twenty seconds. Her eyes had an enigmatic quality to them, and her mouth suggested cynicism.

She sat down on the sofa. "Thank you for seeing me."

"Not at all."

She looked around the room, taking it in with an appraising eye.

"You're a soldier?" Atticus said.

"I am," she replied, her eyebrows kinking up in amused surprise. "I didn't tell you that, though."

"You've just returned from abroad."

"Yes."

"Iraq?"

"Cyprus. I've been back a couple of months, and I've been trying to keep my tan up."

He nodded. "I haven't done too badly if that's all I've got wrong."

She eyed him. "How do you know I'm in the army?"

"You have a military bearing. Your hair is cut short and very neat—that's always a strong indication, especially in a place like Salisbury with so many soldiers. The recent travel is obvious from your tan."

"That could've been because I've been on holiday."

"It could, but, when added to everything else…" He shrugged. "Service abroad is indicated by the evidence."

"It still feels like you're reaching."

He pointed to the timepiece she wore on her left wrist. "That's a G-10 quartz watch. Standard army-issue with a military strap."

"It is. But you *can* buy knockoffs."

"True," he admitted. "But it's another useful piece of evidence. It all adds to the picture."

"Fair enough," she said. "Very impressive."

"Not really," he replied with false modesty. "It's just a question of keeping your eyes open."

"So you can spot the 'trifles'?"

That brought Atticus up short. "Excuse me?"

She stared at him. "'You know my method,'" she intoned. "'It is founded upon the observation of trifles.'"

Atticus sat back, unable to prevent the smile of amusement that crept across his face as he realised what she had just said. "Well played. You know your Holmes."

"'The Boscombe Valley Mystery,'" she said. "Not one of my favourites, but still a cut above the usual. I love all the classic authors—Allingham and Christie and Sayers, especially—but Conan Doyle's my favourite. I read everything when I was little—the novels *and* the shorts—and then I read them all again while I was in Dhekelia."

He chuckled. "It's my turn to be impressed."

"Your little demonstration—does it impress people?"

"Usually."

"And you see yourself as being like him?"

He shook his head, trying to hide his embarrassment at her perspicacity. "Hardly. Some of his deductions are a little too incredible for me. But do I enjoy reading the stories?" He held up his hands. "I do. Guilty as charged."

"You don't need to show off. I'd decided that I wanted you to work on my little problem before today."

"I'm flattered."

"I've been reading up about you. The murders at that house in Grovely Wood—you got that man off, didn't you?"

"I did."

"And then the bodies they dug up at Imber. You solved that."

"I played a part," he said, wanting to say that she was right yet knowing that boastfulness was a bad look; humility was awkward for him as ever.

"What I have for you isn't nearly as exciting."

Atticus took his notebook and a pen. "Tell me about it."

"It's a little embarrassing. I've been seeing a man. I met him online two months ago. We've seen each other quite a lot since then, and I suppose you could say that we're getting serious. He's nice, and we get on well. The thing is, though, I've been married before. My ex-husband was a liar and a cheat, and I promised myself that I'd never put myself in a position where someone could put me through it the way he did ever again. We split up three years ago, and I've been single ever since. It's not that I haven't dated anyone; it's just that I have real trouble trusting anyone. I've never let anyone get close to me, and in the end, they leave." She shrugged helplessly. "It's a problem."

"I can see that it would be."

"But my new… well, my new *boyfriend*, I suppose… He's nice. He's kind; he's thoughtful and generous. He's also married—so there's *that*—but he says that he's going to be leaving her. We get on well, and I don't want to mess it up because I don't trust him."

"And you want me to make sure there are no skeletons in the closet?"

She nodded. "Exactly. I told you it wasn't exciting."

"My job isn't always exciting. There's a lot of sitting around drinking cold coffee while you wait for someone to maybe turn up. I have no trouble taking the job, but it would be unfair of me if I didn't tell you it would be more expensive than it would have to be. I could refer you to someone who would be able to do an excellent job for you at half the price."

"Money's not a problem," she said. "And I don't want someone else—I want you."

"I'm not going to turn the work away if you really want me to do it, but I *do* think it's overkill."

"Like a hammer to crack a nut?"

"Exactly."

"I *want* a hammer," she said. "If I'm going to have a relationship with him, I need to know that there's nothing in his history that might cause problems in the future. I need someone to do that whom I know I can trust. Someone who's good at what they do." She smiled and gestured to him. "Hence me being here."

"Fine," he said. "I'd be happy to do it. What can you tell me about your boyfriend?"

"Do you think I could have a drink before we get into that?"

Atticus put his hand to his forehead. "My manners—I'm so sorry. Of course. What would you like?"

"Coffee?"

"The kitchen's outside—just a minute."

Atticus went outside, filled the kettle, plugged it in and flicked the switch to set it to boil. He was happy to take the new work, even as he knew he was going to have to do the most thorough job possible. The woman waiting in his office was not someone he would be able to distract with demonstrations of his intellect. She had demolished his attempt to impress her, and the only other person who was able to see through his smoke and mirrors in the same way was Mack. Work was work, though, and, since he had been honest about what he would cost and the fact that she could get a report somewhere else for much less, he would charge her the full whack and give her A1 service.

It was her prerogative to choose him to do the work, just as it was his to charge her enough for him to be able to afford to treat Mack to a romantic weekend in Paris.

CHAPTER 10

Mack could have sent one of her junior officers to go and speak to Debbie Campbell. She could think of two officers with training in victim support who would have been able to pass on the news; Francine Patterson, for example, had an especially calming way about her. But Mack was never going to do that. She had long made it her policy not to duck the difficult moments that the job brought her way. Conveying the news of a loved one's death was the most difficult professional conversation it was possible for her to have; she'd never shirked the responsibility so far and didn't mean to start now.

She left Robbie Best to bring the investigation to a close at the cathedral so that the building could eventually be released back to the dean, and hurried through the rain to collect her car. The dean had provided Campbell's address, and she tapped the postcode into her satnav and waited for it to plot a route. The house was in Coombe Bissett, a small village to the south of Salisbury, and it would take fifteen minutes to get there.

She put the car into gear and pulled out. It had been a busier start to the day than she had anticipated, but at least she had negotiated the weekend without killing the kids, and they were now safely at school and ready for Andy to collect them in the afternoon. He had insisted that he would have the children for most of the time on the basis that he didn't want them to be confused by Atticus's role in her life. Mack hadn't wanted that, either, at least not until she had worked out precisely *what* that role was going to be. Atticus was moving a little faster than she would have chosen, and she had recently mooted the suggestion that they go for a long weekend abroad together. She wasn't quite ready for that, but hadn't worked out how to tell him without crushing his confidence. For all his brilliance—or perhaps *because* of it—he had difficulty in reading reactions when they concerned him. He was clumsy when manoeuvring through personal relationships, and Mack knew she would have to navigate for him. She needed to find a way to tap the brakes without sending him into a tailspin of doubt.

CHAPTER 11

Atticus went into town to get lunch. There was a takeaway in the square that did excellent coffee, so he picked up a bagel and an Americano and took them both back to the office. He opened another tin of dog food for Bandit and refreshed his water, and then placed his meal on his desk and sat down.

While he ate and drank, he looked at the notes he had made during his meeting with Nina. Investigators like him were increasingly being asked to research the contacts that clients made online. Catfishing was an issue, with people pretending to be someone that they weren't to deceive others, and nowhere was that more relevant than in the world of online dating. Atticus had read about people who had been bilked of hundreds of thousands of pounds by fraudsters who had used fake identities to seduce them and then, once they were on the hook, ruthlessly deceived them. It was usually women who were tricked by men, but that was not always the case; he remembered an account of an elderly man who had lost more than a million pounds when the younger woman who had bewitched him had emptied his account. One of the investigators he referred work to in Andover had worked on the case of a man who pretended to be a soldier, tricking his mark into paying for fake medical procedures; others persuaded their victims to share intimate images and then used the material to blackmail them; yet others deployed more elaborate schemes involving websites that phished for bank account details.

Atticus woke his computer, navigated to Facebook and typed in Nina Parsons's name. The same glut of profiles was returned as before, but this time, with the benefit of knowing what she looked like, he was able to pick the right one. Her account had been established a year ago with her privacy settings configured so that only friends and family could see her updates and personal information. Atticus sent a friend request to be thorough and then, while he waited for it to be accepted, went to Google and, using the 'site:' qualifier, typed 'Facebook Nina Parsons' and hit search. Facebook users often thought that setting their accounts to private would prevent their information being observable to others, but that was only true up to a point; all comments were public and indexed by Google. Atticus used a software tool to scrape all the comments into a spreadsheet and glanced over them; her account appeared to be dormant, with only a handful of comments over the course of the last few months. That wasn't particularly unusual, and he set it aside.

Nina's boyfriend's name was Robin Wintringham. Atticus navigated to the website of the company he used when he was working on background checks and requested a basic DBS report that would reveal details of his criminal record, including any unspent convictions. He paid the fee and added it to his list of expenses; it would take a day for the report to be issued, but, in the meantime, there was more that he could do.

He went back to Facebook, cleared the search bar and searched Wintringham's name. The name was more unusual, and Atticus quickly found his profile. It had been created ten years ago and was full of the kind of content that it would be almost impossible to fake, at least not without significant effort and expertise. He went further, using a tool that he had bought to identify the connections between Wintringham's account and those belonging to the others with whom he interacted most frequently. He was able to trace an outline of his life and then fill in the spaces with the details: he was married, his Facebook status changing from 'In a Relationship' to 'Married' five years previously; his wife, Laura, was a teacher at Godolphin; he had two young children, both girls, the older of whom went to reception at his wife's school and the other who appeared to be looked after by his mother during the week.

Wintringham was injudicious about the quantity of information he left on his public profile. Atticus was able to find out that he worked as a programmer for a large local website developer with an office near Old Sarum; he played hockey every weekend on the Astroturf pitch next to the cricket club on the Wilton Road; he was interested in cycling, and posted his routes on Strava. This last snippet allowed Atticus to locate the street in Laverstock at which all his rides started and stopped. He opened Google Maps, typed in the address and dropped the Street View icon outside the house. It was impossible to be sure, but it looked like Wintringham's house was one of either 27, 29 or 31 Hill Road. He found a photograph on the Instagram account belonging to his wife and swiped back to a photograph of the family in what looked very much like their back garden. Atticus switched from Street

View to the satellite perspective and was able to match several features in the photograph with the house to the left of the terrace: the fence that divided the garden from what appeared to be a communal parking area and, most tellingly, the large conservatory that belonged only to that particular house.

Atticus noted down everything, dictating his findings into a Word document that he would tidy up when he was finished. He would visit the property on foot to conduct a little surveillance, but he was already about as confident as he could be that Wintringham was who he had said he was; there was nothing about him that appeared to be out of the ordinary.

CHAPTER 12

The Ebble had flooded at Coombe Bissett, with the A354 outside the Fox and Goose closed after being submerged by half a foot of water. Mack's turning was just before the river and, although there were puddles across the road, she was able to drive slowly to the west until she found Northfields, the house where David Campbell and his family lived. The access from the road was behind a set of wooden gates that bore a sign asking drivers not to block the way. Mack ignored that and buzzed the intercom.

"Hello?"

"Can I speak to Debbie Campbell?"

"Who is this?"

"I'm DCI Jones from Salisbury police. Am I speaking to Mrs. Campbell?"

"Yes. Why? Is something wrong?"

"Do you think I could come in?"

"What's the matter? Is it David? What's happened?"

"Please," Mack said gently. "I think it'd be best if I came inside."

The lock on the gates buzzed, and they swung open. The property was larger than Mack was expecting, with an older portion in the middle that was adjoined by two large, modern extensions. A gravel drive led to a garage next to the property, and there was a large wicker love seat on the far side of the lawn. The front door to the house was open, with a woman standing outside it. Mack made her way over to her.

"Mrs. Campbell?"

"Yes," she said. "What is it?"

"Could I come in?"

The woman nodded dumbly, standing aside so that Mack could enter the house. She looked around as she did so, looking for anything that might give her an inkling as to what had happened to her husband. The hallway was pleasant, filled with furniture that looked as if it might have been collected over the course of many years and framed photographs showing the family in happy times. Mack saw a wedding photograph and wondered how long the two of them had been married; she felt the usual discomfort at the news she was going to have to deliver. However long the two of them had been married—thirty or forty years, she guessed from the photo—it had come to an end just a few hours earlier, and Debbie Campbell didn't know it yet.

Debbie had stopped in the hallway. Mack saw that she was confused and unsure what she should do next.

"Could we sit down?"

"Please—this way."

She led the way into the sitting room and gestured to the sofa.

"Can I get you a drink? Tea or coffee?"

She was procrastinating, finding reasons to stop Mack from delivering the news that she must have known could only have been bad.

"I'm fine," Mack said. "You should have a seat, too."

Debbie sat on the armchair, her knees and feet pressed together and her hands in her lap, her fingers shaking.

"I'm very sorry to have to tell you that your husband is dead. He was on one of the parapets of the cathedral tower this morning, and he fell."

"Oh my god," she said, her face crumpling. "Oh my *god*."

"I'm so sorry."

"What am I going to do? I need to tell our children."

There was a telephone in a cradle on the table. Debbie got up, but her knees buckled, and she had to reach out for the back of the chair to stop herself from falling. Mack stood and helped her to sit back down in the chair.

"I'll introduce you to a family liaison officer. They'll be able to assist with things like that if that would be helpful."

She dabbed her eyes. "Thank you." She paused, looking down at her lap before raising her head. "What happened? Was he up there taking his photographs?"

"We think so," Mack said. "We found his camera and equipment."

"In this weather?"

"Yes."

"That project," she said. "That *bloody* project. He was obsessed with it. Once he got halfway into the year, there was no way that he would let anything stop him from finishing. He probably saw this weather as an opportunity to get a really good picture." She closed her eyes, paused to gather herself and then opened them to look at Mack again. "How did he fall?"

"That's what I'm trying to find out."

"He was always careful. He would never have done anything that put him at risk. And you must have been up on the parapet?"

"This morning."

"It was wet?"

"Very."

"But you still wouldn't be able to fall off."

"I don't think so."

"Maybe he was up higher? The weather door at the top of the spire? He said that was sticking and needed to be fixed."

"We don't think so. The weather door is on the other side of the spire. And in this weather? Everything I've found out about him suggests he was a very careful man."

Debbie nodded, her lips pressed tightly together, then covered her face with her hands in an outburst of grief. Mack waited for a moment to let her compose herself once more. She took the opportunity to glance around the room. It was pleasant, with nicely chosen pieces of furniture and a host of framed photographs that showed the Campbells together in several different locations: hand in hand before the Taj Mahal in India; with two young children at Disney World, Minnie Mouse next to them; on the deck of a cruise liner that looked as if it was passing through the Scandinavian fjords.

Mack turned back to Debbie and took a deep breath. "I'm sorry to have to ask," she said delicately, "but, as I said, the question of *why* he fell is what we need to understand.

An accident is one possibility, but, as you've said—and I agree—it does seem unlikely."

"What are you saying? You think he *jumped*?"

"We have to see that as a possibility."

"No," she said with a firm certainty. "It isn't. It's impossible."

"Why do you say that?"

"Because I would've *known*. I've been married to David for thirty-three years. Don't you think that I would have realised if he was depressed?"

"I've investigated similar things before. It's always a horrible thing to say, but I'm afraid I've seen cases where the person involved hid the way they were feeling from their loved ones."

She shook her head. "No. Not David. We don't have secrets." Her voice caught, and she paused. "*Didn't*. And he had too much to live for."

She got up and, steadier this time, crossed the room to the sideboard and picked up one of the framed photographs. She came back and handed it to Mack; it was a picture of the Campbells with a young woman.

"That's Emily, our daughter." She dabbed at her eyes again. "She's pregnant. Due next month. We don't have any grandchildren yet—Emily's had trouble conceiving, and David and I had given up hope. They had IVF, and nothing happened, and then, when they stopped, it happened. It was a miracle—we both thought so. David was excited—*so* excited. He was supposed to go around to help them decorate the nursery after work today. The suggestion that he would kill himself when he had so much to live for…" Her breath came in a shudder, and she had to stop to compose herself again. "No. You can see why I'd say that now, can't you?"

"He didn't mention any problems?"

"No."

"Money?"

"We've got plenty."

"Can you think of anything?"

"He didn't have any concerns. None. The idea that he'd do something like that deliberately… it's impossible. Completely impossible. He must have fallen."

The room fell quiet.

"What happens now?"

"The coroner will have to decide whether to hold an inquest. I think he'll say that the cause of death is unclear and that there should be one. The body will be released for a funeral, and you'll be able to get what's called an interim death certificate that'll help with any administration that needs to be done."

"What about…" She paused. "What about the practical steps?"

"You'll need to find an undertaker. I can recommend one if you like."

"It's all right," she said. "My friend's husband is an undertaker. I'll ask him."

Mack took out her card and left it on the table. "If you need anything in the meantime, please give me a call. I'd be happy to help. I'll arrange for the family liaison officer to be in touch. They'll be able to help you as we investigate what happened." Mack stood and smoothed down her trousers. "Once again—I'm very sorry. I'll let myself out."

CHAPTER 13

The rain had gathered strength over the course of the afternoon, and now it lashed the streets with a vengeance. Alice Morris turned the corner, and a gust of wind, racing at her from the opposite direction, turned her umbrella inside out. She sheltered in an empty doorway long enough to fix it and then stepped back out onto the slick pavement and hurried on her way.

The offices of the Salisbury *Journal* were on Rollestone Street in the centre of the city. The buildings around it were a curious mixture: opposite was an old brewery that had been turned into office space, and a Victorian terrace sat alongside. The office occupied by the newspaper was a seventies addition, an ugly brick three-storey block that had been allowed to fall into disrepair by the landlords. There were four large windows on each floor, but the paint on the frames had peeled off, and the wood had started to rot. The ground-floor windows showed off a selection of photographs that hadn't been changed for years, and the branded boards that would once have been used to advertise the day's papers were empty, stacked against the wall with weeds growing up between them. Alice ruefully thought it an eloquent comment on the state of the local newspaper industry.

She huddled beneath her umbrella as she made her way along the street, opening the door to the office and gratefully stepping inside.

"Afternoon," said Carly, the receptionist who doubled up her work on the front desk by reporting on the council and events at city hall. "You're drenched."

"Cats and dogs," Alice said. "At least we put a warning on the website."

She chuckled. "You seen the comments?"

"No? Why?"

"The usual suspects have been arguing."

"About the *weather*?"

She looked at the screen on her desk. "Lord Salzbrie said it's climate change. Spireman said he's talking out of his arse and that there's no such thing. It all went downhill from there."

They had tried to moderate the comments for a month but had quickly given it up as a waste of time. The usual suspects just found the Facebook posts that they used to promote the stories and commented there instead. Alice was reconciled to it now, and, anyway, it was about the only thing that was lively about the newspaper.

"Have you been at the cathedral?" Carly asked.

"All day."

"How is it?"

"Horrible."

"Poor man. What a way to go."

Alice took off her wet coat and hung it over the banister. "Is Eddie in?"

"Upstairs."

She pushed open the door to the stairs and climbed. The death *had* been horrible. She had been given a call by a friend who worked in the PR department at the cathedral and had been the first reporter on the scene. Workplace accidents were not unusual, and Alice had covered many in two years at the *Journal*, but this one—so Gothically lurid—promised to be something else entirely, with the suggestion that the police were considering suicide as a possible cause of death.

It was funny; Eddie Thorpe had been worrying how they were going to fill the newspaper at yesterday's editorial meeting and had reluctantly agreed to run yet another story on the interminable bureaucracy that swirled around the proposed tunnel that would take the A303 away from Stonehenge. It was a lot of nonsense—Eddie dismissed it as 'yet another crock of Salisbury shit'—but it was relevant to the city, and it was all they had. Now, though, they had been given the perfect lead story. The bypass could be relegated to the inside pages, where it belonged, and they could run with Campbell's death. Alice felt a little guilty at her relief, but she'd been a journalist for long enough to know that selling papers—and clicks—was a cutthroat business.

She climbed the stairs to the newsroom and thought, as she usually did, that that was a rather grandiloquent way to describe her place of work. It evoked images of rooms full of noise and life, of reporters on the phone to their sources or arguing with their editors about the merits of their stories. Alice had been a film buff at college and had daydreamed about what it might be like to be a hack, her expectations coloured by *His Girl Friday*, *All the President's Men* and *The Philadelphia Story*.

The reality was different.

There were three reporters, all of them fresh out of college, with Alice—at just twenty-three—the most senior. Their work was overseen by Eddie and supplemented by an apprentice and a handful of freelancers, including James Ward, the photographer who had been with her to get snaps of what was happening at the cathedral. They shared the space with two desks and three old filing cabinets that Eddie said pre-dated him, and he'd worked at the paper for *years*.

The staff lived in perpetual fear that the owners of the paper would close it down; local news didn't make much money, and newspapers around the country had been swallowed up by conglomerates who then amalgamated them and reduced headcounts to cut costs. Alice had wondered uneasily what she might do if that happened to them and had started to think about going back to college so that she could train for something else. She had friends who were teaching English in far-off climes, and the prospect of decent pay and sunshine were attractive when compared to the dour weather and relative penury that she had here.

Eddie had a tiny office in the corner that looked as if it might once have been a broom cupboard; there was no window and barely enough space for his desk and chair. He was sitting there now, but, upon seeing Alice, he got up and met her halfway.

"Well?" he asked.

"Awful."

"You've got the front page."

She sat down on the edge of the desk. "Feels a bit morbid."

Eddie shrugged. "You know what they say."

"'If it bleeds, it leads.' I know. But it doesn't change the fact he's dead and that he died in pretty much the worst way possible. Do you know how long it would have taken him to hit the ground?"

"Please don't say you've Googled that."

"I was bored. Nearly four seconds. *Four seconds.* That's plenty of time for him to think about it."

Eddie had been a reporter for thirty years. He had worked on Fleet Street when it was still the Street of Ink but had been let go six months earlier when he could no longer square the rampant drinking culture of which he enthusiastically partook with the need to file good copy. He was owed a favour by an old drinking buddy who had moved to the *Journal*'s parent company. He had been given the editor's job after his predecessor quit, citing the exhaustion of covering the stories at Grovely and Imber.

Alice saw Eddie as an example of how not to plot a successful career. He was her opposite: he had started in London and then retreated to Salisbury; she, on the other hand, intended to get the experience she needed here before looking for something more glamorous elsewhere. Alice had been born and raised in Salisbury, but—unlike many of her contemporaries from school whose ambitions did not extend beyond the city limits—she wanted to do great things.

"How much of it have you written?"

"Just notes," she said. "I need to put it together."

"You've got a couple of hours. Photos?"

"James has a couple."

"I'll take a look. Coffee?"

"Love one."

"Get cracking, then. I'll put the kettle on."

CHAPTER 14

Mack followed at the back of the group as they left the station and made their way to the Royal George. The pub, on nearby Bedwin Street, was the venue that they invariably decamped to whenever they had something to celebrate. Today was Bob Bradley's birthday.

They reached the pub and filed inside. The television on the wall was tuned to a Premier League match, with a collection of regulars watching it from the bar. Neil Blyford, Bob's best friend at the nick, took their orders for the first round.

Mack intercepted Blyford at the bar.

"I'll get these."

"Don't be daft, boss."

"No arguments."

She took out her purse, thumbed out two twenties and handed them to the barman. She waited for the first pints to be pulled and then took them over to the corner of the room where the others had taken two empty tables. Mack put the glasses on the nearest table and then sat down. It was a good turnout; Bob had been police for twenty-five years and was a popular fixture at the nick. Robbie Best, Stewart Lynas, Mike Lewis, and Francine Patterson had come from CID, with Neil Blyford, James Boyd, Pete Britten and Sam Collison representing uniform. Another five or six were expected to make their way over once they got off shift.

Blyford and the barman brought over the rest of the drinks and distributed them, together with half a dozen packs of crisps and another half dozen packs of pork scratchings.

"Courtesy of the gaffer," Blyford said, gesturing to Mack.

The others thanked her.

"Long day," Mack said, stretching out her back.

"Been at the cathedral?" Collison asked her.

She nodded.

"It's true, then? He fell off the spire?"

"The tower," Mack corrected him.

"Not that it would've made any difference," Best said. "I don't think he could've made any more mess if he'd tried. He bounced off the wall and then..." He clapped his hands.

They spoke about the day for five minutes before conversation inevitably moved on to office gossip: Ryan Yaxley was rumoured to have won five thousand on the lottery and was still refusing to pay his way at the bar; the travellers up at the hospital site were being investigated for nicking the lead off the church at Britford; Bob Carver had driven his new Tesla into the back of a car at the college roundabout just two weeks after buying it and was blaming Elon Musk.

Francine got up and went to the bar. She was an impressive young officer. She had been a redcap in the 1st Investigation Company of the military police at Bulford before swapping her camouflage for street clothes and joining Salisbury CID.

Mack knew from personal experience that it was a challenge to be an ambitious woman in an environment that was still overwhelmingly male, and had taken Francine under her wing. Francine, for her part, had rewarded Mack's early faith with two years of excellent work, and Mack had recommended that she should be considered for promotion to detective sergeant when the next opportunity arose.

Mack watched as she approached a good-looking man who had just come inside, reaching up to plant a kiss on his lips and then leading him to the table. Mack looked over at Robbie Best and noticed that he had a troubled expression on his face. She knew why: Best had held a candle for Francine ever since she had joined CID, and, until recently, had been labouring under the misapprehension that she was single. It wasn't that she had deceived him or led him on, just that she was private and not keen on discussing her life outside of the nick. Her Facebook status had changed from 'single' to 'in a relationship' the same day that Best had come into the station with a face like thunder, and Mack had joined the dots from there.

"There's someone I want to introduce," she said. "This is Charlie."

Boyd stood up and extended his hand. "The mysterious boyfriend?"

"Nice to meet you," Charlie said, shaking Boyd's hand and then nodding to the rest of them.

Francine was obviously nervous about the prospect of introducing Charlie to her colleagues. Francine knew—and Charlie might not—that they could be a raucous group, especially when they'd had a few to drink. It was early, though.

She was wisely making sure that he was properly introduced to them all before too much ale had flowed.

Mack stood up and offered her hand; Charlie took it.

"Drink?" she asked him.

"Thanks. I'll have a lager." He and Francine took seats beside each other.

Mack went up to the bar and ordered another pint of Amstel. She looked back at the table and noticed Francine holding Charlie's hand underneath the table. Best was putting on a brave face, but perhaps trying a little *too* hard.

They were talking about the death at the cathedral again when she returned with the pint.

"Charlie was walking through the Close when it happened," Francine said.

Charlie picked at a crisp from the open packet. "Didn't see anything. Saw the police and the ambulance, but I only realised what had happened when I got home and heard it on the radio."

"I was saying it was messy," Best said.

"Do you know what happened to him?"

Mack wasn't all that keen on discussing business while a civilian was present, so she shook her head and kept things as vague as she could. "Can't say for sure."

"Could he have slipped?"

"Don't know."

Boyd frowned. "I've been up there, boss. Took my kids. The parapets on those balconies come up to the top of my chest. How'd he go and slip from there?"

"We don't know that he did," she said. "But it's either that or he jumped, and his wife says she has no reason to think he might've been depressed."

Lynas took a sip of his pint and then put the glass down. "That doesn't always mean they're not, though, does it? We've all had cases like that—someone tops themselves, and it takes the whole family by surprise. Maybe it's like that here."

"Maybe," Mack said. "Maybe not."

"Who decides?" Charlie asked.

"It'll be up to the coroner."

Best, perhaps aware from Mack's succinct replies that she didn't want to discuss the case now, looked over at Charlie and changed the subject. "What do you do for work?"

"I'm a photographer."

"Taking photos of what?"

"Whatever takes my fancy. If I could choose, it would be landscapes, but they don't pay the bills. Corporate work, mostly—photos for catalogues, stuff like that. Not nearly as glamorous as what you do."

Lynas nearly choked on his pint. "'*Glamorous*'? Jesus, Franny, what shit have you been telling him?" He swallowed another mouthful and put his glass down on the table. "Mate—what we do couldn't be any farther away from being glamorous if it tried. You think going down the road picking up the bits and pieces of someone who's been in an RTA is glamorous?"

"I don't believe you," Charlie said amiably. "Salisbury's been in the papers. The murders at Grovely? And Imber?"

"True," Bradley said. "But it's not 'glamorous.' Not unless you think standing on Salisbury Plain all day and all night in the pissing rain and wind is glamorous."

"With mud that you find in your boots a week later," Lynas said.

"With weak tea the only thing standing between you and hypothermia," added Bradley.

"All right," Francine said, holding up a hand and chuckling. "Leave him alone. He was only asking."

"How long have you two been seeing each other?" Britten asked.

"It was a year on Sunday."

"Where did you meet?" Boyd asked.

"Online," Charlie said.

Mack glanced over at Best and saw that he was forcing an amiable smile. She felt sorry for him. His wife had divorced him eighteen months earlier, and he hadn't taken it well. Francine was younger than him, and her interest—or the thought that she might be interested in him—had been good for his confidence. Mack wondered whether she should take him out for dinner next week to make sure he was okay. She had known him for years and, at least since Atticus's departure, he was the closest she had to a friend at the nick. He knew about her relationship with Atticus and had been a shoulder to cry on in the aftermath of her separation.

Lewis gestured to the empty glasses on the table. "Who wants another?"

"*Please* don't tell me you're buying," Bradley said.

"Don't sound so surprised."

"You know the last time you took out your wallet?"

"The nineties?" Lynas offered.

Lewis raised his middle finger.

CHAPTER 15

Deadlines weren't usually pressing at the *Journal*. With a couple of recent exceptions, breaking news didn't happen in Salisbury, and that meant that they had all week to prepare for the print edition. Copy was written and edited, and pages were set in plenty of time for Eddie Thorpe to give everything the once-over before approving it and sending it off to be printed. Tonight was different. Eddie had called the printer to tell them they would be filing late and had been told that they could wait until eleven thirty but no longer.

Alice sat down at her desk, opened her laptop and her notebook, and began to type.

A distraught family have paid tribute to a popular local man, 62, who tragically fell to his death from the tower of Salisbury Cathedral yesterday morning.

She read it back. 'Distraught' was too formal; she deleted it and tried again.

A heartbroken family have paid tribute to a popular local man, 62, who tragically fell from the tower of Salisbury Cathedral yesterday morning. David Campbell was taking a photograph on the southern parapet when he fell to his death. The preliminary cause of Campbell's death was confirmed as multiple injuries following a fall from height.

She flexed her fingers and typed out a final paragraph.

In a statement, his wife Deborah described Mr. Campbell as being a 'great father' and said that 'he had worked at the cathedral all his life.' She has asked for privacy so that the family can come to terms with their loss.

She reclined to straighten out her back and read the piece through. It was good, if a little impersonal. She reminded herself that they had an excellent photograph of Campbell from the archive at the cathedral, and that his broad smile would do much to bring his personality across. She had already finished a piece on his life for page three, and that, together with a second photograph of him changing the anemometer at the tip of the spire—so far above the ground that it made her queasy to look at it—would add extra colour.

She scrolled back to the start with the intention of tightening up the flabbier sentences when she saw Carly in the doorway.

"What's up?"

Carly held up a Jiffy bag. "Parcel for you."

"What? It's late."

"Must have been put through the letterbox."

"By whom?"

She shrugged. "Sorry—didn't see."

"When?"

"Don't know. I just noticed it."

Carly brought it over and handed it to Alice. The bag looked as if it was brand new, and had been sealed at one end with an adhesive strip. She turned it over and looked at the front: her name had been printed onto a label, and the label had been fixed—perfectly dead centre—on the packet. The package wasn't heavy and was perhaps thirty centimetres long and twenty-five centimetres wide.

Carly looked over Alice's shoulder. "Expecting anything?"

"No," she said. "I don't think so."

She slid her finger into a loose gap at the end of the package and wriggled it until she had torn it all the way open. She turned the packet on its side and tipped the contents onto her desk: it was a glossy black plastic case with a single piece of A4 paper folded in half.

"What is that?" Carly said.

Alice picked the case up and examined it. It had a clear plastic sheath around it, and a label had been affixed to the spine. A name and date had been written in black ink on the label.

Campbell, David / 21 June

Alice opened the case.

A videotape was inside.

She got up so quickly that she knocked her chair over. "Eddie?"

"What?"

"Come here a minute."

Eddie had his office door half-closed and, when he opened it, a cloud of smoke drifted into the newsroom. He took the cigarette from his mouth and dropped it into a mug of cold coffee that had been left on someone's desk. "What's up?" He came over to where Alice and Carly were standing.

"Look at this." She handed over the envelope and the videotape and watched as he examined them. "A video?"

"Look at the name on the side."

He turned the case over. "Weird."

"Do you think we need to call the police?"

"Why?"

"Because we get this on the day he died?"

Eddie shook his head. "We don't even know what it is."

Alice took the piece of paper and unfolded it. Two sentences had been printed in bold type:

It is mine to avenge; I will repay. In due time their foot will slip; their day of disaster is near and their doom rushes upon them.

Carly looked over Alice's shoulder. "What? What does that mean?"

Alice went to her computer and tapped a key to wake the screen. She went to Google, typed out the first dozen words and searched. The first result was from Biblehub.com and identified the words as from Deuteronomy.

"That's…" She stared at the paper, and the sentence drifted away.

"Weird?" Carly offered.

"Very weird." She put the paper down and picked up the case. "Do we have something here that'll play this?"

"Not a chance," Eddie said. "We used to have a player, but it was chucked out years ago."

"eBay?" Carly suggested.

Alice laid the case down on the desk and ran her finger over the black plastic. "I think my dad's got one in the attic. God knows if it'll work. I'll give him a call."

"Don't forget you need to finish the piece for the front page."

"Give me ten minutes."

She picked up her chair, sat down and flexed her fingers. She needed an extra paragraph to fill the space on the front page and had decided that she would include a reference to the photography project that Campbell had been working on all year.

She started to type, but her attention was snagged by the shiny black cassette box next to the keyboard.

PART 2

Tuesday

CHAPTER 16

Carl Jeffers parked his car next to the shipping container that was used as his office and pushed the button to open the boot. His dog, Jess, leapt out and proceeded to run in a series of circles, throwing up sprays of muddy water as her legs powered through the puddles that had gathered overnight. It was still raining, just as hard as it had yesterday, and the forecast was the same for the rest of the day and tomorrow. The Avon had burst its banks, and the floodplain between the main river and the carrier was underwater. The level recorded by the gauge at Harnham Bridge was still climbing, and Jeffers had started to wonder whether they might see the businesses on the southern side of Southampton Road flood again. It had happened four years ago, and there had been the threat then that the road itself might flood. Salisbury's traffic was bad at the best of times, but if the main road into the city was forced to close, it was going to be awful. Jeffers drove in that way from his home in Alderbury. The diversion through downtown would mean he'd have to get up an hour earlier, and he wasn't keen on that at all.

He got out of the car, his boots sinking into an inch of mud, and then squelched across to the container. He removed the padlock and opened up, switching on the light and filling the kettle with water that he'd brought from home in a two-litre plastic bottle. He pushed back the sleeve of his waterproof jacket until he could see his watch: it was five thirty in the morning, and he was expecting a dozen fishermen to come and enjoy the fishery today. He was here a little earlier than normal so that he could walk the banks from one end to the other and make sure that everything was as it should be, and that access was even possible. He picked up his shotgun, put a handful of shells into his pocket, stepped back outside and locked up the office again.

Jeffers was the water bailiff for this stretch of the river. His role was to maintain the river for the fishermen who travelled from all over the country to enjoy it. He arrived early every morning and spent the first hour walking to the trout farm that marked the eastern limit of the angling association's land and then walking the mile and a half back to New Bridge Road, which was the western boundary. He had the shotgun to shoot the cormorants that would, if left unchecked, decimate the fish that the association had released into the river to maintain stocks. The bird wasn't a native species, and, because of that, Jeffers was allowed to kill them. It was a different matter with herons, and the heronry in nearby Britford was a problem for which there was no easy solution. He would fire a shot to scare them off when he saw them, but he knew that the clever buggers just waited to return at the end of his shift.

With Jess at his side, Jeffers passed the church, older even than the cathedral that he could see if he turned back to the west, and trudged through the slop of the mud. He stopped to check on the repairs to the wooden platform that he had made last week, satisfied that the planks were strong enough for the fishermen who would set up there so that they could cast out into the deepest part of the river.

He reached the weir that governed the flow of the water at the trout farm, splitting it in half so that the farm had enough for its purposes, and then turned back. He retraced his steps, passing the church and then the first and second bridges that the farmer used to take his cattle to and from the water meadows. He went by the car park with his office and the two fishing lodges. Jess wriggled beneath the fence that guarded the bridge over Manor Ditch, and Jeffers used the stile, continuing along the paved track until the old eel house came into view. The building stretched across the river from one side to the other, a single span on raised stone piers and then a sluice house, built at a right angle so that the whole building was arranged in the shape of an L. The bonded red bricks and dark tile roof stood out against the water and the greenery that surrounded them.

The structure was in a state of some disrepair. Some time ago, Jeffers had removed some of the ivy that had engulfed the walls and had found that one corner was collapsing. The river current had undermined three of the six stone piers upon which the sluice range stood, and the roots of an ash were damaging the foundations. Jeffers had been concerned; the building regulated the flow of the water and, if it had collapsed, the water levels on the city side of the sluice would have plunged and damaged both the upstream and downstream habitats. The Environment Agency was looking into the possibility of making repairs, but every morning that Jeffers approached it, he did so in fear that more of the structure would have been damaged.

The interior of the sluice house contained machinery for operating the sluices, including several large cast-iron gears that were used to raise and lower them. Jeffers looked inside and saw something in the flow.

He thought at first that it was a deer. There were plenty of them here, and it wasn't all that long ago that a fawn had fallen into the river and drowned. The body had been swept down the river by the current until it came to rest against the sluice; Jeffers had had to loop a rope around its neck to haul it out.

He carefully stepped inside the building and saw that it wasn't a deer, he stepped closer still, and his stomach fell as his worst fears were realised.

It was a man.

CHAPTER 17

Francine Patterson was woken by the buzzing of her phone on her bedside table. She snaked out a hand, probing the table with fingers still clumsy with sleep, and upended a half-empty glass of water that she had left there last night to help prevent the hangover that she had known would be waiting for her when she awoke.

"*Shit*," she mumbled.

She found her phone and snoozed the alarm. She blinked the sleep from her eyes until she was able to focus on the time: six thirty. She usually set two alarms—one at six and the other at half past—and she had either forgotten to set the first one or had slept through it, and now she was going to struggle to get to the nick in time to start the early turn at seven.

She felt movement on the other side of the bed and remembered that Charlie had come home with her after they had gone out with the others for a curry last night.

He groaned.

"You don't need to get up," she said. "Go back to sleep."

"What's the matter?" he mumbled.

"I'm on the early shift, and I'm late. And I've got the hangover from hell."

She shuffled over to the edge of the bed, slid her feet down to the floor and stood. Her head throbbed, and she felt vomit bubbling up at the back of her throat. She staggered into the bathroom, knelt in front of the toilet and brought up whatever it was that she had had for dinner. She took a moment before she was sick again, a third heave bringing up nothing more than a mouthful of bile. She wiped her mouth with the back of her hand and flushed the foul-smelling vomit away.

It had gone pretty well last night, she thought, all things considered. The others had taken to Charlie well and, after early nerves that she would have been the only one to notice, he had held his own with their banter. She had noticed that Robbie Best had been uncomfortable. That was a shame; Robbie was nice and had been kind to her when she'd swapped uniform for CID, and, although she found him attractive, she had already been seeing Charlie when his marriage had ended. She would've liked to have been able to say something to make him feel better, but had no idea where to start without it being embarrassing for them both.

She ran the shower so that the water could warm up and went back into the bedroom to pick up the towel that she had dumped on the floor yesterday. Charlie was still in bed, his face lit by the glow of his phone as he scrolled down the screen.

She bent down for the towel. "How drunk was I?"

"Quite drunk."

"You were drunk, too—right?"

"I think so."

"The others?"

"You weren't the worst. Whose birthday was it? Rob?"
"*Bob.*"
"They had to carry him into a taxi."
"And everyone else?"
"Not as bad as him, but all pissed. Relax. You didn't do anything to disgrace yourself."

She started to unbutton her pyjama top and then, with a little blush of self-consciousness, paused and went into the bathroom. She remembered Charlie taking off her shirt last night and then, as she closed her eyes and tried to remember everything, was as sure as she could be that they had had sex. She grimaced, it wasn't their first time, but they were early enough in their relationship that she was worried that the experience might not have been up to scratch. She glanced through the crack between the door and the frame and saw that he had put his phone down on the bedside table and lain down again.

She undressed and stepped into the shower, letting the water soak through her hair and run down her shoulders and back. She squeezed out a handful of shower gel and scoured herself clean, then took her toothbrush and scrubbed her teeth until the taste of the vomit was replaced by mint. She turned off the shower, then dried herself with a towel before wrapping it around herself and creeping back into the bedroom to find clean clothes that she could wear for work. Charlie was snoring lightly. She crept around the bed so that she could look down at him and allowed herself a smile; he looked happy and comfortable, his chest rising and falling with each breath. She reached down to pull the duvet all the way up so that his shoulders were covered and then went to the wardrobe, taking out the navy-blue wool skirt suit that she had had dry-cleaned last week and a white shirt that she could just about get away with without ironing. She grabbed fresh underwear and went back into the bathroom to change. It was six forty-five, and she had a short drive to get into the office. She was going to be late, but hopefully not too late for it to be a problem.

* * *

Francine pulled into the car park at the side of the building at Bourne Hill at six minutes past seven. She took her bag and umbrella from the passenger seat, locked the car and made her way into the office. Sergeant James Boyd was waiting for her at her desk. He had been working the night shift, from eleven until seven. The rota had everyone on the team cycling through the three shifts—early, late and night—changing from one to the next every two days before they had two days off.

"What's up?" she said to him.

"How's your head?"

"Sore. How do you know?"

"You don't remember me being there?"

"No…"

"We had a complaint. I had to go out and calm things down."

"What? Really?"

His face broke into a wide grin. "No, you tit, not really. Although I'm a little concerned you think it's *possible* that you all might have disgraced yourself. Can't wait until Bradley rolls in."

"He's off today. Lucky bastard."

"Bet you wish you'd thought of that."

"Don't rub it in."

Boyd put on his jacket and picked up the rucksack that he'd left on her desk. "Time for me to go. I'll walk you down to your car."

She frowned. "What? Why?"

"Because we've just had a call from uniform. I'd deal with it, but I'm done for the day."

"Where?"

"You know the old sluice house on the river down by Churchill Gardens?"

"Think so," she said. "Why? What's happened?"

"Bob Carver just called in. There's a body in the water."

CHAPTER 18

Mack was still sleeping when Atticus woke. He swung his legs off the mattress as gently as he could so as not to wake her. She had been out with colleagues from the nick for Bob Bradley's birthday and had texted him late and said that she wanted to see him. He had offered to go over to hers, but she had replied and said that there was no need: she was outside. She was a little the worse for wear and had fallen asleep almost as soon as he had helped her upstairs to the bedroom. He had wakened her so that she could take two aspirin with a pint of water, and then lay down next to her, listening to her breathing as she fell into a deep and dreamless sleep.

He freshened up in the bathroom, then went back into the bedroom to change. He clipped the lead to Bandit's collar and led the way down the stairs and out to the car. He took out his phone and went to his notes. He found the address that he had discovered for Robin Wintringham, copied the postcode and pasted it into his map's search bar.

* * *

Atticus drove across town to Laverstock and arrived at Wintringham's address at a quarter to eight. Hill Road was one of the new developments that had sprung up around Salisbury over the course of the last few years, and the houses—neat and tidy, with fresh red bricks and slate-covered porches over their front doors—looked pleasant as the sun broke through the clouds and shone down on them. The land registry record that Atticus had purchased confirmed his earlier deduction: Wintringham was the owner of number 27. He drove down the slope that gave the road its name and found a space at the side of the road where he could leave his car and continue his observation on foot.

Atticus recalled the research that he had conducted, and, in particular, the layout of Wintringham's property in relation to its neighbours. The house was on the left-hand side of a block of three, with a short drive to the side that led to a large parking space. Atticus followed the drive, jumping to peer over a wooden fence that enclosed the back garden. It was a simple space, a rectangle of lawn with a large conservatory extending out from the house. Atticus was able to see into the windows on the first floor and saw a girl in school uniform looking out before turning her head and mouthing something to someone whom Atticus couldn't see.

"Excuse me?"

Atticus turned to see that a woman had emerged from around the corner of the fence. She was looking at him with obvious suspicion, and he guessed that the girl in the window must have alerted her to him peering over the fence.

"Hello."

"What are you doing?"

"I'm from Carter and May," he said, using the name of the first estate agency in town that came to mind. "We're letting agents for one of the houses over there, and we've had a complaint about noise."

Her suspicion was allayed and replaced with a prying officiousness. "From which property?"

"That one," he said, pointing at the back of number 27.

"Really? The Wintringhams? No—that can't be right."

"That's definitely the house."

"I find that hard to believe."

"Why do you say that?"

"Because they're a very nice young family. Two little girls, both good as gold. They're not the sort of people to create a disturbance. Who made the complaint?"

"I'm afraid I can't tell you that."

"Well, whoever it was, I'd suggest that they might be making a mountain out of a molehill. This is a good street. Everyone knows everyone else, and nothing's too much trouble."

"That's good to hear. Sorry to have disturbed you."

He set off back to the street and had turned left to go and get his car when the door to number 27 opened, and two girls emerged from within. The first was dressed in school uniform and the second in a padded coat that looked as if it would be snug in the brisk weather. They waited by the door until their father, two bags slung on one shoulder and a set of car keys in his hand, stepped out to join them. Atticus recognised Robin Wintringham and gave what he hoped was a sympathetic smile as he stepped to the side to let the girls make their way down to the car parking space where he had just been. Wintringham returned the smile with a wry shake of the head, presuming, perhaps, that Atticus had children and could empathise with the rigours of getting them ready and out of a morning.

Atticus walked to his car. He knew that the woman who had questioned him was probably still in the car park and, although he thought it was unlikely that she would repeat the story that he had given her to Wintringham for fear of embarrassing him, it wasn't worth waiting to find out.

CHAPTER 19

Alice parked outside her parents' home and finished the rest of the strong black coffee in her flask. She had found it difficult to sleep, and now she was paying the price. Her dreams had been unusually vivid: her first had seen her falling from the tower of the cathedral, and then, once that had woken her up, she hadn't been able to stop thinking about the tape that had been delivered to the office. The fact that it had been labelled with the dead man's name was strange and, given the timing, ominous.

She got out of the car, went to the front door and knocked.

Her father opened it. "Morning, sweetheart."

He crouched down and picked up the video cassette recorder that he'd placed on the floor earlier.

"Thanks," she said.

"No idea if it still works," he said, handing it over.

"Do you have the leads?"

He bent down again and collected a plastic bag, depositing it on top of the recorder. "Should all be in there. What on earth do you want it for?"

"We were sent a tape last night, but we don't have anything to play it on."

"Sounds intriguing. Everything all right at work?"

"All good," she said. "I'd better get into the office—thanks for this."

"No problem, love. Want a hand getting it to the car?"

"It's all right—I can manage."

"See you at the weekend."

* * *

Alice parked the car in Salt Lane car park and carried the VCR the rest of the way to the office. Eddie Thorpe was already in the newsroom.

"Well done," he said. "You found one."

"No idea what I'm supposed to do with it."

Eddie snorted, muttered something about millennials and took the recorder from her and carried it into the conference room. They had a television on a stand there, and Eddie slid the VCR onto the shelf beneath the screen. Alice looked at the nest of cables and wires in the bag and shrugged her shoulders. Eddie connected the VCR to the television, found a power cord and plugged that in, too, then switched the power on and stood back. The display blinked on. He took the tape from its box and pushed it into the slot. The mechanism whirred as the tape was drawn back into the machine; Alice was suddenly fearful that it would be chewed up and ruined.

"Shouldn't we test it on something else first?"

"It'll be fine."

He pressed play, and the two of them pulled up chairs and sat down.

The screen was filled with static and then bars of white that rolled from the top to the bottom. An image emerged: a room,

THE RED ROOM

lit in luminous red, with a bed shot from above and to the side. A boy was on the bed. He was naked.

Alice felt very uneasy. "What *is* this?"

Eddie didn't answer. The atmosphere had changed quickly. Their initial curiosity was gone; their scepticism had been replaced with confusion and, in Alice's case, dread. She wondered whether she should reach over and press stop but found that she couldn't. Her hands stayed in her lap, fingers laced together, and her eyes stayed on the screen.

The boy's mouth opened as he said something to whoever else was in the room but out of shot. There was no sound on the recording, but it was obvious from his eyes, wide as saucers, that he was frightened.

"Maybe you were right," Eddie said. "We need to think about what we should be doing with this. Maybe we *should* get the police."

A second person stepped into shot. It was a man, also naked, but he was looking away from the camera so that they couldn't see his face. He said something to the boy, who shook his head. He tried to stand, but it looked as if he was suddenly dizzy. He teetered on the edge of the bed before the man put his hand on his shoulder, and he settled back down. The man sat down next to him and, for the first time, turned and showed his face. He said something to someone off camera; he looked confident and eager, and his arousal was evident. He laughed and turned his attention to the boy.

Alice reached forward quickly and pressed stop.

The man's face was still turned to the camera, frozen and caught amid the bands of static.

Eddie stared. "Is that who I think it is?"

"It's him. It's *definitely* him. It's David Campbell."

CHAPTER 20

Francine drove into Britford, taking the bridge over the Avon cut and then turning down a rough track that ran between opposing lines of mature elms. There were two old fishing lodges at the end of the track and, to the right, an open area of parking for anglers who had visited the river to fish. A shipping container had been left at one side of the space, a door cut into it and a sign fixed to the outside advertising it as the office where fishermen could buy day passes for the fishery. There were four cars parked in the space: a silver Toyota four-by-four, a lime-green Mondeo, a Fiat and a police patrol car. She parked behind the Toyota and opened her door. The car park was unadopted, and the rough surface had been turned into mud by the rain. Francine made her way gingerly around the car to the rear, opened the boot and sat on the edge while she took off her shoes and changed into her waterproof boots.

She stopped to get her bearings: the two lodges were to her left, a deer watched her from the edge of the flooded field to her right, and there was a bridge across the river straight ahead. She had called Bob Carver on the way, and he had told her to go left, taking the track that allowed access to the lodges. She did, noting the lights in the window of the house on the right. There was a narrow concrete bridge that spanned a ditch, and then a gate with a stile to the side.

She crossed the bridge and climbed the stile. The river was to her right, with brambles to the left. The city was close; the spire of the cathedral was visible above the trees. The track had been paved at some point in the past, but it had not been maintained; weeds had punched through the concrete, and chunks of it had been allowed to disintegrate. The river had burst its banks, and long stretches of ground had been submerged. A pair of ducks paddled against the flow, and a bright splash of blue, so vivid as to be almost indigo, signalled a kingfisher as it darted low across the water.

Francine turned the corner and saw a building that she remembered. The playground in Churchill Gardens was on the other side of the water; her parents had taken her there when they were younger. A modern weir had been built across the water and, behind that, it was possible to see the red brick of the old sluice house. She had never had reason to visit it, and it was strange to see the structure from this direction and from close up. The river spread out on this side of the range, the surface whitened with froth as the current pushed out through the sluices.

Francine saw a uniformed officer—Bob Carver—and he raised a hand in greeting as she approached.

"Morning," she said.

"Morning."

"What have we got?"

"Dead body found in the water this morning."

"Where?"

"This way."

Carver led the way upstream to an opening that offered access to the large cast-iron gears that worked the sluices. Francine saw a man waiting for them, a shotgun leaning against a tree. A dog had been tied to a post, the animal pacing back and forth as far as its lead would allow.

"Who's he?" Francine asked, inclining her chin toward the man.

"The water bailiff. He found the body."

"Where?"

Carver pointed into the opening. "In there."

The inside of the structure was gloomy, and it took Francine a moment for her eyes to adjust. It was loud, too, with the water rushing through the sluices, through the channels and then into the pool on the other side. There were six sluice gates, three of which had been raised for the water to flow through. The river shot through the gates, emerging on the other side in a cascade of spray. Francine looked down and saw that the concrete surface was slick with water. She was careful not to slip as she made her way to the edge so that she could look down into the channel.

The body of a man was floating there, pressed up against the gate by the flow of the water. He was of slight build and dressed in clothes that had seen better days: a leather jacket, ripped jeans, battered boots.

"How did he get in there?"

"I asked the bailiff—he's not sure."

"Would he fit through the sluices?"

"Maybe."

"Do we know how long he's been in the water?"

"Jeffers—the bailiff—says he was off yesterday and didn't check inside here the day before that."

"Up to two days, then?"

Carver nodded. "Looks like it."

She looked back down into the throbbing water. "I'll need to call the coroner."

Carver nodded. "We're going to need another couple of lads, too. Fishing him out isn't going to be easy."

CHAPTER 21

Salisbury was a small city, and Alice had worked for the *Journal* long enough to have built up a reasonable contacts book. Her closest police contact was Detective Sergeant Mike Lewis at Bourne Hill, and she had called and said that he needed to come to the *Journal*'s office as soon as he could.

He arrived at the office at eight and rapped on the door until Carly went over to open it.

"Morning," Alice said.

"It's early," he grouched. "What did you want to show me?"

"In the conference room."

"What is it?"

"I need to show you—this way."

He frowned, but then saw the expression on her face. "All right."

She led the way up the stairs and took him into the room with the VCR and the TV. Eddie was sucking on a cigarette, blowing smoke through the partially open window.

"Eddie," Lewis said.

"Mike."

"Alice says you have something for me."

She pointed to the VCR. "We were sent a video last night. You need to see it."

"Go on, then. Let's have a look."

Alice paused, wondering whether she should warn him that the footage was graphic, then realised that was foolish and just pressed play.

CHAPTER 22

The sluice house had been quiet when Francine had arrived, but that didn't last for long. She knew that the death of the man in the water was likely to be classified as unnatural and that they would need to have at least a DS at the scene. She called the station and spoke to Nigel Archer, explaining what had happened and that they were going to need a couple of additional men so that they could get the body out of the water. Archer arrived at the scene half an hour later with Constables Sam Collison and Philip Newman. He toured the sluice house and surrounding area with Francine and decided that it would be better to report up to the duty detective inspector—it was Robbie Best this morning—for additional support and guidance.

Best sent over a crime scene investigator, and Jeffers unlocked the gate so that he was able to drive his van as close to them as the flood allowed. He took out his camera and started to take photographs. Francine watched him as he went about his business, making sure that he had shots of the body from several angles so as not to miss anything.

Jeffers had found a windlass and had lowered the sluice gates to ensure that the flow of water was a little less fierce. He was resting now with a roll-up cigarette. "Aren't you going to get him out?"

"We will."

"When? What are you waiting for?"

"The pathologist."

"Why'd you need him?"

"We can't rule out foul play. We'll need advice to work out the cause of death, and he'll be able to make sure we get him out in a way that doesn't disturb trace evidence."

"Foul play? What does that mean—murder?"

"Much too early to say, but… yes, of course, it's possible."

"Murder? Here?" He lit the cigarette and put it to his lips. "No chance."

"Why'd you say that?"

"I know the type of blokes who come down here. I just can't see it."

Francine gestured into the building. "Do you recognise him?"

"Haven't seen his face yet."

"His build, though? His clothes?"

Jeffers shook his head. "I wasn't here yesterday, like I told the other one, but we didn't have no one in the book who was due to come down and fish, so, whoever he is, I'd say there's a good chance he's not a member."

"Not supposed to have been here, then?"

"That's right. You'd need to be a member—we haven't done day tickets since before COVID. People take advantage, though. You get some who'll come down later when they know I'm not likely to be around. Gypsies—they come down. That might've been what he did."

"What about at night? Does anyone fish then?"

"Not supposed to, but they do. Good time to go after chub. You use a stinky bait like cheese paste and you'd be surprised what you can get out."

"What about the day before yesterday?"

"Like I said, I *was* here then. I had half a dozen down, but none of them were dressed like him." He drew down on his cigarette. "Never had nothing like this happen in all the years I've been here."

"How long's that?"

"Thirty years."

"Who do you work for?"

"London Anglers Association."

"They own the land?"

He shook his head. "Lord Radnor owns it. We rent it from the estate—have done since the sixties."

Francine looked back to the spire of the cathedral and saw the bank of angry dark cloud that was rolling over the city behind it. Her phone buzzed in her pocket and, taking it out, she saw a warning that yet more rain was imminent. She looked at the time on the screen and wished the pathologist would get a move on.

CHAPTER 23

Mack reached over for her phone and silenced it, lying back and closing her eyes as she remembered what had happened last night. Bob Bradley's birthday drinks had been predictably messy, and she had made her escape at last orders just as the others were conspiring about where they could go next. There was talk of a lock-in at the Pheasant—or was it the Wig and Quill?—and, knowing that going along with the others would be a certain way to a much worse hangover than the one she was already going to get, Mack had made her excuses and headed over to see Atticus.

She blinked open her bleary eyes and saw the empty water glass on the bedstand. She remembered him insisting that she drink it—all of it—before they went to bed. She had done and, as she lay back and assessed how she felt, she found that her headache wasn't nearly as bad as she might have expected given the number of pints she had put away.

Mack looked the other way and saw that the bed was empty. She reached out a hand and felt the indentation where Atticus had lain; it was cold. She turned back to the bedstand

and took her phone, opening her messages to see if he had left anything for her. He hadn't, but she remembered that he had said something about getting an early start. He'd told her he'd been given a new job, that it wouldn't be difficult and that he ought to be able to get it finished in a day if he put his mind to it.

It was seven. She would grab a quick shower, get dressed and then stop off at Boston Tea Party for breakfast on her way to the office. She fancied something greasy and unhealthy.

* * *

Mike Lewis called Mack during her walk to the nick.

"Morning, Mike. What's up?"

"Sorry to disturb you, boss. I'm at the *Journal*. I got a call from Alice Morris. She said she had something I needed to see. She was right. You need to see it, boss. You need to get over here now."

"Now? *Right* now? I was going to stop and get some breakfast."

"Sorry, boss. I don't think this can wait."

CHAPTER 24

Francine watched as Professor Allen Fyfe, the home office pathologist, made his way along the sodden track to join them.

"You'd think I would've learned by now," he grumbled, pointing down.

His brogues and the bottoms of his trousers were thick with mud, and he was soaked through despite his umbrella. Francine remembered the same complaints when Fyfe had attended to the bodies that had been discovered at Imber. He was much more comfortable in his inspection rooms at the hospital than out in the field, especially when the weather was unpleasant.

"Thank you for coming, Professor."

"What've we got?"

"Dead body inside the sluice house. Looks like it's been in the water for a while."

Fyfe went over to the opening and looked inside. "Bloody hell. We can't leave him in there getting bumped around like that. We need to get him out."

"We've just been waiting for you," Archer said.

Fyfe told them that they should get started. Collison had drawn the short straw and was going to be the one who got into the water to manoeuvre the body while the others pulled him out. Francine watched as he pulled on a pair of waders that Jeffers had fetched for him from the shipping container back near the fishing lodges, hauling them up so that he was covered to halfway up his chest.

"It's going to be bloody cold," he grumbled as he went to the edge of the channel and sat down.

Jeffers gestured down into the channel. "Are you sure you wouldn't rather I did it?"

"Better that it's us," Francine said.

"We'll need you to help pull him out," Archer said.

"It'll be slippery on the bottom. There'll be mud and silt down there, and the current will be a bastard. Be careful."

Collison pushed off the edge and lowered himself into the water. It was deeper than it looked, and the glossy surface came up to the top of his chest. The water tried to shove him downstream, and he had to set himself against it. Archer passed him the end of a coil of rope, and Collison carefully looped it around the torso of the dead man. He fed it beneath his arms, secured it around his back and then gently floated the body away from the edge.

Archer and Jeffers took the other end of the rope.

"Ready?" Archer said.

"Ready," said Jeffers.

"Ready," said Collison.

"*Pull.*"

It was a joint effort: Collison tried to ensure that the body didn't scrape against the side of the channel, getting his arms around the dead man's waist and boosting him up; Archer and Jeffers and Francine pulled, hand over hand and inch after inch, heaving the dead weight out of the water and then up and over the side. They grabbed him beneath the shoulders and pulled him all the way out, leaving him face down on the concrete floor. He was sodden, and water pooled beneath him and ran back down into the channel again.

"Give me a hand," Collison said.

Archer reached down and locked his hand around Collison's wrist, grunting with the effort as Collison scrabbled up, his boot finding something to wedge against so that he could boost himself over the edge and out. He remained where he was, on hands and knees, and gathered his breath.

Fyfe stepped forward. "Let's get him over there," he said, pointing to a spot where the curve of the riverbank had been flattened out.

The body was limp. Archer took the arms and Jeffers took the legs and, between them, they moved it to the spot that Fyfe had indicated. They lowered the body to the ground and turned it over and, for the first time, Francine was able to look at the man's face. It was angled slightly upward by a small overbite, and his skin was tanned by the weather, with a lattice of tiny veins across his fleshy nose and pitted cheeks. He was unshaven, with water clinging to the unkempt bristles, and his lips were chapped. His clothes looked as if they would have been dishevelled even before he entered the water; they were torn, and a rip in his shirt revealed an expanse of tattooed skin.

"Recognise him?" Archer asked Jeffers.

"Never seen him before."

"Not a fisherman?"

"Not a member, put it that way."

Francine put a hand to her cheek.

Archer noticed. "Franny? What is it?"

"I know who he is. I've nicked him before." She closed her eyes and tried to remember the details. "Rough sleeper, used to doss down in the Maltings, record for petty crime—mostly shoplifting. I picked him up after he took a bunch of clothes from the tailor's on New Street. He flogged them for heroin he got off Tommy Quinn in the Friary. He had a couple of grams he'd hidden in his sock."

"Name?"

"He's Polish…" She scrunched up her face, then put her hands together as she remembered it. "They called him Lucky Lucjusz."

"Not *that* lucky," Collison said as he peeled off the waterproof trousers.

She tried to remember his surname. "Lucjusz… Lucjusz… Lucjusz Kajetan."

Fyfe knelt and started to make a quick examination. "The deceased is male, late forties to early fifties."

"How long has he been in there?"

"A body in the water will decompose more slowly than would be the case if it were on land. It's the cold—it delays things. You'll see the usual post-mortem changes—discolouration of skin and soft tissue, bloating, putrefaction. It just takes longer."

"When, then?" Archer said. "A day? Two days? The bailiff wasn't at work yesterday and didn't look in here the day before."

Fyfe nodded. "A two-day window, then. That's about right."

Francine was impatient. Fyfe's caution was as predictable, and as annoying, as ever. "Best guess?"

Fyfe sucked his teeth. "Anywhere between twelve and eighteen hours."

"Cause of death?"

"Most likely drowning, but I'll have a look." He stood up. "I need to move him. Putrefaction accelerates once a body is taken out of the water. I need to get him into the fridge."

CHAPTER 25

Atticus followed Wintringham, picking him up at the end of the road and then discreetly tailing him as he headed into town. He stopped at Godolphin to drop off his eldest daughter and then continued to Bishopsdown, where he delivered his youngest to an older woman Atticus recognised from Wintringham's social media as his mother. The house was on the same estate as the one that Mack had shared with her ex-husband, and Atticus was irrationally concerned that Andy Jones would see him and confront him for breaking up his marriage.

Atticus had expected Wintringham to drive over to Old Sarum for work, but he didn't; he turned around and headed into the city, leaving his car at the Maltings and hurrying on to Fisherton Street on foot while sheltering beneath a small umbrella. Atticus parked up, put Bandit on the lead and followed, staying a decent distance behind him. Wintringham stopped in Waterstones, where he browsed the shelves for ten minutes. He went outside again, turning left and walking the short distance to St. George's Mall, where he diverted to WHSmith. He came out and retraced his steps to Boston Tea Party, the large coffee shop on the High Street. Atticus sheltered in the doorway of an empty shop where he could watch without being easily noticed. Wintringham ordered a coffee and a pastry and then chatted with the barista who served him.

Wintringham came back outside, and Atticus followed him once more as he made his way up Crane Street to the medical practice at the back of the Lush House car park. Atticus waited behind a car and watched as Wintringham went into the surgery, spoke to the receptionist and then disappeared.

Atticus waited for a minute and then started back to his car. There was nothing about Wintringham that gave him any cause for concern. He was just as Nina had described him: a father of two children with what appeared to be a normal, mundane life. There wasn't much else for him to do. He would go back to the office and write up his report, add the relevant links to the social media profiles that he had used, and then, when he had received the DBS check and the entry on the land registry for the Wintringhams' house, he would bundle it all together with his invoice and send it over to Nina.

It was boring work, but it paid well, and Atticus wasn't in the habit of turning down easy money.

CHAPTER 26

Francine drove back across the city to the nick. Fyfe had arranged for the body to be taken to the hospital, where he would go through the motions of confirming what they already suspected: Lucjusz Kajetan had fallen into the water and drowned. He said that he would test the blood for the presence of alcohol and drugs; Francine remembered Kajetan and was confident that he would have been under the influence of one or the other—or both—when he died. It all seemed grimly predictable: another unfortunate who had fallen on hard times and was dead because of it.

Francine was cold and damp and in need of a hot drink. Robbie Best was in the kitchen, filling the kettle at the tap. She paused, worrying that it might be awkward, but he defused any possible awkwardness with a friendly smile as he held up a tea bag. "Want a brew?"

"Please. It's bitter out there."

Best flicked the switch on the side of the kettle. "How was it?"

"Unpleasant."

"You get the body out?"

She nodded. "Remember Lucjusz Kajetan?"

"Name's familiar. Where do I know him from?"

"Rough sleeper. I nicked him for possession. It's a sad story—came over from Poland twenty years ago and set up as a builder, got in too deep with the bank and lost it all. He ended up on the street with a drug habit, which is where he was when I pulled him. He got a suspended sentence and disappeared. I heard on the grapevine that he'd gone to Andover, but maybe not."

"What was he doing in the river?"

"I think he might have been sleeping in the sluice house and fell in. It's dark and slippery, and if he was pissed or high, like he probably was… I don't think it'd be too hard to go over the edge and drown."

"What does Fyfe think?"

"He's going to take a look at the body and let me know."

The kettle boiled. Best took out two mugs from the cupboard, dropped a tea bag into each and was about to pour the water when they heard footsteps approaching from outside.

Mack stopped in the doorway. "Meeting in the conference room in fifteen minutes," she said. "Grab everyone who's here, Robbie. No exceptions."

"What is it, boss?"

"David Campbell," she said. "It *definitely* wasn't an accident on the tower yesterday."

CHAPTER 27

The memory of what she had watched at the *Journal*—and what it might mean—was fresh in Mack's mind as she went through into the same space that they had only recently used as the Major Incident Room for the Imber enquiry. There was a long table with enough chairs to seat twenty. Mack had brought the package with the video and, once the evidentiary requirements had been taken care of, had asked the IT department to digitise the footage so that it could be more easily distributed and viewed. They would also ensure that it was stored safely in the event that it became important evidence in any subsequent investigation into the events leading up to the death of David Campbell. There was a screen on the wall, and Mack took out her laptop and connected it, thumbing the remote to the correct input so that she was able to share her screen.

She went to one end of the table, pulled out the chair and sat down. She tried to get her thoughts in order as she waited for the others to arrive. She was buzzing with the adrenaline of a new challenge, a death that had been tragic until this morning, when it had suddenly become much more than that: now it was mysterious and most likely sinister.

Debbie Campbell had been convinced that her husband had not taken his own life, and now, considering what she had seen on the video, Mack was inclined to believe her.

Suicide was possible, but, if it was, then blackmail was involved.

Murder was in play, too.

Robbie Best marshalled those officers who were working the day shift and sent them into the conference room. Nigel Archer took the seat to Mack's right, and Francine Patterson took the seat next to him. Archer had only just been promoted from detective constable, his career already characterised by huge ambition and the willingness to put in the hours that others might not have been prepared to invest. Francine's hair was damp, and Mack had noticed mud on her trousers; she had been told that a body had been found in the river and that Francine had been the first detective on the scene.

DC Stewart Lynas sat down at the opposite end of the table. He was ambitious, too, but, unlike Archer and Francine, Mack wasn't sure that he had the ability to back it up. He was the son of wealthy parents who had not stinted on his education, sending him to a succession of expensive private schools. These had given him an overinflated sense of self-worth and a habit of looking down on others but had been unable to improve a sluggish intellect.

She tapped her knuckles against the table. "All right, quieten down. We've had a development on the death of David Campbell at the cathedral. We *had* been working on the assumption that he had either fallen by way of an accident or that he'd jumped. An accident always felt like a bit of a long shot, and there's been a development overnight that makes it even less likely."

She looked around the table at the faces of her officers. They were all rapt, Campbell's death was already grotesque, but the suggestion that it might have been something other than a dreadful accident gave it an edge that had been missing before. The suggestion of a darker motivation raised the stakes.

Mack turned to her laptop and moused over to the folder that she had been given by the evidence handler. The envelope that had contained the tape had been photographed and then transferred to a sterile container and filed. Mack double-clicked the folder and then clicked again on the sub-folder that was labelled with the details of the envelope. She picked a photograph taken from above and gestured to it on the screen.

"At some point yesterday," Mack continued, "this package was delivered to the offices of the *Journal* on Rollestone Street."

She dragged the image of the package to the other side of the screen and opened two additional top-down photographs of the video cassette: one showing the label and the other showing the back. She opened another folder and clicked on the images that showed the case, with Campbell's name written on the slip of paper that had been pushed down against the spine.

"The tape was in the case," she said.

Best pointed to the image that showed the label. "David Campbell?" he said.

"That's right. He's on the tape. You need to see this first."

She clicked again and opened a photograph of the piece of paper.

"'It is mine to avenge,'" Best read out. "'I will repay. In due time their foot will slip; their day of disaster is near and their doom rushes upon them.' What is that? From the Bible?"

"Deuteronomy chapter thirty-two, verse thirty-five."

"Didn't Jack leave Bible verses with Atticus after he left Miller's body?" Francine said.

Mack nodded. "He did."

She clicked back, jumped across to the folder that had the digitised version of the video and double-clicked it. The file opened and auto played, showing the room with the bed, everything lit in red. No one spoke as the boy appeared in the shot and then the man. He turned so that his face was exposed to the camera.

"Shit," Best said.

Mack pointed to the screen. "I haven't had it absolutely confirmed yet, but I'm about as confident that we can be that that is Campbell, albeit maybe twenty or twenty-five years ago. We'll have to ask his wife, but that can wait for now."

"And the boy?"

"Young," Mack said. "Hard to say how young, but I wouldn't be surprised if he was under sixteen."

"Definitely under sixteen," Lynas said.

Mack moved the cursor to the top right of the video and closed it.

Archer laid his palms flat on the table. "And this went to the *Journal*?"

She nodded.

"Why?"

"We don't know, but it'd be a very big coincidence that Campbell happens to fall to his death on the day that this video comes to light. An accident was always unlikely. He knew the cathedral well, and they've made it safe up there. He slipped?"

She shook her head. "No."

"Blackmail?"

"That'd be my guess. Maybe Campbell was sent this by someone who was trying to make money. Either he didn't have the money, or he was worried that the tape would come out anyway."

"Or he paid it, and they still put it out."

"Possible."

Lynas clucked his tongue. "What about the verse?"

"I don't know," Mack said. "But Franny is right. It does remind me of Jack."

"Could it be him?"

"We never made it public that he was into the Bible," Mack said. "I mean, it *might* just be one of those things, but I don't know…"

Lewis leaned back. "So it's murder?"

Mack spread her hands. "There's no evidence that there was anyone else up there with him."

"No CCTV?"

Best shook his head. "Checked. None once you get through the door at the back of the nave and start to climb the tower."

"What about the cameras they *do* have?" Archer said.

"We've reviewed them, didn't see anything that would suggest that someone else was up there."

"That's not to say that we can rule it out," Mack said. "I think it's less likely than suicide, but we need to eliminate it." She paused. "We don't have any choice but to open an enquiry. I want it to be discreet at the moment. Campbell's wife lost her husband yesterday, and the last thing I want is for her to have to worry about this until it's absolutely necessary." She gestured to Francine. "Can you very carefully get a crop of the video that shows just his face—nothing else if you can help it—and take it over to her and get her to confirm that it's him?"

"And if she asks where we got it from?"

"We can't shield her from it completely. Maybe just try to be vague. Tell her we've seen a video of him from a long while ago that he might have found embarrassing. Tell her that she doesn't have to see it, but that we need her to confirm that it's him."

Francine nodded. "It's possible she knows something about it and didn't want to say."

"Maybe. See how she reacts. And ask her if she had any reason to think that he might've been blackmailed. Had he moved money out of a joint account or asked if she had any he could use—anything like that."

Archer pointed to the screen. "What about the package?"

"That's got to be our focus," Mack said. "We need to find out who delivered it." She pointed at Lynas. "Go and check all the cameras on Rollestone Street. See if there's anything that shows someone dropping a package off. They don't think it was there before lunch, and they found it around ten. Eight hours. That's your search window."

Lynas said that he would get to it right away, Mack didn't doubt that he would find the task menial and beneath him, but she had decided that he was going to have to get used to doing the running around before she gave him the more interesting and consequential jobs.

"What about the boy?" Archer said. "Who is he?"

Lynas scratched his cheek. "We're saying that's twenty years ago? He'd be mid- to late-thirties now."

Mack shrugged. "Look for mispers around the time. You can dig out the files from Imber—we already spent hours on it. No point doing the work twice."

"And if nothing shows up?"

"Public appeal?" Archer suggested.

"Not yet," Mack said. "Not without making things a million times worse for Mrs. Campbell."

He nodded his agreement. "Hold off until we don't have any other choice."

"Agreed." Mack nodded to Best. "Can you sort forensics? We need to get everything looked at—the envelope, the video, the box, the paper. We'll need disqualifying prints from everyone at the *Journal*, so get that done and then see if there's anything else. Maybe we get lucky and there's a hit."

"Will do."

Mack stood. "Good. I don't want to make a song and dance about this yet, so let's not talk about it out of school."

Best drummed his fingers on the table. "Look, I don't want to sound the alarm unnecessarily, but do you think this could be connected to Imber?"

"Go on."

"We had missing girls there. I don't know—seems like that video was shot at around the same time they were killed. Maybe they had it away with boys, too."

"We can't rule anything out. See if you can find a match with the boy in the video and the girls we dug up in the graveyard. Anything. Think laterally. Go on—get to it. Dismissed."

THE RED ROOM

The team dispersed. Mack stayed where she was for a moment, thinking about what Best had said about Imber. The thought had crossed her mind, too, and she wondered whether she should mention what they had discovered to Atticus.

CHAPTER 28

Atticus had been surprised to receive the text message from Mack asking if he was available for lunch. He had spent a quiet morning writing up his notes following his background check on Robin Wintringham. He had prepared a short two-page report that laid out what he had found—or, precisely, what he *hadn't* found—and had just about finished it when his phone buzzed with Mack's invitation. He had given the dog a quick walk so that he could relieve himself and then had walked to the market square. Mack had suggested that they meet at Henderson's and was waiting for him at a table inside.

"This is a pleasant surprise," he said as he sat down. "Is everything all right?"

"I thought it would be nice to see you," she said.

"Really?"

"I don't need a reason for that, do I?"

"Of course not."

Mack wouldn't admit that there *was* a reason, but Atticus could see that she was agitated: the glasses on the table held cutlery and paper napkins, and Mack had taken out one of the napkins and torn it into squares. She was fidgeting, too, and a tightness in her neck suggested stress. Atticus's instinct was to point out what he had noticed, but, for once, he managed to hold his tongue.

"What are you having?" she asked him.

"A sandwich," he said, rising before she could. "I'll get them. What do you want?"

"You choose."

He went to the counter and ordered two sandwiches—the cheese and tomato that she liked and a pastrami for him—together with drinks. He paid for them and went back to the table.

Mack had taken out a second napkin and was in the process of shredding that one, too.

Atticus couldn't hold his tongue any longer. "What is it? Something's up."

She sighed, pushed the pieces of the napkin into a pile, and nodded. "I could do with your opinion."

"Work?"

She nodded. "You know I've been looking into the man who fell from the tower of the cathedral?"

"What about him?"

"I don't think it was an accident."

His eyes widened. "Really?"

"This doesn't go any further—right?"

"Of course not."

"Atticus—I'm serious."

"It's strictly between us."

She leaned forward a little. "A package was sent to the *Journal* yesterday. We only found out about it this morning.

It was a video of Campbell from fifteen or twenty years ago. He was doing things with a boy that he really oughtn't have been doing."

"Have you seen it?"

She nodded.

"Cheese and tomato and pastrami?"

The girl from the counter had their sandwiches and two cans of Diet Coke.

"Thanks," Atticus said, smiling as she set the food and drink down on the table.

Mack waited until she had gone back behind the counter.

"This video shows up on the day that he falls off the tower and dies?" She spread her hands over the table. "I mean—come *on*. You can see why I don't think it was an accident now, right?"

"Blackmail?"

"That'd be my guess."

"He's blackmailed, and *then* he jumps off the tower." Atticus's mind started to race with questions and angles that would have to be investigated; he held up his hand, as much to tell himself to slow down as anything. "Right—give me the details. When did they get the package?"

"Yesterday afternoon or evening."

"Can they be more specific than that?"

"No. That's the best they can do."

"How was it delivered?"

"We think by hand. It wasn't posted."

"So it was delivered yesterday afternoon or evening, and Campbell died in the morning. Why would they do that?"

"Maybe he didn't pay?"

"Or maybe he did. Maybe someone wants to ruin his reputation. His death wasn't enough."

"Suicide, then?"

He paused again, prodding a finger against his untouched sandwich.

"Atticus?"

"Someone pushed him?"

"Why?"

"There's an argument. It gets physical."

"Why would there be an argument on the cathedral tower? It's hardly convenient."

"I agree, but humour me. Would anyone have known he was there?"

"He was taking photos for a project. He's been up the tower at the same time every day all year. He blogs about it."

"*That's* interesting." Atticus paused. "We need motive, means and opportunity—predictability gives us opportunity."

"But means and motive? I don't know." She toyed with the napkin again. "Let's say it's blackmail, and he *didn't* jump. Why murder him? It couldn't be that he didn't pay. Maybe you'd kill him, but like that?"

"The lack of discretion? Yes—strange. But how about this— maybe whoever pushed him *wants* the attention. They want this to make the news. It's why the video was sent after he was dead. It's about publicity."

"*Not* blackmail, then?"

"It's the most likely motive, but it wouldn't have to be that. Maybe someone wants to kill him *and* ruin his reputation."

"Murder him twice," she suggested.

"That's a nice way to put it."

"There was something else, too," she said. "There was a piece of paper in with the tape. It had a Bible verse printed on it. 'It is mine to avenge; I will repay—'"

He finished for her. "'—In due time their foot will slip; their day of disaster is near and their doom rushes upon them.' Deuteronomy thirty-two, verse thirty… thirty…"

"Five," Mack said. "Thirty-five."

"And that was in the package?"

Mack sighed. "Yes."

"Right. *Okay.*" He clapped his hands together. "*Now* I get it—you think this is Jack?"

"He referred you to a Bible verse when Miller was left."

"And gave me a Bible with all his favourite verses highlighted."

"Was that one of them?"

"No, but the Bible's not short on revenge. Especially not the Old Testament. He'd have *lots* to choose from."

"So—what do you think? Could it be him?"

"I don't know. You never made the fact he left verses for me public, did you?"

"No. Did you tell anyone?"

He shook his head. "I can see why you think I might be interested."

She pushed her food away and looked at him. "Are you?"

"Of course."

"Why?"

"Because…" He started, noticed that Mack was looking at him quizzically, and stopped.

"This all goes back to Burns. You went after him like a dog with a bone, then Imber, and you haven't really stopped."

"Because I knew Burns was guilty. And because there's more to what he and Miller and York did than we've found out so far."

She was watching him carefully as he spoke, and he found it unnerving.

"Okay."

Atticus reached across the table and took her hand. "What is it?"

There was concern in her face as she squeezed his hand. "You'll always be honest with me, won't you?"

"Of course," he said. "What is it, Mack?"

"I'm always here if you want to talk."

He shook his head. "Where's all this coming from?"

She squeezed his hand again and let go. "All right. I just wanted to make sure you knew that."

"I do."

"Good. And thank you. I'm grateful for your help."

"Could you call the cathedral for me? I'll go up to the tower and have a look. Tell them I'm coming and to let me up."

"There's nothing there. We've been over it from top to bottom."

"So there's no harm in me having a check, is there?"

Atticus could see from Mack's body language that she was reluctant. Atticus knew that her decision to involve him would be rescinded if she knew that he had butted heads with Murphy yesterday, she had been too drunk to ask him about the interview last night, and he hadn't volunteered his account of it. He would have to tell her about it eventually—especially given that Murphy looked like he had her in his sights, too—but it could wait until tonight.

"I don't know," she said.

"Just a quick look. Up and down in half an hour."

She sighed.

"You wouldn't have spoken to me about it if you didn't want my help."

"I wanted to *talk* to you about it. That's a *long* way from wanting you to get involved."

"It's up to you. But a second opinion might help you get a little closer to what happened."

"I suppose I could say that you're consulting again."

He thought of what Murphy had said and ignored it. "Just like before."

"But please—don't embarrass me."

Atticus picked up his sandwich, opened the wrapping and took a bite.

"I'll be good."

CHAPTER 29

Atticus went back to the office, took Bandit into the courtyard for five minutes so that he could relieve himself, and then walked the short distance to the cathedral. Mack had called ahead, and one of the guides who led the tours up to the tower was waiting for him in the cloisters.

"Mr. Priest?"

"That's right."

"I'm Clive Mouton. You want to go up the tower?"

"Please."

"Anywhere in particular?"

"I'd like to see the parapet Mr. Campbell was on when he fell."

"I thought the investigation was finished?"

"I'm just checking a couple of things before we close the file."

Atticus didn't know whether Mouton had been told that he wasn't a policeman, but, if he didn't know, Atticus wasn't minded to correct him. It would be a useful misconception and would make securing his cooperation a little easier. Mack had explained that Mouton was one of the witnesses who had seen Campbell falling from the tower, Atticus didn't expect that he would be able to extricate anything from him that he hadn't already provided to the investigation, but it would be helpful to be able to have his perspective.

"This way," Mouton said, going through the door and into the nave of the cathedral. They crossed over to the doorway in the corner of the building that was used for the tours. "Have you been up the tower before?"

"I haven't. Would Mr. Campbell have come this way?"

"Definitely."

"Any other ways up?"

"A couple," Mouton said, "but those doors are kept locked."

"Where?"

"There's a door in the north transept and another in the sacristy."

"Would you be able to show me later?"

"If it'd help."

Atticus was looking for CCTV cameras and had spotted half a dozen between the entrance and the doorway through which they were about to pass. Mack had said that they had checked the recordings and hadn't seen anything that would suggest that anyone other than Campbell had climbed the tower yesterday morning.

"It was suicide, wasn't it?" Mouton said.

"Seems most likely."

"Awful."

"Did you know him?"

"We all did. He was a popular man. He'd been here a long time."

Mouton took a key from his pocket and unlocked the door. Atticus followed him into the waiting area with the lockers on the left-hand side and the passage on the right that would continue up into the rest of the building.

"No cameras in here?"

"No," Mouton said. "There's no need. The public can't come up unless they're with a guide, and the door is locked."

Atticus followed Mouton up the stairs, across the passage that ran along the wall of the nave and then up more stairs until they reached the clock. They climbed again, paused for a moment while the bells chimed the quarter hour, and then climbed the final set of stairs that brought them to the top of the tower and the four doors that led out onto the parapets.

Atticus tried to orient himself. "Which door?"

Mouton pointed to the door on the right. "That one." He walked over and turned the handle. The door was unlocked, and he opened it, stepping aside to let Atticus pass. Atticus stepped through and onto the narrow parapet on the other side. He looked over the edge of the balcony to the roof of the refectory below. He could see that what Mack had said was likely correct; it would be very difficult for anyone to fall over the barrier accidentally. It would have had to have been an intentional act on Campbell's part. He thought about the other possibility—that he was pushed—and found that prospect less likely now.

"How big was Campbell?"

Mouton frowned. "Sorry?"

"Was he a large man?"

"Yes. A couple of inches taller than me."

"How old?"

"Early sixties."

"Fit? Unfit?"

"Very fit. You know he was in the army? The discipline never left him. He was in good shape. Ran a marathon every year to raise money for the cathedral and worked out two or three times a week. Why?"

"Just wondering about whether he might have climbed up onto the railing and then slipped. More likely if he was frail."

"Frail is the *last* word I'd use to describe him."

Atticus looked at the balustrade. The fact that Campbell was still fit and strong made foul play less likely. It would have taken effort to get him up and over the barrier, especially if he was struggling.

Was it possible?

Yes.

Likely?

No.

Atticus stood with his hands on the metal bar and looked out over the city. The rain started to fall again, but he ignored it, closing his eyes and concentrating on the explanations for what might have happened here the day before.

Three options.

An accident? That seemed unlikely. There was no reason for Campbell to have put himself in a position where he might fall. Everything Atticus had been told about him suggested that he was careful.

Foul play? Also unlikely. Atticus had been unable to find any evidence to suggest that there was someone on the tower with Campbell yesterday morning, and, even if he wasn't alone, it was difficult to see how it would have been possible to get him into a position where he could be tipped over the edge.

Suicide, then. More likely. Campbell was being blackmailed and, fearing the ruination of his reputation, he had come up to a place that he loved and taken his own life. But the blackmailer had released the footage anyway. Atticus tried to find the weaknesses in the argument but could see only one: that Campbell's wife had detected nothing to suggest that her husband was considering taking his own life. Atticus agreed with what Mack had suggested; there was no guarantee that she would have realised his intentions, especially when the thing that Campbell wanted to avoid—his shame—would have been guaranteed if he had been honest.

But, saying all that, Atticus still felt the nag of doubt.

He needed to see the tape.

CHAPTER 30

Mouton took Atticus to the doors that he had mentioned in the north transept and sacristy. The transept was first. Atticus tried the handle.

"It'll be locked," Mouton said.

It was.

Atticus knelt and, ignoring the looks of confusion from the worshippers and tourists who were ambling around the building, leaned in close to examine the wood around the keyhole for any suggestion that the lock might have been picked.

"What is it?" Mouton asked him.

Atticus ignored him. The wood was old and had been scratched and scraped over the course of its life, but there was nothing that looked new. They went to the sacristy, and Atticus confirmed that that door, too, was secured. There were cameras covering both doors, and, as he looked up and down the nave, he doubted whether anyone who might have wanted to do Campbell harm would have been able to use either door to climb the tower without being seen.

Atticus thanked Mouton for his help and exited the nave, walking through the cloisters and then going outside. The rain was falling more heavily now, but Atticus had an idea and was distracted from the fact that he was getting wet by his desire to test it. He skirted the cathedral until he reached the Trinity Chapel at the easternmost side of the building. He remembered from walking the dog that the walls here were covered with a lattice of scaffolding across the whole flank. The exterior of the Lady Chapel and its vast stained-glass window were accessed by way of six levels of boarded platforms, each level reached by a ladder. The nave was also being maintained, and another nine platforms reached up from the roof of the chapel to the points of the three decorative pillars that stood at the eastern end of the main building. There was no obvious means of access to the tower that sat over the junction of the nave and the north and south transepts, but that was not reason enough for Atticus to abandon the suspicion that nagged at him as he looked up at the building.

What if there was a way into the tower from the outside?

The bottom of the scaffolding had been protected behind a series of interlocking portable fences that had been erected all the way along the length of the wall. Atticus followed the fence until he came to a gate; he looked around and, seeing no one who might oppose him, tried the gate and found that it was unlocked. He pushed it all the way back and passed through the opening, turning left and then right until he saw the ladder that led up to the first platform ten feet above him. He climbed it, reaching the wooden boards and then taking a second and third ladder until he was thirty feet above the ground. He was up close to the stained-glass window that celebrated prisoners of conscience, the view into the cathedral obscured by the coloured glass to the extent that the people inside were no more than indistinct shadows.

Atticus climbed the next ladder, then the next and, finally, the ladder that took him up to the platform that allowed access to the apex of the roof. He was high up here; the boards continued around the top of the cathedral and, hidden from the ground on the southern side of the building, he saw two stonemasons who were working on the weathered marble piers. They both saw Atticus as soon as he climbed up to the platform, and the man who was closest stood up and picked his way around the boards.

"What are you doing?" the man said angrily.

Atticus held up his hands. "It's okay."

"You can't be up here."

"It's fine."

"No, it's not. Who are you? You need to get down right away."

"I'm with the police."

"Oh." The man stopped. "Because of David?"

"That's right. We're looking into what happened."

"You still shouldn't be up here, mate, especially not by yourself."

He smiled. "I'm not by myself now, am I? The two of you are here."

"Come on. That's not—"

Atticus interrupted him. "Could you answer a couple of questions for me?"

"You need to—"

Atticus cut across him again. "What's your name?"

"Tristan."

"The dean knows I'm up here, Tristan, but feel free to go and have a word with him if that'd make you feel better."

He fidgeted uncomfortably. "What was your name?"

"Atticus Priest."

"And you're police?"

"That's right."

"And what do you want?"

"Just a couple of questions."

"Go on, then."

"Are you up here every day?"

"Yes."

"What time do you start?"

"Usually around nine."

"Yesterday?"

He shook his head. "Didn't come up—not after what happened."

Atticus hadn't expected to find out anything useful, but that wasn't why he had asked his questions; he needed a delay while he looked for what he was really interested in.

"I remember reading about a workshop in the attic, above the nave—is it still there?"

"Yes. Why?"

"Have you ever been inside?"

"No. It's not being used at the moment."

"Where is it?"

Tristan pointed across the leadwork roof to a hatch that Atticus hadn't noticed.

"Could you show me?"

Atticus followed the stonemason around the platform until he reached the outward bulge that marked the start of the choir transept. The hatch was made of wood that was banded with iron straps; it had received a battering from the weather over the years. It had a handle and looked as if it was secured by way of a mortice.

Atticus gestured to it. "Locked?"

"Never tried it."

Atticus stepped around him, reached for the cold iron knob and turned it.

The hatch opened.

The space inside was dark, and Atticus was unable to see anything once the gloom swallowed up the daylight.

"Where does it go?"

"It's above the nave, but, like I said, I've never been in."

"But it might run to the tower?"

"I mean, it *might*, but—"

Atticus took out his phone, activated the flashlight and shone it inside. He could see a little farther now, but still not enough to satisfy his curiosity. The tower was still at least a hundred feet away; the only way to see whether it was possible to access it through the roof was to go in and check.

Atticus took a step over the threshold, and the mason grabbed his arm.

"You can't go in," he said. "Not without someone from the works department."

"So either come in with me or go and get someone."

The man turned back to his mate and called out that he was going to have to borrow his phone. Atticus took his opportunity, he shook the man's hand off, and, shining the torch down to light the way, he stepped inside.

CHAPTER 31

Atticus held his phone out in front of him in the hope that the torch might light the way enough for him to see where he was going. He remembered reading an article about a secret workshop in the roof that was used by the stonemasons and glaziers who had been involved in restoration work across the life of the building. The attic space was full of the beams that supported the roof. Long cross braces stretched from one side of the space to the other, with more modern—yet still ancient—metal trusses locking everything into place. The wood was old—hundreds of years old—and Atticus breathed in its aroma. The attic was furnished with one vast table that would have been used by masons and glaziers working on larger items that couldn't easily be brought up from the ground.

Atticus counted his steps to the other end of the workshop and reached fifty; he guessed that he still had the same distance again before he reached the start of the tower.

The room ended in a triangular wall formed by the angle of the roof. Atticus shone his torch up and saw that there was a door in the wall, and that it was open. He shone his light down on the floor and carefully stepped over the sill and into the next room beyond.

"Hey," he heard from behind him. "Stop! You can't just go in there."

It was the mason; Atticus ignored him and carried on.

The second room was an attic that didn't look as if it had ever been used. A wooden gangway led down the middle of the space, with the false ceiling of the nave bulging upwards. Holes had been drilled into the lime so that water could drain in the event that there was ever a fire. He followed the gangway as it took him above the presbytery. He tried not to focus on how high above the floor of the cathedral he was and hoped that access to this space was not restricted on account of it being unsafe. He didn't know, but couldn't stop walking; he felt that he was close to making a discovery that could be important in determining what had happened to Campbell. His single-mindedness—Mack would call it impetuosity—might land him in trouble, but the game would be worth the candle if he could give her an explanation as to what might have happened on the tower yesterday morning.

He came to the end of the roof space and tried to picture the plan of the cathedral. It was laid out in the shape of a cross, with the tower atop the junction where the nave and the north and south transepts met. He guessed that he had travelled beyond the choir transepts and that he must now be near to the tower.

He shone his torch ahead and saw another door in the wall. It was made of wood and looked as old as the beams behind him. The door had an iron handle; Atticus covered his hand with the sleeve of his jacket and tried it. The handle turned, and the door opened. Atticus knelt and shone his torch on the door, checking the wooden frame for signs of damage and finding none. He focused on the lock itself; it was antique, although newer than the door. He got in closer and recognised a double-acting tumbler design. His knowledge of locksmithing was extensive, and he knew that this lock would have dated from around the mid-1700s. He concentrated his light on the decorative plate that protected the keyhole and saw a scrape, a straight line that started at the hole and extended an inch below it. Atticus held the torch as close to the door as he could and then leaned in even closer; it was impossible to say for sure, but the scratch looked recent. He covered his fingers with his sleeve and very carefully touched the iron handle, gently pulling the door back so that he could look at the bolt. It was undamaged. He would need to have the door removed so that he could look at the mechanism; he made a note to himself to mention it to Mack when he spoke to her.

He went through the doorway and emerged onto a landing before a set of stairs that he remembered from his visit to the tower earlier.

Satisfied, he turned and retraced his steps, passing through the second and then the first door and returning to the hatch that opened onto the roof. The masons were still there, but a third man—someone Atticus hadn't seen before—had joined them.

The newcomer approached him. "What do you think you're doing?"

"Who are *you*?"

"The deputy clerk of works. Who are you?"

"I'm with the police."

"I just *called* the police. They said there's no one supposed to be here."

"I'm a consultant," he said patiently. "Speak to DCI Jones."

"Don't worry, mate—I intend to."

"She'll explain everything." He turned and pointed into the dark attic. "There's a door at the end of the gangway in the second room, just before the staircase in the tower. Please don't go inside, and *definitely* don't let anyone touch it. I'm going to arrange for a crime scene investigator to come out and see if there are any fingerprints on the handle. Do you understand?"

"Fingerprints? What do you mean?"

"When's the last time that you went in there to have a look?"

"Beyond the workshop? Never. It's not safe."

"And was the door locked or unlocked?"

"We never go in there," the clerk repeated. "We don't use that door. I have no idea whether it's locked."

"Please listen carefully," Atticus said. "Don't go inside now. Absolutely do not touch *anything*. There could be evidence there that'll help us to understand what happened to your boss."

"What do you mean? Evidence of *what*?"

"I need you to meet the CSI and show him where he needs to go. All right?"

The man looked baffled, his earlier indignation with Atticus for trespassing inside the building now replaced by confusion.

"Is that all right?" Atticus repeated.

"Yes. I'll show them."

"Good man." Atticus smiled. "Is there anything else?"

All three men looked completely bemused.

"No? Good."

Atticus went over to the ladder and started to descend before any of them could raise any further objections. He knew that he had gone a little further than he ought, and that Mack was going to be angry, but, on the other hand, he had made a breakthrough. He still wasn't sure how anyone would have been able to force someone as large as Campbell over the side of the parapet, but, on the other hand, he had demonstrated that it was possible that someone *could* have joined him in the tower without having to use the internal doors that were covered by cameras. There might have been a perfectly good reason for the scratch on the lock, but there was a chance that the damage had been done while someone was trying to pick it.

He reached the ground, went through the gate in the fence and looked up at the cathedral. He took out his phone and called Mack.

It went to voicemail.

"It's me," he said. "I need to speak to you."

CHAPTER 32

Alice had been busy all morning, pushed on by the adrenaline of working on a story that she knew was going to be big. Eddie had told her they were going to include a piece about the video with Campbell. He had recorded it on his phone before the police arrived and said he wanted her to write up something they could illustrate with a still. He was going to write a piece from the point of view of the newspaper, explaining how the tape had come to be in their possession. He was particularly interested in the scripture that had accompanied the tape and wanted to include a photograph of it that he'd taken before the police had removed everything to the station.

Alice had been surprised that he would be that ballsy, but reminded herself that he had ink beneath his fingernails and that life on a provincial paper after time spent breaking stories on the *Sun* and the *Mirror* had to be depressing. He had never spoken about it, but she suspected he had been bruised by the end of his career in London and that he saw his job at the *Journal* as a backwater where he would see out the last few years before his retirement. He was an old newshound at heart, and this was his chance to publish something important again.

"Shit!"

The shout came from Eddie's office. She looked up from her desk and saw that he was standing, the handset of his phone held out in front of him.

"Shit, shit, *shit!*"

For a moment, Alice thought he was going to crash the phone against his desk. He didn't. He replaced it, and then, a moment later, he came out into the newsroom.

"Sorry," he said. "Lost my rag for a moment."

"What was it?"

"I was speaking to Andy Clarke," he said.

"Who?"

"My boss. He's taken an interest in Campbell."

"What did he say?"

"He said he'd heard we'd been sent a video of Campbell and that, if we wanted to run anything on it, we had to clear it with head office first. I said I wanted to cover it, maybe find a still we could use to illustrate it, and he said no. It was the lawyers, he said. They'd had a think and said that there was no way we could do it. We can't mention the scripture, either."

"What? Why?"

Eddie waved a hand in irritation. "Reporting restrictions. Don't want to impede the investigation. Blah, blah, blah. It's all bollocks. What about freedom of expression, I said? What about the right to impart and receive information? He told me to get back into my box."

"How does he even *know* about the video?"

"*We* didn't tell him," he said bitterly, "and the only other people who know are Old Bill. Someone must've put pressure on them to make sure we don't print anything they want kept quiet." He reached into his pocket for his packet of cigarettes. "Anyway. You might as well leave the video for now. I'll push him on it again tomorrow."

Alice had plenty of other work to be getting on with and would have carried on all the way through her lunch break, but Eddie insisted she go for a sandwich to clear her mind before they all knuckled down for what would probably end up being a very long day. He was going out for a walk, he said, and she should, too. She didn't protest; she had dry-cleaning to pick up from Waitrose and could grab a bite to eat while she was there. Alice hadn't had the best night's sleep, and a couple of shots of caffeine and a sandwich would help her negotiate the rest of the day. She told him where she was going, grabbed her coat and set off.

It was still raining, and she grabbed an umbrella from Carly at reception before stepping outside and hurrying to the car park on Salt Lane. She drove onto the ring road but saw, to her annoyance, that there was a long queue of traffic waiting to get around the roundabout at St. Marks.

She turned on the radio but couldn't focus on it. Her thoughts drifted. It was obvious now that Campbell's death wasn't accidental, and that it was much more likely that he had killed himself after being blackmailed by whoever had delivered the tape to the office. DCI Jones had questioned them all at length about whether they had any idea who that person might have been; she asked whether there had been any other communication, and whether they had any cameras that might have recorded any footage that could help. Eddie had answered in the negative to all three questions, and Jones and Lewis had departed with the proviso that they would need them all to come down to the station and provide statements to that end.

Alice reached the obstruction on the road—a broken-down bus—and pulled out to go around it. It took only another few minutes to reach Waitrose, and she parked up and hurried inside. She collected her dry-cleaning and then stopped by the café for an egg and cress sandwich and a coffee to go. She put the umbrella up again, shared a rueful expression with an old man who didn't have one, and set off back to the car.

She had reversed into a space between two others, and the angle meant that she didn't see that something had been left next to the driver's side door until she was almost alongside. She knelt: it was a waterproof satchel of the sort used by bicycle couriers. She stood up again and looked around her for any sign of the person who might have left it there. The car park wasn't busy, and the only people that she could see looked to be going about their business: shoppers either going into or leaving the stores; a man in a Waitrose uniform pushing a long line of trolleys.

Alice picked up the satchel, opened the door to the car and put her dry-cleaning and lunch onto the passenger's seat. She lowered herself inside, put the satchel on her lap and opened it.

She felt a twist of anxiety as she reached down into it and withdrew a Jiffy bag. It was the same as the one that had been delivered to the office yesterday: brand new, her name printed on a label and the label fixed in the middle of the packet.

She knew she should put it down and call the police, but she couldn't.

She slipped her finger into a gap at the end and carefully peeled back the adhesive strip. She turned the packet up and shook it so that the cassette box inside slid into her lap. She reached a hand into the envelope and drew out a piece of paper, folded once down the middle. She unfolded it and read.

'If you do wrong, be afraid, for he does not bear the sword in vain. For he is the servant of God, an avenger who carries out God's wrath on the wrongdoer.'

She turned the cassette box onto its side and read the label.

Kajetan, Lucjusz / 15 May

CHAPTER 33

Atticus left the lawns of the cathedral and made his way to North Walk, the road that marked the southern perimeter of the cathedral and its grounds within the Close. He continued to the junction with Bishop's Walk and then walked west, looking for any security cameras that might offer footage that would help him to prove the validity of the theory that he was considering. He came to Sarum College, passed through the ornate iron gate with the lantern atop it, and looked up at the side of the building. There was a camera fixed to the wall just beneath the eaves of the roof, and, as he squinted up at it, Atticus saw a green light that suggested that it was powered and operating. The college was connected to the cathedral and offered courses on theology and ecclesiastical history, among other things. Atticus went inside, buffeted by a warmth that was the opposite of the cold and wet outside.

The reception was empty, but there was a small bell on the desk that gave a melodic tinkle as Atticus pressed his hand against it. He went over to a rack of leaflets advertising the courses that were planned, picking out one—

Reading Scripture Together—that promised to illuminate the Book of Jonah. Atticus had just opened it out to read when he heard footsteps and turned to see a woman.

"Can I help you?"

"I hope so. I'm with the police. I'm looking into what happened to the man who fell from the tower yesterday."

Her smile faded. "Dreadful. Completely dreadful."

"It was," he said, slotting the leaflet back into the rack. "You have a camera on the wall outside."

"Yes."

"Do you know whether it's recording at the moment?"

"It is. We had lead taken from the roof a month ago. The police said we needed to improve our security, so the camera was put up after that."

"Do you think I could have a look?"

"Can I ask why you're interested in it?"

"It's to do with what happened on the tower."

She looked shocked. "You think it might have recorded it?"

"Probably not," he said, smiling reassuringly at her. "He was on the other side of the tower when he fell. I'm just being thorough. I doubt I'll be long."

* * *

The woman took Atticus into a room behind her desk with a computer sitting between stacks of books on a small desk. She switched on the machine, waited for it to boot up and then, after consulting with a colleague on the phone, managed to navigate to the portal that showed the footage from the camera outside.

"I'm afraid I've never used it before. I'm not sure how much help I can give you."

"It's fine," Atticus said. "I can manage from here."

"I'll just be outside. Let me know if you need anything."

Atticus waited for her to go and then reached back and pushed the door so that it was nearly closed. He turned back to the screen, considered the interface and then navigated to the calendar that showed the last two weeks' footage. That, at least, was a good start; not every camera would retain that many days' worth of content. The feed from the camera was uploaded to the cloud, and Atticus double-clicked on the icon to access yesterday morning.

He scrolled back to the evening before Campbell's death and pressed play. There was a reasonable distance between the camera and the cathedral, and, although the paths were lit, it was impossible to make out any detail from the figures who occasionally passed along them. Atticus increased the playback speed by three times, and then focused his attention on the area around the scaffolding. He saw a man walking just inside the boundary of the cathedral grounds and then what looked like a man and a woman taking a seat on one of the benches that were arranged inside the wall. The two of them stayed on the bench for twenty minutes before they stood and retraced their steps. The clock in the corner of the screen showed eleven p.m., and Atticus knew that the gates to the Close were shut at around that time.

Eleven became twelve and then two, and there was no sign of any activity. The minutes went by in chunks, and Atticus started to worry that his theory would be disproved.

The clock showed two fifteen when he was rewarded: the figure of a person, their features invisible in the dark, passing through the gap in the wall and then leaving the path to make a direct approach to the scaffolding.

They headed for the gate that Atticus had used earlier, and he watched, agog, as the figure knelt where the padlock that fastened the gate would have been placed. It didn't take long, the gate opened, and the figure rose and stepped inside, hidden by the fencing for a moment before Atticus caught them again on the first ladder. It was even more difficult to see anything now that the figure's dark clothes were up against the stone, hidden by the night and sheltered by the scaffold and the boards, but he could see movement as the figure progressed up the second ladder and then the third.

Atticus leaned forward, his nose just a few inches away from the screen, and watched as the figure climbed all the way up to the uppermost platform and then headed in the direction of the hatch in the roof that Atticus had used a few hours earlier.

Atticus scrubbed back in the footage and played it again, straining his eyes for anything that might give him an idea as to the identity of the figure scaling the ladder. It was in vain, it was too dark, and the figure was too far away from the camera to reveal anything other than the fact that they were wearing black. Atticus knew from before that the fence was around six and a half feet tall and, judging by how high up the fence the figure reached, he estimated that they were between five feet eight and five feet ten. It was either a woman who was a little taller than average or a man who was right around the median for his sex.

He let the footage play, keeping an eye on the time in the top left of the screen so that he could reference it to the moment that Campbell fell to his death. The angle of the camera didn't show the tower, and, even if it had, the parapet from which Campbell had fallen was on the other side; he wouldn't be able to see him fall, but he hoped that he might see something else that would give him a clue as to what had happened.

He focused his attention on the top of the roof, especially the area of the door that led into the passage that he had used earlier.

Night became dawn, and then the gates to the Close opened. Cars started to crawl down to the Cathedral School. A van parked, and the driver emerged to set a ladder against the wall of one of the buildings. A DPD driver looked for the address of his delivery. People made their way across the lawn.

Atticus blinked, trying to maintain his focus as the clock in the corner of the screen showed seven and then eight. At ten past eight, a clutch of people came into view and gathered in front of the cathedral, perhaps talking about the news that someone had fallen to their death. A police constable wandered from one side of the shot to the other.

Midday came and went.

Dusk fell, and then it started to grow dark.

The woman from the bookshop shuffled up behind him.

"Anything useful?"

Atticus paused the playback. "Maybe. I just need to concentrate for a moment."

"Sorry, love. I'll leave you to it."

Atticus pressed play again and kept his eye on the screen as the clock showed seven and then eight.

At twenty past eight he saw what he had been waiting for: it was dark again, but he noticed movement on the ladder and, after three minutes had passed, a figure emerged through the gate in the scaffolding. They stayed off the main path and left the cathedral grounds at Bishop's Walk, turning left and continuing north, then turning right on North Walk and disappearing out of sight in the direction of St. Ann's Gate.

Atticus scrubbed all the way back to the arrival of the figure in the early hours of the morning. There was a button at the bottom of the screen that allowed him to select a clip from the footage and then attach it to an email; he sent it to himself, and then, in an abundance of caution, he played the footage again and recorded the screen with his phone. He did the same for the fifteen-minute period that showed the figure's departure.

He was checking the recording on his phone when it rang with an incoming call.

It was Mack.

He pressed answer. "I've been trying to—"

She cut across him. "Where are you?"

"At the cathedral. I think I've found—"

Her voice was tight with tension. "I need you to come in."

"Why? What's happened?"

"There's been a second package."

He felt a buzz of excitement. "When?"

"This afternoon. It was left next to the reporter's car when she went to Waitrose for lunch. I'm going to the office now. Can you come?"

"Are you sure? You didn't want me to—"

"Just get over there," she said. "We'll deal with it later."

He stood up. "I'm on my way."

CHAPTER 34

The *Journal*'s office on Rollestone Street was close to the nick. Mike Lewis led the way, with Mack and Francine Patterson alongside him; they were approaching the office when they saw Atticus hurrying toward them from the other direction.

They met him at the door.

"Tell me everything," Atticus said without preamble.

"I've told you everything I know," Mack said. "They've had a second package. Came this afternoon."

"How?"

"Didn't say."

"Another video?"

"They said it looks the same as the first."

"And a verse from the Bible?"

She nodded.

Lewis was quiet. Mack glanced over at him and saw that he was glowering in Atticus's direction. She knew that she wouldn't be able to continue justifying Atticus being included on an ad hoc basis, and that, if she wanted him to work on the case—if she thought the circumstances warranted it— she would have to revive the consultancy arrangement that they had used before. The others would gossip about his involvement and what that might mean, but putting things on a professional footing was something that she would need to do sooner rather than later.

Atticus turned to the door. Mack laid a hand on his arm. "Information only gets released to the press—or to anyone—when Beckton says. All right?"

She couldn't tell whether Atticus realised that she had chided him on account of Lewis, but he nodded his agreement. "I know."

"Keep it in mind," Lewis muttered. "You've got form for messing things up."

* * *

They tried the door to the office, only to find that it was locked. Atticus rapped his knuckles against the glass pane and then waited until he saw movement from inside. The door was unlocked and opened, and Eddie Thorpe stood in the doorway.

"Come in."

They did, and Eddie shut the door after them. "Thanks for coming, Mack." He turned to Lewis. "Mike, Francine." He turned to Atticus. "And you are?"

"Atticus Priest," Mack said. "Atticus—this is Eddie Thorpe. The editor."

Eddie squinted at Atticus. "Of course. You were on the Grovely case."

"He's working for us as a consultant," Mack said. "I'd be grateful if you'd answer his questions just the same as you'd answer mine."

"Of course."

"Where's the package?" Atticus said impatiently.

"You'd better come up."

They went up to a conference room on the second floor. Alice Morris was sat at the table, and a television on a trolley had been set up at one end. An old VHS recorder sat beneath the TV. Mack saw an opened Jiffy bag on the table in front of the woman.

"You didn't open it…" Atticus said.

"Excuse me?"

"The package. You didn't—"

She cut over him. "I'm sorry, who are you?"

"Mr. Priest is working with the police," Eddie said. "This is Alice—she works at the paper."

"And you're the one who got the package?"

"Yes."

"And you touched it?"

"Obviously, but I was very care—"

"I *wish* you hadn't."

"As I said, I was very careful."

"Wearing gloves?"

"No. But I was—"

"Have you watched it?"

"Some of it."

Mack gestured with her hand that Atticus should throttle back. "It would have been better if you'd waited," she said. "There could be forensic evidence on it that will help us to find out who sent it."

"I *did* tell her," Lewis said, looking over at Mack in fear, perhaps, that she might blame him. "I asked her to call us straight away."

"Hang on." Eddie shook his head. "This has to be cooperative. We're involved here—the newspaper is involved, and Alice is involved *personally*—and I'm not going to let things head off in another direction without us."

"The investigation has to come first," Mack said.

"Of course it does, but we want to be able to run the story. I've been doing this for long enough to know that the nationals are going to be all over this like flies on shit when it gets out, and we all know that it *is* going to get out. I'm not going to sit around and let them scoop us. I can tell you now—that's *not* going to happen."

Mack raised her hands to mollify him. "It won't. You have my word. We have to be careful how and when we release information, but this is your story to break. Okay?"

Eddie looked at Alice and then back at Mack. "Okay."

"I'm sorry," Alice said. "This has been difficult for us to negotiate."

"How's that?" Mack said.

"We've been told that we have to be careful what we publish."

"By whom? Someone at the police?"

"No," she said. "The owners of the paper."

"It's just internal politics," Eddie said. "We don't need to bother them with that."

Atticus was clearly itching to gather up as much information as he could. "There was a Bible verse?"

Alice nodded and pointed to the piece of paper on the desk.

Mack looked down and read aloud: "*If you do wrong, be afraid, for he does not bear the sword in vain. For he is the servant of God, an avenger who carries out God's wrath on the wrongdoer.*"

"It's from Romans," Alice said.

Atticus waved a hand dismissively. "Chapter thirteen, verse four."

Francine came around the table so that she could examine the cassette box.

"How was it delivered?" Atticus asked.

"I went to Waitrose at lunchtime," Alice said. "It was in a waterproof bag next to my car when I came back."

"Do you still have the bag?"

She nodded. "It's downstairs."

"Did you see who left it?"

"No."

"No one who looked suspicious?"

"No."

"You didn't notice anyone following you?"

"No," she said. "No one."

Atticus turned to Mack. "You'll need to check CCTV in the car park."

"We will."

Francine gasped.

Mack turned. She had her hand over her mouth.

Eddie looked at her with suspicion. "What?"

Francine shook her head. "Nothing."

"I don't believe you. What is it?" He pointed down at the name on the box. "Kajetan—do you know who that is?"

Francine bit her lip and looked over at Mack for help.

"We'll need to discuss this back at the nick, Eddie," she said. "We'll share everything that we're able to share."

"Really? I can't help feeling that we're being pushed to the side."

"This is a police matter," she said, a little more sternly. "I've promised that we will let you have what we can, and we will. But you need to keep in mind that a man has died in suspicious circumstances, and finding out what happened to him must be the priority. Okay?" She waited, and, eventually, Eddie gave a grudging nod of assent. "Good." Mack pointed to the tape player. "We'd better have a look."

Eddie walked around the table and pressed play on the recorder. The screen was filled with a blizzard of static. They waited until the interference dissolved away and the footage that had been recorded became visible. Mack watched carefully: the bed; the naked bricks of the wall behind it; the blood-red glow that came from lights that were below the shot, a red that was so deep as to be almost purple, brightest at the foot of the wall and faintest at the top.

Atticus spoke without taking his eyes off the screen. "Is this like the first video?"

"You haven't seen it?" Eddie asked him.

"Not yet. Is it?"

"Looks like the same place," Lewis said.

A man, naked apart from his underwear, came into the shot and sat down on the bed. He looked to be in his mid-forties and was solidly built. He had tattoos down both arms and another on his chest.

"Stop it there," Mack said.

Eddie pressed pause, and the image froze save for the thin bands of static that rolled from the top to the bottom of the screen.

The man was looking straight into the lens.

Mack thought she recognised him.

* * *

They left the office and set off back to the station. Mack could see that Francine was bursting with whatever it was that had excited her when they had watched the video; they turned the corner onto Bedwin Street and then stopped outside the alms house.

Atticus was fizzing with excitement. "You know him," he said to Francine. "Don't you?"

"It's Lucky Lucjusz."

"Who?" Atticus said.

"I've seen him before, too," Mack said. "Where?"

"I nicked him," she said. "But that's not it." She spoke slowly and deliberately, trying to keep a lid on her obvious excitement. "He's dead, boss. We pulled him out of the river this morning."

CHAPTER 35

They continued back to the station, sharing the cover of two umbrellas. Atticus walked alongside Mack and was distracted, trying to sort out the developments that had quickly cast the death of David Campbell in an entirely new light. He had initially agreed with her: his death had looked very much like suicide. The discovery that he had made by way of the security camera footage cast doubt on all of that, and now this—a second possible victim, with a second tape—made things look very different indeed.

Atticus was left with the sensation that there were depths to what had happened that they hadn't even *begun* to plumb.

He could see that Mack shared his animation, but there was a trepidation on her face that he knew was inspired by the fear that they were about to be plunged into their third major murder enquiry in the last two years. Francine looked to share the anticipation, although not the misgivings; she was new enough in her CID career to be insulated from the practical considerations with which Mack would need to grapple. Lewis was excited, too, but he knew it was tempered by an irritation that Atticus was involved in the investigation that he was making no effort to hide.

They stopped at the doors to the station. "Go and get the others," Mack said to Lewis. "Meeting in the conference room in ten minutes."

Lewis said that he would take care of it and went ahead.

"Can you give me a minute with Atticus, Franny?"

"Of course, boss. See you upstairs."

She followed Lewis into the building.

Mack and Atticus stayed outside, the rain thrumming against the umbrella that Atticus held over both of them.

"Shit," Mack said. She looked out over the Greencroft and the playground where a mother was pushing a child in a pram, and then turned to him. "Would I be right in thinking you'd like to be involved again?"

"Very much so."

"Same as before? Your company invoices, not you?"

"I'd do it for free."

"No, it has to be professional."

Atticus knew that he ought to tell Mack about his interview with Murphy. He knew that Murphy would be very much against the idea of his involvement in the investigation, but, given that he had said he was going back to London, Atticus was prepared to operate on the basis of out of sight and out of mind. He didn't know what Mack would say if she learned of Murphy's reservations, but there had to be the possibility—the likelihood, even—that she would change her mind. Atticus knew that it was selfish, but this case was so intriguing that he was prepared to hold his tongue. The thought that Murphy was investigating Mack, too, gave him the most pause;

he concluded, again, that it wouldn't matter if he waited a day or two before telling her.

"Come on, then."

"I'm in?"

"You're in."

Atticus folded the umbrella and shook it off. "Thanks."

"Just *try* not to show off."

"Can't promise," he said and, as she frowned, he tried to reassure her with a wink that just deepened her scowl.

CHAPTER 36

Atticus followed Mack through the CID room and into the same conference suite that they had used for the Major Incident Room in the Imber investigation. It still hadn't been cleared of everything from that case: the map of Salisbury Plain that they had stuck to the wall had not been taken down, and there were files of witness statements and other evidence stacked in the bookshelves. Atticus took a seat and waited for Lewis to corral the others who would be working on the enquiry: Robbie Best and Nigel Archer came inside first, both perplexed as they looked at Atticus; Francine Patterson sat next to him; Stewart Lynas followed her, double taking as he noticed Atticus and then exchanging a look of incredulity with Archer that he made no effort to hide. Lewis came next and then Mack.

She shut the door and went to the head of the table.

"Right," she said. "First things first—for reasons that will soon become obvious, the Campbell case is going to be more complicated than we thought. There are aspects of it that are starting to look as if they might be very troubling, and I've asked Atticus to consult with us again in the same way that he did for the murders at Imber. Everything is the same as it was then—please treat him as a member of the team."

"Really, boss?" Lynas said. "No disrespect, Atticus, but—"

"It's funny," Atticus cut over him. "Whenever someone says that, it usually means the complete opposite."

"I'm fine with him being here," Best said. "I'm sure he'll play nicely."

"*Really*, gaffer?" Lynas said. "It's a distraction."

"He'll be reporting directly to me," Mack said. "For reasons that, as I said, will become obvious in a moment, I think we should be open to the offer of help. Right?"

Atticus looked around the table: Lynas didn't hold his eye, and Archer looked to be stifling his objection.

"Good," Mack said, keen to put potential disagreements to the side so that they could move on. "We've had a development in the case—*several* developments, actually. You've probably heard that we had a body in the river at Britford this morning. Francine went out and took charge of getting him out. Franny?"

She cleared her throat. "I recognised him—Lucjusz Kajetan. Polish immigrant, used to run a building business until it went under. His life went off the rails after that, and I ended up nicking him for possession. Last I heard, he was sleeping rough in the car park underneath Sainsbury's. We had Fyfe out to have a look, and his initial assessment was that he drowned. No obvious signs of trauma on the body. It seemed likely that he was sleeping rough in the sluice house, got pissed or high or both, slipped, fell in and drowned." She looked over at Mack. "But we don't think that now."

"No," Mack said. "We don't. A second video was sent to the *Journal* today. It's the same set-up as the first—a man in the same location as before with what looks like a teenager. Francine recognised Kajetan. On that basis, it's impossible that either his death or Campbell's was accidental. We've had two bodies in two days, with videos of the dead men in very compromising situations sent to the paper both times."

"Blackmail, then?" Lynas said. "Blackmail and suicide?"

"Maybe," Best said.

Atticus shook his head. "No."

Lynas turned to him. "What?"

"Two murders."

Lynas exhaled and, when he spoke again, his usual superciliousness was coloured with disdain. "That's ridiculous. How can you say that? You can't be sure."

"Of course I can."

"Why not blackmail?" Best said. "That's what we're looking at for Campbell."

"No," Atticus said firmly. "Campbell may or may not have been blackmailed, but he was *definitely* murdered. And Kajetan."

Lynas appealed to Mack. "Come on, boss. Not this again."

Mack was looking at him uncomfortably. "Atticus?"

Atticus had forgotten how disagreeable he found Lynas; the man's public-school arrogance blinded him to deficiencies that were obvious to everyone else. Robbie Best had said once that Lynas was 'a legend in his own lunchtime,' and Atticus agreed. He remembered what he had promised Mack and tried to keep the scorn from his voice.

"I'm sorry, Mack. There are a couple of things I haven't had a chance to tell you yet—I was going to call, but then you told me about the video."

She frowned. "Tell me now."

He held his palms together and worked out how to explain what he was thinking in as efficient a way as possible. "Let's assume Campbell was being blackmailed. Can I accept him jumping off the tower in shame? Yes. Definitely. But Kajetan's different. He was homeless, so blackmail doesn't make sense."

"It still *could* be," Lynas protested.

"Whatever," Atticus said. "But committing suicide by drowning? *That* would be unusual."

"Rubbish," Lynas said.

"What? You think he drowned himself?"

"Why not?"

"Because it would be very uncommon."

"It happens." Lynas looked at the others as if appealing for support. "You remember the woman who died in the river at the back of the Maltings? That wasn't an accident, was it? She drowned herself."

"I didn't say it *couldn't* be suicide," Atticus said. "I just said it would be *uncommon*. Do you know the percentage of suicides by drowning last year?"

Lynas folded his arms and leaned back in his chair. "I have no idea."

"I do—less than three percent. What about death by falling?"

Lynas shrugged. "I'm sure you'll tell us."

"*One* percent. So, if we are looking at two suicides, it'll be two of the most unlikely methods in terms of relative prevalence. Possible? Yes. Likely? No. Not likely at all. We have to proceed on the basis that these could be murders. It would be nice if they weren't, but, even then, we've still got evidence that the two of them were filmed having sex with partners who look very likely to be under the age of consent. And whether it's murder or blackmail and suicide doesn't make a huge difference in practical terms to how we're going to have to deal with this—it's salacious either way, and the press is going to be all over it."

"The *Journal*, for certain," Lewis said. "Both tapes were sent to them. Both had Bible verses about revenge that'll make it even *more* salacious, especially when they connect it with Jack from before."

"Is the *Journal* onside?" Lynas asked.

"They've said that they'll cooperate with us," Lewis said, "but it'd be naïve to think that we're going to be able to keep a lid on it for long."

Mack nodded her agreement. "This is going to have cut-through. It's definitely prurient enough. The media will be interested. Beckton is going to want this cleared up before the nationals and the TV get wind of it."

"Absolutely," Lynas said with conviction. "That's why it's irresponsible to talk these up as murders when there's no evidence to suggest it."

"I agree with Stewart," Lewis said. "They look like suicides to me."

Atticus couldn't stop the impatient roll of his eyes.

Lewis noticed. "You haven't changed a bit."

"Neither have you," Atticus said. "You're as slow and predictable as ever."

"Piss *off*." Lewis turned to Mack in exasperation.

Atticus looked at her, too, mouthed an apology and then cut across her attempt at mollification. "It's murder—I guarantee it."

"You keep saying that, but you have *nothing* to back it up."

"Fine," he said. "There's the similarity with Jack, for a start."

"He didn't leave videos," Lewis said.

"No, he didn't. But he did speak to me about the Bible, and that's never been made public."

"Tenuous."

"Yes, on its own, but not when you add it to everything else. I went to the cathedral today and went up to the tower for a look around. I couldn't find anything that made me think Campbell's death wasn't what you think—that he jumped. It's obviously not an accident—it's too hard to fall from the parapet without meaning it. That leaves us with two possibilities: Campbell killed himself, or someone else threw him over the side. But Campbell was big, and he was in good shape."

"So pushing him over the edge wouldn't have been easy," Best said.

"Absolutely. I agree. That's why I thought murder was unlikely, especially when there was no obvious way for anyone to get up on the tower without being seen."

"We checked the cameras," Best said. "They don't show anything."

"And I checked the only other doors that would let someone get up to the tower. Both were locked."

Best gestured for him to continue. "Why do I get the feeling there's a 'but' coming?"

"There is. I went outside and walked around the grounds. The east side of the cathedral has scaffolding all the way to the top. I had a look and saw how easy it would have been to climb up."

Mack closed her eyes. "Please don't say what I think you're about to say…"

CHAPTER 37

Atticus spread his arms helplessly. "I had to look, and it was as easy as I thought it would be. There's a gate in the fence at the bottom, and then it's just a question of climbing the ladders up to the roof."

Mack put her head in her hands. Atticus continued before she could speak, hoping that *what* he had discovered would quickly cancel out any qualms she might have had about *how* he discovered it.

"I found a hatch that opens into an old stonemasons' workshop above the Lady Chapel. I went inside and followed it, went through a door into an attic space and then ended up at another door. They were all unlocked, although I don't think they should have been. I can't say for sure because it was pitch black, but it looked to me like there was a scratch on the last one that might have been from someone picking the lock."

"That doesn't prove anything at all," Lynas said.

"It does. The one thing that always mitigated against there being someone else involved was that we didn't see anybody apart from Campbell going up to the tower. But finding out that you can get up there from the outside changes everything. It *would* be possible for someone to get up to the tower without being seen."

"Are there any CCTV cameras in the tower?" Lynas said.

"Not once you're on the stairs," Mack said.

Lewis shook his head. "So this is still speculation. All you've shown is that it *might* be possible. That doesn't mean that anyone actually *did* go up that way."

"Yes, you're right." Atticus tried hard to ensure that his patient reply didn't sound exaggerated and sarcastic. "So I went back outside again and found a security camera on Sarum College that's pointing at the east side of the cathedral. I was there this afternoon—I reviewed everything from the evening before Campbell died. Robbie—could you pass me the remote for the TV, please?"

Best took the remote control and slid it across the table. Atticus turned on the screen, took out his phone and found the two clips from the camera that he had emailed to himself. He cast his phone to the television and tapped to begin playback. They saw the shape of the cathedral in the gloom of the night.

"What are we looking at?" Lewis grumbled. "There's nothing."

"Wait."

Francine pointed at the screen. "Look there—by the fence."

"Keep watching."

Atticus found that he was holding his breath as the figure went through the gate in the barriers and climbed the ladders to the roof. Atticus let the footage continue until whoever it was had disappeared out of shot.

He stopped the playback.

Mack pointed to the screen. "The time on the screen—is it right?"

"I think so."

"Six hours before Campbell fell."

Atticus nodded. "Give or take."

"What are we supposed to do with that?" Lewis said. "It could be anyone. It's not even clear whether it's a man or a woman."

Mack ignored his grumble. "Do we see them come down again?"

"Yes," Atticus said. "Much later."

"Can we see it?"

Atticus opened the second clip and played it until the figure descended the ladders.

Mack pointed to the time on the screen. "They were up there for *hours*."

"They stayed out of sight until it was dark again. Most likely they hid in the attic space."

The figure on the screen stepped out through the gate in the fence and crossed to Bishop's Walk.

"I can't make out anything useful," she said. "Any other cameras?"

"Not at the college. I didn't have time to check between there and Exeter Street, though."

"The school's down there," Francine said. "They could have a camera."

"There's the dentist, too," Mack said.

"And an architect?" Lewis offered.

"Maybe one of them has a video doorbell."

"Let's check *all* the cameras in the Close," Mack said. "All of them. We're due some luck. We might be able to wrap this up before there's any more chaos."

Atticus chewed his lip.

Mack saw him. "What?"

"I'm not optimistic. Think about how this has been planned." He pointed at the figure on the screen. "Whoever that is, they're careful. Clever, too. They knew that they would've been filmed if they'd followed Campbell when he went up the tower, so they found another way. And I think they knew there's a camera at the college. They knew they couldn't avoid it altogether if they wanted to use the ladders, so they worked around it. Look at how precise they've been. Look at the route they chose to get back to North Walk. The quickest way would've been to follow the path diagonally up, but they didn't do that. They took the long way to make sure there was distance between them and the camera. And then, even when they got closer, they were looking down the whole time. It's hard to be sure, but it looks like they've covered their face, too. *Look.* They scouted this all out. This has been planned. They know the places they need to avoid, and I'll bet you whatever you like that they knew exactly where the cameras are on the way back to Exeter Street, too. I don't think those will show us anything."

"So how did they know about the other way up to the tower?" Lewis said.

"Could it be someone who works at the cathedral?" suggested Francine.

Atticus gave a nod. "That would be a good place to start. There's something else to check, too—I remember reading something about the cathedral offering a tour of the secret rooms in the attic just after COVID. They had a budget shortfall and were looking for ways to make it up. It might be worth seeing if they have a record of everyone who's been up there."

Best noted it down. "I'll check."

"What about Kajetan?" Atticus said. "Much as I'm loath to take anything Fyfe says without a very large dose of scepticism, what did he say about the cause of death?"

Francine gave a shrug. "Not much. No sign of anything that would suggest it was suspicious."

"He didn't know what we know now, though," Mack said. "When's the post-mortem?"

"Tomorrow morning."

Atticus turned to Mack. "I'd like to go."

"We'll both go."

Mack brought the meeting to a close. Atticus could see from the way that she was glaring at him that she was irritated about something—he guessed it was the fact that he had blindsided her with what he had found at the cathedral—but there had been nothing else for it, and he hoped that she would forgive and forget, just as she usually did.

"Mack," he said, "can I have a word?"

"I've got to go and see Beckton. What is it?"

"I need to see Campbell's video."

"Franny," Mack called out, stopping Patterson at the door, "could you show Atticus the first tape?"

"Of course, boss," she said. She turned to him. "I've got it on my computer. This way."

Atticus turned back to Mack, but she had left the room and all he saw was her back as she made her way down the corridor to Beckton's office. He winced; he supposed that she *had* told him that she didn't want him freelancing and that she didn't want surprises, and she probably thought that he had already let her down. He knew he had to try harder, but it was difficult when he had the scent of the chase.

CHAPTER 38

The enquiry team knew that they were going to be working longer days as the investigation gathered momentum. Francine had come on shift at seven that morning and would normally have clocked off at five, but it was half past eight when Mack told her and the others that it was time to knock off for the night. She would have been happy to stay, but Mack was not the kind of boss who required staff to stick around when there was no good reason for it. They had made a good start in establishing the structure of the team that would be responsible for the investigation, and Francine had been given the responsibility for setting up the database that they would use to collate and cross-reference the information and evidence that would be collected. It was known as the Home Office Large Major Enquiry System, and very much a case of a product's name being crowbarred to fit the acronym that had been chosen for it. HOLMES 2 allowed all the officers on the team to both input and interrogate data at the same time. Francine's role as disclosure officer would require her to assess the incoming data, determining whether the information met the disclosure test so that it could be provided to the defence in any subsequent trial that came out of the investigation.

Francine snagged her jacket from the back of her chair. Atticus was sitting in it and watching the video of David Campbell. She had given him access after the meeting, but that was an hour ago, and he was still going over it.

"Find anything?"

He didn't take his eyes off the screen. "Nothing useful."

"Do you think it's him?"

Atticus paused the recording. "Who? Jack?"

She nodded.

"Yes," Atticus said. "I think it's possible."

"Why, though? What do Campbell and Kajetan have to do with Miller?"

"That's what I'm trying to work out."

"Jack said that Miller was involved with Burns and York—right?"

Atticus pushed away from the desk and swivelled the chair so that he could look up at her. "That's right."

"And he said that the three of them were abusing kids."

"He said they were being paid to do it," Atticus added. "And that he was involved."

"How? As one of the kids?"

"Maybe. Or maybe he was a customer. Or maybe he was working with the three of them. It's impossible to say."

"So this is Jack getting revenge?"

Atticus looked at the screen and breathed out. "That's where I'd put my money."

Francine put on her jacket. "Switch off when you're done."

He turned back to the screen. "Will do."

Francine left him and paused at Mack's open door. "See you in the morning, boss."

Mack looked up. "Will do. Get a good night's sleep. We're going to be busy tomorrow."

CHAPTER 39

Francine went down to the car park and drove back to St. Ann Street, pleased to see that there was a space for her to park on the road outside her house. She had a little two-bedroom house that was just a hundred yards from the Close by way of St. Ann's Gate. She had bought it a year ago, using the inheritance she had been left when her father passed away. The estate agent who had showed her around had described it as 'compact,' and it certainly was that; there was a study, sitting room and kitchen on the ground floor and two small bedrooms and a bathroom above. It was quaint, though, and although owning a property that was hundreds of years old presented ongoing challenges—her mother warned her it would be like maintaining the Forth Bridge—she was happy to accept that rather than living in one of the boxes that were being constructed at great pace as the city slowly spilled out at the sides. She had a view of the spire from her front door, too, and she stopped to look at it as she reached for her door key. The red light at the top glowed out, and the floodlights lit the stone in amber. She thought of Campbell falling to his death and shivered a little.

She opened the door and went inside, taking off her boots and hanging her jacket on the banister. She went into the kitchen and opened the fridge to see what she had for dinner and was dithering over the remains of Sunday night's lasagne or a microwave chicken chasseur when she heard a knock on the door.

She went back down the hall and opened it: Charlie was outside with a bunch of flowers.

"Oh," Francine said.

"Sorry… are you busy?"

"No, of course not. Did you say you were coming over? Did I forget?"

"I thought I'd surprise you." He held up the flowers. "I thought these might help you feel better."

"The hangover?" She waved that aside. "I'm fine now—but thanks, they're lovely." She stepped aside. "Want to come in?"

He did, taking off his shoes and coat and then giving her a kiss.

"I was just going to cook dinner," she said. "Have you eaten?"

"Not yet. I'm starving."

She took out the tray of lasagne. "There's enough here for the two of us."

He looked over her shoulder. "You've got salad leaves, carrots, tomatoes… I could make a salad to go with it."

Francine put on Radio 4 just as *The World Tonight* began, the presenter trailing ahead to what they would be discussing. The chancellor had delivered a mini budget that afternoon, and there had been a development in a doping scandal involving racehorses that Francine had been following.

Charlie took the packet of tomatoes from the fridge and tipped them out onto a chopping board. "How was your day?"

"Long."

He started to halve the tomatoes. "Anything interesting?"

She nodded. "Body in the river."

He stopped. "Where?"

"You know the sluice house on the Avon?"

"Other side of the river at Churchill Gardens? Other side from the playground?"

She nodded.

"What happened to him?"

"Looks like he drowned, but we won't know for sure until they do the post-mortem tomorrow."

"You had to deal with it?"

"I was the first detective there."

They listened to the discussion on the radio as the chancellor's plans for dealing with inflation were skewered by an expert on fiscal policy and then derided by an opposition MP.

"Got any mustard?" Charlie asked. "I'll make a dressing."

"In the cupboard," she said, pointing.

The discussion on the economy ended, and the presenter handed over to the newsreader for a summary of the day's news.

Francine opened the oven and slid the lasagne inside.

"A man who fell to his death from the tower of Salisbury Cathedral has been named as David Campbell."

"Turn it up," Francine said.

"Mr. Campbell, who was sixty-three, was the clerk of works at the cathedral. He was pronounced dead at the scene."

"That's what we were talking about last night," he said.

She put her finger to her lips as the announcer continued.

"While the police have indicated that they believe Mr. Campbell's death to have been an accident, the Health and Safety Executive will be conducting an enquiry to ensure that the proper procedure was followed."

The announcer moved on to the next item.

Charlie whistled. "You're going to be famous."

"Hardly."

"Why are they reporting it?"

"Duh," she said. "He fell off the tower. It's macabre."

"I guess." He shivered. "What a way to go. Wouldn't have been how I'd do it."

"Do what?"

"Top myself."

"We're not so sure that's what it was now."

"Him topping himself?"

She went over and turned the radio down.

"What, then? An accident?"

"It would've been hard to fall unless you did something really stupid, and, by all accounts, he was careful."

"Suicide, then."

She shrugged.

Charlie laid the knife on the chopping board. "*Murder?* Seriously?"

"Atticus thinks so."

"Atticus? Who's that?"

"I haven't told you about him?"

"I think I'd remember a name like that."

"He used to be in CID until he got fired or resigned for using drugs—depends on who you ask. Mack's brought him in as a consultant."

"Is that usual?"

"Not at all. He's seeing Mack, too. Makes it more complicated."

"She hired her *boyfriend*?"

She nodded. "With form for doing drugs. I know."

"Why would she do something like that?"

"Because he's seriously clever. Weird, too, and hard to deal with, but you can't argue with the fact he gets results. He found things out at Grovely and Imber that no one else did. And he found things at the cathedral that we'd missed."

"And he thinks Campbell was murdered?"

"He thinks someone climbed the tower just before Campbell fell. We thought he was alone, but it looks like we might've been wrong about that." She paused, her cheeks flushing. "Shit. I didn't tell you that, all right?"

Charlie used the back of the knife to push the tomatoes into the bowl with the rest of the salad. He gave a knowing wink. "Tell me what?"

Francine hadn't had a serious boyfriend since she had joined the force, and she could see that she was going to have to be careful with what she told Charlie. She trusted him, but that didn't mean that he might say something that he shouldn't. He might not mean to do harm, but it would put her in a difficult position.

Charlie spooned mustard into a bowl and slowly whisked in olive oil. "Poor bastard, either way—whatever happened to him."

Francine thought back to the clamour that had accompanied the discovery of the bodies at Imber, and coming home to watch footage from helicopters that had been flown over the churchyard during the excavation. She was tempted to tell Charlie about the video that had been sent to the *Journal*, but she knew that that information hadn't been released to the public yet and that it would be unprofessional to discuss it with him.

But… *still*.

Charlie finished the salad and edged around her, his hands on her hips, as he made his way to the fridge. He opened it and, with a happy clap of his hands, took out the bottle of Chablis that she had put inside to chill the day before yesterday. He found two glasses in the cupboard and a corkscrew in the drawer. He uncorked the bottle, poured out two large glasses and gave one to Francine.

"Cheers," he said, leaning around and planting a kiss on her lips. "Sounds like you need this."

CHAPTER 40

Mack had gone into her office after updating Beckton with what had happened. Atticus watched her over the top of the screen on Francine's desk. She was busying herself with the administration that accompanied any large enquiry and was so lost in the minutiae that she didn't notice when he went over and knocked on the door.

"Yes?"

"Can I have a word?"

He started to close the door so that they could have some privacy, but she told him to leave it open. He looked at her quizzically before noticing her knowing gaze out to where the others were working at their desks and understood: a shut door might suggest intimacy, and she wasn't ready for the others to reach that conclusion.

"Sorry," he said quietly.

She spoke more loudly. "What's up?"

"Are you staying late?"

"Beckton wants me to send him the details by email. It'll take me an hour, maybe two."

Atticus kept his voice low. "After that?"

Stewart Lynas stopped at the open door. "Night, boss."

"Night. See you tomorrow."

Atticus waited for him to go. "Want me to cook?"

Mack got up from behind the desk and went to the door. She looked around him and, seeing that the office was empty, reached across and laid her hand on Atticus's arm. "Go back to mine and let yourself in. You know where the keys are."

"Shall I wait so we can walk back together?"

"Better if we don't. Better, for now, if we keep this—*us*—to ourselves."

He wanted to protest, but he saw how awkward this was making her feel. "I'll see you later, then."

She very quickly ran her fingers down his arm and then went back to her desk.

* * *

Atticus walked to Mack's rented house in Harnham. It was a small two-bedroom property that she could just about afford. Mack and her husband still had the mortgage on the family home in Bishopsdown, and taking on another property had, she had confided, put their joint finances under strain. Atticus had been tempted to suggest that it would all be sorted out once they divorced but had managed to hold his tongue; even he realised that that would have sounded hopelessly self-interested. Mack didn't speak about her relationship with Andy, and although Atticus wanted her to tell him what she was thinking about it—and what she was thinking about *them*—he knew that particular conversation could only happen at her instigation.

Mack kept the key in a lockbox that was fixed to the wall, and the combination was the birthday of her daughter. Atticus felt awkward as he turned the dial and opened the box; he still hadn't been introduced to her children. He had suggested they all go to the park last weekend, but Mack had quickly dismissed the idea. She had seen his hurt feelings and had been tender in explaining that the time wasn't right and that it would just confuse them.

There wasn't much food in the fridge. Atticus took out a tray of chicken breasts that were just within date and then collected an onion, the last two cloves of garlic, a piece of ginger, a can of chopped tomatoes, a bag of rice and jars of turmeric, cumin and dried chillies. He took out a wok, tipped in the last dregs from a bottle of cooking oil and heated it up. He chopped the onion and garlic, tossed them into the wok, and, once those were hot, added the chicken, the spices and the chillies. He tipped in the tomatoes and lowered the heat so that the curry would simmer rather than boil.

He ran the sink to wash up the things that he had used and thought about Mack telling him to leave work without her. He knew why: she was still nervous about advertising the fact that the two of them were seeing each other. Atticus was less concerned about what the others thought—it was the opposite: he *wanted* them to know—but it was different for her. She worked with them every day, and, if they knew that she and Atticus were romantically involved, it could lead to them doubting her judgement. He had complained to her about a similar situation during the Imber investigation and, knowing how difficult he found it to put himself in someone else's shoes, she had explained: she had already gone out on a limb to bring him onto the team, and the last thing that she'd needed then, as now, was for someone to suggest that her motives were coloured by her feelings. Atticus found it impossible to navigate topics like this, but wondered whether it would have been the same if the roles had been reversed. Mack had often suggested that a career in the police was more difficult for a woman; was this the kind of thing that she meant?

He cleaned the utensils and the plates that he had used, stood them in the rack and wiped his hands. His condition made it difficult to be as sensitive to Mack's concerns as he knew she would have liked and, although he had told himself that he would try to be better, he knew that it was going to be a challenge. He was lucky, then, that Mack was sympathetic; Atticus couldn't imagine many partners sharing her patience.

CHAPTER 41

Atticus heard Mack's key in the lock and looked at his watch: it had taken her nearly two hours to finish in the office. She came into the kitchen-diner and sat down at the little table.

She took off her shoes. "What a day."

"Are you okay?"

"Robbie wanted to talk to me, and then Beckton called me back. I couldn't get away."

"I've eaten," Atticus said. "There's a plate for you in the oven. I'll get it for you."

"Thank you."

Atticus went to the oven, put on a glove and took out the bowl with the rest of the curry. He took it over to the table, along with a knife and fork, and set it down in front of her, then sat down on the chair across from hers.

"What did Robbie want?"

"He was concerned about you." She held up a hand to stop his protest. "Don't be defensive. It wasn't like that. He wasn't negative."

"He can leave that to Lynas and Lewis."

"He actually *likes* you. He just wanted to tell me that he has reservations after what you said at the meeting."

"After I said *what*?"

"Going off and doing your own thing again. At the cathedral… I mean, come on. He has a point. You know that's not the way we work."

"I got carried away."

"You *always* get carried away. Robbie knows how good you are. That's why he's concerned. He's worried you'll find out something really important and it'll be inadmissible because of *how* you got it. If it's not done right…" She let the sentence drift and sighed. "If it's not done right, it could be damaging. He's not sure if it's worth the risk."

He looked at her, saw that she was annoyed, and, for a moment, he worried that she might have decided to take him off the case.

"You're right. *He's* right."

"It's not as if you're just a consultant we've brought in to help. You've worked with most of them before. You have a history. And they all know about us."

That brought Atticus up short. "Really? But you said—"

"At least I *think* they do," she interrupted. She sighed, wearily this time. "I know you miss details like that when it comes to you because of…" She fenced for the right word that wouldn't insult him.

"Because of my condition."

"Yes, because of that. None of them will bring it up with me, but they're talking. And because of that—and because Beckton might not agree with my decision to bring you on again—you have to be especially careful not to piss them off. Beckton won't need an excuse to get rid of you, but he'll criticise me for my decision, too, and, with everything that's going on with Andy and the kids—and with us—it's not something I can afford. Understand?"

"Yes. I need to stop and think."

"You promise? No more impetuousness?"

"Promise. I'll run everything by you."

"Good."

Atticus could see that she was tired, and that it wasn't just the fatigue that came with a long day. She was in charge of the investigation, and he could see that the weight of it was bearing down on her. Most detectives, even of senior rank, would never have to deal with the media attention that would be aroused by a case that became a *cause célèbre*. Mack had had the misfortune to have been given two big investigations to deal with in the last two years, and now he was quite sure that she was about to receive a third.

"There's something else," he said.

She looked dejected. "What is it now?"

"Don't worry—it's not the investigation. It's Murphy."

"I forgot you went to see him. Sorry. I got distracted."

"Don't worry about it. It's fine."

"What did he say?"

"He's not my biggest fan. And he wasn't happy with me consulting during Imber."

"I cleared it with Beckton," she protested.

"I know you did. But I doubt you told him about my clearance not being revoked when it should've been. And he thinks the billing arrangement was set up to be deceptive."

"He doesn't care that you helped us to clear up the murders?"

"Like I said—he's not a fan."

"You didn't…" She stopped.

He grinned. "Tell him what I thought of him?"

"*Please*, Atticus…"

"But he's *so* mundane."

"You have to play the game. Someone like him… It's easy—you just flatter his ego and you'll have him eating out of your hand. The other way, though? A man like him won't take well to someone who makes him feel inferior, and you have a particular knack of giving people the idea that they don't impress you."

"And that's because they usually don't."

"Fine. I know. But you need to learn to keep that to yourself."

He got up and went around her chair so that he was behind her and started to massage her shoulders. "He's going to ask why you brought me back for Imber."

"So he won't be a fan of you working on this." He felt her muscles tense and took his hands away.

"No," Atticus said, "but he's in London for the rest of the week. There's no reason why he'd know."

"Until he comes back," she pointed out.

"We can cross that bridge when we come to it."

She sighed and rested back in the chair again.

He kneaded her shoulders again. "We might have worked it all out by then."

"I wish I could believe that. What you were saying in the meeting—do you really think it's murder?"

"I do," he said.

"And Jack?"

"Francine was asking me about that," he said. "I think it's possible. The verses from the Bible... it'd be weird if it was someone else. You're sure that was never made public?"

"Not by us," she said.

"In private?"

"I can only speak for myself, and I haven't spoken to anyone outside the investigation about it."

"Someone from the team?"

She sighed. "I don't think so, but can I say for certain?" She spread her hands helplessly. "Of course not."

"The post-mortem might help," he said. "We need to look and see if there are any similarities with Miller."

"Be careful with what you say. Fyfe's already said he thinks Kajetan was an accident, and he won't take kindly to you coming in and asking questions."

"He just doesn't like his mistakes being pointed out to him."

She lowered her shoulders so he could really dig his fingers in. He could feel the knots in her muscles. "Did you hear what I said about making people feel inferior?"

"I did. I know. And I'll be nice."

She turned her head and looked back and up at him. "Do you want to stay?"

"Can't. I need to see to the dog."

"You could bring him over, you know."

"You said the lease said no pets."

"It does, but is anyone really going to find out?"

"Look at you—breaking all the rules."

"Are you sure you don't want to stay?"

"Tomorrow," he said. "I want to spend a little time going over my notes when I get back tonight, and you *need* to eat. Go on—before it gets cold."

"Okay."

He lowered his head and kissed her. "I'll see you in the morning at the hospital."

"You will. I know you don't like Fyfe, but please try to be civil with him."

"It's not that I don't like him. It's more that I have absolutely no respect for him."

"*Atticus.*"

PART 3

Wednesday

CHAPTER 42

Atticus was up at six, early enough to go for a longer walk with Bandit so that the dog was tired out for the rest of the day. He followed the longer of their usual loops: through the cathedral grounds, up into Harnham and then around the cricket pitch, then following the river to the Old Mill pub and taking the town path through the water meadows and back into the city and home. He took out his phone and filleted his inbox as he walked, deleting everything until he looked down with satisfaction and saw that there were none left. His smugness was only temporary, though; moments after he shoved it back into his pocket, his phone buzzed and beeped with an incoming message.

He took the phone out again, opened his mail client and saw it was from Nina Parsons. She wanted to come back into the office to discuss the report on her boyfriend that Atticus had prepared. She said, with apologies, that she was leaving the country on military business tomorrow and that she wouldn't be able to relax while she was away without having had the chance to clarify a couple of points.

Atticus opened his calendar: he had the PM for Kajetan first thing and had blocked out the rest of the day to dig into the case for Mack, but he would be able to find thirty minutes for Nina without too much bother. He hadn't had the chance to provide her with his invoice yet, either, and this would be a good opportunity to do that.

He tapped to reply to the message and said that he was available at midday if she could come to the office again. He sent it and, a moment later, she replied: that was fine, she said. She thanked him for fitting her in and closed with a breezy 'see you later' and an informal 'Nx.'

Bandit scampered over the bridge that led into Queen Elizabeth Gardens and chased a duck until he was up to his chest in the water. Atticus called him back and, after trotting out of the river and shaking himself dry, the dog ambled up and waited as Atticus fitted the lead to his collar.

"Time to get back. It's going to be a busy day."

CHAPTER 43

Max Mason had been following the same morning routine for years. He was woken by his butler, Ross, at five minutes past seven, with a breezy "Good morning, sir," as he crossed the bedroom and opened the curtains. He brought a tray over to the bed with his breakfast—eggs Benedict and a cafetière of strong black coffee—and copies of the *Sun*, the *Mail* and the *Times*, together with a printout of his diary for the day ahead. Mason allowed himself a moment for his eyes to adjust to the sunlight and then shuffled up the bed, allowing Ross to put two cushions behind his back so that he could sit more comfortably.

"How are you this morning, sir?"

"Not bad," he said.

"You wanted me to remind you about the Wednesday Morning Club."

"Yes, that's right. Thank you. Are they all coming?"

"No one has said otherwise."

"Good. Thank you."

Ross dipped his head and made his way out of the bedroom. Clarendon was a large house, and, given the fact that

Mason was approaching eighty, it wouldn't have been possible to live here without help. There were two cleaners, a chauffeur, a handyman and two gardeners, with Ross as the glue that held them all together. All of them worked for Mason on a full-time basis, and it gave him a sense of pride to think that he was supporting them and their families. He had been born in the area and had never been tempted to leave it for somewhere that might have been seen as more glamorous; he had a *pied-à-terre* in London and a house in Florida, but he spent most of his time here. Even now, though, and after all these years, the fact that he had people working for him was still apt to bring him up short. It was quite something when he considered where he had come from.

He finished his eggs and got out of bed, making his way slowly to his en suite bathroom. He relieved himself and then went to the window and looked out over the grounds. The manor house was in Redlynch, south of Salisbury, and Mason had bought it at the end of the eighties when his fame had provided him with more money than he really knew what to do with. The estate had cost him three million, and he had spent the same again on renovating it and its outbuildings, plus a further two to buy additional land from a farmer who owned the neighbouring fields. It had been a huge outlay, yet it had still proven to be a shrewd investment. Mason's banker had arranged for the property to be valued, and the report had come back suggesting that, if he were ever to sell, offers would need to include seven zeroes.

Mason's rise from humble beginnings had been stratospheric, and the story was one that he never tired of telling. The poverty of his youth and the snubs that might have set him back had given him a chip on his shoulder, and the house and its grounds and everything else that he had accumulated were the ultimate denunciation of those who had doubted him. He had been born in Broad Chalke to Roman Catholic parents, the youngest of eight. His father had worked on a farm, and all the family could afford was a tiny two-bedroom house in the village. He had been an abject failure at school and had left as soon as he could and taken a job as a labourer. He worked on the Southampton docks and then found a job as a concert promoter. He found that his brashness was perfectly suited to show business, and his swift rise through radio and then television seemed preordained. Success had piled upon success, and now Mason enjoyed a position as television royalty, one of the best-loved celebrities in the country. It would have been easy to look out at the lawn and the lake and the hundred acres beyond that and feel that he didn't deserve it, but that kind of doubt was alien to him. There had been some good fortune along the way, but Mason had worked hard to get where he was and, as far as he was concerned, he deserved every last scrap of it. You could make luck with hard work, and that's what Mason had done.

He went into his dressing room and opened the wardrobe with his suits. He had more than twenty, each made to his precise measurements by his tailor on Savile Row. They were his trademark: he had them in all the colours of the rainbow, from electric blue to bright yellow to lime green. He never allowed himself to be seen in public when he wasn't looking his absolute best, and people had come to associate him with the striking colours that he matched with similarly garish shirts and ties. He ran his finger along the rail; each suit was freshly dry-cleaned and cloaked in a protective plastic sheath. He stopped at a three-piece that was ketchup red. He took it down, tore off the plastic and laid it across the back of the chair that sat in front of his make-up table. He took down a shirt of the same hue and then added suede shoes, also in red. His guests this morning all had an idea of what to expect of him, and Mason had never been one to let anyone down.

CHAPTER 44

Atticus dropped the dog back at the flat and drove over to the hospital. It was eight o'clock, and the car park was beginning to fill with staff and people visiting patients. Fyfe's office was behind the mortuary, reached by way of a series of functional corridors that led to the basement of the hospital. Atticus reached the door to the two post-mortem suites and held down the doorbell. The lock buzzed, and he pushed the door open and went through. Mack and Fyfe were in the reception area.

"Morning," Atticus said.

Fyfe turned. "Morning."

"Morning," Mack said. "I was telling Professor Fyfe that you were going to come over. He was just telling me that he was able to move up the PM to yesterday evening."

"I was hoping to be here for it," Atticus said.

"I'll run you through the results," Fyfe said, as defensive as always. "Very straightforward. Could probably have done it by email, to be honest."

"Nothing like seeing the evidence in person," Atticus said with a smile. "Shall we get started?"

Fyfe found each of them a disposable gown and handed out pairs of nitrile gloves and hair nets. They put them on and followed Fyfe into the examination room where the post-mortem had been carried out. Kajetan's body was laid out on the examination table. He was naked, the dark ink on his arms contrasting starkly with his pasty-white flesh and the gleaming steel beneath him.

Fyfe went up to the table and stood at the head of the body. "It's straightforward, as I said. Kajetan wasn't subjected to prolonged attempts at resuscitation, and there hasn't been significant decomposition. I pressed down on his chest and saw exudation through the mouth and nose of pink froth. The manifestation of the subject's last attempts to breathe on a mixture of residual air and water, plus oedema fluid in the lungs and a very clear sign of drowning."

"But not conclusive," Atticus said. "You see it in drug overdoses and congestive heart failure."

"True," Fyfe said, making it obvious that he was humouring him. "But add it to the fact that he was found in water? I think we can say with a *very* high degree of confidence that he drowned."

"Anything else?"

"Mud in his nostrils and mouth and in his scalp. Washerwoman's hands, too." He pointed down at Kajetan's pale and wrinkled hands.

"You'll be pleased to know that I can't disagree with any of that. He was certainly drowned." Atticus approached the body. "How long do you think he was in the water?"

"Hard to be sure," Fyfe said. "Somewhere between one and two days."

Mack came up to the table, too. "That ties in with what the water bailiff said."

Atticus decided not to ask whether Fyfe had been made aware of that when he visited the river. He suspected he would find that in Francine's report, and that Fyfe—lazy as always—had tied in his findings to match what she had said.

Fyfe gestured down at Kajetan's chest. "I could open him up to have a look at the lungs, but I don't think it's warranted when cause of death is as obvious as this."

Atticus pointed. "What about that? He's bruised around the neck and shoulders."

"He is," Fyfe said. "Likely caused after death. My operating hypothesis is that it was caused by him being jostled against the concrete in the channels by the current."

"Really? Are you sure?"

Atticus knew that Fyfe found him confounding. He had contradicted the man's findings when they had found the bone on Salisbury Plain, and that had just been the most recent of their disagreements. Atticus had never been impressed with Fyfe's abilities, and as always, he was struggling now with keeping his opinions to himself.

Remembering his promise to Mack, he smiled as benignly as he could. "I'm not trying to be impertinent—just trying to encourage a vigorous examination of the facts. You're confident he drowned first?"

"Yes—on the balance of probabilities." Fyfe said it with less certainty this time.

"So you should welcome an open exchange of views. I'm sure you'll still be right at the end of it—and your conclusion will be bolstered by the process."

Fyfe turned to Mack and spread his arms in a silent plea for help.

Atticus noticed the smile that was playing on the corner of her lips. "It can't hurt, can it? Go on, Atticus."

Atticus nodded his thanks. "So—we can agree that he drowned. But *how*? It's either natural causes or foul play. Can we agree on that?"

"Of course."

"So it all comes down to the bruising. You say that he was alive when he went into the water and that the bruising was caused by him being bumped around."

"That's the most likely outcome," Fyfe began. "Indeed, you might—"

"It's the *least* likely," Atticus said over him. He turned to Mack. "What do we know about bruises?" He didn't allow her a chance to answer. "A bruise is a collection of blood, visible to the naked eye as an area of discolouration, usually after trauma."

"That doesn't help you in the slightest," Fyfe said.

"Yes, it does. Blood seen in the tissue after death can be misinterpreted. What we have here is very significant bruising. Look at it." He pointed at several key spots. "I read a study last year that examined whether blunt force trauma delivered *after* death could cause blood and tissue damage that was indistinguishable from bruising produced *before* death. The study showed that producing post-mortem bruises, like these, requires considerable force. Even when they used a mallet, the resulting bruise was always smaller than would have been the case before death."

Mack looked down at the bruising. "What are you saying?"

"I'm saying that bruises as extensive as this could not easily have been produced by jostling a dead body against the sluice house."

"Fine," Fyfe said. "*Fine*. I'll play along. Let's say he had a heart attack. He falls into the water, still alive, and he's bruised before he drowns."

"Possible," Atticus conceded. "But more unlikely than the alternative."

"Being?" Mack said. "That he was murdered?"

"That he was attacked in the sluice house, leading to the bruising, and then drowned."

Fyfe snorted. "You're speculating."

"Maybe. But maybe not." He turned to Mack. "I think you should tell him about the videotape."

Fyfe frowned in confusion.

"A tape was sent to the *Journal* yesterday," Mack said. "Like the one for Campbell. Given the context, we have to assume that this is either suicide or murder."

"You didn't tell me that," Fyfe protested.

"Sorry," Mack said. "It's a fast-moving enquiry."

"Well, yes," he blustered. "Obviously, it changes everything. I can't see how this was suicide. I mean, it's possible, but—"

"Very unlikely," Atticus said. "What about David Campbell?"

"I looked at him two days ago. I'm sending the report over today."

"The potted version?"

His face puckered a little. "He was a mess. Falling from as high up as that? Not pleasant."

"Cause of death?"

"Impact. Obviously."

"Any sign of struggle?"

"Not easy to see with all the other injuries, but no—no obvious signs."

"What about toxicology?"

"I've taken blood and urine. They'll be tested next week."

"Same for Kajetan?"

"Yes. I know what we'll find for him—alcohol or drugs. Probably both."

"Can you expedite the tests?"

"Why? What are we looking for?"

"Kajetan probably *was* out of it, I agree, but there's no suggestion that would be the case for Campbell. It was early in the morning, and he wasn't a drinker. He was also fit and healthy. It would've been difficult to get him over the edge of the parapet."

"Meaning what?" Fyfe said. "You think he was pushed?"

"Let's say he was. He would've put up a fight, wouldn't he? Unless…"

Mack finished the sentence. "Unless he was drugged."

"Maybe," Atticus said. "I'd like to check."

CHAPTER 45

Alice had forced herself to get out of bed without snoozing her alarm and had gone to the gym so that she might start the day properly. She hadn't worked out for over a week, and it had started to bother her; she found it embarrassingly easy to find a reason to ignore her early morning routine, but she always felt bad when the day ended and she hadn't done any exercise. She had been one of the first into the building that morning and had done forty minutes of cardio, followed by a few gentle laps of the pool.

She reversed the car onto the drive, taking it back until the proximity warning bleeped and then applying the brake and switching off the engine. She took a moment to sit quietly, closing her eyes as she realised just how tired she was. It had been a hard week so far. David Campbell's plunge from the cathedral tower was three days ago, and there had been a lot of follow-up work to do even after the story had run. Subsequent events had changed the complexion of the story radically, and she had been running to catch up ever since.

She breathed in and out, grabbed the plastic bag of groceries from the passenger seat and reached for the door. She had stopped at the Marks and Spencer outlet at the petrol station to pick up some muesli and fresh fruit, and the thought of breakfast made her hungry. She would make herself a bowl, listen to the *Today* programme on Radio 4 and then get into the office.

She crossed the short path across her front lawn to the door and let herself in. There was a pile of post on the doormat, but she needed to eat, so she stepped over it and went into the kitchen. She had bought the house six months earlier. It was her first property, and she had been thrilled to move out from her parents' and into a place of her own. The costs of the transaction had been steep, and the mortgage was at the limit of what she could afford. She had had no choice but to be frugal with furnishing the place, and her father had hired a van and driven her down to the IKEA in Southampton, where he had helped her buy the things that she needed right away. There was the Grönlid sofa and Ypperlig coffee table in the living room; the Hemnes sideboard and Malm ottoman bed in the bedroom. The rooms still looked bare, but Alice couldn't afford everything she wanted straight away. But she had a list and would work her way through it, item by item, as funds allowed.

Alice put the bag on the counter and took out the muesli and fruit. She poured the cereal into a bowl, chopped the strawberries and grapes, added milk and then ambled back into the hall. She looked down at the post: there was an envelope that looked as if it might contain a bill, two packets from Amazon that probably contained the books on the cathedral that she had ordered and, hidden beneath them, the corner of a yellow Jiffy bag.

She set her bowl aside, then knelt and reached for it, her hand freezing before she touched it. She went back into the kitchen, took out a freezer bag and put her hand inside it. It wouldn't be as good as a glove, but it would do for now. She went back to the front door and very carefully picked up the package, gripping it between thumb and forefinger at its edge. She took it into the kitchen, set it down on the counter and then stared at it: there was a label on the side that faced up, and her name had been printed on it, just as had been the case with the package that had been delivered to the office. It was the same brand of Jiffy bag as before, and the shape of it suggested that something similar was inside.

Lewis had told her to call him at once should anything like this happen, but, as she reached for her phone, she stopped.

Wouldn't the police just take it away?

Would she even be told what was inside?

She felt awkward, as if ignoring the instructions that she had been given was going to get her into trouble, but mastered her unease for the sake of what she might find, and what *that* might mean for what was looking like the story of a lifetime—and what that might mean for her career. She would say that she had opened it without realising what it was.

She took a knife from the knife block, slid the tip inside the seal, then drew it back with just enough force to cut through the paper but not enough to cause unnecessary damage. She lifted the parcel and tipped it up, careful not to touch the contents as they slid out and onto the counter. It was the same as before: a black plastic box of the sort used to store videotapes.

She turned the case and saw that it, like the others, had a label that had been pushed into the plastic sleeve that lay against the spine.

Hartnett, Dominic / 31 August

There was a sheet of folded paper, too. She opened it out.

Whoever kills an animal must take restitution, but whoever kills a human being is to be put to death.

She exhaled, looked back at the cassette box and the note and forgot all about her breakfast. She took out her phone and scrolled through the contacts. She found the entry for Lewis, called the number and waited for it to connect.

CHAPTER 46

Atticus had asked Francine Patterson to search the Police National Database for everything that could be found about Lucjusz Kajetan, and when he got back from the hospital and woke his computer, he found that there was an email waiting for him. He opened the report attached to it and scanned it. The database held records of Kajetan's cautions and convictions, and Atticus saw that there were a *lot* of them: most were for possession of controlled substances, along with one for assault. There was a witness statement that Kajetan had made when he had been interviewed by Francine after his most recent arrest for possession. He told her that he was born in Warsaw in 1973 and that he had arrived in London at the turn of the century. He had lived in London for five years, working for a Polish builder, and then, after marrying a local woman, he had moved down to Salisbury and set up his own business. Things had been good until the financial crash; the banks called in their loans and, with no one starting any new projects, the business was choked of the funds it needed. After limping on for a year, it died. Kajetan's house was repossessed, his marriage failed, and, with nothing left, he ended up on the street.

Atticus gave a low whistle, and Bandit, who had been sleeping in the other room, lifted himself off the mattress and trotted over.

"Another walk?"

The dog bounded with excitement as Atticus put on the harness, clipped the lead to it and led the way down the stairs.

* * *

Atticus and Bandit walked through the city, along the High Street and then onto Fisherton Street, eventually turning right and following the signs to the office where the Shopmobility team hired out their wheelchairs and scooters. The office was on the ground floor of the two-level car park at the Maltings, beneath Sainsbury's. Atticus continued around the corner until he reached the area used by the local homeless as a place to shelter and sleep. The council had been trying to move them on for months, and Atticus remembered the consternation when they had installed metal fencing to prevent access to the areas that they favoured. There had been a campaign in the *Journal* about it, he recalled, and the fencing had been removed.

There were three men and two women there as Atticus approached, surrounded by the detritus of the terminally poor: empty cans of cheap lager, empty bottles of supermarket own-brand cider and fragments of glass from crushed vials that crunched underfoot. They had spread out a series of mismatched duvets to soften the concrete, and there were orange carrier bags from the nearby Sainsbury's, some stuffed with empty food wrappers and more empty cans. They had a cooker that ran off a bottle of Calor gas, and one of them had found, and moved in, an armchair that was now accommodating a sleepy-looking Labrador. Bandit wagged his tail enthusiastically at the prospect of an introduction to the dog, but the Labrador stayed where he was and closed his eyes.

Atticus had been down here regularly when he had been a detective. There were usually six or seven rough sleepers, and, although the precise membership of the group varied from time to time due to some moving on and others passing away, Atticus had been able to form useful relationships with several of them over the years. He approached now and saw a man he recognised.

"Ricky," he said.

The man looked up at him. "Haven't seen you for a while."

"Months."

"Still police?"

"Not anymore. I'm working on my own now."

"Doing what?"

"Private detective."

"For real? Like on the telly?"

He smiled with self-deprecation. "Don't you read the papers? I'm famous."

"Bollocks you are."

"How are you?"

"Same as always."

"I thought you were waiting for a room at Alabare?"

"I had one for a week," he said.

"And?"

"They kicked me out." He shrugged. "Caught me shooting up, and that was that. There's no way I'm ever going to stop. Don't *want* to stop. Anyway, it doesn't matter—I've got everything I need."

Ricky had been a soldier, like so many of the other men and women who ended up down here. Their military careers came to an end and, without preparation or training for their transition to Civvie Street, they fell between the cracks and were forgotten.

"I'm looking for information on someone who used to sleep down here. Do you think you could help me?"

"Depends," he said.

"On what?"

Ricky put his hand out.

Atticus took out his wallet, opened it and removed the little wad of notes that he kept inside. He peeled off a ten and gave it to the man. "Same again if you can help me."

"Fair enough—what do you want?"

"Do you know Lucjusz Kajetan? The police nicked him here for possession three or four months ago. He had a nickname. They called him—"

"Lucky," the man interrupted, then gave a hacking laugh. "Lucky Lucjusz. He thought that was hilarious."

"Did you know him?"

"Same as I know any of the others around here. People come; people go. You'll get blokes turn up and sleep down here for a few nights; then they'll get a bed somewhere until they get kicked out and end up here again."

"What can you tell me about him?"

"Not much to say. He's Polish, used to be a builder, I think, until his business went under and his life went to shit."

"Did he ever give you any reason to think that he had enemies?"

Ricky shrugged. "Don't think so. He's a good bloke. Hard not to like him."

"*I* don't like him," said the man to Ricky's right. His name was Jezza, and Atticus remembered him as being an airman who had, if memory served, seen action in Afghanistan. He was rolling a joint.

"Why not?"

"Has a temper on him. You wouldn't want to be around him when he was in the wrong sort of mood."

"Shut up," Ricky said. "He's all right."

The dog reached out with a paw and scratched itself on the snout.

"When was the last time you saw him?"

Ricky paused for a moment, his face puckering as he gave thought to the question. "Last week, I think. The police come around here and move us on every now and again. Like you said, Lucky got nicked not all that long ago, and I think it freaked him out. He said he'd found somewhere else to kip where he wouldn't get trouble."

"Did he say where?"

"Not to me," Ricky said. "You get somewhere good, somewhere you might get a bit of peace and quiet, you don't always tell anyone else. You keep it to yourself."

"*I* know," Jezza said, putting out his hand. "He told me. But you're going to have to pay me if you want me to tell you, though. Nothing comes for free."

"Nice try," Atticus said. "I know where it was—the old eel house on the river."

Jezza finished rolling his joint and lit it. "S'right." He didn't seem remotely concerned that his ploy for Atticus's money had failed. "He told me last week."

Ricky was confused. "Why are you here asking about him if you already know where he is? Has he done something wrong again?"

Atticus watched their faces for a reaction. "He's dead. He was found in the water yesterday."

Both men reacted as Atticus would have expected: with surprise, if not necessarily shock. It wasn't unusual for the men and women who ended up down here to find themselves in medical difficulty, and death would be a more regular occurrence here than would have been the case in the world outside.

"What happened?" Ricky asked.

"The police aren't sure. Might have been an accident—he gets drunk; he slips; he falls in and drowns."

Jezza was looking at him shrewdly. "But that's not what you think. You were asking whether he had any enemies."

"That's the other possibility. Ricky said he didn't. What do you think?"

Jezza cocked an eyebrow, smiled suggestively and put out his hand again.

Atticus took another ten-pound note and held it out. Jezza reached for it, and Atticus pulled it back. "You first."

The man stared at Atticus, then smiled, baring a mouthful of blackened teeth. "Fine. There was a bloke down here, back end of last week. He was like you, asking around about Lucky. Had a picture of him from before—didn't recognise him until he said that he was Polish, and then it could only really be him.

He told me he was a lawyer and that he was looking for him because one of his relatives had died and left him some money in a will."

"And you told him where he was?"

He nodded. "He gave me fifty notes."

"When was this?"

"I said—"

"You need to be precise," Atticus interrupted. "*Exactly* when?"

"I have no idea, mate. One day is the same as any other. I don't even know what day it is today."

"Tell me what happened."

"I already said—a bloke came down here asking where he could find Lucky, and I said I thought he was down on the river." He took a draw on his joint.

"Don't do that now," Atticus said. He reached out and batted the joint from his fingers.

"Hey!"

Atticus took out two more ten-pound notes and added them to the first, holding them up so that Jezza could see what he stood to make by cooperating. "What did he look like?"

Jezza picked up the joint and screwed up his face as he tried to remember. "Younger than me. Thirties. Dark hair. About your height."

"What was he wearing?"

"Jeans, I think. And a leather jacket."

"Was there anything about him that was unusual?"

"Not that I can think of."

"Anything at all."

He sucked his teeth. "I didn't think he was a lawyer. He didn't have that kind of air about him, if you know what

I mean. He had an *edge*. I said I'd help him if he'd make it worth my while, and the way he reacted made me think that he wasn't someone that I'd want to piss off. I mean, he paid up—generous, too—but I got the feeling that he might have a nasty side."

Atticus knew that there was no point in pushing things too much further. He gave him the notes and a business card that he took from his pocket. "There's another hundred in it for you if you can think of anything else that helps me to find him."

"What about me?" Ricky protested.

"You too." He took out a second card and handed it over, plus the additional ten he'd promised him. "Here's my number. Call me if you think of anything useful."

CHAPTER 47

Max Mason waited in the library as his guests arrived. He could hear the crunch of the wheels of their cars as they rolled to a stop on the gravelled turning circle in front of the house, and then Ross's voice as he welcomed them and showed them through into the drawing room. Mason's chef—a Frenchman named Claude whom he had poached from the kitchen of Michel Roux—had prepared coffee and pastries, and Ross had brought out a humidor with a selection of cigars from Mason's extensive collection. Mason listened to the buzz of conversation as his guests greeted one another and waited for their host's arrival.

The Wednesday Morning Club had been a fixture in Mason's diary for the last forty years. He cultivated social contacts the way a gardener might attend to his garden; he added new members who he thought might add colour to his collection and pruned those for whom he had no further use. A few of the men—and they were always men—whom he had invited had turned out to be disappointments, but, by and large, Mason had extracted value from the weekly gatherings. On the one hand, it did his ego no harm at all to have the great and the good of local society under his roof and enjoying his hospitality; he remembered where he had come from and remembered the snubs that his father had received when he had tried to advance himself. On the other hand—and more importantly—the connections that he had made during those countless mornings together had stood him in good stead. The men who came to him had nothing to do with the glitz and glamour of Mason's life in London, but they were all important in the local community. The complement changed over time, but it had included businessmen, doctors, lawyers, judges, army officers and men from the police. Mason was a spider, weaving a web that stretched out from Salisbury to all corners of Wiltshire and beyond. His guests willingly flung themselves into its strands, all of them attracted by the glow of his celebrity.

There was a knock.

"Yes?"

Ross opened the door. "Everyone is here, sir."

"Thank you."

Mason straightened his jacket, fastening the last button but one, and then crossed the hallway to the reception hall and then the drawing room. His guests were waiting for him: Allan Ellsworth, the owner of a local estate agency, was pouring coffee while talking to Craig Loome, a landlord who owned a swathe of the industrial park near to the airfield; Connor Gallagher, a retired judge who still enjoyed extensive connections at the High Court in London, was sat in an armchair opposite Chief Superintendent Alexander Beckton; Richard Claire and William Mackintosh, both involved in finance in London, were chatting by the big mullioned window.

Mason clapped his hands. "Good morning, gentlemen. How are we all doing?"

The others turned to him; they were sycophantic toadies to a man, but, rather than be irritated by the transparency of their obsequiousness, Mason found it amusing. It was almost flattering; the son of a farmhand, a former labourer and stevedore who didn't have a pot to piss in while he was growing up, was able to hold court and attract the great and the good of Wiltshire society to his door. It was another sign of how far he had come.

He went to the humidor, opened the lid and took out an Arturo Fuente Opus X, a big seven-inch stogie that cost fifty pounds. He went to where Beckton and Gallagher were sitting and held out the ebony box; Gallagher passed, but Beckton obliged, taking out another of the Arturos.

"How are you both?" Mason said as he took a cutter and snipped off the end of his cigar and then Beckton's.

"Very good, Max," Gallagher said.

"I saw the show at the Palladium," Beckton said.

"*The Royal Variety*?" Mason waved a hand dismissively. "Things aren't what they used to be. Do you know the first year I did it?" Beckton shook his head. "Seventy-five. Nearly fifty years ago. The bill in those days… my god, it put last weekend to shame."

Mason noticed the way that Gallagher and Beckton both leaned in toward him, big smiles fixed to their faces as he regaled them with stories from his career. He had long since realised that he had that effect on people and had always taken advantage of it; the stories he could tell told of a different time, of gossip and intrigue, when celebrity meant something, rather than the ephemeral fluff that passed for glamour these days. He could make them feel part of something exclusive, give them a glimpse into the world that would otherwise have been closed off to them. His career had been long enough for him to *embody* show business, and it was catnip to those with boring, dull, provincial lives.

He took out his lighter and offered to light Beckton's cigar. "How are things with you?"

"Still dealing with what happened at Imber."

"What happened with the Met?" Gallagher asked.

"They sent a man from the counter-terrorism team," Beckton said. "It took a lot of effort to persuade him that it had nothing to do with that."

"This is Richard Miller?" Mason said.

Beckton nodded.

Mason had heard about Miller's death from Beckton on the occasion of his last visit. He had explained that Miller's body had been found in the back of a car and that the suggestion was that he had been involved in a murder connected to the deserted village at Imber. Mason had prompted him for more information, but Beckton had been a terrible bore and told him that it was under investigation and he had to be careful what he said.

No harm In trying again. "Have you found out how he was involved?"

Beckton drew down on his cigar and then blew the smoke up toward the ceiling. "It's still not clear. Miller confessed to a robbery in Londonderry when he was in the army. We charged him and bailed him, and then he was found dead in the back of a car on New Street."

"Found by the private detective."

Beckton nodded. "Priest."

"Do you know why he was left there?" Gallagher asked.

"We still don't know. Someone—the murderer, most likely—called Priest and told him that Miller was involved with the two men who we think were responsible for the Imber killings. This person—whoever he is—thought Miller would get away with it, so he decided to take matters into his own hands."

"How extraordinary," Gallagher said.

Beckton blew out another mouthful of smoke. "That's one way of describing it. We still don't have any idea who he is."

"But you're investigating?"

"We are," Beckton said. "With help from the Met. They've accepted it's not terrorism, but Miller was an MP, and they have to be seen to be treating it seriously. It's made things much more difficult for us, of course. That's the thing with the Met—they come down to a place like this and think that we don't know what we're doing. You know my dad was an officer?"

"I don't think you've ever mentioned that," Mason said.

He nodded. "Down here, too—Salisbury. He got to detective inspector before he retired. Did a case with the Met back in the seventies. It was the same then, too. He said they treated them like country bumpkins. You know what they called them?"

Mason shook his head.

"Swedes—like turnips. It hasn't changed."

Mason told Beckton to enjoy the cigar and got up to circulate around the room. He had been to Imber, and the thought of the bodies in the graveyard sent shivers up and down his spine. He had followed the investigation through the reports in the newspapers at first, swiping through the pages from front to back with the morbid curiosity of a rubbernecker at a car crash. The reporters had run out of fresh material as the investigation foundered, and Mason had taken advantage of Beckton's friendship in an attempt to get the inside line. Beckton had been coming to the house for several years, but, in truth, Mason had always found him rather dull. Beckton was a senior officer, though, and now Mason was prepared to hold his nose in the hope that he might be able to learn something that would otherwise have been beyond him.

He noticed that Beckton had been eyeing the crystal decanter on the table with the Glenfiddich. He indicated it with a flick of his fingers. "Fancy a Scotch?"

Beckton feigned reluctance. "Surely it's too early?"

"Never. That's the Grande Couronne—twenty-six years old. I picked up in an auction in London for… well"—he grinned—"it wasn't cheap." Mason raised a hand, and Ross was alongside almost before he could lower it. "Pour the chief superintendent a glass. I'll take one, too."

"Right away, sir."

Mason watched as Ross went to the table and selected two tulip-shaped glasses with tapered necks, perfect for allowing the concentrated aroma to hit the nose through a narrow rim.

"So," he said to Beckton as Ross unstopped the decanter and poured, "bring me up to date about Imber. I'm dying to know what's happened since you were last here."

CHAPTER 48

Atticus went back to the office, made Bandit comfortable in the second room and spent ten minutes reviewing the file that he had prepared for Nina Parsons. He got up from his desk at a little before midday and went to the bay window, where he could look down on the street below. He saw Nina making her way along the pavement and then passing beneath him, where she would turn right into the passageway that led to his door.

The bell rang, and he went down to let her in.

"Mr. Priest," she said.

"It's Atticus."

"Atticus," she said, smiling, "thanks for seeing me on short notice."

"Not a problem. You said you were going away?"

"Estonia."

"You're Royal Welsh?"

"First Battalion. How'd you know?"

"I had a case before I left the police—an infantryman from Tidworth crashed his car outside the barracks after a night out. He was Royal Welsh—just rotated back from Eastern Europe."

"Well, that's me."

"The weather won't be quite as nice as Cyprus."

"No, it won't. You'll have more of a challenge next time."

"How do you mean?"

"You'll have to find something else to impress me with other than what my tan might tell you."

She wasn't criticising him, but rather, judging from the sparkle in her eye, was very gently ribbing him for his earlier attempt to impress.

"You're never going to let me live that down, are you?"

"Probably not."

Atticus wasn't sure, but he was left with the impression that she was flirting with him. "Well," he said, "unless you have some other work you'd like me to do, I'm not sure that our paths will cross again. I've finished looking into Mr. Wintringham for you." He held up a copy of the report that he had printed out.

"Do you have time to go through it with me?"

"Of course."

"Tell you what—why don't I have a quick flick through it while you make me a coffee?"

Atticus clapped his hands together. "I'm *so* sorry. That's the second time I've been a terrible host. How do you take it again?"

"White, no sugar."

"White, no sugar. I'll just be a moment. Here."

He handed her the report so that she could take it, then got up and made his way to the kitchen outside. He filled the kettle and flicked the switch to set it to boil, then prepared the mugs with coffee granules and milk. He found that he was impressed once again with Nina's assurance; she had had no problem calling him out on his attempts to show off, and her easy banter was the same today as it had been before. It was unusual, especially in a client; coming to see an investigator was out of the ordinary and disconcerting, and the prospect of discussing intimate personal matters would have made most people cringe. It was much like going to the doctor with an embarrassing condition. Nina did not show any of the usual symptoms of nerves, though, and Atticus found himself wondering whether her poise might be thanks to her career as an officer. Those in the military often had that same self-possession; perhaps she held a more senior rank than he had assumed. It made him curious, and he decided to check once he had a moment.

His phone chirped with an incoming text just as the kettle boiled. He took it out of his pocket, saw that it was from Mack—*Call me!*—and resolved to get back to her as soon as he was finished here; it wouldn't be long. He poured the hot water into the mugs and took them back into the office. Nina had got up from the sofa in the bay window and was standing next to the desk when he returned, looking at one of the large whiteboards that he had fixed to the wall. He had used the board to note down his thoughts on the continuing investigation into Alfred Burns, only recently wiping it away. He had returned to the office last night and had doodled a series of inchoate thoughts on the deaths of Campbell and Kajetan, trying—and failing—to find anything to connect them beyond the peccadillos that had been exposed by the videos that had been received at the *Journal*.

The scribbles would have made no sense to anyone else, and Nina showed no interest in them. Atticus handed her one of the mugs, and she took it over to the bay window and sat down once more.

"Thank you," she said, then proffered the printed report. "You didn't find much."

"There's not much *to* find. He's a fairly normal man. I didn't find anything that says he's anything other than what he told you he was. Married, two kids, mortgage on his house with Barclays, drives a sensible car, shops at Waterstones and has coffee at Boston Tea Party."

"You followed him?"

He nodded. "I went to his house, spoke to one of the neighbours, who said that the family was very nice, and then followed him into the city."

"What about online?"

"That's pages five and six," Atticus said, gesturing to the report, "but the précis is the same: standard Facebook profile of long standing, reasonably active, posts a little too much about his family to be safe; has a Twitter account but doesn't use it; posts pictures of local landscapes taken from a drone on his Instagram. None of it is even remotely controversial."

She flicked through the pages, scanning the screen-caps that Atticus had taken from his various profiles. "It's funny," she said. "I'm relieved he's what he said he is, but I can't help feeling foolish that I've had you go to all this trouble when I should just have trusted him."

"It was no trouble at all," Atticus said. "And I don't blame you. You had a bad experience—it's not unreasonable to try to do everything you can to make sure it doesn't happen again."

"Yes—you're right." She stood, opened her bag and slid the report inside. "Can you email a copy to me as well, please?"

"Of course."

"And a copy of your bill? I'll pay before I fly out."

Atticus stood and took her outstretched hand. "Why are you going to Estonia?"

"There's a battlegroup out there—we're training them in how to use NATO gear. Can't really say much more than that."

"Of course."

She paused at the door. "I meant to ask you—did you get out to Imber during the investigation?"

"I did," he said. "Several times."

"What did you make of it?"

"It's one of the strangest places I think I've ever been. You must have been?"

"When I was training, but that was years ago. You're right about it being weird, though. It's the buildings that they just left, as if they were always going to come back… I found it a bit spooky. And the bodies were found in the graveyard?"

"They were."

She shook her head. "Awful what they did. Awful."

Atticus opened the door for her. "Let me know if there's anything else I can do for you."

"I will," she said. "And thanks for taking care of this so promptly. I appreciate it."

* * *

Atticus watched Nina walk back up New Street, took his phone from his pocket, woke the screen and saw that Mack had sent another two messages after the first. The first asked him to call her back, the second asked again, and the third—in all caps—practically *demanded* it.

He called her.

"What is—"

She didn't let him finish. "Where are you?"

"At the office. I had a meeting with a client."

"You need to come in."

He noticed the edge to her voice and guessed immediately what it was. "There's been another video?"

"At Alice Morris's house this morning. She's bringing it into the nick."

"Wait for me," he said, reaching for his jacket. "I'll be there in fifteen minutes."

CHAPTER 49

Atticus hurried to Bourne Hill, negotiated the woman at the desk and rushed up to the CID room. The desks were empty, and he could see and hear the activity in the enquiry room.

He went inside. The team were taking the seats around the table.

Mack saw him and turned. "Good. We're all here."

Atticus pointed at the open envelope on the desk. "Another?"

"Another."

"Who opened it?"

"They did. The *Journal*."

"What? Didn't we tell them not to?"

"We did," Lewis said. "It was Alice. She said she wasn't thinking."

"Did she touch it?"

"Just the envelope," Lewis said. "Not the tape or the case or the note."

Atticus muttered a curse and turned to Mack. "Where's the tape now?"

"It's being digitised."

"When will it be ready?"

She went over to the computer on the desk and tapped the keyboard. "Now."

Mack cast the laptop's screen onto the larger screen on the wall and double-clicked on the most recently added file. The video player opened with the same background that had become familiar from the two previous videos: the bed, the bare brick wall behind it lit from below by red uplighters on the floor. The footage ran for thirty seconds without anyone appearing in it, but then a man crossed into the shot from the left and sat down on the edge of the bed. He was bare-chested and, sharing a conversation with someone off camera, he gave a laugh that carved lines around his mouth and nose.

"Stop the tape," Best said.

Mack did, freezing the frame with the man looking straight into the camera with a grin on his face.

Atticus recognised him. "You know who that is?"

Best pointed down to the label on the case. "Dominic Hartnett."

"Yes—and?"

"Shit." Mack's jaw fell open as she realised. "The MP for Devizes."

Atticus jabbed his finger at the screen. "He's younger, but it's him."

Best took out his phone and, after a moment, turned it around so that the others could see the display. He had found Hartnett's website: the MP was standing with his hands behind his back and a smile on his face. His hair was grey now—it was dark brown in the video—and his skin was wrinkled with age, but there was very little doubt that the two images were of the same man.

Atticus's thoughts ran around his head in crazy circles, and he had to close his eyes in order to try to corral them. "What day is it today?"

"Wednesday."

"There was a vote in Parliament yesterday evening."

"How do you know that?" Best said.

"It was on the radio. I had it on in the background last night. Things—random things—stick in my mind." He took out his phone, opened a browser and navigated to the website that listed how individual MPs had voted in the chamber. "He wasn't there."

"So?" Lynas said.

"So it was a three-line whip. He *had* to be there, and he wasn't."

Best held up his phone. "I've got the number for his constituency office."

"Call it," Mack said.

Best placed the call and, after waiting for it to connect, introduced himself and asked if it was possible to speak to the MP. Atticus couldn't hear the response, but, as the conversation continued, Best shook his head and turned his face away. He thanked the other person for their help, asked them to stay on the line and then muted his microphone and put the phone on the table.

"He's dead."

CHAPTER 50

Atticus sat bolt upright. "How?"

"You were right—he wasn't there for the vote last night. They couldn't get in touch with him, so they went to the place in Fulham he has for when he's in Parliament. He was in bed. Dead."

"*How?*"

"They think he had a heart attack."

"He didn't have a heart attack," Atticus muttered.

"They said it didn't look suspicious."

Atticus ignored that. "I need to go and see for myself."

"No," Mack said. "You can't. That'll be for the Met."

"They'll mess it up."

Mack stared at him and shook her head.

"What about the post-mortem?" he said. "Someone from here needs to go."

Mack held up a hand to try to calm him. "First things first—we need to make sure Murphy knows. That's two dead Wiltshire MPs in less than two months. And Hartnett's apartment is on their patch. I know it's frustrating, but we don't have any choice."

Atticus threw up his hands. "But Murphy is *hopeless*."

Mack held his eye until he remembered to take a breath. "This is what we're going to do. I'm going to go and speak to Beckton. I don't know what he'll want to do about it, but that'll be for him and Murphy to decide. I'd suggest you speak to the tech department and make sure that the other two videos have been put somewhere convenient so that we can all look at them. Okay?"

"What? Why?"

"I want to make sure we can get to them as easily and conveniently as possible."

Atticus realised what Mack was suggesting: she anticipated, as did he, that Murphy would return with reinforcements and take control of the investigation from top to bottom. Atticus would definitely be barred from offering his assistance; it might lead to the freezing out of the officers from Salisbury, too. Mack was hinting at a way that he could remain involved: if he were to have a copy of those videos, then he could continue to investigate them even if he was no longer on the team.

"Good idea," he said. "I'll do that. What about the message?"

Mack held up an evidence bag with a piece of A4 inside.

Atticus read: "'Whoever kills an animal must take restitution, but whoever kills a human being is to be put to death.'"

"Leviticus," Francine said. "Chapter twenty-four."

"It's him," Atticus said. "It has to be."

"Jack?"

"It must be. There's too much pointing in that direction to ignore it: the scripture, the kids in the videos."

"Let's say it is him," Lynas said. "Why is he including the scripture with the tapes? Because he's religious?"

"Maybe," Atticus said.

Mack eyed him. "But you don't think so?"

"I don't know. He could be—it's possible. But if he is, he's butchering the meaning. None of the verses actually *condone* revenge. At best, they say it's not our place to intervene and God will sort everything out."

"No one is suggesting he's rational," Best said. "Maybe he has his own spin on them."

Atticus shook his head. "*I* think he's rational."

"So?"

"I think he's including them because he knows that when they get out—and we all know they *will* get out, eventually—it's going to make the story even bigger than it would already have been. Think about what the hacks from the nationals will say when they get wind of it? It'll be like catnip for them."

Lynas frowned. "You think he *wants* publicity?"

"It wouldn't be unusual. I can think of a dozen killers who craved notoriety. David Berkowitz, Richard Ramirez, Dennis Rader—what did they all have in common?"

"Apart from the fact that they were psychopaths?" Best said.

"Apart from that. They sent letters to the cops and the newspapers because the thing they wanted most of all was a public image."

"You don't think he's like *them*, though?" Best said. "I mean—those are all serial killers."

"He's killed multiple times," Atticus said. "So there's that. But no, I don't think he's like them. His victims aren't random. There's an agenda. He's choosing them. It's something to do with the videos."

Atticus sat back, put his hands on his head and laced his fingers. The room was quiet as they digested the implication of what had just been discussed.

Best tapped his knuckles on the table. "What do you want the rest of us to do, boss?"

"Work on the leads we've been following."

Lynas raised a hand. "I've got something on that."

"The cameras near the *Journal*?"

He nodded. "I went up and down Rollestone Street, looking for cameras. There's a surgery on the other side of the road from the office. They have a camera above the door that looks out onto the street." He paused and shrugged. "I went through the footage carefully. Nothing."

Atticus frowned. "There must be *something*."

"There isn't. The staff from the paper go in and out, but it was raining all day—*really* heavy, remember?—and there was hardly anyone around. The only people who went in through the front door were the editor, the reporter, the receptionist and another bloke they told me was the photographer. That's it. If you don't believe me, you can go and check it out yourself."

"Then how was the tape delivered?"

Lynas spread his arms. "I don't know—with the post?"

"No," Lewis said. "I checked with the receptionist, and she's sure it wasn't that."

"Do we trust that she's right?" Atticus said. "It looked disorganised there when I went in."

"It is disorganised," Lewis said, "but she was sure. The post comes in the morning, and she says it wasn't there then. It could've been a courier…"

"But then they would've been on the camera," Lynas finished, "and they weren't."

"We need to get to the bottom of that," Mack said.

The talk of cameras spurred a thought. "What about the cameras around the cathedral?" Atticus said. "Anything after he went by the college?"

"No," Best said. "The only one that was working was up high above the door to the school. We've got him going by, but his face was covered. You were right. He knew how to get through without letting us get a good look at him."

"I'm not surprised," Atticus said.

Best held up a finger. "There's one other thing. I checked with the cathedral to see if they had a record of everyone who went up on the tour of the attic. They only did it twice—six people each time. I checked them all, and none of them ring any alarm bells. One family—mum and dad and three kids. Four of the others were women from the Women's Institute. The other three didn't look likely, but I checked them out to be sure, and they all have alibis."

Atticus slumped back in his chair. He had hoped that they might be destined for a little luck, but it seemed not.

Mack brought the meeting to a close, making sure that everyone was assigned a task and dismissing them with the injunction that they clear their diaries: there was going to be a lot of overtime until they were able to find out who was behind the deaths.

CHAPTER 51

Mack went to Beckton's office but found he wasn't there. She went to his secretary and asked her to ensure he called her as soon as he returned, explaining that it was important they speak before the end of the day. The secretary said she would see to it; Mack thanked her and went back to the CID room.

The door to the enquiry room was closed. She looked through the opaque window to the side and saw a blurred figure in the glass.

She knocked on the door, waited a moment, and then opened it.

Atticus was standing with the boxes of documents that had been generated during the enquiry set out on the floor by his feet. The table was covered with papers, and Atticus was standing over them, taking a picture of each before replacing it with the next and repeating the process.

"Shut the door," he said without looking up.

She did. "What are you doing?"

"What does it look like I'm doing? I'm copying as much of this as I can. Pass me Miller's statement—it's in the box over there."

THE RED ROOM

She opened the lid and took out the statement. "I'm not sure this is a great idea."

"You suggested it."

"I meant the videos—not all this."

"I've already emailed myself the videos," Atticus said, checking the images on his phone. "It's not enough. I need these, too. I need all of it, really. The statement, please. Give it to me."

Mack went around the table and looked over his shoulder. She saw he had just finished photographing the last page of James York's statement. She dropped Miller's on top of it.

"You think there's a connection between Imber and now?"

"I think it's likely."

"What, though?"

"York and Burns abused and murdered teenagers. We know that. Miller was involved, too, beyond what he admitted to, anyway. Jack told me that."

"And we believe him?"

"Why wouldn't we?"

"Go on."

"All three videos involve kids."

"True. But we've got nothing beyond that."

"What did Jack say to me?"

"That Miller wasn't just guilty of the murders in Londonderry."

He gestured for her to continue. "What else?"

"That the three of them were being paid to abuse the girls."

"What did he tell me—the exact words?"

"I can't remember, Atticus. I'd have to—"

He spoke over her. "'I don't know the names of the customers.' That's what he said. 'The *customers*.' What if

Campbell, Kajetan and Hartnett were involved in it, too? Maybe it was a business—what if you could buy the kids? What if they were being prostituted?"

"But why would they have been filmed?"

"Look where the camera is—up high, in the corner. I'll bet you anything you like that the three of them didn't know it was there."

"So they could be blackmailed."

"We know Alf Burns was into blackmail. Or maybe it was so the tapes could be used for protection. Or leverage."

"Okay," she said. "Okay. Let's assume, for the sake of argument, that I buy that. Who's topping them? Who's sending the tapes? You *really* think it's Jack?"

He stared at her as if she had just asked a stupid question. "It's him."

"Next question, then. How's he got the tapes?"

"Don't know."

"And why's he sending them to the paper?"

Atticus was about to answer, but, before he could speak, there was a knock at the door.

"Hold on," Mack said. She put Miller's statement back into the box. "And that one," she hissed to Atticus, pointing at York's statement. She waited until he had put it away before raising her voice again. "Come in."

Murphy opened the door. "DCI Jones," he said. "Mr. Priest. What are you doing?"

"Discussing the enquiry," Mack said.

Murphy turned to Atticus. "With him?"

"That's right."

"Why?"

Mack paused.

"It's true, then—you brought him back again."

"Atticus works for us as a consultant. I cleared everything with the chief superintendent."

"I just spoke to him about that," Murphy said. "And other things. But never mind—it can wait." He came inside and drummed his fingers on the top of the nearest cardboard box. "I've just got back from London. And DCS Beckton's been speaking to my boss. There's not really any point beating around the bush—we'll be taking over."

"How much?"

"All of it. You've had two MPs murdered in the space of six weeks. You're out of your depth."

Atticus stiffened. "And you're not?"

Murphy glowered. "Thank you, Mr. Priest. We won't need you anymore."

"You don't know what you're doing. You're going to make a mess."

Murphy pointed at the door. "Out."

"No." Atticus shook his head. "I'm not going anywhere."

"Yes, you are. But not too far, please. I've still got some questions I want to ask you."

"I answered your questions."

"Not satisfactorily. I'll be in touch."

Mack could see that Atticus was close to losing his temper. She reached a hand out and rested it on his elbow, but he brushed it off.

"Mack doesn't need your help," Atticus told him. "And handing the investigation over will slow things down and cause confusion. This is *local*. Can't you see that? The dead men all have connections to Salisbury. There's no reason for you to be involved other than politics."

"I'm afraid politics is an excellent reason for us to be involved."

Mack tried again. "Atticus."

"No, Mack. You know as well as I do that this is wrong."

Murphy folded his arms. "Go on, then. Indulge me. What do you think happened?"

"You've seen the tapes? The three dead men all featured in them. At first I thought it was blackmail and then suicide, but it isn't that. They were *murdered*. It's Jack—he's getting revenge. They were killed, and then the tapes were sent to the newspaper to discredit them. Killing them isn't enough. Throwing Campbell off the tower of the cathedral isn't enough. The motive here is *intensely* personal. Jack wants them dead, *and* he wants their reputations ruined."

"Speculation. We won't get anywhere with random guesses."

"You think I'm going to stop looking into this?"

"Yes—I do."

"I won't."

Murphy's brows lowered. "Yes, you *will*. Interfering with an investigation is a crime. I'd like you to leave the building now, please. I don't know the details of your *arrangement* with DCI Jones, but I'm sure we can take care of any formalities. That can all be dealt with later. I need to speak to her privately now about how we can work together from now on. And you need to leave."

Mack listened to the way Murphy sneered 'arrangement' and knew that he knew about them. Atticus must have realised, too, but was seemingly too angry to respond.

Mack tugged him aside. "Atticus—come with me."

"Don't be long," Murphy said to her. "There's a press conference tomorrow morning, and I need to talk to you about it."

CHAPTER 52

Francine was exhausted when she got home, and there were no spaces outside the house where she could park. She drove along St. Ann Street until she found somewhere she could leave the car and, ignoring the fact that her permit wasn't valid this far down the road, she pulled up to the kerb and walked back to the house. It was only when she opened the door that she remembered that Charlie had offered to cook dinner for her. The light in the kitchen was on, and she could hear the radio, tuned to the channel that played the nineties indie tunes that he preferred. The music was loud and, as she slipped off her boots and hung up her jacket, she recognised the Manic Street Preachers.

"Hello?" she called out.

The volume on the radio was turned down, and Charlie stepped into the doorway. He was wearing her apron and, as she smiled at the incongruity of it, he gestured to the slogan printed onto the front.

"'Wine goes in, wisdom comes out,'" he read. "Recent events would suggest otherwise."

"Very funny."

"We could put it to the test tonight?" He reached for the counter and held up a bottle of red. "I had a bottle of this last year. It's bloody nice."

Francine followed him into the kitchen and saw that he had already gone to an effort to make the evening special: he had laid the table with cutlery for three courses and had lit a candle that flickered above the two settings.

"Look at all this," she said.

He pulled out her seat and, with a theatrical sweep of his arm, indicated that she should sit down. He went to the counter and brought out the first course: mussels with chorizo, beans and cavolo nero.

"So," he said, sitting down and pouring out two glasses of the wine. "How was your day?"

"Difficult." She took a bite of the mussels. They were delicious, and she said so.

"Thank you," he said. "So what happened?"

"You know the death at the cathedral?"

"The bloke who fell off the tower?"

She nodded. "It wasn't an accident. We're sure about that now."

"You said that someone went up the tower with him."

"It's not just that."

She knew that she should keep her mouth shut, but she had been thinking about it all day, and she knew it would help her to relax if she could tell someone else about it, too.

"A video was sent to the *Journal* on the day he died. An old videotape—VHS."

"Why would that have made him jump?"

"It's a sex tape."

"With him in it?"

"When he was younger."

"Oh."

"That's not all. The boy in it was borderline legal—hard to say, one way or the other. Teenage."

"Seriously?"

She nodded.

"So why push him off the tower?"

"Maybe he wouldn't pay. Maybe the blackmailer wanted him dead and his reputation ruined. We don't know."

Charlie rose and cleared the plates away and then replaced them with the main course: baked sea bass with lemon caper dressing. Francine finished her glass and refilled it, Charlie held his out, and she topped that up, too.

She swallowed a mouthful. "That's not all. You mustn't tell anyone *any* of this."

"I won't."

"I'm *serious*. I'll be in the shit if anyone finds out."

"Not a word," he said. "Promise."

She exhaled; talking *was* helping, as was a decent meal. "There have been two more videos and two more deaths." She dug into the sea bass. This, too, was excellent, and she felt herself relaxing even though the subject matter was anything but.

"Shit, Franny."

"I know. Remember the body in the river yesterday?"

He nodded. "The guy who drowned."

"His name was Lucjusz Kajetan. Another video was sent to the *Journal*. The same as before—another sex tape. Teenage girl this time."

"So he didn't drown?"

"He definitely drowned," she said. "But maybe it wasn't an accident. And then we got another tape today. Dominic Hartnett."

"Who's that?"

"Another MP."

Charlie's mouth fell open, and he set down his fork.

"I *know*," she said, "it's nuts. He died last night in London. They're saying it was a heart attack, but a video was delivered, so it obviously wasn't."

"Do you have any idea who might have done it?"

"No. None."

"How do you go about investigating something like that?"

"We look at the victims and see if there's anything in their pasts that might give us an idea about who might have wanted to kill them. Or we try to find out where the videos came from. It looks like they were shot in the same room." She caught herself; she had already gone too far. "I can't say anything else about that."

He took away the empty plates, opened the fridge, and with a melodramatic "Ta-da!" he brought out the dessert: a white chocolate and cardamon tart.

"You didn't buy this from a shop?"

"How dare you," he said in mock offence. "Iceland doesn't do these."

They finished the bottle of wine and took their time over the tart. It looked good and tasted even better.

Francine cut off a slice with her fork, put it in her mouth and savoured it as it dissolved on her tongue. "You can see why it's messy now?"

"I can."

"Promise to keep it to yourself?"

He laid his fork down and looked her in the eyes. "Of course."

"Because I probably shouldn't have told you."

Charlie stood, went to the cupboard where Francine kept her alcohol and took out a bottle of whisky. He found the glasses and poured out two generous measures. He brought the glasses back to the table, gave out one to her and held the other up for a toast. She touched her glass to his and took a sip; the whisky burned her throat as it slid down into her stomach.

"Thank you for doing this," she said. "It's been a tough day. Just what I needed."

"My pleasure."

Francine got up and took the plates to the counter. It was a running joke in her family that she was the messiest cook imaginable, with a reputation for leaving her working surfaces strewn with dirty pots and pans and utensils and smeared with whatever ingredients she was working with; Charlie, by contrast, had cleaned up as he worked, and there was no sign that he had prepared a meal for them both at all.

"I was going to do the washing up," she said, "but you've done that, too."

He shrugged. "I can't stand leaving a mess."

She went to the table, sank what was left of her whisky and reached down for his hand. "There must be another way I can thank you," she said.

PART 4

Thursday

CHAPTER 53

Atticus had intended to go to Mack's overnight but found that he wasn't in the mood. He worked until three, studying the papers he had copied in the hope of finding something that might now be cast in a different light, and then—disappointed with his lack of progress—retreated to bed, where he managed a couple of hours of unsatisfactory sleep. He woke just before dawn, decided that he might as well get up and get started again.

He made himself a cup of strong black coffee and took the mug to his desk. He connected his phone to his computer and set about copying across the photographs that he had taken of the documents that were being used in the investigation. He hadn't had the luxury of time when going through the boxes, and, apart from the fact that the photographs had been hastily taken and were often badly framed, he knew that there would be plenty that he had missed either because he was rushing or because he didn't know that they would be relevant. He would need Mack's help with that.

He navigated to the folder where he had stored the digital copies of the videotapes that had been delivered to the *Journal*.

He had been unable to quieten his mind, his thoughts continually returning to the three dead men. It was possible that one might have killed himself in shame or through fear of being exposed, but not two and certainly not all three. They had been murdered, and he was sure it was Jack. There had to be something that would give him a clue as to what had happened and, with little else to go on, Atticus knew that his best chance of making a breakthrough lay in the footage.

Atticus double-clicked on Campbell's video and watched it. It was unpleasant, but he forced himself to watch every frame in the hope that something might give him an angle he could pursue. He got to the end of the footage and let it run. There was a minute of static that filled the screen before it disappeared, to be replaced by black. He reached for his mouse but then decided not to stop the playback. The entire tape had been digitised and, with nothing else presenting itself, he settled back in the chair and kept his eyes on the screen in the event that there might be something else that had been missed. The black continued, interrupted intermittently by flashes of static and horizontal bars that rolled from the top of the screen to the bottom. Atticus kept watching, occasionally nudging the mouse to bring up the counter so that he could gauge how long he had left.

Ten minutes went past.

Twenty minutes.

The city awoke. Atticus heard traffic passing on the street outside the window but ignored it, his attention fixed on the monitor.

An hour passed, and then an hour and a half.

He could have fast-forwarded through it all, but that would be a shortcut that might not be worth taking. It was a long shot that he would find anything, but he had little else to go on, and he didn't want to miss something because of his impatience.

Three hours passed before he got to the end.

Nothing.

Atticus double-clicked to close the player and got up.

Bandit was sitting behind him, patiently waiting for his walk.

"Come on," Atticus said. "We both need some fresh air."

CHAPTER 54

Mack made her way into the meeting space that had been chosen for the morning's press conference. It had been hastily arranged, but, despite the short notice, the room was full of journalists from the press and TV. The leaking of the news of Dominic Hartnett's death—and its possible connection with the murder of Richard Miller—had meant that the media caravan had decamped to Salisbury for the third time in two years. Mack had delivered the briefings on the previous occasions and, although she was relieved that the responsibility had been passed to Murphy this time, she still felt a burn of irritation that the Met had muscled onto their patch and taken charge of an investigation that should have remained with local officers. She shared Atticus's annoyance in that regard, but, whereas he was unable to keep his anger to himself, she would bite her tongue and let Murphy get on with things. It had been difficult enough to advance in her career as far and as fast as she had, and she didn't want to torpedo her prospects by giving Murphy or Beckton any reason to be aggrieved with her.

The two men came into the room together. Mack had seen Mary Winkworth, the constabulary's media liaison, in the room that the two officers had used for preparation and knew that they would have been primed with answers for the most obvious questions that would be received. There wasn't very much that they would be able to discuss, and Mack had wondered about the good sense of having the conference at all, but it had been decided that something had to be said, even if it would be obvious under even the gentlest questioning that they had nothing substantial to go on by way of a lead.

A table had been set up with two seats behind it. Beckton took the seat to the left and Murphy the seat to the right.

"Hello, everyone," Beckton began. "Thank you for joining us today. I'm Chief Superintendent Beckton from Wiltshire Police, and I'm here with my colleague Detective Chief Superintendent Lee Murphy from the Metropolitan Police. What I intend to do today is read out a short statement of the facts as we know them so far. We will then be available for some brief questions."

He took a sip of water from the glass on the table, cleared his throat and then continued.

"Just after midnight last night, officers from the Metropolitan Police were called to a flat in the Fulham area of London. The body of a fifty-five-year-old man was found at the scene. A Home Office post-mortem was carried out this morning, and police are now treating the incident as suspicious. Formal identification has been carried out by the family of the deceased, and I can confirm that it is Dominic Hartnett, the member of Parliament for Devizes. You will be aware that the member of Parliament for Salisbury, Richard Miller, was murdered six weeks ago. Although we have yet to demonstrate a link between the two deaths, we are proceeding on the basis that they might be connected. I'd like to hand over to DCS Murphy now—he's a member of the Metropolitan Police's anti-terror task force and is responsible for the investigation of those two deaths."

Murphy thanked Beckton and leaned forward so that he could speak into the microphone.

"Thank you, Chief Superintendent." He cleared his throat, and Mack saw, with satisfaction, that he was nervous. "I've been in Salisbury working on the investigation into Mr. Miller's death for the last few weeks. The death of Mr. Hartnett is suspicious, and I want to assure everyone that it will receive the closest possible scrutiny. We are examining the last few weeks of both men's lives in the event that we might be able to find a connection. Obviously, Mr. Hartnett's death is very recent, and our enquiries have only started in the last few hours. Mr. Miller's death—his murder—was some time ago and, as you would expect, things are a little more advanced on that front."

There was a shout from one of the journalists. "So who did it?"

"We don't know that at this time," Murphy said. "As I say, Mr. Hartnett was only found last night, and the initial suggestion was that he had passed away from natural causes. That may not be the case, and hence we are now treating his death as suspicious."

"Why? What made you change your mind?"

"I'm not able to discuss that at the moment," Murphy fenced.

"Don't you think the public should be told?"

"Not at the risk of jeopardising an ongoing investigation. We'll provide additional information when the time is right to do so."

"Who did it?" asked another reporter.

"We don't know," Murphy said.

"You must have *some* idea," the same journalist called back. "Or a lead, or *something*."

"As I say," Murphy repeated patiently, "it's very early in the investigation. We have several lines of enquiry that we are looking to pursue, but you'll understand when I say that we're unable to go into any detail on them now. However, there is one appeal that I would like to make. We would like to speak to the person who has been in contact with a local man, Mr. Atticus Priest. This person, who uses the name 'Jack' when speaking to him, had information regarding the death of Mr. Miller, and we believe he might also have information on the deaths of Mr. Hartnett and two local men—David Campbell and Lucjusz Kajetan. We would ask him to make contact with police." Murphy gave a nod. "Thank you. We're happy to take a few more questions."

A forest of hands shot up. Murphy pointed to a woman at the front of the room.

"You mentioned the two local men who died this week." She looked at her notes. "Campbell and Kajetan. What can you tell us about them?"

"We're not in a position to speculate upon that," Murphy said.

"What about James York and Alfred Burns? The police investigation into their deaths suggested that they were involved with Miller. What's going on here, Mr. Murphy? It doesn't feel as if we've been given anything like the full picture."

"I've told you everything I'm able to say at the moment."

"That might be so, but it's not going to fill local people with much confidence, is it? I've lost count of the number of murders that have happened in the city during the last two years—this is the third time I've been back here in that time. It's *Salisbury*, not the Bronx."

Beckton leaned into the microphone. "It's true that there have been a series of deaths here. There are no two ways about it—we've been unlucky. But I can say with confidence that the murders in Grovely Wood have nothing to do with the deaths that we are investigating now."

"And the murders at Imber?"

"We can't comment on that at the moment," Murphy said.

A reporter whom Mack recognised from before put up his hand. "What about the videos?"

The surprise was evident on Murphy's face. "Sorry?"

"Have you read the paper this morning?"

"No," Murphy said. "Sorry. Who are you?"

"Ian Bird from the *Sun*. We received a video last night that we understand was also sent to the Salisbury *Journal*. A man who looks very much like Mr. Campbell is shown having sex with a teenage boy. Could you comment on that?"

Murphy took a moment to gather himself.

"DCS Murphy?" Bird pressed. "You must've seen the video?"

"I can't comment on anything beyond what has been said already."

"We ran a still from it in the paper this morning. I can let you have a copy afterwards if you'd like."

The offer raised laughter from the other reporters. Both officers were obviously uncomfortable and, with a look over at Winkworth, they pushed back their chairs and stood.

Winkworth came to stand in front of the table, covering the officers as they made their retreat. "Thank you for coming," she said. "You all have my number. Please do call if there's anything else that you need."

Mack got up and made for the exit with the others.

"DCI Jones, hang on a minute."

Mack turned and saw that Bird was hurrying to reach her. Mack had found him charming and completely untrustworthy during their previous interactions, his cheerfulness a mask that he used to disguise the fact that he was an ambitious snake who had been working her in the hope that her guard might slip and he might learn something useful.

"*That* was a waste of time," he said.

"Not much to say at the moment."

"What about the video?"

"Can't comment on that."

"Look. I've got it here."

His phone was in his hand. He tapped the screen and showed it to her before she could get away. She looked down: it was a still of the room that had become familiar from the three videos. Campbell was on the bed, looking right into the camera.

"We only ran the still," Bird said, "but the video is disgusting."

"How did you get it?"

"Can't say."

"You need to speak to DCS Murphy about that."

"We will," Bird said. "My editor tried to speak to him earlier. Can you give me *any* idea what's going on?"

She shook her head. "Nothing more than what you just heard."

"There's other footage, isn't there?"

"Why would you say that?"

"There was a message with the video. It said that if we ran this, we'd get more."

Mack didn't want to have to lie, but she couldn't very well confirm that he was right. She smiled in a way that she hoped included a little innocent nonchalance and shrugged. "I can't talk about the case. You really will have to speak to DCS Murphy." The queue shuffled forward enough for Mack to spy a way out and, with a cheerful farewell, she passed through the door and used her key card to swipe open the door that led to CID.

CHAPTER 55

Mack went back to the nick and was shanghaied by Beckton's secretary as soon as she stepped through the door.

"Boss wants to see you upstairs."

Mack wasn't surprised in the slightest and took a moment in the bathroom to compose herself before taking the lift. Beckton was a proud man, and he wouldn't have enjoyed being caught on the hop like that. Mack didn't know Murphy at all, but it had been obvious that he had also found the experience of being surprised in front of the press to be an excruciating one. The two of them would be looking for someone to blame and, as Mack's father had often been fond of saying, 'shit runs downhill.'

She braced herself and knocked on the door.

"Come."

She went inside. Beckton was sitting behind his desk, and Murphy was pacing.

"How did he know about the tapes?" Murphy said.

Mack closed the door behind her. "He says the one with Campbell was sent to them."

"You spoke to him?"

"He grabbed me on the way out."

"Do you know him?"

"Not really. He covered the Imber enquiry."

"And?"

"And he says it came with a message promising more if they ran it. His editor has been trying to speak to us."

"No one spoke to *me*," Murphy said.

"Or me," Beckton said.

The door opened, and Beckton's secretary appeared with a copy of the *Sun* in her hand. Beckton thanked her, took the newspaper and opened it onto pages two and three. He laid it out on the desk so that they could all see it. The top half of the left-hand page was taken up with a still image that she recognised from the first video: Campbell's grinning face was frozen, his eyes sparkling as he looked into the camera, the red light behind him lending him even more of a demonic aspect.

Murphy threw his hands up. "How can they just run that?"

"I know," Beckton said. "They've crossed a line. The CPS can deal with it."

Murphy stabbed a finger against the photograph. "How did they get it?" He turned to Mack. "*How?*"

"I have no idea."

"*Speculate.*"

"Like I said… it was sent to them last—"

"I know it was sent, but by whom?"

"I think it's obvious."

"Yes," Murphy said, staring at her. "I agree. Your boyfriend."

Beckton looked from Murphy to Mack and back again. "What?"

Murphy stared at her. "Tell him."

Mack took a breath. "Fine," she said. "I'm in a relationship with Atticus. I'm sure DCS Murphy will say it's an abuse of my position, and perhaps it is, but I'd suggest that it might be better to save that discussion for another day rather than have it distract us now."

Beckton held her eye and then nodded. "I agree. But, just for the record, and just so it's clear, you've never given me a reason to doubt your professionalism."

"Thank you, sir."

He looked to Murphy. "And you might want to think carefully before you impugn the reputation of one of my senior officers."

Mack thought for a moment that Murphy was going to insist that they discuss her behaviour there and then, but—perhaps because of Beckton's vote of confidence, or perhaps because he recognised that she was right, and they couldn't afford the diversion—he muttered something under his breath and shook his head.

"Well?" Beckton said. "Could it have been him? He strikes me as the sort of man who'll throw his toys out of the pram if he doesn't get his own way."

Mack knew Atticus well enough to know that his hand was rarely stayed by whatever he had been told to do or not do, and, although she doubted he would do anything to damage the investigation, he could go off-piste if he disagreed with a decision and thought that he knew best. Could he have been frustrated with the pace or direction of the investigation and decided to take things into his own hands? She really hoped not.

"No," she said. "He wouldn't do that."

"Who, then?"

"The *Journal*?" Beckton suggested.

Mack shook her head. "Doesn't make sense. They're desperate to break the story themselves. Why would they let themselves be scooped?"

"No," Mack said. "It's not Atticus, and it's not anyone on my team, and it's not the *Journal*. It's him. *Jack*. He's upped the ante. Things aren't going as fast as he wants, so he's changed his tactics."

"Maybe," Murphy said.

"Probably," Mack corrected him.

"And we think this is him?" Beckton said. "Jack, I mean?"

"Atticus does," Mack said.

Beckton turned to her. "Call the *Sun* and tell them we need to see what they've been sent."

"Yes, sir."

Murphy turned back to Beckton, putting his back to Mack and ignoring her as if she weren't there. "We'll have to decide when we can make it public."

Mack went back out into the corridor and set off for the CID room. She would call the newspaper, but, before that, she needed to speak to Atticus.

CHAPTER 56

Atticus found it difficult to keep his attention on the screen. His eyelids had grown heavy from lack of sleep and, as he blinked them to try to stay awake, the footage on the Kajetan tape ran to the end and stopped.

He froze.

He blinked.

He didn't know if he had imagined it, but he thought he had seen something just before the tape ran out. He reached for his mouse, scrubbed back for ten seconds and pressed play. He stared hard at the screen; there was nothing of interest, just more of the unending black that had taunted him for the last three hours. The counter ticked up to the end, and then, just a moment before it came to a stop, something new *was* there: a woman standing on a balcony and, behind her, a row of houses.

His eyes were tired. He rubbed them.

Atticus scrubbed back again and clicked play, waited until he got to the footage and then hit pause. The clip was short and contained little other than the woman smiling at the camera and a bird flying over the tops of the houses. He selected the start and end of the clip and copied it, then uploaded it to YouTube, not because he intended to publish it but because it made it easier to use the FFmpeg tool to break it down into a collection of still images that would be easier to examine than the video itself. The length of the clip was just under a second, and the tool turned the video into thirty-two still images. The shot jerked a little to the left and right, suggesting that the camera had been handheld when the footage was taken. Atticus examined the still images one by one in an attempt to find anything useful that might have appeared in only one of them, but, despite the small variations in the field of vision, there was nothing useful.

He selected the image with the greatest clarity, printed it out and laid it on his desk. He took his magnifying glass from its sleeve and subjected the printout to a minute examination. The image had been taken from the third or fourth storey of a building and showed the street outside and the buildings opposite. He saw a row of apartment buildings with black balconies and one with an extruding bay window that had been painted white. The buildings were of varying heights and designs, with unusual tiled roofs that did not look like the sort that would have been used in the United Kingdom.

Somewhere in Europe?

He could see a much larger and more modern building behind the terrace, and, behind that, a blue sky crisscrossed with aircraft contrails. The foreground of the image included a white car, a sign from an estate agent, an unusual cast-iron lamp that was attached to one of the buildings, the number of one of the properties—62—and a pavement that had been laid with some sort of dark grey stone slabs. The street appeared to be narrow, without trees or freestanding streetlamps.

Atticus copied the most noticeable features of the image—the polished wooden door, the extruding white bay window, the balconies—and ran them through a reverse image lookup. The results provided nothing useful.

He enlarged the licence plate of the car. The letters and numerals were not discernible, but he was able to see that they were dark red in colour. Atticus opened a browser and navigated to a website dedicated to licence and registration plates found all around the world. He selected Europe, then went through the countries until he found a match; Belgium was the only country that he could find that used that particular colouring. It wasn't conclusive, but it was a start.

He went out to the kitchen in the hall and boiled the kettle.

While he waited for it to boil, he went back to his screen and focused on the estate agent's sign. It was attached to the wall at ground level and, when he enlarged it, he was able to make out part of a business name, a phone number and a word in French—VENDU—that added to his suspicions that the picture was taken in Belgium. He opened another browser and searched the phone number, bringing back a website for Calao Consulting, a real estate agency based in Brussels. The name and logo matched what he could see on the sign.

Belgium.

Brussels.

He was getting somewhere.

He heard the kettle click off and went back to the kitchen, then made a cup of strong black coffee and took it back to his desk. Bandit was waiting for him, his tail wagging and his lead in his mouth. Atticus scrubbed him on the back of the head, took a slurp of coffee and sat back down.

THE RED ROOM

He visited the agency's website and saw that the business had only a single office in the Forest district of the city. That was helpful; he doubted that they would work on properties that were outside of their patch. He looked at the properties on their website now and plotted them on a map, showing the districts of Ucce, Forest, Anderlecht and Sint-Jans Molenbeek. He opened Street View and wandered through those areas, finding that they often included dark metal balconies and buildings that had been constructed with similar materials. His quick scout did confirm that the streets in Brussels were unusual for often having a distinct style of streetlamp that varied from district to district. The variation was *so* distinct that an open-air museum had been established to celebrate the various styles. He visited the museum's website and spent half an hour reviewing the contents. He saw the ornate nineteenth-century lanterns that were prevalent in the older parts of town, the bronze gas lamps that could be found in Schaerbeek, and the orange 1970s orbs that had been installed on the outskirts.

He returned to Street View and examined the areas that were served by the agency. He looked for the streetlamps and saw that in neighbourhoods like Forest, with broad streets and newer buildings, they were not fixed to the sides of the buildings and were more modern in design. It was only in the more densely built areas in the middle of the city that they were found on the buildings; these areas had similar designs, too.

Atticus narrowed down his search to the area around Barrière de Saint-Gilles. It was easy from that point, and it only took him another ten minutes to locate the particular lamp, the dark glossy door and the house that was marked with 62.

He rotated the camera and looked back at the building from which the video must have been taken: 75 Albaniëstraat.

It was a four-storey building with two large windows on each floor, a narrow sliver that was jammed in between a similarly narrow building to its right and a larger neighbour to its left. The bricks had been painted magnolia, and its door and window frames were made from varnished wood.

Atticus dragged the mouse to angle the camera and looked up at the two windows on the top floor. The video had been shot there—he was certain of it—and now all he needed to know was by whom.

CHAPTER 57

Max Mason gazed into the camera and delivered the same closing line that had made him famous: "Thank you very much, ladies and germs. *I've* been Max Mason; *you've* been amazing. I'll see you again next time for more…"

The audience roared out: "*Couples Clash!*"

Mason bowed. "Good night!"

He waved and held his smile until his cheeks ached. He waited until the floor manager counted down from three and announced that they were out.

The audience continued to applaud.

Mason clapped them, turning through a half circle so that they were all included. "Thank you," he called up to them. "Thank you. You were easily the best audience we had today."

Laughter rolled down from the gallery, the audience humouring a joke that he had used on countless occasions in the past. They had recorded two episodes of the show this morning, and the audience had been the same for both.

Mason made his way to the side of the studio. His assistant, Clara, was waiting with a bottle of water.

"How'd I do?" he asked her.

"You were brilliant. They loved it."

He cranked off the top of the bottle and took a swig. "I would've loved for them to have won the jackpot."

"I can't believe they didn't get it."

"I know. How long is an Olympic swimming pool—who doesn't know that?"

"What did they say? Twenty-five metres?"

"Twenty-five metres," he said. "Come on. Ridiculous. That cost them thirty grand. Thirty! They were kicking themselves—I almost felt bad for them." He set off toward the backstage area, and Clara followed. "I *definitely* felt bad for us—would've been great telly."

Bob Nicholls, the floor manager, was waiting by the door. "Good job, Max. Two good ones in the can."

He gave a heavy theatrical sigh. "And back tomorrow for another two."

"You love it."

He winked. "I love what they pay me."

The studio had been constructed within what had once been an old warehouse on the banks of the Thames. Max's production company had purchased it forty years ago when it had been ready to fall into the river, and he had gambled by sinking every last penny in his name into the renovation. It had been the shrewdest thing that he had ever done. *Couples Clash* had shown signs of promise, but it was only when he'd moved the recording here that its success had really taken off. Mason had gone from having nothing to his name but a speculative project in an unseemly part of the city to having a beautiful new studio and a contract that had paid him more every time it had been renewed. And, what was more, the area around the studio had been gentrified in the same way as all the other run-down ex-industrial quarters in London, with the result that the property, bought for a song, was now worth thirty million.

The studio itself was a large open space with four rows of raked seating that surrounded the contestants' chairs and the lectern from which Mason presided over affairs. Each audience was composed of three hundred members of the public who had been given a seat by way of a raffle. The contestants were picked from the audience in a process that was reputed to be random, but which was anything but. They had quotas to meet, and each episode was sure to include the necessary demographic qualities to ensure that all the relevant boxes were ticked. That was something that had changed during Mason's career, and he wasn't sure it was for the best.

The backstage area was a warren of corridors that led to the production suite, storage areas and changing rooms.

Mason gestured for Clara to keep up. "What have you got for me?"

She walked briskly to match his pace. "They want you on *This Morning* to discuss the retrospective."

"When?"

"Next Wednesday."

"Am I free?"

"You are."

"Book it in. Next?"

"The People's Choice Awards are next week. A little bird tells me you're going to get a gong."

"For what?"

"Quiz show."

"Who's getting the Bruce Forsyth Award?"

"Ant and Dec."

"Tell them I can't make it." They turned the corner and arrived at the door to his dressing room. "Anything else?"

"Corporate gig for Vodafone."

"Fee?"

"Hundred thousand."

"Do it. Next."

"The BBC asked if you'd do a vox pop for a show they're doing with Jonathan Ross."

"Can't stand him, not interested. Next."

She put her phone away. "That's it."

"Good. Thank you. What do I have on for the rest of the day?"

She took the phone out again. "Lunch with Mic at the Ritz and dinner with George at NOBU."

"Good," he said. "I'd forgotten about that."

"I've left a suit and a clean shirt on the hook inside. The car's coming to get you in an hour."

Mason went into the dressing room and closed the door behind him. He had a rule that he was not to be disturbed when the door was closed. This was his sanctuary, a space where he could relax after however many hours he had just spent pandering to the public. The false jollity, the catchphrases, the legendary rapport with the audience that was supposed to be natural, but which was, in fact, just one more pretence from a career that had been built on a stack of them; the whole thing was exhausting. He took off his jacket and the shirt that had grown damp with sweat after he had stood underneath the stage lights all morning. He removed the rest of his clothes and showered, drying himself off with a monogrammed towel and then pulling on the robe with the same mark—the intertwined *M*s—on the breast pocket.

His backstage requirements were modest: a pot of fresh tea and the day's newspapers. He had flicked through the broadsheets before recording started this morning, leaving him with the trashy redtops. The teapot had been refilled with a fresh brew; Mason poured himself a cup and took it, and the papers, to the sofa on the other side of the room.

Clara went through the papers before giving them to Mason every morning and marked anything that she thought might be relevant with sticky tabs: yellow tabs were stories that mentioned him, while red tabs were those that mentioned people on the list that Mason provided to Clara, usually rivals whom Mason enjoyed seeing in difficulty. There had been nothing of note in the broadsheets, and only a handful in the tabloids.

He checked the yellows first: a sniffy review of his autobiography; a short article trailing the anniversary of *Couples Clash* that was due to run over the weekend; a recipe for pulled pork that he had provided to one of the supplements; an account of his sponsored cycle ride around the country that had raised six million for charities. There were more red tabs than yellow today, and he finished his tea while enjoying the travails of celebrities and other public figures who had attracted his ire over the course of his career.

He picked up the *Sun* and was flipping through to the single red tab when he glanced at the photograph that accompanied a story on pages two and three. He was about to turn the page when something in the photograph caught his attention.

It looked like a still from a video, with a room that was lit with deep red light. There was a bed in the centre of the shot with a topless man sitting on it.

Mason felt a queasiness that came out of nowhere.

He read the headline:

SEX TAPE SENSATION OF CATHEDRAL DEATH MAN

Mason stared back down at the still image. It didn't look as if it had been taken recently.

There was a knock on the door.

Mason quickly closed the newspaper and tossed it on top of the others. "What is it?"

It was Clara. "Just checking you're getting ready. The car will be outside in ten minutes."

"I'll be ready," he said.

He stared across at the paper and felt the pinprick of pressure in his temples that always heralded one of his headaches. He closed his eyes until the pressure eased, and then got up. He couldn't deal with that now. He needed to have lunch with his agent and then meet his son for dinner. He hadn't seen George for weeks, and the last thing he wanted was to spoil the evening by worrying about something that was probably, he hoped, a fuss about nothing.

But, even as he told himself that, he knew that the image was a problem and that it was not going to be something that he would easily forget.

CHAPTER 58

Atticus wiped down Bandit's muddy paws, filled his bowl with biscuits and changed his water and then went back to his desk. He navigated back to the folder where he had placed the three videos and double-clicked on the file with the footage that he had been examining.

His phone rang. He picked it up, expecting to see that Mack was calling, but didn't recognise the number. It was probably a marketing call, so he killed it and put the phone down.

He pressed play.

The phone rang again.

Atticus grabbed it. "I'm not interested."

"That's no way to speak to an old friend."

He froze.

The voice was disguised, like before, but Atticus knew: it was Jack.

He put the call on the phone's speaker. "You've been quiet."

"I've been busy."

"I'm sure you have."

"See the press conference?"

Atticus took a digital recorder from the cubbyhole underneath the surface of the desk. "I did."

"They want me to get in contact with them." Jack chuckled. "Why would I want to do a thing like that?"

Atticus hit the button on the device to record and put it down next to the phone. "It was you, then? Campbell and Lucjusz and Hartnett? You killed them?"

"They got what they deserved. They're dead, *and* everyone knows what they did. I know you might not agree, but *I* think that's justice."

"Are we going to find anyone else?"

"I told you, didn't I? The last time we spoke."

Atticus pushed the recorder a little closer to the phone. "I can remember exactly what you said. I asked if it was just York and Burns, and you said that there were others."

"And I'll get to them all eventually."

"Wouldn't it be easier to just tell the police?"

There was anger in Jack's reply. "They can't be trusted. They didn't help then, and they won't help now. Nothing has changed. I thought we agreed on that."

"They'll find you in the end. You'll make a mistake, and they'll find you."

"Probably. But I'm *good*."

"Are you?"

"You have no idea who I am, do you?"

"I don't."

"I have the deepest respect for you, Atticus, and if *you* can't find me, well… I'm not likely to lose sleep over the police, am I?" He paused, then chuckled again. "Listen to me. So rude. I hope you don't think I'm insulting your girlfriend."

The reference to Mack and their relationship was deliberate: *I know all about you.* It was a tactic that he had used on their previous call, too.

Atticus ignored it. "Tell me about the videos."

"What do you want to know?"

"Where did you find them?"

"Do you remember Derek Burns?"

"Alf's brother. He disappeared."

"He knew that they'd come after him, so he ran and took them as insurance. But he was an amateur. He wasn't hard to find."

"*'Wasn't'?* Past tense?"

"He knew about what Alf had done, and he did nothing about it. That made him culpable."

"You killed him?"

There was no answer. Atticus went to the window and looked out onto the darkened street. There was no sign of anyone there.

"How many tapes do you have?"

"More."

"Where are they?"

Jack tutted. "No, no, no—*that's* not going to happen. I need them. How long do you think it'll be before the police talk about what's on the tapes? About the red room?"

"I don't know."

"Soon. They're stuck, and they'll have to appeal for help. They'll describe the room and hope that someone will come forward and say that they were there, that they know where it is. Can you imagine how anyone who's ever been there will feel? They'll *panic*." He chuckled. "They'll lose their shit.

It'll be in their heads all day and all night. They won't be able to sleep. They won't be able to kiss their wives or hug their kids without thinking it might be the last time. I don't have a tape for everyone who's ever been inside, but *they* won't know that."

A line of cars had formed up outside, with cars trying to exit the multi-storey car park and others jammed up against the two sets of lights that stood between them and Brown Street.

"You're the only one smart enough to stop me," Jack continued, "but I don't think you will."

"Is that right?"

"You hated Burns. Why do you think I got in touch with you in the first place? You knew there was a risk that he'd wriggle free, and he did. That's what I mean—the police can't be trusted even when they do mean well. Don't tell me that the thought hasn't crossed your mind that this way—*my* way—is better. I give them what they deserve. I punish them for the things that they did."

"There's a line between justice and vengeance."

"*Boring*, Atticus. You don't believe that, and neither do I. Their guilt isn't in question. It's right there on the screen. And you know what makes it worse? They would've forgotten about the children they hurt as soon as they'd finished with them. They used them and tossed them aside like it'd never happened. Not a second's thought. They wouldn't have lost sleep then, would they? Now they will."

The queue started to move.

"What do you want?"

"Just to speak to you. What I do can be lonely."

"You still haven't told me *why* you're doing it."

"Isn't it obvious?"

Atticus was looking up at the multi-storey car park when he thought he saw a shadow moving across the roof. He grabbed his phone and ran for the door, startling Bandit into thinking that he was about to get a bonus walk. With an apologetic "Stay, boy," to Bandit, he let himself out, pulling the door shut behind him. He took the stairs two at a time, fumbled with the lock and, once he had got the door open, barrelled out into the passage and then the street. There were two flights of stairs that offered access to the five floors of the multi-storey; Atticus thought that the figure he had seen had headed toward Exeter Street, so he went right, dodging between two cars and then skipping back as a motorcyclist had to skid to a halt to avoid hitting him. There was a cacophony of horns behind him as Atticus shouldered the door open and started to climb; he took the stairs two at a time and then, when his thighs started to burn, just one. He was gasping for breath when he reached the top floor, shoved the kick bar to open the door and staggered out into the cold early-morning air. A car was pulling out of a space on the other side of the roof; Atticus ran for it but saw that it was driven by an old lady who gaped fearfully at him as she went down the ramp. There were a dozen other cars, but none were occupied, and there was no one else save him on the roof.

He went to the spot where he thought he had seen the figure. It was directly opposite his window and, as he looked down, he saw that Bandit had clambered onto the sofa and was looking out, perhaps wondering where his master had disappeared to in such a hurry. Atticus looked left and right and saw nothing; he looked down and saw a pair of footprints that had been left on the damp concrete and the smouldering end of a cigarette.

He remembered that he was still clutching his phone. He looked at the screen and saw that the call had ended. He was still looking at it when an incoming text was announced with a buzz and a chime.

> NOT YET. WAIT UNTIL I'VE FINISHED.

CHAPTER 59

Mason would have liked to have gone straight back to Wiltshire, but he had a long-standing lunch appointment with his agent that he couldn't postpone. Mic had booked them a table at the Ritz, knowing that it was one of Mason's favourite places to eat, and was waiting for him as the endlessly deferential maître d' accompanied him to the back of the room.

She stood, beaming at him as he approached. "Max, so good to see you. How are you?"

"Good," he said, thanking the maître d' as he pulled out a chair for him.

The man put his hands together in an expression that managed to look particularly obsequious. "Your usual?"

Mason was thirsty, and the thought of something alcoholic was tempting after the discovery that he had just made. "Yes, please."

Mason tried to pay attention as Mic ran through the news that she was obviously excited to deliver. She was gleeful, announcing a slew of potential new endorsements that would amount to several million pounds over the lifetime of the deals;

Mason was perfunctory in his enthusiasm, his mind fixed on what he had read in the newspaper. He couldn't stop his thoughts drifting back to the picture and what it might mean.

"What is it, Max?"

He looked up. "What?"

"You don't seem pleased."

Mason managed to force a smile. "I'm sorry. I *am* pleased—*delighted*. I've got a couple of things on my mind, that's all."

"Anything I can help you with?"

"It's just something at home. It's all under control."

The waiter arrived at the table with their drinks: Mic had a glass of Krug, while Mason took a tall glass with the drink he always ordered when he came here: a Bull Shot combining vodka, sherry and vegetable juice with herbs, sauces and spices.

Mic raised her glass. "Cheers, then."

"Cheers," Mason said. "And, really, thank you—I can see you've been working hard on all this, and I'm grateful."

He tried to be more present for the rest of the meal but was relieved when the plates were cleared away and he was able to make his excuses and leave. He called his chauffeur, Steve, and told him that he was ready to be picked up and, after thanking Mic again, he left cash on the table to cover the bill and made his way outside to where his Bentley Flying Spur was waiting.

Steve got out and opened the door. "Back home, sir?"

"Yes," he said, then added, "just give me five minutes. I need to make a quick call."

He walked in the direction of Green Park and found a quiet alley off Piccadilly where he would be able to make the call without being bothered by anyone who might recognise him.

He found the number and tapped the screen to dial it, putting the phone to his ear as he walked a little deeper into the alley.

Harry Summers picked up at once. "*Max*, this is a surprise."

"Is it?"

"Yes—why would you say that? We don't have anything in the diary for you, do we?"

"I need to see you."

"Okay. Where are you?"

"London."

"I'm afraid I'm at the house in Wiltshire—"

"I'm coming back this afternoon," Mason said, cutting across him. "I'll be there around five. Make sure you're in. This can't wait."

CHAPTER 60

Mack had been at the nick all day, working with Murphy to ensure that his team had everything they needed as they formally took over the investigation into the death of Miller; they also took responsibility for the deaths of Campbell, Kajetan and Hartnett. Mack had already formed an opinion of Murphy as someone with an unfortunate mix of bombast and incompetence, and the time they spent together only reinforced that. He swanned around the CID room, dispensing instructions with an air of easy superiority, oblivious to the fact that most of the things he wanted doing had either already been done or were in hand. He made no effort to smooth over the friction that had been caused by him taking control; Mack had watched her team with pride as they got on with their work without complaint. They would convene in the pub after work to put the world to rights, and none of the London interlopers would be invited. Mack decided that she would take the initiative and arrange the drinks herself.

She was composing a WhatsApp message to the others when her phone rang with an incoming call. She checked the screen, saw that it was Atticus and went into the bathroom so she could take it in private.

"What's up?"

"I need to see you."

"What is it?"

"Not on the phone."

"I'm really busy, Atticus."

There was a manic edge to his voice that suggested he was having—or about to have—an episode. Mack could have asked him to explain why he needed to see her, but she knew him well enough to know that that would make him impatient, and that he would become more and more insistent until she gave in.

"I *need* to see you. He called me."

"What? Who?"

"*Jack*."

"When?"

"Just now."

"Shit."

"There's something else, too. Maybe more important. But you need to come here."

"Okay, okay. I'm coming."

"Come *now*, Mack—I'm serious. I've made a breakthrough."

CHAPTER 61

Mack went through the passageway to the courtyard at the back of the building and climbed the metal steps so that she could knock on the door that led into Atticus's bedroom. She was rewarded with a bark from Bandit before the dog moved the curtain out of the way and pressed his damp nose against the glass; Atticus followed soon after, cursing as he tripped over something in his way.

He opened the door. "What took you so long?"

"I came as soon as I could," she said.

He stepped aside and gestured that she should come in. "I've got something to show you in the office."

Atticus went through with Mack following and Bandit trotting alongside. Mack's heart sank as she saw that Atticus had made a dreadful mess: there were papers strewn across the desk and the floor, splayed-open ring binders on the table, and the whiteboards had been wiped clean and then filled again with notes that made no sense, decipherable only to a mind like Atticus's. He was standing by the desk, his hands opening and closing, his eyes blinking a little more often than normal, and his jaw clenching and unclenching. She had seen him like this before; he was on the precipice of an episode.

"Have you taken your pills?"

"Not today."

"You know you need—"

"Forgot. Too busy. And I needed everything sharp and focused. The pills slow me down."

"They also stop you from ending up in hospital. Where are they? In the bathroom?"

"Never mind them. I need to show you this."

"I'm not looking at *anything* until you take them."

She opened the door and started to cross the landing to the bathroom.

"*Fine*," Atticus said after her. "In the cabinet above the sink."

Mack found the plastic bottle of Prozac that bore a label with his details. She had Googled to learn how the pills might be helping him and learned that some doctors believed it gave those on the spectrum a better chance of controlling their impulsiveness. She opened the bottle, tipped out two pills and carried them, together with a glass that she filled with water at the sink, back into the office.

"Take them now, or I'm going back to the nick."

He muttered under his breath but put the pills in his mouth. Mack stood, her arms crossed, and waited until he drank from the glass and then, giving her an ironic shrug, opened his mouth so that she could confirm that he had swallowed the pills.

"Happy?"

"Go on, then—start with Jack."

"He called me. Disguised his voice again, like last time. He said he killed the three of them, that there are more and that he isn't going to stop. I recorded the call. I'll play it to you."

He dug a recorder out from underneath a pile of papers, switched it on and played back the call. Mack listened intently. It was the first time that she had heard Jack's voice and, even though it was distorted, she felt an immediacy that she hadn't felt when Atticus had recounted their first call.

Atticus went to the window and pointed across the street to the car park. "He was there. He was watching me."

"Did you see him?"

"He was gone by the time I got there, but he was definitely there. He texted me. Look."

He handed her his phone and showed her the message.

"I found this, too."

Atticus held out a small plastic freezer bag. Mack looked at it and saw the dog-end of a cigarette.

"How do you know that was his?"

"It was still lit when I got there. It'll be worth testing for forensics."

She took the bag. "I'll get that done." She pointed to the recorder. "I'll need to take that, too. Murphy will want to listen to it."

"Fine," Atticus said.

She looked at him curiously. He would normally have grumbled about that but had agreed as if it was of trifling importance. She could see that whatever it was he had discovered was exciting him much more than the conversation with Jack.

"Go on, then," she said. "What else is there?"

CHAPTER 62

Atticus went to his laptop, tapped the keyboard and woke the screen. It displayed an image of a woman standing on a balcony with a terrace of tall houses behind her.

"What is that?"

Atticus didn't answer. He clicked his mouse and the image moved, the woman smiling at whoever was behind the camera for less than a second before the frame froze once more.

Atticus pointed. "That was recorded at the end of Kajetan's tape."

"What?"

"It was there *before* what we saw was recorded over it. I investigated how tapes work. You can get machines that wipe them—they erase the original recording before the next recording re-magnetises the tape with new, stronger information. Either the machine didn't work all the way to the end, or they got sloppy, but this clip was left."

She stared at the woman looking out at them from the screen. "And you think whoever that is might be involved in all this?"

"Impossible to say. Maybe whoever filmed Campbell bought a job lot of second-hand tapes, wiped them and then used them. Or maybe this was a one-off, and this is a personal tape that was wiped and re-used."

"We'd prefer the latter."

"We would."

"So we need to know where that"—she tapped her finger against the screen—"was filmed."

He grinned. "Brussels. Seventy-five Albaniëstraat in Barrière de Saint-Gilles."

He took a piece of paper and put it down on the desk next to the keyboard. It was a screengrab from Google Street View. Mack looked from the image on the screen to the screengrab and saw that, although the images had been taken at different times, it was definitely the same building.

"I bet you can't wait to tell me how you worked that out."

"Maybe later," he said, so excited by his discovery that he was prepared to postpone a demonstration of his brilliance. "Once I figured out where the building is, I just needed to know who might have owned it at the time that video was filmed. I contacted the Belgian Federal Ministry of Finance and asked for a search of the land register and got lucky. The most likely owner was always going to be a Belgian, and we would've had to fly over there on the off chance that he or she might have been able to remember who visited the property twenty years ago when the video was taken. But it *wasn't* owned by a Belgian. It was owned by an Englishman."

"Go on," she prompted.

He took out a second piece of paper and laid it down on top of the first. It was a printout of an official document that bore the logo of the Belgian government and the headline KADASTER. The contents were in French, but it looked like a record of the owners of the property listed as 75 Albaniëstraat.

Atticus had ringed one of the names in red ink.

"General Sir Harry Summers," he said. "Originally commissioned into the Intelligence Corps, Parachute Regiment after that. Multiple tours in Northern Ireland and then the Balkans."

"And in Brussels because of NATO?"

"Commander of the Allied Rapid Reaction Corps during the Kosovo War. Came home after six years. Retired a decade ago and set up a very successful private intelligence business. Corporate clients, a hundred staff, multi-million-pound contracts. Companies House says they had a turnover of a hundred million last year."

Mack looked at the still from the video and laid a finger on the woman smiling into the lens.

"And she is?"

Atticus took a third sheet of paper and handed it to Mack. It was a printout of a website from Tatler's, a restaurant in the New Forest that Mack had visited before. The photograph was from the website's 'About' section and showed the chef-proprietor, Samantha Summers. It reported that she had started the restaurant, but had passed away several years ago. The woman in Brussels was younger than the woman in the picture—maybe twenty years younger—but it was obvious that it was her.

Mack put the paper down on the desk and exhaled. "Shit. Why do I get the feeling this is going to get worse before it gets better? Why would footage shot in a property belonging to Summers end up on a dead man's sex tape?"

"It could be a coincidence."

"But you don't believe in coincidences."

"No. I don't."

She could see from the gleam in his eyes that he was excited by the discoveries that he had made, and that she was going to have to rein him in for fear of him doing something outrageous. During the last case on which they'd worked together, the mystery of the bodies at Imber had taken a turn with the revelation that Miller had been involved, and that had required a delicate touch that, for all his brilliance, Atticus just did not possess.

This had the potential to be even more sensitive.

"You don't do *anything* with this," she said.

"I know. I'm not stupid."

"Where does he live?"

"Big place out near Sixpenny Handley. Hawthorne Manor."

Mack exhaled. "I need to go and speak to Murphy."

"Really? Are you sure that's a good idea?"

"He's in charge of the investigation. I don't have a choice."

"I disagree."

"Atticus…"

"Just go and have a look. You don't have to do anything else. Tell Murphy you were checking it out and leave it up to him to arrange an interview."

"Just like that?"

"Come on," he said. "Where's the harm? You're just being thorough. The last thing you'd want to do is to waste his time with something that you haven't checked out first."

"And I suppose that's something you'd be up for helping me with?"

THE RED ROOM

"I have nothing on this afternoon. Bandit could do with a walk, and the countryside is lovely down there." He shrugged. "I don't know—sounds like it might be something I could help you with."

She stared at him. "Please tell me you're not going to put me in a difficult position?"

"I won't," he said. "Trust me—for once?"

CHAPTER 63

Harry Summers lived in a house at the centre of a near-thousand-acre estate two miles northeast of Sixpenny Handley and eleven miles south of Salisbury. Mason's driver took him straight there, turning off the road and passing through the open gates with the sign on the left-hand pillar that announced Hawthorne Manor. The area was picturesque, and the entire estate set within an Area of Outstanding Natural Beauty. There was open farmland all around and then the oak forests of Cranbourne Chase, the big house set in the hollow of the landscape. Mason didn't pay any of it the slightest bit of attention; he had read and reread the story in the *Sun* over and over again, looking at the picture of the red-lit room with the bare stone walls and knowing, with a certainty that filled him with dread, that he had been there.

Steve parked the car and stepped out and around so that he could open the door. Mason got out just as Summers opened the door to the house and made his way down the flight of stone steps to the gravelled turning area.

"Max," he said, shovelling on the charm, "how are you?"

"I'll be better once I've had a chance to ask you some questions."

"Come inside."

Mason told Steve to wait in the car and followed Summers to the front door and then into the house. He looked around as they passed through the entrance hall and saw the pictures of Summers that had been hung on the wood-panelled walls. There were photographs of him with local and national dignitaries, all of them speaking to the fact that he was a man of influence. His military background bestowed upon him an air of unflappable sangfroid, and his career—brimming with tales of derring-do with which he never tired of regaling his company—had given him authority among the many retired senior officers who had made Salisbury and its neighbouring villages their home. The jaw-dropping success of the business that he had set up following his retirement had given him gravitas in London, too, meaning that his reputation was assured in both town and country.

"Cup of coffee?" Summers said.

"No."

"Something stronger?"

"*No.* This isn't a social call."

"I didn't think it was. It's about the report in the newspaper today?"

"What else? What's going on, Harry?"

"Nothing you need to be concerned about. I can help put your mind at ease."

Mason's stomach sank. He realised that he had been holding onto the hope that the whole thing was an unfortunate misunderstanding, that the image he had seen in the paper did not show the room he remembered from twenty years ago, but Summers's suggestion that there was nothing to worry about had the opposite effect.

"It's right, then? The picture *was* what I thought it was? The red room?"

"Yes."

"How did it get into the paper?"

Summers sat down on one of the leather sofas and indicated that Mason should do the same. "You know about the man who died at the cathedral?"

Mason lowered himself onto a nearby Chesterfield. "Of course—they thought he killed himself. Jumped off the tower."

"David Campbell. He was a customer from twenty years ago."

"So why was he on film?"

"There used to be another man in the business with me and my partners. We found out recently that he was using a hidden camera to record our customers. We think he had a mind to blackmail them, although he never did—at least not as far as we know."

"Who is he?"

"You don't need to be concerned about him."

"I disagree."

"Because he's dead, Max."

"You *killed* him?"

"There's no need to go into what happened, but let's just say I don't tolerate betrayal, and I take the privacy of my customers seriously. *Extremely* seriously."

"How many customers did he film?"

"No more than a handful."

"And not me?"

"No, Max. Not you."

"How can you be certain?"

"Because the videos we found were all made in the autumn of 1999. You didn't start going out to Imber until after that."

"Late 2000."

"There you are, then. Months later. You have nothing to worry about."

"Is that why you stopped using the house in Imber?"

"Because of that?" Summers shook his head. "No, that was a business decision—things are much easier to scale online."

Mason remembered: the house at Imber had been closed down not all that long after his final visit. The operation had changed, with personal participation curtailed in favour of streams distributed on the dark web and, these days, paid for by way of cryptocurrency. The aesthetic—the red room—had been kept.

"Anything else, Max?"

"You haven't explained how the newspaper has the video. You said he was dead."

"We're looking into that with all the urgency you'd expect."

"You're holding something back. Remember who you're talking to, Harry. I'm not just anyone."

He nodded. "No, you're quite right—you're not. The situation with my colleague was very unpleasant, as you can imagine. We dealt with the problem, but we couldn't find all the recordings we think he made. There was a brother involved, and he's gone missing. We think he might have the tapes, and now *he's* trying to make money off them."

"You're guessing."

"Educated guessing, and I'm afraid it's the best I can do at the moment. One thing I can say with absolute certainty, though, is that you were never filmed. We were able to speak to him before he died, and he was clear about that."

"You believed him?"

"We were persuasive, and he had no reason to lie. There's nothing—and I really do mean *nothing*—that would implicate you. You have my word on that, Max."

"I'd like to say that makes me a little more confident, but I can't. I trusted you. It was all about discretion. That was the selling point, *especially* for someone like me. You've let me down."

Summers spread his hands. "I understand why you would say that. I'd feel the same."

Summers kept agreeing with him, and that made it more difficult to remain angry. "What about the police? You said you had connections there."

Summers nodded. "I do. It has to be managed with discretion, but we have sources who'll let us know of anything that might be helpful."

Mason thought of Beckton. "I have a connection. Senior."

Summers shook his head. "Keep it to yourself. It's in hand. Why bring any attention onto yourself by asking questions? There's no point. Leave it to us." He stood. "Now—are you *sure* I can't get you a drink?"

Mason stood, too. "I need to be getting back. I'm filming again tomorrow."

"We're planning another performance soon. Two very pretty girls who'd be right up your street. I'll tell you what—why don't I see about you having access to the stream for free? I feel bad that you've been worrying. Let me start to make it up to you."

That was tempting.

"Sort this mess out first," Mason said. "Then we'll see."

CHAPTER 64

Atticus had reviewed the manor house on Google before making the twenty-minute drive to the south. It was grand and had been bought by the general after his corporate intelligence company had made profits in what had turned out to be just the first in a series of stellar years. Atticus had downloaded the particulars from the website of the high-end estate agents who had been engaged to sell it and had noted from the land registry details that the asking price—more than £18.5 million—had been exceeded by thirty per cent. The *Evening Standard*'s society page suggested that Summers had been caught up in a three-way auction with a well-known singer and a *nouveau riche* dilettante who had recently received the fruits of a multi-million-pound inheritance and wanted the estate as a place to run a shooting business. Summers had bid aggressively to close the deal.

Atticus pulled over at the side of the road within sight of the track that the map suggested led to the property.

He turned to Mack. "How much are you comfortable with?"

"I'm not comfortable with any of it."

"You don't have to be here. I can take Bandit on my own."

"And what happens when someone sees you?"

"I was walking the dog, and he went after a deer. I'm very sorry to have trespassed, but I would've lost him if I didn't go after him."

"What's the point?" Mack muttered. "We need to speak to him, not look around his gardens."

"So let's do that."

"And Murphy?"

"You're a DCI," Atticus reminded her. "Do you need to ask his permission before you do anything?"

"No," she began. "No, but—"

He cut across her. "Tell him this was just speculative, that it's almost certainly nothing, and you didn't want to waste his time."

Atticus had known that Mack would be tempted. She wouldn't have agreed to come out here with him without at least considering the idea that they might go a little further than they had agreed and try to speak to Summers. He knew her well enough to know that she would have been fuming at her replacement as the head of the investigation; he had seen that she had no respect for Murphy, and had no doubt that the fact that he was male and from outside the area would have exacerbated her irritation. Atticus had tempted her with the prospect of a breakthrough that she would be able to wave in the faces of those who doubted her; Murphy and Beckton wouldn't be able to complain that she had gone off the reservation if she could show them that her initiative had brought them closer to understanding what had happened to the three murdered men.

Atticus might have given thought to the propriety of taking advantage of how well he knew Mack, but that wasn't something that came naturally to him; and, besides, it wasn't as if he was suggesting something that wasn't important. The fact that he would get to come along and speak to Summers himself had been in his thoughts, too. Murphy would never have allowed it, and he wouldn't be able to get a gauge on the man without sitting opposite him where he could watch his body language for useful tells.

Mack sucked on her teeth. "I suppose we could see if he's in."

Atticus nodded. "Where's the harm in that?"

"Who does the talking?"

"You do," he said.

"Sure?"

He put a finger to his lips. "Not a word."

CHAPTER 65

Mack led the way to the pillars that accommodated the gates for the property. The gates were open, but, rather than walk down the track unannounced, she pressed the intercom.

They waited a moment before the speaker crackled into life. "Hello?"

"Hello," Mack replied. "Is that Harry Summers?"

"No. Who is this?"

"Detective Chief Inspector Mackenzie Jones from Salisbury CID. Is Mr. Summers at home?"

"What do you want?"

"We're making some enquiries, and Mr. Summers's name came up. We'd like to speak to him, and it'll be much easier if we do it here rather than asking him to come to the station. Is he around?"

There was a pause, and Atticus thought he could hear hushed conversation. He and Mack shared a glance, but, before he could say anything to her, the intercom crackled with static once more.

"He's got twenty minutes before he needs to go out. Will that be enough?"

"Plenty," she said.

"Follow the drive and park in front of the house."

They went back to the car. Atticus turned off the main road, passed between the pillars and through the gate. The estate was reached by way of a single-track road that was hemmed in between a converted farm building and a row of new houses. Another car approached them. It was a big Bentley Flying Spur, and it took up all the width available; there was a passing space behind them, and Atticus reversed back into it. The driver of the Bentley didn't acknowledge them as he passed.

"Who's that?" Mack said, craning her neck to watch the Bentley.

Atticus glanced up at the rear-view mirror. The car turned the corner and passed out of sight. "No idea. But there's obviously a lot of money here."

The track continued between hedges that divided otherwise open farmland for three-quarters of a mile. The halfway point saw a Dutch barn and a parking area where tractors and equipment were stored, and then, as they continued, Atticus saw the beginning of the estate proper; the farmland turned into lawns and then manicured gardens. The manor house was to the left, bracketed by a long barn to the northeast and formal gardens, with topiary and striped grass to the south.

They reached the parking area at the rear of the house, and Atticus rolled the car to a halt next to a brand-new Land Rover Discovery. The two of them looked from the car to the house and then to the immaculate grounds.

"A *lot* of money."

They got out of the car and started toward the house. The front door opened before they were halfway there, and a man dressed in red tweed trousers and a salmon-coloured shirt came out to meet them.

"Detective Chief Inspector Jones?"

"That's right."

Summers put out his hand, and Mack shook it. "Harry Summers. Good to meet you." He turned to Atticus. "And you are?"

"Atticus Priest."

Summers shook his hand, too. "Police?"

"I'm a private investigator."

"He's a consultant," Mack explained. "He has some experience with the case that we're investigating, and I thought it would be helpful to have him here this morning."

Summers released Atticus's hand and gave him another broad smile. "Absolutely. Please, come inside—I only have twenty minutes, but you're both very welcome."

Summers led the way through the house. The entrance hall had doors to what looked like the drawing room, a grand flight of stairs to the first floor and an arch that led down into a library. The walls were panelled in oak and hung with pictures of men and women who looked as if they might have been connected to the house in years gone by; small plaques beneath them identified previous owners and family members. Other framed photographs showed Summers with politicians and the occasional celebrity that Atticus, who had little time for such people, half recognised.

"Can I get you both a coffee?"

"Yes," Mack said. "Thank you. That would be nice."

They continued into a vast dining hall with a table that would have been big enough to seat twenty and then into the kitchen. Atticus couldn't help but be impressed with the property. He knew how much Summers had spent on it, and it served as a reminder of how successful he had been since he had retired from the military. His experience had evidently been put to lucrative use in his new business.

"Thank you for agreeing to see us, Sir Harry," Mack said.

"Please—it's Harry. I'm not one for formality. Take a seat."

Summers filled a kettle and stood it on one of the hot plates of the large Aga that warmed the kitchen. Atticus looked around the room and saw more examples of Summers's wealth. The pictures on the wall were of his family, while those arranged on the large dresser that stood against the wall showed him in uniform during his years of service. Atticus wandered over so that he could look at them more closely.

"You had a very interesting career," he said.

Summers nodded. "Certainly can't complain."

Atticus saw photographs of him in ceremonial garb with the Queen; in conversation with the host of the *Today* show on Radio 4; crossing the line at the end of the London Marathon; in a mud-smeared uniform as he stood with a rifle before a tank. Atticus picked up a photograph of Summers as a younger man standing with a group of officers in what he guessed was a parade ground at Sandhurst. Summers was watching him, and Atticus thought he detected discomfort.

"How can I help you?" Summers said.

Mack was looking at Atticus too, her frown suggesting that he should stop interfering with the general's things. He took the hint and put the photograph back on the shelf.

"It won't take long," Mack said. "Just a few questions. I'm grateful you've found time for us."

Atticus clenched his jaw. Her deference was irritating; he knew why she was treating him carefully—he was an important man who could have caused them enormous trouble if his feathers were ruffled—but he was impatient and wanted to get stuck into the questions. Mack's equanimity also cast light on the fact that it was something that *he* lacked, and that annoyed him, too.

Summers took the kettle from the Aga, poured hot water into the cafetière and then stood it on the tray with three mugs and a plate of biscuits. He brought it over to the table, set it down and took a seat next to Mack.

"Fire away."

"This is going to sound a little unusual," Mack said. "I'd like to show you a picture if that's all right?"

Summers pushed down on the plunger of the cafetière. "Of course."

Mack opened her bag and took out the still image of the woman on the balcony of the house in Brussels. She put it on the table. Summers poured the coffee, replaced the cafetière and put on a pair of glasses so that he could examine the photograph.

Atticus watched his face carefully.

"Where did you get this?"

"Do you recognise it?"

"Yes, of course," he said. "That's Samantha."

"Your wife?" Atticus said, taking over.

"Ex-wife."

"Where was it taken?"

"Brussels. Must be twenty years ago."

"What were you doing there?"

"I was based there. I was the UK representative to NATO."

"And where in the city was it taken?"

"Our house in Barrière de Saint-Gilles. Up on the balcony." He tapped his index finger against his lips. "I don't remember this as a photograph, though. I'm pretty sure we were messing around with a camcorder."

"You're right," Atticus said. "That's a still from a video."

Summers looked at the image and shook his head. "How on earth did you get it?"

"We can't tell you that," Mack said.

"What? No, Detective Chief Inspector, that won't do."

She put her hands together. "Very sorry, sir, but I can't go into that at the moment."

Summers shook his head with exasperation. "How extraordinary. How is it relevant?"

Atticus ignored the question and asked another of his own. "Can you tell us where you've been over the last week?"

"Why?"

"Please—just answer the question."

"No, I'm sorry. Why are you asking me that? Am I being investigated for something?"

"No," Mack said. "Not at the moment."

"Meaning that you *might* investigate me in the future?" He folded his arms in a classic pose of defence. "You said this was a simple matter. Do I need to speak to my lawyer?"

Atticus could see that the conversation was sliding out of control. He looked at Mack and saw that she could see it, too.

"We're not investigating you, sir," she said, "but if you feel you need a lawyer, then you—"

Summers snapped across her. "I don't need a lawyer because I've done nothing wrong. My goodness—this is a strange thing to drop on someone like this. If you must know, I've been at my flat in London. I was in the office yesterday and the day before, and I went out to the theatre with my girlfriend. My PA will be able to confirm that."

"Thank you, sir," Mack said. "That's very—"

Atticus couldn't stay silent any longer. "The videotape of your wife in Brussels—do you still have it?"

"Of course not," he said. "Who keeps *videotapes*? I imagine it was thrown out years ago."

"Are you sure?"

"I'm not *sure*," he said. "But it's the kind of thing Samantha would've done. And it would've been years ago, as I said."

"We need to be sure about what happened to that tape."

"Yet you won't tell me why!"

He was losing his temper, his earlier urbanity pierced by the indignation of a senior officer unused to being put on the spot like this by two civilians. Atticus would have loved to push him a little closer to the edge, to prod and poke him until he forgot where he was and said something he might regret, but Mack put up a hand to forestall him.

"Thank you, Sir Harry. We have enough to be getting on with."

The moment had passed, and Summers's courtliness returned, albeit with a hint of hauteur about it. "I'm sorry—shouldn't be so impatient, but it's frustrating when you can't tell me what it's about." He handed back the sheet with the image of his ex-wife. "It's a worry that you can't tell me how you came by this."

"I understand. I'll be very happy to tell you more when I'm able." She got to her feet, and Summers and Atticus followed suit.

Summers put out his hand, and Mack shook it. "Thank you, Detective Chief Inspector."

"*Do* ask your ex-wife, though," Atticus said.

Summers withdrew his hand and stared bleakly at Atticus. "She's dead."

"Oh," Atticus said. "I didn't know."

"Cancer. Five years ago."

"We're very sorry to hear that," Mack said.

"Yes," Atticus said. "Very sorry. But do let us know if you think of anything that might be helpful."

Summers held Atticus's eye. "I will."

CHAPTER 66

Bandit was excited to see them as they made their way back to the car. They got inside, turned around and drove away from the house.

"Did you *really* have to do that?" she said.

"Do what?"

"Wind him up."

"Putting someone under a little pressure is the only way to test whether they're telling the truth."

"Fine. And? Was he?"

"What do you think?"

She sighed in exasperation. "That's why I brought *you* along."

"You first."

"I don't think he told us everything."

Atticus tapped both hands against the wheel. "He *definitely* didn't. Did you see how he changed? Friendly and affable when we arrived."

"But nervous."

"Yes," he said. "He did a good job hiding it, but there were signs. His posture was stiff, his arms were folded and the whole coffee thing? Who offers coffee when they've just said they've only got twenty minutes? It was an excuse to turn away from us, to give his hands something to do to stop him from fidgeting."

"None of that's unusual. You know what it's like when you interview someone—they always think that they must've done something wrong. It's human nature."

"It is," Atticus said. "And that might have been the reason for it. But did you notice how he changed once we showed him the picture of his wife?"

"He was vague."

"Very vague."

"You think he's lying?"

"He repeated questions before he answered them—he was giving himself time to think. He spoke in fragments of sentences—that's the same. The bluster at the end? Manufactured. He was trying to hide his reaction by distracting us with something else."

"He pressed his finger to his lips, too—did you see that? He was literally telling himself not to answer."

"Very good," Atticus said. "You've been paying attention."

"Jesus," she said, rolling her eyes. "Could you be any more patronising?"

"Sorry. Didn't mean it like that."

"You're hopeless," she said. "But never mind."

They reached the end of the drive. Atticus waited for a car to go past and then followed the road to the north.

Mack drummed her fingers against the dash. "Could he be involved?"

"In the murders?" Atticus drew in a breath and then exhaled. "We can't say that. All we *can* say is that a tape that he used to record his wife twenty years ago *was* used again to record David Campbell. That's suspicious, at the very least."

"Fine—let's play it out. Say the same tape was used twice. How did that happen? Maybe his ex-wife threw it out. Maybe she gave it to a charity shop, and they sold it to whoever used it again."

Atticus gazed out into the gathering darkness at the side of the road.

"Atticus?"

"Possible," he said.

"But unlikely?"

"I think so."

"I need to speak to Murphy and Beckton. I can't sit on it any longer. I wouldn't put it past him to call the nick and make a complaint."

"I'll drop you off."

"What are you going to do?"

"Bandit's never going to talk to me again if I don't give him the walk I promised."

She looked across the cabin at him.

"What?"

"Nothing," she said. "Do you want to come over later? I wouldn't mind talking it over with you."

"When?"

"Ten? I'll be back by then."

"Ten it is," he said.

CHAPTER 67

Atticus dropped Mack at the station and then drove back to the office. He let Bandit out of the back seat, took his lead and knelt to hook it to the dog's collar.

"Who's been a patient boy?" Atticus said as the dog pushed its muzzle into his neck, licking his cheek and ear.

He walked to the cathedral, unclipped the lead and watched as Bandit sprang away. His gaze was drawn up to the spire and then down to the tower; the floodlights from below splashed it in white light that was visible from miles around.

Bandit raced toward him at full speed, dodging to the side at the last moment and then haring away again.

Atticus looked absentmindedly at the floodlights until he realised what he was doing and blinked the brightness away. He didn't believe what Summers had told them, or at least didn't think that he had been frank with them. He couldn't say for sure how Summers might be involved in what had been happening, but he knew that if he was, then the longer they waited, the greater the opportunity Summers would have to come up with a credible story and dispose of anything that might speak to his involvement.

Bandit rushed by him at full pelt just as Atticus's phone rang. He took it out, expecting to see that Mack was calling, but, instead, it was a number he didn't recognise.

He answered it. "Hello?"

"Mr. Priest?"

"Yes," he said. "Who is this?"

"Harry Summers."

Atticus switched the phone to his right hand and started toward the nearest vacant bench. "I didn't give you my number."

"It's on your website."

"So it is." Atticus sat down. "How can I help you?"

"I've had a think about that video you were interested in."

"Yes?"

"I wonder—I know this is going to be inconvenient, but would you be able to come back out to the house to see me?"

"Couldn't you come into the station? DCI Jones is the one you need to speak to."

"Can't, not really. I'm going away tomorrow for a week, and I'd much rather get this off my chest now."

"I'm sure she'd see you tonight. I could call her if—"

Summers spoke over him. "I don't want to be seen going into the police station. And I'd rather this wasn't *official*—do you know what I mean? I'd rather it was you. Of course, you can speak to her yourself when we're finished, and I'll be happy to cooperate if she thinks that'd be useful. I'm hoping that won't be necessary, though. I think—I *hope*—I can put your mind at ease."

Atticus bit down on his lip. It was an unusual offer, and one that made him suspicious. Summers had become unfriendly during the questioning, especially toward him, and it was difficult to understand why he would invite Atticus back to his house.

"When?"

"Now? Are you free?"

Atticus watched as Bandit gambolled happily across the grass. He hurtled at Atticus again, swerving around the bench and then slowing right down, his belly low to the ground as he sprang away once more.

"Mr. Priest?"

"Okay," he said. He looked at his watch. "I've got a couple of things to do first. I'll be with you in an hour."

"Thank you. I appreciate it."

Atticus ended the call and then tried Mack's number. It went straight to voicemail. Atticus ended the call and drummed his fingers against his knee. Mack had explained that she would be seeing Murphy and Beckton, and she was probably still with them now. How long would she be? An hour? Two? He knew that he ought to wait until he had spoken to her, but that would require patience that he didn't have. Summers's offer was intriguing, and he wanted to understand why he had made it. There was a reason he wanted to speak to him and not Mack, and Atticus couldn't work out what it might be; an unresolved question like that was agony for him, and he needed to have it answered.

He called Mack again and, this time, waited to leave a message. "It's me," he said. "I just had a call from Summers. He wants to talk to me. I know I should wait for you, but he says he's going away tomorrow, and he doesn't want it to look 'official.' Anyway, I just wanted you to know that I'm going to go out there, and I probably won't be back until after ten. I'll come straight to you when I'm done."

He called Bandit back to him, gave him a biscuit and re-attached his lead, and went back to the office.

CHAPTER 68

Atticus fed Bandit, changed his water, and then tried to call Mack again, with the same result. He took his spare digital voice recorder and slipped it into his pocket and went down to get his car. He sat down and fastened his belt and rested his hands on the wheel, reluctant to start the engine. He knew why: he was suspicious of Summers's motive but, at the same time, unable to resist his invitation. It was as if a lure had been dropped into the water and, even though he knew that taking it would be a bad idea, there was nothing he could do to stop himself. He reminded himself that, beyond the video, there was nothing to suggest that Summers was involved in any of the crimes that they were investigating. That might have been true, but, as he turned the key and started the engine and moved out, it didn't ameliorate the sickening feeling in the pit of his stomach that he was wandering into a situation without really appreciating what it might mean.

***

Atticus followed the same route that he had taken with Mack that afternoon, arriving at the house at half past eight. He gazed at the house, which was now bathed in the silvered glow of the moon. Light escaped between the curtains of the windows on the ground floor. Atticus parked the car next to the Land Rover Discovery they had noticed earlier, opened the door, stepped out onto the gravel, and started over to the door. It opened before he was halfway there, and Summers stepped out.

"It's cold," he called over. "Come in."

Atticus hurried across the gravel as Summers stood aside. "Evening."

"Thank you for coming," Summers said. "Please—let me have your coat."

Atticus shrugged off his jacket, and Summers took it, hanging it on a hatstand that was next to the grandfather clock that Atticus had noticed that afternoon.

"We'll go through to the drawing room," Summers said. "This way."

The library was straight ahead, but Summers turned right and showed Atticus into a vaulted room that was dominated by a stone fireplace, the stone blackened by soot that must have gathered over time. Wooden beams supported the ceiling, and the polished floor was softened by large rugs. There was a huge bay with leaded windows, and a chandelier glittered overhead. Speakers in the ceiling played Vivaldi at low volume.

Summers indicated that Atticus should take one of the armchairs and went over to a table next to the window.

"Can I pour you a drink?"

"I'm fine," Atticus said.

THE RED ROOM

"No, that won't do. I've got a *really* good twenty-five-year-old bottle of Ardbeg that I was going to open tonight. Let's have a glass."

It wasn't a suggestion, Summers had decided, and that was that. He took two heavy glasses, opened the bottle and poured out two generous measures. He brought the glasses over, gave one to Atticus and kept the other one for himself. He found a remote control on the table, muted the speakers and raised his glass.

"Cheers."

Atticus touched glasses. "Thank you."

"So," Summers said, crossing one leg over the other. "You were interested in the videotape."

"We are—have you had a chance to think about it?"

"I have, and I remember what happened to it. My wife took it to a charity shop in town."

"When was this?"

"We divorced ten years ago—must've been around then."

"Ten years."

"Yes—what about it?"

"You have a good memory."

He looked at Atticus and smiled. "I suppose so."

"To remember something like that? It's a bit random, isn't it? And you couldn't remember it this afternoon."

"I just needed to put my mind to it," he said. "It's come back to me now. We had a collection of videos. I used to be a video buff. I had an old JVC camcorder, used to bring it out all the time, usually to do with the children, of course. Sports day, Nativity plays, learning to ride a bike, my daughter's first gymkhana—you name it. We had a wardrobe in one of the bedrooms with a box full of tapes. Samantha took the box and gave them to a charity shop in town."

"Why did she do that? Family memories. She'd just get rid of them?"

"I transferred them to DVD," Summers said. "There was no point in keeping the tapes after that. They were just taking up space."

"So why not just throw them out?"

"I suppose she thought the charity might be able to get something for them."

"For used VHS tapes? Really?"

"She never liked to just bin something if she thought it might have value."

Atticus sipped his drink and looked at Summers over the top of his glass. It was a decent enough story, with—fortunately for Summers—no way for Atticus to disprove it. It smelled very much like the sort of explanation that he might have cooked up after he had been questioned earlier that afternoon.

"You asked me to come all the way here to tell me that? Wouldn't it have been easier to tell me or DCI Jones on the phone?"

"I wanted to give you the opportunity to ask me anything else you might want answering, and it's easier to do that face to face."

Atticus had the impression that Summers had brought him out here so that he could better assess his reaction to the story that he had just provided, plus any others that he was preparing to tell. He was surer now than he had been that Summers was being economical with the truth; he was lying, or—at the very least—holding something back. He decided that it was worth turning up the temperature a little to see how he reacted.

"I hope you don't mind me saying that it all seems a little unlikely."

Atticus watched for a change in Summers's demeanour and was rewarded with several tiny defensive movements: a stiffness in his posture, a dab of his finger to the side of his face and then, as he noticed that Atticus was observing him, a classic crossing of the arms.

"I don't think it's unlikely at all. We had some videos, we didn't need them anymore, we got rid of them. End of story. You haven't even told me why it's so important."

"That'll be something you can discuss with DCI Jones."

"I will."

Summers stood and went to the table where he had left the bottle of Ardbeg. He finished his drink and poured another, then turned back to Atticus.

Atticus smiled pleasantly. "I don't know, Harry. I can't help thinking you're hiding something."

Summers didn't offer Atticus a refill. "Why would I want to do that?"

Atticus kept his eyes on him. "I don't know. Why would you?"

The easy smile on Summers's lips disappeared, and his brows lowered into a scowl. "Can I give you a word of advice, Mr. Priest?"

"Please do."

"You should be careful about the way that you present yourself to other people."

"Should I?"

"You really should. You have an unfortunate tendency to rub people up the wrong way."

"Sorry you feel that way."

"But it's not just me, is it? I have a business that works with law enforcement, among other things."

"I know. I've looked into it—the business, your background."

"And I've looked into *you*. I know about your career. Your dismissal."

"My *resignation*."

"Semantics. You resigned before they could fire you. I know all about it. I have a friend in Wiltshire constabulary who was able to let me have a look at your annual appraisals. They were dreadful. I mean… *really* dreadful. I'm surprised you lasted as long as you did. You're clearly intelligent, but you don't play well with others."

"Am I supposed to be impressed?"

"With what?"

"That you were able to get my appraisals."

"Not at all."

"What is it, then? You're trying to intimidate me?"

He laughed. "Don't be so *paranoid*. I just want you to know that I've got my eye on you. I don't enjoy having my character called into question. It's important to me—my integrity and my reputation—and anyone impugning either can expect a response."

Atticus stood. The convivial atmosphere had always been tenuous, but the façade had fallen away completely now, and Summers's icy threats were evident even to him. It was time to leave. "Duly noted. Thank you for your time this evening. I'll make sure that DCI Jones is up to speed the next time you see her."

"I doubt there'll be a next time," Summers said. "I can't imagine what else she might want to ask me."

Atticus made to leave the drawing room and collect his jacket from the hatstand in the hall, but, as he approached the open door, he saw that a man was waiting just the other side. He was bigger than Atticus, with an obvious solidity that spoke of hard muscle. His forehead had an atavistic slant that ended with heavy eyebrows, and, beneath small and pitiless eyes, his nose was squashed flat to his face.

Atticus was about as sure as he could be that he had seen him before. It had been dark that night in Alfred Burns's flat, and his recollection had been scrambled a little by the blow to the head that had knocked him out, but he would have laid a sizeable bet that the man in front of him now was the man who had attacked him.

"Mr. Doyle," Summers said, "would you show Mr. Priest to the door, please?"

The big man nodded but didn't immediately step out of the way. He blocked Atticus for just long enough for him to be sure that his presence there was not an accident but a threat; if Atticus continued to make a nuisance of himself, or if Summers concluded that he was being harassed, then the next interaction would be with his pet gorilla instead of him.

Doyle glared at him, then took a step back so that Atticus could make his way out and into the hall. He took his jacket from the hatstand and went to the door.

Summers followed. "Thanks for coming, Mr. Priest. Pass on my best wishes to DCI Jones. I doubt she has any other questions to ask me, but, if she does"—he spread his arms—"then of course I'd be happy to answer them."

The smile was back on Summers's face now, but he made no effort to disguise the fact that it was a pretence. Doyle opened the door, and Atticus stepped outside. The door slammed shut behind him before he had taken even a handful of paces toward his car.

CHAPTER 69

Atticus made his way down the drive, turned onto the A354 and started back in the direction of Salisbury. He couldn't stop thinking about the conversation with Summers; he was sure that the general was lying to him, and that he'd invited him to the house to assess and then threaten him. Atticus was sure that he had already come off second best in an encounter with Doyle and had no wish to arrange a repeat performance, but he was not about to be daunted by threats.

He reached the turning for the nature reserve at Martin Down, saw a lay-by and, without really thinking about it, pressed down on the brake and pulled over. He gripped the wheel tightly and ground his teeth. He had been given a problem to solve and was surer than ever that Summers had information that would help him to do that; he wouldn't be intimidated into turning away. He checked his mirrors, then swung the car around and drove south again, turning off the road at the junction for the manor house and then turning left, following a short drive that gave access to the rear of one of the cottages that came with the estate. There was a space at the end where it was possible to park two cars; the space was empty, and Atticus reversed into it. Save the fact that he was going to need to trek northwest for a mile to get back to the house, it was a good place to leave the car.

He opened the glovebox and took out one pair each of the nitrile gloves and overshoes that he kept there, putting both into his pocket. Better to have something and not need it than to need it and not have it. He wasn't intending to break in—probably—but he knew himself well enough to know that it was a possibility if he found something that looked like it might be interesting. He reached inside the glovebox again and took out his penlight and the leather sleeve that held his collection of lock picks. He put those in his pocket, too.

The moon hung overhead, a glowing gem amid the dark of a sky that was, for the first time in days, without cloud. He would have much preferred the conditions of the last week so that visibility was not quite as good, but there was nothing to be done about that now. He would just have to make his approach a little more carefully.

He joined the drive and started walking. He followed it for the first half a mile before clambering over a gate and continuing through the fields and then the oaks that enclosed the house. He reached the start of the formal gardens and found a spot among the topiary that allowed him to watch without being seen from the house. The lights were still on and, as he watched, the glow from one of the bedrooms on the first floor dimmed as someone walked in front of the window. Atticus kept his focus on that window; the person returned, their shadow thrown out into the middle of the square of light that was cast on the grass, and closed the curtains.

He tried to recall the map of the estate that he had studied before coming here with Mack. The house and gardens were ahead of him, with a long range of brick stables behind them and to the northeast. There was another lawned area to the rear of the house and then the first of a series of cottages that would once have been tithed to the men and women who worked on the land. There was a chapel behind those buildings and then nearly a thousand acres beyond that.

Atticus wanted to look around the grounds and the other buildings. That might involve breaking in and risked severe consequences were he to be caught. He doubted that he would be able to resist it but knew that he'd have to wait until he was confident that Summers was asleep.

He looked at his watch and wondered when the general would turn in. He lowered himself to the ground and settled in to wait.

PART 5

Friday

CHAPTER 70

Atticus crept closer, taking a wide path to avoid exposing himself directly to the house. He took advantage of another line of neatly kept trees, moving along it until he reached the stone wall that encircled the formal gardens. The drive that he had used to get to the parking area at the back of the house was to his right; he went left, staying down low and working his way around the western side of the building. There was a large barn there, the door was unlocked, and Atticus peered inside. It looked as if it was used to store the machinery that was used to keep the grounds in order: he saw a sit-on mower, a roller, then strimmers and blowers and brush cutters and other pieces of agricultural machinery that he didn't recognise. None of it warranted a second look, and there was nothing else of interest inside. He backed out, carefully pulled the door closed and went around the side so that he could look at the back of the house.

He heard footsteps across gravel and stepped back so that he could hide behind the barn. It sounded like the movement was coming from the direction of the door that he had used to get inside earlier. He followed the long edge of the barn and then picked his way between the shrubs and the trunks of the smaller trees that he found on the other side until he was able to peek through the vegetation.

Summers and Doyle were walking to the north, following a path that skirted the lawn in the direction of two cottages and, beyond those, the old chapel. Atticus watched and waited, wondering whether this was the opportunity to look around the house. He remembered that the door was on a latch and wondered whether it might have been left unsecured; even if it *was* locked, it would still have been easy enough to get inside. He agonised over it for a moment before deciding that it was too risky: he didn't know how long Summers and Doyle would be away, and he didn't want to have to rush. He was curious, too, to see what the two men were doing outside at such a late hour.

He waited until they were out of sight and then followed, making his way across the gravel as quietly as he could before he reached the path they had taken. He stopped there for a moment, listening for any sign that Summers or Doyle might be coming back. He heard nothing and, after waiting another beat to be sure, he continued to follow them. The path went north beneath the shelter of another two large oak trees and then continued between a pair of lawns to a junction where it intersected with a path running east to west. Summers and Doyle turned right, following an avenue of trees, then turned left and carried on until they reached the chapel. Summers paused at the door, reaching into his pocket for a set of keys, then opened it. The two men went inside.

Atticus looked around for somewhere that he could wait without being seen when they came back out. There was another path bracketed by hedges, but he would have had to cross an open area of lawn to get there, and the risk of exposure was too great. He decided his best option was to go left at the intersection of the two paths rather than right, and to find a spot between the trunks of the trees where he would be able to watch.

He had a good vantage point from here, where he was able to look across the lawn to the chapel. It was a gable-ended stone building topped by a pitched roof with a stone ridge. An arch was set around the timber door, with a small window above that showed the red glow from a light inside. Atticus waited in the trees for ten minutes, looking for anything that might give him a clue as to what Summers and Doyle were doing. He thought that he could hear conversation but couldn't be sure.

The timber door opened again, and the two men emerged.

"He's a troublemaker," Summers said. "I'm not sure we're in a position to take the chance that this goes away, especially not now."

"What do you want me to do?"

Summers rubbed his scalp. "We've got to move the stuff."

"I'll take care of it. Where shall I take it?"

"Put it in the van for now and find storage in the morning. There's a place up at South Newton."

"Black Hole Storage."

"That's it. Get a unit and dump the gear. We'll leave it there until this mess goes away."

"What about him?"

"Who—Priest?"

"I could sort him out tonight, boss. I know where he lives."

"I know you do, but we can't. What if he told someone he was coming out here? What if he told his girlfriend? It wouldn't take a genius to work out that I'm involved. No. He gets a reprieve for now, but we need to keep an eye on him."

"And after that?"

"I don't care. Do what you want to him. I've been up all day dealing with this shit, and I'm done in—move the stuff and tell me when it's been done tomorrow."

"What about the girl?"

"Just take care of it."

"I'll go and get the van and get started."

Doyle left Summers and headed east; Atticus guessed he was going to the farm that he remembered from the satellite map. Summers set off back to the house. The path would take him very close to Atticus's hiding spot, and he had no option but to hope that the gloom between the trunks of the trees would be enough to shield him. Summers approached and then stopped, close enough that Atticus would almost have been able to reach out and touch him.

He waited, watching Summers as he began walking again and made his way back to the house, and then, once the coast was clear, he turned back to the chapel. He reached into his pocket, pulled out the nitrile gloves and overshoes and put them on. The timber door looked as if it was decades old, pitted with knots and whorls that felt rough through the synthetic rubber as he laid his palm against the wood. The door had been fitted with a substantial hasp, which was then secured with a padlock. Atticus reached into his pocket for the leather pouch and took out a long, straight pick. He slid it into the padlock and, once he felt a little resistance—indicating it had been inserted fully—he twisted it to the right. It took him twenty seconds to pop the lock; he removed it from the hasp and then slowly and carefully pushed the door open.

The interior was about as different from what he had expected as it was possible to be. There was a flagstone floor, an ancient timber above the door and a single window on the eastern end of the building that still retained fragments of stained glass. It wasn't the architecture that gave Atticus pause for thought, though; rather, it was the modern equipment that was arrayed around the space. There were two professional video cameras, each mounted on a pedestal; there were microphones and foldback speakers; two video monitors for visual feedback and a mixing desk for sound. A bed had been placed in the middle of the room, the cameras arranged so that they could cover it from two separate angles. Uplighters had been placed at the bases of the walls; Atticus went to the socket that provided them with power and, heedless of the risk that the illumination might be visible from the house, flicked the switch to turn them on. He had known what to expect and was not disappointed; the lights were fitted with coloured bulbs that filled the room—the *studio*, he corrected himself as he acknowledged the sickening feeling in his stomach—with a deep blood-red glow.

He switched the lights off and took out his flashlight. Beyond the equipment, there was nothing else of note. The bed was covered with a duvet and, when he lifted it and looked beneath, he saw that the sheets had been recently changed. He looked beneath the bed and saw a wooden crate; he dragged it out, opened the lid and looked inside: there were handcuffs and a selection of sex toys. He bit down on his lip; he knew what had happened here from the videos that he had seen this week. Those were old, though, from twenty or twenty-five years before, and the thought of how many films must have been shot here—or in places that looked just like this—was enough to make the blood rise in his cheeks. Summers had owned this property for only five years, meaning they had developed their aesthetic somewhere else and then imported it. It was as if the red lighting was the brand for their filth; the thought of it made him sick.

He heard an engine from outside, and, remembering Doyle, he hurried to the door.

CHAPTER 71

Harry Summers walked back to the house. It was after midnight, and he was angry. He had always been a man who liked to be in command of events and, recently, it felt as if things had run away from him. Control had been important in the military and then as he made the switch to business, and to lose it—as he most certainly had—was difficult. Max Mason insisting that Summers see him on short notice had been bad enough, and having to put up with his self-important bluster and bombast had been a test. But the visit by DCI Jones and her tame private investigator had been something else; he had suffered their impertinent questions and Priest's knowing looks and asides while maintaining his pretence as the perfect host, confused and concerned about what he was being told.

He had decided to bring Priest back to the house again so that he could gauge how much he knew—and how much danger Summers was in—without the detective chief inspector around. He had concluded the answers were 'too much' and 'enough.'

Summers had been aware of Priest ever since he had been involved in the police investigation against Alf Burns. That had been inconvenient, and, the more Summers had come to think about it, Priest's relentless hounding of Burns had been the inflection point for everything that happened next. Burns's legal difficulties had led to financial difficulties, and they had led, in turn, to his foolish attempts to blackmail Summers, Miller and York. Burns had been killed because of that, and Summers had hoped that that might have been the end of the matter.

It wasn't.

He had been wrong.

It had just been the *start*.

Priest's investigation had revealed some of their old operation at Imber. Summers had moved them out to Hawthorne Manor years ago, within months of buying the house. Imber had served a purpose in the early days, but they had outgrown it. It had always felt amateurish, and the fact that they couldn't control it meant that it was riskier than Summers would have liked. His new place had allowed them to install a purpose-built studio and, as technology moved on, to take it entirely online. It was discreet and professional and safe.

But the police investigation in Imber had been effective enough to mean that their past put them at risk, and it had eventually meant there was no choice but to find a fall guy. York had terminal cancer and was the obvious choice; a razor blade slipped to him by a corrupt lawyer was all they needed. Miller would have needed to take his medicine, too, but it should have been limited to what happened in Londonderry. He had been out to the house to talk it through on the night he died; Summers still hadn't been able to get to the bottom of what had happened to him, but the fact that his body had been deposited outside Priest's office suggested that he—and the police—knew more than Summers did, and that rankled.

Doyle had suggested that he pay Priest a visit. The two of them had met before, at Alf Burns's flat, and it had been a pity that Doyle had only knocked him out. He could have topped him then, and that might have avoided all the present difficulties. Summers was a good judge of character, and, although he could see that Jones was dangerously sharp in her own right, it was Priest who gave him cause for the most concern. Summers had told Doyle to stand down, but he wondered now whether that had been a mistake. Murdering Priest now would be a brazen move, and one that could easily have him implicated as a suspect, but perhaps it would be better than letting him continue to tug and pull at the loose threads that Summers had been unable to snip. If he kept doing it—probing and prodding and making a nuisance of himself—there was no way of knowing what he might turn up.

And now old customers were being murdered, and Burns's old blackmail tapes were being sent to the press. Summers had no influence over events, and that bothered him more than anything else.

CHAPTER 72

Atticus looked out through the door. The noise of the engine wasn't coming from the house, but—as he had guessed—from the direction of the farm. He slid outside and edged around the chapel until he could look behind it. There was a paddock between the building and the farm, and a van was approaching, the headlamps bouncing up and down as the wheels negotiated the uneven surface. Atticus shut the chapel door but knew that he wouldn't have time to lock it again; he left it as it was, checked back to the house to be sure that Summers wasn't in view, then crossed back over into cover again. He found the same spot in the trees as before and waited as the van edged through a gap in the fence and reversed until the cargo doors were next to the chapel door.

Doyle got out of the cab and paused, evidently confused at finding the door unlocked. Atticus held his breath and froze as Doyle turned and looked out over the lawns. He knew that he was well hidden, but there was a moment when Atticus was afraid that Doyle had seen him; he tensed, ready to run if Doyle were to make a move in his direction.

He didn't.

Instead, he turned back to the door, pushed it all the way open, then went inside. He emerged a moment later with one of the large cameras cradled in his arms. Atticus watched as Doyle opened the doors at the rear of the van, carefully lowered the camera inside and then went to get the tripod. Atticus waited for Doyle to put the mixer and then a second camera into the van, and then left the undergrowth, moving quickly with his head down until he was alongside the vehicle. He took out his penknife, unfolded a serrated blade and made a quick and forceful strike into the sidewall. He pushed the blade deeper into the tyre and yanked it to the side. Air rushed out through the split in the rubber; it was loud at first—Atticus was sure that Doyle would hear it—but then quieter, a low hiss that was less obvious.

Atticus heard Doyle's footsteps and saw the van's suspension dip as he put something heavier inside. He walked back inside. Atticus knew that Doyle would notice the tyre eventually and that now was the time to beat a retreat. He reached the path and followed it back to the house, looking up and seeing that two of the windows on the first floor were now lit.

He hid in the gloom beneath the boughs of one of the old oaks and put in his earbuds. He took out his phone, and, shielding the light of the screen with a cupped hand, he called Mack. He felt a buzz of nervousness as the call rang. She was going to be angry with him.

She picked up. "Where are you? You said you'd come over and—"

He cut across her. "Did you get my voicemail?"

"No. Why?" She paused. "And why are you whispering?"

"There's something you need to see."

"It's past midnight. What is it? Where are you?"

"At Summers's house."

She didn't respond.

"It's not what you think," he said. "He called me, and he asked me to come. I sent you a voicemail, but… well, you didn't get it."

"What did he say?"

"He lied through his teeth and then threatened me, but it doesn't matter. I've found a room that looks just like the one in the videos. The red room."

"You 'found' it? *Please* don't tell me you've broken the law." She paused. "What am I talking about? Of *course* you broke the law."

"I didn't. Summers invited me here, and I had a look around the grounds afterwards. I suppose, technically, it might be described as trespassing…"

"'Technically'? You're there without permission. That's the *definition* of trespassing."

"And it's a civil matter, not criminal. Anyway." He took a beat. "*Anyway*—it was worth it. Summers and a man who works for him went inside the chapel, and I looked inside, through the door. He's got a little film studio, and it's been made to look like the one in the videos."

"What good does this do us? What do you want me to do? Come over and ask him nicely if he'd show me?"

"No, Mack. You've got grounds to suspect there's evidence relating to an indictable offence on the premises."

"You don't need to teach me what PACE says," she said, referring to the Police and Criminal Evidence Act.

"It's definitely connected to the three deaths, and Summers knows we're onto him. They're moving everything out. You need to get here before it all disappears."

"How? I've got no grounds to be there save what you've told me, and you only know that because you're there when you shouldn't be."

Atticus stopped. He thought he heard something. He frowned, closed his eyes and concentrated on listening as carefully as he could.

Had he?

There was nothing now, nothing obvious save the call of a night bird from somewhere in the dark overhead.

But that wasn't it.

It was the sound of breaking glass.

"Atticus."

Atticus looked back up at the house and saw that another light had come on downstairs.

"Atticus, are you still there?"

"Something's happening."

He stepped out from behind the tree and then ran across the grass to the main house. He reached the wall and edged around it until he was outside the door that he had used earlier. That door was still closed, and there was no sign of broken glass. He continued, reaching the corner of the house and another door that he recalled as opening into the storeroom next to the ground-floor office. There was a pane of glass in this door, and it had been smashed; the door, when he touched it, swung open.

"*Atticus?*"

He heard a loud cry from somewhere in the house.

CHAPTER 73

Atticus pushed the door back with his fingertips and stepped into the dark space beyond. His recollection of the plan of the property was right; the space was used as some kind of store, with shelving on the walls and a low unit pushed up beneath the single covered window. There was an open door to his right; he stepped through it into the office and then froze at the sound of an angry shout from somewhere upstairs.

He only had to pass through the office and the boot room to get to the hall, and from there it was just a short distance to the stairs that would take him up to the first floor. The master bedroom was above the kitchen, with the bay window perhaps ten metres away from where he was standing now.

He heard voices.

Two men: one of them angry, the other afraid.

Atticus crept forward, passing between the desks in the office and gently opening the door to the boot room. An exterior door was to his left. There was a sink in the corner and, beneath it, a cupboard. He opened it and found a plastic box that had been used to store a variety of tools that could be used for household maintenance. He took it out and picked up a screwdriver with a heavy plastic handle, wondering whether it would serve as something he could use to defend himself. He put it down, reached into the box again and took out a hammer.

Atticus stepped into the hall. There was a second flight of stairs directly to his right that ascended to the landing on the first floor.

The voices were clearer now. He could make out what was being said.

"Put it down," Summers said.

"You don't remember me, do you?"

"How would I? I've never met you before."

"Yes, you have. But I was younger then."

Atticus started up the stairs. They were made of dark hardwood, with ornate balustrades and a curved handrail. The treads were old and loose, and they creaked as he put his weight on them. Atticus froze, but the voices continued. He resumed climbing.

"What do you mean?" Summers said from the floor above.

"Tell me you remember me."

"I don't."

Atticus reached the landing. It was grand, with high ceilings and large windows that were covered by thick curtains. The floor was covered by a plush carpet that meant he could approach the master bedroom without making a sound. Eleven doors opened onto the corridor that ran along the middle of the house, some of them grand and imposing.

The voices were coming from the master bedroom.

"It's too late for that."

"For what?"

"For playing the innocent."

"Put that *down*."

Summers muttered something, and there was the sound of a scuffle, then a thud as something heavy fell to the floor. There was a shriek—from Summers, Atticus thought, but he wasn't sure—and then another thud.

He reached the doorway. His heart hammered in his chest, and he could feel sweat on his palms beneath the gloves and in the small of his back. He waited for a beat and then turned and looked into the bedroom.

A figure, dressed in black and with a knife in his hand, turned to face him.

CHAPTER 74

The man was dressed in black from head to toe. He was of average appearance: his hair was dark and of a medium length, worn in a practical cut; his blue eyes were a pale, almost greyish shade; his features were neither overly sharp nor overly soft, lending him an ordinary appearance. He would have been entirely unexceptional were it not for the knife in his hand.

"Atticus," he said, "why did you have to come back? You should've kept driving."

"How do you know my…" He stopped, the pieces of the puzzle locking into place. "What do I call you? Jack?"

"That'll do."

Atticus looked at the knife and saw that the blade was stained red. Summers was spreadeagled across the floor, his arms and legs splayed wide. A slowly expanding pool of blood leeched out from beneath his torso.

"Put it down."

Jack shook his head. "Can't do that. I'll take it with me. But I don't want to hurt you."

Atticus raised the hammer with one hand and held up the other, as if that might be enough to ward him off. "What have you done?"

"He got what he deserved. You saw what they were doing. Miller, Burns and York? You've seen the videos. You *can't* disagree with me. Summers was involved from the start. He had the money and a place to film when they couldn't use Imber." He stepped away from Summers. "He's as guilty as sin, and he got what he deserved."

"You need to stop. They'll catch you in the end."

"No, they won't. They haven't got a clue."

"*I've* found you. They will, too. Give up."

"When I'm done. But not now—there's more to do. There are others."

"Customers?"

"Men who paid to abuse kids. I've got a list of them, and I'm going to work through it from top to bottom." He took a step toward the door. "Get out of my way."

Atticus heard a car rolling across the gravel drive and saw headlights raking the room through the uncovered window.

"I told you," Atticus said. "You can't run."

Footsteps approached the house across the gravel, and then there was a heavy knock on the door. "Police—is anyone inside?"

Jack raised the knife and turned his wrist so that the tip of the blade was pointing at Atticus's chest. He jabbed it at him, forcing him to step back, then darted through the open door and turned left, hurrying along the corridor to the landing. He took the stairs two at a time, the treads creaking in protest.

"*Police!*" came the shout from below.

Atticus was frozen. Jack had a knife, and Atticus had no desire to be stabbed. On the other hand, he knew that Jack was cunning and cautious, and there was a good chance that he would disappear forever if he was allowed to leave now.

Atticus had no choice; he *had* to know who he was.

He followed, sprinting along the corridor and onto the landing, then descending the stairs as fast as he could. The police sounded as if they were outside the door to the entrance hall. Jack had come in through the office store and would be able to use that to get outside again. And, thanks to the angle of the house, he would be invisible to the officers who were trying to get inside.

"Mr. Summers?" the voice called out. "Atticus? *Open the door.*"

Atticus reached the foot of the stairs, ran into the library and leapt up the three steps to the entrance hall. He stopped, removed the gloves and overshoes, undid the latch and opened the door. Bob Carver was on the threshold.

"The owner of the house has been stabbed," Atticus said.

"Where is he?"

"Upstairs."

The blue and red lights of a patrol car pulsed against the walls of the house and cast enough light for Atticus to glimpse a figure running north, between the trees that bracketed the path that ended with the chapel.

Atticus stepped around Carver and ran.

CHAPTER 75

Atticus put his head down and sprinted, passing the two cottages and following the path toward the chapel. He slipped on a patch of wet grass, his legs sliding out from underneath him so that he crashed down onto his side. He got up again and ran, reaching the path and pressing on as fast as he could.

He heard an exclamation from ahead and then a dull thud. He came around the corner and saw Doyle and Jack on the ground next to the van. Doyle was struggling to get astride Jack, and, as he managed it, he used his knee to press down on Jack's left arm. Jack's top was pulled up, and Atticus saw a scar, a couple of inches long, on the lower-right side of his belly. Doyle punched down at Jack's head: once, twice, and then a third time. Each blow was hard, with all of Doyle's weight behind it, and blood splashed on Jack's face.

"Hey!" Atticus yelled.

Doyle turned at the sound, his face twisted with fury. He turned back to Jack and drew back his fist to deliver another blow, but didn't notice Jack scrabbling with his free hand, his fingers probing for the knife that must have fallen from his grasp. He found the tip of the blade, then the handle. Doyle saw, but too late; Jack swung his arm up and around, burying the knife into Doyle's torso, the point slicing in between his ribs. Doyle gasped. Jack pulled the knife out and then plunged it in for a second and then a third time.

Doyle stiffened, his arms falling limply to his sides.

Jack lay back and gasped for breath. His face was smeared with blood.

Doyle groaned and slumped to the side. He slid off Jack's body, bounced off the van and then hit the path.

The knife had fallen from Jack's hand again and lay on the path next to him. Atticus used the toe of his boot to push it away and knelt next to him.

"It's over."

"Why are you... doing this?" He coughed, and blood bubbled out of the corner of his mouth. "You want... you want... same thing as me. Burns, York... Miller... the others..." He swallowed the blood, his words slurring. "Just the same..."

"Not like this."

Atticus heard footsteps from behind him and glanced around as another uniformed officer—Pete Britten—raced up to them. He slowed and stopped and muttered a curse.

"What's happened?"

"This is Jack," Atticus said, then pointed at Doyle. "He works for Summers. Jack stabbed him."

Britten took his cuffs from his belt, opened the bracelets and secured Jack's wrists.

Atticus sat down next to Jack.

Britten spoke into his radio. "Bravo November four-five to Control. I need an ambulance to Hawthorne Manor."

Atticus closed his eyes.

"Ambulance is already on its way, four-five."

"I need another one. I need the on-call DI, I need CSI, I need the Major Incident Team… I need *everyone*."

CHAPTER 76

Atticus got up and went over to check Doyle. He put his fingers to his neck and felt for a pulse.

Britten looked over. "And?"

"Dead."

They both heard footsteps and turned to see another uniformed officer approaching.

"Sarge," Britten called out, "over here."

It was James Boyd. He changed direction and swore as he saw the two bloodied men.

Britten explained what had happened. Jack looked as if he was unconscious now. Boyd radioed Control to see where the ambulance was and was told that it would be with them in ten minutes. The two officers made sure that Jack was breathing before Boyd stood and turned to Atticus.

"Anything I need to know?"

"Look in the chapel."

"Why?"

"You'll see."

He did as Atticus suggested. "Empty. What am I looking for?"

Atticus went inside, went over to the plug and switched on the lights.

The room was bathed in red.

"Shit," Boyd said.

"The dead man's name is Doyle. He worked for Summers. He was moving the kit from here into the van."

"Why?"

"There was a little too much heat here for them."

"Let me just try to get this straight," Boyd said. "Are you saying that Summers and the bloke outside—Doyle… Are you saying that they're responsible for making the videos?"

"They were involved."

"And what are you doing here?"

"Summers asked me to come over to see him tonight. I was outside when all this kicked off."

Boyd reached out and put a hand on Atticus's shoulder. "Better go up to the house. Mack's on her way. You'll have to explain it to her."

* * *

Atticus left the chapel and walked back to the house. An ambulance and two other patrol cars were parked there, and he could hear the howl of more ambulance sirens and patrol cars in the distance. Atticus saw a man being stretchered out of the door and loaded into the back of the ambulance. He drew nearer and saw that it was Summers.

Bob Carver was standing at the door.

"How is he?"

"Alive."

"Is he going to make it?"

"They don't know."

Atticus stepped back, waiting for the paramedics to shut the doors and for Carver's attention to be distracted as they got into the cab and started the engine. The door to the house was closed, and rather than have Carver notice him opening it again and going inside, he made his way around the house and used the door that Jack had forced. Atticus went upstairs, emerging on the top landing and orienting himself with his memory of the plan of the property.

The door to Summers's bedroom was open; it was the only room that was lit, with a warm glow falling out across the carpet. Atticus took it all in quickly: the duvet on top of the bed was disturbed; a glass of water on the bedstand had been overturned; and the bloodstain on the floor had grown a little larger.

He left the room and checked the others. The bedrooms had been made up, but none of them were being used. A door at the end of the corridor was closed and, when Atticus tried the handle, he found—to his irritation—that it was locked. He was going to try to pick it when he heard a car outside. He went back to the master bedroom, glanced out of the window and saw another patrol car and, beyond that, the lights of several additional vehicles approaching along the long drive.

They drew nearer, and he saw that Mack's car was bringing up the rear.

Time to leave.

CHAPTER 77

Atticus went back outside and stepped around the corner of the house as Mack pulled up in the parking area. He went with Carver to join her.

"What's going on?" she said. "I passed an ambulance on the way in—what happened?"

"The owner of the house has been stabbed," Carver said.

She looked to Atticus. "Summers?"

Atticus nodded.

"Dead or alive?"

"Alive," Carver said. "But it looks bad."

"What happened?"

"It was Jack," Atticus said. "He broke in and attacked him."

"You saw him?"

"I was in the room with him. He ran when the first patrol car arrived. We got him, though."

"Where?"

Atticus pointed. "By the chapel. He was jumped by one of the men who work for Summers. There was a struggle between the two of them—Jack knifed Summers's man, but he's taken a beating. Britten and Boyd are with him."

A second ambulance arrived and slowly made its way through the gardens in the direction of the chapel.

"What does Jack have against Summers?"

"The videos. Summers was involved with Miller and the others. Jack killed Miller, he killed the customers—Campbell, Kajetan, Hartnett—and he tried to kill Summers. He admitted it."

"You've spoken?"

"Yes, but not for long. You'll need him to repeat that in an interview."

"And if he won't?"

"He'll talk to me."

"That's not going to happen, though, is it? You're not police."

Robbie Best pulled up in his car, got out and listened carefully while Mack updated him. Atticus paced, anxious to return to the chapel. He needed to be doing something. The police would search the house and the grounds and, although Atticus was desperate to be involved, he knew that Mack wouldn't—*couldn't*—allow it.

Mack finished with Best and turned to Atticus.

"Show us where he is," she said.

Atticus led the way, following the strobing blue lights of the ambulance to the chapel. One of the paramedics was crouched over Doyle; he looked for a pulse, shook his head, and covered the body with a sheet. The other medic was with Jack. He had been propped up against the side of the van, his cuffed wrists in his lap, while the woman checked him over.

Mack stopped dead. "Shit."

"What is it?"

"*Shit*. That's Francine's boyfriend."

Atticus frowned. "What do you mean it's her boyfriend?"

"I can't remember his name. I met him in the pub this week." She turned to Best. "You were there—Bob Bradley's birthday. That's him, isn't it, or am I going mad?"

Best stared. "You're not going mad. It's definitely him."

"What's his name?"

"Charlie."

They watched as Jack—or Charlie, or *whoever* he was—was helped up.

Mack put her head in her hands. "Someone's going to need to tell Franny."

"Can't be a coincidence," Best said.

"Of course it's not," Atticus said. "He's used Francine to get a line into the investigation. *Jesus*. How much has she told him?"

Mack frowned at him. "Maybe she hasn't told him anything. She knows this is sensitive."

"And you've never shared anything out of school?"

She glared at him, then turned to Best. "Follow the ambulance to the hospital."

"Will do."

Mack gestured to Atticus with her finger. "Walk back to the house with me."

She set off, and he followed.

"You've done it again," she muttered.

"Done what?"

"Messed up! I told you not to let me down, and you said—you promised—that you wouldn't."

"I told you," he reminded her starchily. "Summers called me. He asked me to come. I tried to let you know, but you didn't pick up."

"I was with Beckton and Murphy."

"Did you listen to my message?"

"Yes, but you still should've waited. You know I would have told you it needed to be done properly. By a police officer who's prepared to respect the rules."

"I thought he might have called me because he was panicking about what you might know, so he brought me over so that he could get a sense of it without it being official. And I thought *if* he was panicking, it would potentially be too good an opportunity to wait until tomorrow when he might not have been."

She cut across him. "You really should listen to yourself sometimes. The shit that comes out of your mouth. You can try to dress it up however you like. We had a plan, and you ignored it."

"I know, and I've said I'm sorry." He knew that Mack was going to tear a strip off him, but he was growing frustrated that she wasn't paying attention to the progress that had been made. "Look—you can beat me up about it for as long as you like once this is over and done with, but, for now, you need to focus on what we've found out. It's *done*. It's *over*. You can put this whole thing to bed tonight. We wanted to find out what's been going on, and now we have. Jack has been murdering the men who made the videos and the men who were in them. Summers was involved in making them."

"You could have caught either of them in the act, and it wouldn't make a blind bit of difference if the evidence is inadmissible because of how you got it. Let's assume he doesn't die and we have enough to build a case against him—"

"We do," he said.

"Let's *assume* that we do." She pointed back up the garden to the house. "Look at this place. It cost eighteen million when he bought it. Eighteen million! He has enough money to afford the kind of lawyer who'll make *us* look corrupt when we get him to trial. There are rules that we have to follow about evidence. I know you find them tedious, but there we are—they exist, they're there for a reason, and we *can't* ignore them."

"I haven't done anything wrong. He asked me to come, and I came. That's it."

"Fine. When did this all happen?"

"Just after midnight."

"Why were you still here, then?"

Atticus was quiet for a moment. "I see what you mean. Yes. We'll have to think of a reason to explain that."

She put her head in her hands.

"I'll say I forgot something, came back to get it, went to the door, saw that it had been forced."

"And called me."

"Yes," he said, hoping that she might be prepared to play along. "I heard a scream and went inside to see if I could help. I saw a man with a knife. He ran. I chased him. Look, Mack—we can argue later, but, right now, you need to search the property."

"How are we going to do that? We can't ask Summers for permission."

"Say that there's a risk that evidence would be destroyed if we had to wait to get a warrant?"

Mack thought about it, then shook her head. "No. We've already taken enough risks in getting to where we are now. We'll make an expedited application for a warrant. We need to be sure that we do this by the book." She stared at him meaningfully. "No more shortcuts."

The ambulance drove by them, following the path back to the house.

Atticus turned back to Mack. "How much have you told Francine?"

"About what?"

"About Summers? About what I found on the tape?"

She shook her head. "No. I haven't seen her today."

"So how did Jack know that Summers was involved?"

"I don't know. Maybe—"

"Don't say coincidence," he cut over her. "He's out here the *same* day that we find out about Summers."

"It's possible."

"No, it's not. He's got close to Francine to keep an eye on the investigation. You need to find out exactly what she's told him."

"Could he have been watching you?"

"And then followed me here?" Atticus closed his eyes and tried to recall whether there might have been a car on the road with him out to the estate on either of his two visits yesterday. "I don't know."

"We'll ask him," she said. "He'll need to be checked out, but once we have the green light, we'll get him in the interview room and see what he's got to say."

They both noticed another car as it came around the house and slowed as the driver looked for a spot to park.

Atticus squinted at it but was blinded from seeing who was inside by the glare of the headlamps. "Who's that?"

"Looks like Murphy," she said. "He'll want to take over here."

"What about Francine?" Atticus said.

"I'll go and see her now. Want to come?"

"Okay."

She pointed to her car. "Get in before Murphy sees you."

CHAPTER 78

Mack drove to Francine Patterson's place on St. Ann Street. She parked in an empty space and then led the way back down the hill to the house. There was a light on in the downstairs window.

She put out a hand and took Atticus by the elbow. "I'll do it. This is going to be very difficult for her, and I don't want her to feel like it's her fault."

"Can I come in and listen?"

"Be gentle."

Mack knocked on the door. Francine opened it and blinked out at both of them. Her face was pale, and her eyes were damp.

"Is it true?"

"How do you know?"

"Robbie called me. It *is* true, then? About Charlie?"

"Yes," Mack said. "I had a look as they loaded him into the ambulance. It's definitely him. Can we come in?"

A hand fluttered up to her throat. "Sorry. Of course."

She stepped back to allow Mack and then Atticus to come inside. They went into the kitchen.

"I feel like I've been punched in the face," Francine said.

"Sit down. Atticus—make us all a brew."

Francine distractedly told him that the teabags were in the cupboard above the sink. He found them, filled the kettle and flicked the switch to set it to boil.

Mack quickly recounted what had happened at Summers's house, that Charlie looked to have broken his arm and that he had been taken to hospital.

Francine put a hand to her mouth. "Are you sure he did what you say he did?"

"I was there," Atticus said. "He was in the house with a knife."

"My god."

Mack reached out and grabbed her wrist. "It's fine. It's not your fault."

"I still feel like a complete fool."

The kettle boiled. Atticus put tea bags into three mugs and poured in the hot water. He put the mugs on the table and opened the fridge for the milk.

"It's off," Francine said. "Charlie was going to pick up a bottle on his way over."

"I'll have it black," Mack said.

There were only two chairs at the table, so Atticus stood with his back against the wall. "How did you meet him?"

"Online. I've got a profile on Bumble. He sent me a message." She waved a hand vaguely. "It was all totally normal."

"He's very smart," Atticus said.

"Is Charlie even his real name?"

"We don't know yet," Mack said. "We'll find out when we speak to him."

"When?"

"Depends what the doctors say—later this morning or this afternoon."

"Can I be there?"

"Probably best if you aren't."

Atticus looked around. "Where's your phone?"

"Why?"

"Can I see the messages he sent?"

Francine looked down and bit her lip; Mack thought she might be about to cry. "This is going to be so embarrassing," she said.

"It's important. We—"

Mack looked up at Atticus and gave a gentle shake of her head. "We can wait until later for that."

Francine breathed in and out and, when she looked up again, there was steel in her eyes. "What can I do to help, boss?"

"Are you sure? I don't mind if you take a little time to get yourself together."

"I'd rather get straight back into it, if it's all the same. Doing something useful will take my mind off it."

"Okay—that's good. We need to get a search warrant for Summers's house. Liaise with Robbie—you'll need to go and wake a judge up."

She nodded.

Mack gripped her hand. "And it's *not* your fault. No one blames you. There was no way of knowing."

"I know," she said, although the tremor in her voice suggested that she hadn't yet been able to persuade herself that that was true.

"We'll get to the bottom of it. Call Robbie, go and get the warrant, and we'll take it from there."

CHAPTER 79

The search team assembled at the property at nine. Mack got out of her car and finished what was left of the coffee that she had brought with her from the office. She had managed to grab an hour or two of sleep on the sofa in the break room, but she knew that she was going to be working for hours in a row as the investigation picked up speed, and that she was going to need caffeine to stay upright.

Murphy and his team arrived, parking next to her and exiting to join the others who were milling around. There were a dozen of them, a mixture of plainclothes—from Salisbury and London—and uniform. Atticus had wanted to be here too, but Mack had vetoed it. Murphy had made his feelings about him very obvious, and it made no sense to antagonise him. Mack felt vulnerable, too; she knew that her feelings for Atticus— and her confidence in his ability to make breakthroughs that were beyond everyone else—could sometimes blind her to his methods. There were occasions when the ends justified the means, but it felt as if parading him in front of Murphy now would be asking for trouble. He had been predictably outraged, but she had won him over with a promise that she would share anything useful that they discovered with him.

Still, she had arrived at the house with a sense of trepidation, half expecting to find Atticus waiting for her. Thankfully—and for once—he had been good to his word.

Robbie and Francine had applied to a judge to obtain the warrant that they would need to search Summers's property. Robbie had made the application with Francine, taking contemporaneous notes to provide the audit trail in the event that the warrant was disputed at trial. They had visited the judge at home and reported that she was easily persuaded by their evidence and that the process had been over in less than fifteen minutes.

"Ladies and gents," Murphy said now, clapping his hands together to bring them to order. "We've had a development. DCI Jones will bring you up to speed, and then we're going to be busy."

Mack briefed them all so that they understood the background to the search and why a warrant was necessary. She explained first that she had questioned Harry Summers following the discovery that images of his ex-wife had been found at the end of one of the videos that had been sent to the *Journal*. She said that he had then been attacked here yesterday evening, leaving out the information that Atticus had been the one to interrupt the assault and likely saved his life. She had briefed Murphy at the nick earlier, and he was now aware that Atticus was responsible for the discovery. He had also made it plain that he was going to want to discuss Atticus's continuing involvement in the case—'despite his clear instructions'—with Beckton.

They were each assigned a part of the house to search, and set off.

Mack was paired with Francine, and the two of them set off through the gardens to the buildings at the rear. There were two barns that it was necessary to clear, and it looked as if both had been converted: the first was being used as accommodation, while the second looked to have been adapted to provide office space for Summers's business.

"What was Summers like when you spoke to him?" Francine asked her as they started to look through the first cottage.

"Polite."

"How did he explain his ex-wife being on that tape?"

"He didn't. He couldn't explain it."

"And you believed him?"

"I didn't think he was telling us everything."

"What did Atticus think?"

"The same."

They cleared the first cottage and moved into the second. The interior of the building had been divided into two separate sections: the first provided two large conference rooms, a kitchenette and staff break-out areas; the second was reserved for an extra-large office. There was a huge desk with two external monitors that looked as if they would have cost the same as reasonable family cars, and the walls were bedecked with sporting memorabilia, including signed shirts, a pair of football boots in a Perspex case, and a football, complete with the signatures of the 1966 England World Cup winning team, displayed on a pedestal. Other framed photographs showed Summers with the great and the good from the worlds of entertainment, sports and politics.

"Look at all this stuff," Francine said, pointing up to a pair of boxing gloves in a clear case, a plaque beneath them noting that they had been used by Mike Tyson in his defeat of Frank Bruno. "It must've cost a bomb."

"He's not short of money."

Mack tapped the keyboard to wake the two screens, but the computer to which they were attached was locked.

"Boss," Francine said, "look at this."

She was on the other side of the office, bent over a circular coffee table that held an open lever-arch file. Mack crossed over to look at it and saw that it held a thick stack of papers. The page at which it had been left open was a printout of a spreadsheet that looked as if it recorded a list of payments. The payments started in 2020, and the recipient of at least half of them was listed as KBank.

"KBank," Mack muttered.

"Kasikornbank," Francine said with a nod of confirmation. "It's Thai, isn't it?"

"The bank that Alfred Burns used in Bangkok. That's where Miller and York said they were making payments after he blackmailed them, isn't it? What are we saying? Burns was blackmailing Summers, too?"

Mack took out her phone and snapped a picture of the spreadsheet so that she could show it to Atticus. She was sure, now, that he was right in his suggestion that Summers was involved with Miller, York and Burns and that his ignorance about the videotape was feigned. The sense that they were closing in on a breakthrough that would throw the whole case open was now too tantalisingly close to ignore.

"Come on," she said, pointing to the door. "Let's see what they found in the chapel."

They reached the door when Mack heard a muffled noise from somewhere beneath the floor.

"Did you hear that?"

Francine had stopped, too. "I think so. What was it?"

"It sounded like a voice."

They both stood still and listened.

It was clear this time: a muffled shout, coming from somewhere beneath their feet.

Mack looked around. "There's got to be a cellar."

They each looked around the room, searching for a trapdoor or any other means of access that would allow them to get down to a basement. There was no obvious opening. Mack went back to the desk and heaved it to the side, hoping to see something beneath it, and finding nothing save freshly scuffed floorboards. She went to the sofa, pushing that away from the wall and finding nothing.

The noise came again.

"Shit," Francine said. "There's someone down there."

There was a cupboard on the other side of the room that was secured with a padlock. Mack found a heavy metal paperweight on the desk and took it over, raising it up and bringing it down as hard as she could so that the edge caught the shackle. The metal was dented but didn't break. She hit it again and again, and then, with the fourth blow, the shackle came away from the body and she could open the door.

Mack had been wrong: it wasn't a cupboard.

It was a set of stairs that led down into darkness.

She took out her phone and switched on the flashlight. The beam wasn't strong enough to cast light all the way to the bottom, but Mack thought she could make out another door.

"Stay here," she said. "I'm going to have a look."

She started down the stairs, taking them one tread at a time and listening carefully for anything that might suggest danger.

There came another muffled cry; it *was* a person. Mack was sure about that now.

She reached the foot of the stairs and turned to face another wooden door. This one was locked, but the key had been left in it. Mack turned it and, with the phone held up so that the light shone inside, pushed the door open. The room beyond was cramped, not much more than a cubby, and the flashlight could reach all four walls. Mack shone the light down and saw a girl. Her hands and feet had been secured with plastic ties, and a cloth had been stuffed into her mouth and then held in place with tape.

Mack's heart raced.

"Franny!" she yelled. "There's a kid down here."

The girl said something, but her words were rendered unintelligible by the cloth. Her eyes were wide with fear.

Mack knelt beside her. "It's all right. My name's Mack. I'm with the police. Let me get this off you."

She gently peeled away the edge of the tape and pulled it back, trying not to yank the strands of blonde hair that had been caught in the adhesive. She removed it all, dropped it to the side, and removed the cloth from the girl's mouth.

"Everything's going to be fine," Mack said. "You're safe now."

CHAPTER 80

Mack remembered seeing a pair of scissors on the desk upstairs and told Francine to bring them down. Mack used them to cut through the ties and then put her arm around the girl's waist and helped her to stand. She took her to the stairs and helped her to climb up to the ground floor.

Francine was waiting, and bit down on her lip as the two of them emerged. Mack could see the girl more clearly now: she couldn't have been much more than fifteen or sixteen and was dressed in a dirty T-shirt and tracksuit bottoms. Her feet were bare, and her wrists and ankles were chafed from where she had struggled against the plastic ties. She blinked her eyes against the light; Mack realised that she might have been kept down there, in the pitch dark, for hours.

"Franny," Mack said, "can you get her a drink of water?"

Mack took the girl to the sofa and indicated that she should sit down. She sat, too, turning her body so that they were almost facing each other. She reached out and took both of the girl's hands in hers.

"What's your name, love?"

Her voice was hoarse. "Maria."

"What's your surname?"

"Zankovetska."

"Where are you from?"

"Ukraine."

"All right. That's good. Do you speak English?"

"I learn it."

"I'm Detective Chief Inspector Jones, although you can call me Mack. My friend over there is Francine. She's a policewoman, too. A detective—like me. Like I said—you're safe now."

She shook her head, her eyes wide. "I'm not. What about them?"

"'Them'? Who do you mean?"

"The men. The men who…" She swallowed, unable to finish the sentence.

"You're *safe*," Mack said. "There are a lot of police officers here apart from us. They're outside now. A dozen—more than a dozen. And we know what happened."

The girl squeezed Mack's hands tight. "The *men*. They…" She choked up again.

"Do you mean Mr. Summers?"

She shook her head. "Don't know names."

"The men who kept you down there have been sorted out. I *promise*. You're safe, Maria. You don't need to worry about them, not anymore. We won't let *anything* else happen to you."

Francine brought over a plastic beaker of water and gave it to the girl. She gulped it down quickly, as if worried it would be taken away.

"Maria," Mack said, "I'm just going to leave you with Francine for a moment. Is that okay?"

The girl shook her head and tightened her grip on Mack's hand.

"Francine," Mack said, "come over and say hello."

Francine knelt in front of the girl and rested a hand on her knee. She smiled. "You can call me Franny. I'll stay with you, I promise."

"And I'll be back in a moment," Mack said. "I just need to tell the other officers that you're here."

CHAPTER 81

Mack left Francine in the cottage and hurried back to the rally point at the front of the house. Murphy was waiting there, along with a detective constable from his team and Robbie Best. All three of them turned as Mack crunched through the gravel and made her way over to them.

Best had a clear plastic evidence bag in one gloved hand. "Look at this, boss." He held the bag up so that Mack could see what was inside: a leather-bound book.

"What is it? Address book?"

"Don't know. It was in an office upstairs." He unsealed the bag and carefully removed the book. Mack put on a fresh pair of gloves and took it. "Turn to C."

Mack did as she was told. The page contained eight names, all ordered alphabetically.

The name at the top was David Campbell.

"Now go to H."

Mack flicked forwards, found the page behind the tab for H, and found another six names.

At the top, once more, was a name that she recognised immediately: Dominic Hartnett.

She didn't need to be told what to do next, and flipped forward another two tabs until she reached K. There were only three names listed, but Lucjusz Kajetan was the second of them.

Murphy was watching her. "Any idea what that might mean?"

Mack tried to order her thoughts. The investigation had multiplied over the course of the last day, and it was difficult to keep track of the angles that were shooting off in all directions. She needed to write down her thoughts before they ran away with her; she needed to speak to Atticus even more.

"DCI Jones?"

"I think this is a customer ledger. I think Summers has been running some sort of dirty video business, or whatever passes for that online."

"From the studio in the chapel?"

"Yes, and probably for years—at least twenty. I think he used to run it with Burns, York and Miller."

"And the man who attacked Summers last night?"

"It's Jack," she said. "I think he was one of the children they abused, most likely at Imber. He killed Miller and three customers and then went after Summers when he learned he was involved."

"And how did *you* work that out?"

"Sir?"

"How did you know to come out here and speak to him? Priest was involved again, wasn't he?"

"He was, sir, but with respect, I think that's going to have to wait."

"No, Detective Chief Inspector, I don't agree with that at all. I gave him explicit instructions to—"

"Please," Mack cut across him, "*please*, for once, just *shut up*."

"*Excuse* me?"

"Shut up and *listen*. We found a young girl in the cellar of one of the cottages. She was tied up, and the door was locked."

Murphy's mouth fell open. "Shit. Where? Which cottage?"

Mack pointed. "There. It's not really a cellar—not big enough. More of a crawlspace. I've no idea how long she's been down there."

"Is she okay?"

"No, she's not. She's traumatised. I don't even want to think about what she's been through. Francine Patterson is with her now, but we need someone from the child abuse investigation team down here pronto. We'll need a translator, too—she's a Ukrainian refugee, and I don't know how well she speaks English."

"I'll sort it out," Best said.

"She'll need to be checked out at the hospital, too."

"Has she said anything?" Murphy said.

"She's scared. I haven't been able to get much out of her yet."

Murphy muttered another curse. "What a mess. You really think this goes back to Imber?"

"I do. We know Burns was blackmailing Miller and York, and we know they killed him for it. I found bank statements in the cottage saying that Burns was blackmailing Summers, too. All four of them must have been working on the business together until they fell out."

"We need to speak to Jack," Murphy said.

"Have you heard from the hospital?"

"They've given him the all-clear on the concussion."

"When can we question him?"

"After lunch."

"And Summers?"

"They operated on him. He lost a lot of blood. They've intubated him. It's fifty-fifty."

Mack knew they needed to speak to him, but she couldn't stop thinking of the girl in the cellar. She wouldn't have been remotely upset if he never recovered.

The officers dispersed to carry on with the search. Mack wandered over to the trees that fringed the parking area and took out her phone. She saw she had three missed calls from Atticus and knew that he would be beside himself with agitation and anxiety.

She tapped his number, and he answered on the first ring.

"What's going on?"

She updated him on what had been found.

"What about Summers?"

"Not in a good way."

"And Jack?"

"He's been cleared for interview. It'll be later."

"I want to be there."

"Murphy won't go for that."

"Persuade him."

"How?"

"I'm a witness," he said.

"And he'll see that you're interviewed about that, but I can't see any chance that he'll let you be involved."

"I *need* to be there, Mack. No one else has the experience with him as I do."

"I'll speak to Murphy," she said, "but don't hold your breath."

CHAPTER 82

Even by recent standards, it had been a busy morning.

Mack had stayed at Summers's house until lunchtime. An officer from the child protection unit had arrived to help with Maria Zankovetska, but she had refused to leave the cottage unless Francine went with her. Mack was happy to approve that and watched as the girl was checked out by the paramedics before going with Franny to the hospital for a more thorough examination. They would need to take a statement from her, but it could wait. In the meantime, they had established that her parents had both been killed by shelling in Kramatorsk and that her older brother was in the military. Mack worried it wouldn't be easy to find a relative who could be responsible for her and that they would have to rely upon Social Services.

Robbie Best had investigated the man Jack had stabbed to death outside the chapel. He had a wallet in his pocket, and the name on his driving licence and credit cards was Paul Doyle. They had run a PNC check and had been rewarded with a litany of previous convictions: public order and violence offences, including assault and criminal damage. Best reported that Doyle had been a soldier and that he had been jailed for eighteen months after a court martial in Osnabrück found him guilty of mistreating Iraqi prisoners at an aid depot near Basra. Doyle had been dishonourably discharged upon his release and employed by Summers shortly thereafter. A check of his DNA matched a sample taken in Derek Burns's flat in Andover; Atticus had been attacked there and, although the incident had never been recorded because Atticus shouldn't have been in the flat at all, Mack knew they had found the man who had been responsible.

Mack went through the office to the custody suite where suspects were held until they were ready to be questioned and then to the interview room at the end of the corridor. Murphy was sitting at the table with papers and photographs spread out in front of him.

She cleared her throat, and he looked up. "DCI Jones."

"Afternoon, sir."

"So—Jack."

"It's probably Atticus you need to be talking to," she said. "He's the one who has been in contact with him."

"I'm not having him anywhere near this investigation. We still need to talk about what he was doing at the house last night." He waved a hand as if swatting away an irritation. "I understand Jack has been in a relationship with one of your officers."

"Yes, sir—DC Patterson. She knows him as Charlie."

"I can understand why Jack might want a relationship like that—it's an excellent way to get an idea of what we're thinking."

"Francine says she didn't tell him anything."

"Come on, it's human nature. She would have said *something*."

"Maybe," she allowed. "But I will not see this as an error on her part."

"What about Priest? Why's Jack interested in him?"

"Jack—*Charlie*—knew Atticus was the one pushing to investigate Alfred Burns, and he obviously had a reason to want him brought to justice. He told Atticus that he was involved with what Burns, Miller and York were doing. We didn't know what that meant then—being 'involved'—but we can make an educated guess now."

Murphy took notes. "Charlie called Priest after you'd arrested and released Miller and told Priest that there were others involved in what was going on—more than just Miller, Burns and York."

"Yes. And he said that he was involved. He must be one of the kids. You'll have to ask him."

Murphy took out his notebook and scribbled a line. Mack looked at him and wondered whether he was equipped for a conversation with Charlie. She knew that Atticus's own interactions with him had been cursory, but he had reported that the man seemed unusually smart.

"I want you to come in with me," Murphy said. "It's my interview, but we'll benefit from having your knowledge of him."

CHAPTER 83

Mack sat quietly with her hands in her lap as Charlie was brought into the interview room. His face was a mess: one eye had been closed shut, and there were cuts and bruises everywhere. He moved gingerly and winced as he lowered himself into the chair. There were two cameras in the room: one focused on all three of them from above and to the side, while the second focused only on Charlie. Murphy had a ring binder with him and he set it down on the table, opening it and taking out several pieces of paper: a map and crime scene photographs Mack recognised from Summers's house.

"Okay," Murphy said. "Let's get started. This interview is being both audio and visually recorded and may be given in evidence if your case is brought to trial. At the conclusion of this interview, you'll be supplied with a form explaining what will happen to the recordings and how you may gain access to them. We're in interview room 2 at Bourne Hill Police Station in Salisbury. The time now is one in the afternoon, and the date is 15 February. I am Chief Superintendent Lee Murphy of the Metropolitan Police, and I'm with Detective

Chief Inspector Mackenzie Jones of Wiltshire Police. I know that we don't have your full name yet—it would be helpful to have it."

"Thomas Chandler."

"Not Charlie?"

"No."

"Or Jack?"

"No. It's Tom. Call me Tom."

"I must caution you that you don't have to say anything, but that it may harm your defence if you don't mention when questioned something which you later rely on in court. Anything you do say may be given in evidence. The interview is being audio and visually recorded, as I said, so the content of our discussion will be played in court at any subsequent trial if it gets to that. Do you understand?"

"Absolutely."

"And I understand that you've decided you don't need a solicitor."

"I don't."

"I just need to be *very* clear about that."

"Don't want one."

"Thank you."

Murphy flicked through his notebook while Mack watched Tom. He was eerily calm.

"Okay, Tom. Shall we start with what happened at Hawthorne Manor earlier this morning?"

"There's much more to talk about than that."

"Is there?"

"We'll need hours if we're going to get through it all. What about what happened to Richard Miller?"

"You'll talk about that?"

"Happily. And the three men from this week. I'll give you everything, but—no offence—I need someone else to be here when I do."

"Who?"

"Atticus Priest. Is he here? In the station?"

"He's not. Mr. Priest isn't a police officer."

"I know that. But I'll need him to be here if you want me to talk. Go and get him, please."

"I can't do that. He's not a police officer. It's impossible."

Mack leaned forward, knowing exactly what Tom was about to say and impressed, in advance, with his astuteness.

"I have mental health issues, Mr. Murphy, plus I've been hit in the head. I'm worried that I won't understand what you're asking me. I want Atticus to be here as my appropriate adult."

Murphy didn't reply at once. Mack could see the tension in his body—he clenched his jaw, and his fists were bunched in his lap—and he looked down at the papers on the table before looking up into the camera, his face darkening with a scowl.

"Fine." He looked at his watch. "I'm going to stop the interview here, and we can pick it up again later. It's ten past one."

CHAPTER 84

Atticus took Bandit for a walk down by the river in Churchill Gardens. The water had risen with the amount of rain that had fallen over the last few weeks, and now it had spilled over the banks, flooding over the path and encroaching on the children's play area. A swan, baffled by its change in circumstances, paddled in the lake that had been used for football the last time Atticus had brought the dog here.

He had needed to get out of the office. Mack had told him that the interview with Jack—or Charlie, or whatever he was really called—was due to commence at one, and he knew that he would obsess about it if he didn't give himself a distraction. As he'd stood staring out his window earlier, Bandit had padded over to him and nudged his leg with his muzzle; Atticus would have liked to credit the dog with the anticipation to have known that he would need to get out, but he knew that Bandit just wanted to go and cock his leg. It didn't matter. Fresh air was an excellent idea, and Atticus didn't need persuading.

He picked up the stick that Bandit had collected and tossed it into the water, watching as the dog threw up clouds of spray as he pursued it. The exercise was good, but not enough of a distraction for him to be able to forget the interview. He knew that Mack had a good grasp of the case and had spent an hour last night making sure she had everything that she needed with regard to Atticus's interactions with Jack, but it could only ever be a substitute for him being present for the interview.

Bandit returned with the stick clenched between his teeth. Atticus leaned down to take it, but the dog hopped back and, before Atticus could retreat, shook himself dry.

Bandit dropped the stick and waited patiently for Atticus to pick it up.

"You've got to be kidding. After that?"

The dog looked up at him with pleading eyes.

Atticus picked up the stick and heaved it away again, sending it end over end until it landed with a splash in the middle of the lake. Bandit paused at the edge of the water, decided the stick was too precious to ignore, and then bounded after it again.

Atticus took out his phone to check the time just as it buzzed with an incoming call.

He didn't even check to see who it was. "Mack?"

"Where are you?"

He barely heard her. "How did it go? It can't have finished already?"

"Where are you? Please say you're in Salisbury."

"Churchill Gardens."

"Get to the nick."

"Why?"

"Because your friend said he'd tell us everything, but only on one condition—you need to be in the room, too."

Atticus couldn't stop chuckling.

"I know," Mack said. "Hilarious. Murphy finds it *particularly* funny."

"He's playing with us."

"I know he is," she said. "But can you get here—please?"

"Wouldn't miss it for the world." He put his fingers to his lips and whistled. "I'll be there as soon as I can."

Bandit trotted back to him. He had swapped his stick for an even larger one, dragging it through the water and then up the slope. Atticus clipped the lead to the dog's collar and gently worked the stick out of his mouth.

"Sorry, boy. They need me after all."

CHAPTER 85

Mack was waiting for him in reception when he arrived.

"Is Jack here?"

"His name isn't Jack. It's Thomas Chandler."

"And he's ready to confess?"

"Only if you're in the room as his appropriate adult. He's saying he's worried he might be concussed."

"Oh, that's delicious. I bet Murphy *loved* that."

"He's not thrilled."

"I should've been here from the start."

She took his arm. "Don't be a dick." She looked at him. "Okay? Can you do that?"

"I want answers as much as you do," he said. "We just need to let him talk—that's it."

"Good."

"I'll rub Murphy's nose in it afterwards."

"Atticus."

"Kidding," he said, although he wasn't. "Where is he? Interview room?"

She nodded.

"Better get up there, then."

* * *

Mack took Atticus to the interview suite. Murphy was waiting in the corridor and indicated that they should follow him into one of the rooms. It was empty.

"I just want to put it on record that this is absolutely *ridiculous*. I've been a policeman for twenty years, and this is the first time that I've had to deal with a shitshow like this."

"You can say what you like about him," Atticus said, "but he's smart. He knew he'd be caught eventually, and he's prepared for it. This will be part of his plan."

Murphy folded his arms. "I don't care. If he thinks he's going to be able to give me the runaround, then…" He paused, breathing in and then out again. "Then he's going to get a nasty surprise. I'm not going to pander to him."

"You *should*," Atticus said. "Humour him. He wants to confess."

"But only to you."

"He thinks we have a connection. It'll be worth going along with him if it means we can clear everything up. It might stick in the craw to play his game, but remember what's at stake."

Murphy bit down on his lip. Atticus could read him easily enough: he was balancing his distaste for him on one hand and the possibility that he might be able to help on the other. Murphy reminded Atticus of other young officers he had come across during his interactions with the Met. You only got to his rank if you had the right upbringing, or you were driven by ambition. Murphy was a working-class grafter who had outpaced his contemporaries with ruthlessness and hard work. He might not like Atticus, but if he thought he offered him an advantage in solving the case, then he would take it.

"There are going to be some ground rules if we're going to do this," he said.

"Fire away."

"One—you're there as his appropriate adult. You're *not* interviewing him."

"Understood."

"Two—anything he says stays confidential. You don't tell *anyone* outside of this building."

"I don't have any friends," Atticus said. "No one to tell."

Murphy's brows lowered. "Three—this is not a joke, just a laugh, or some sort of *riddle* that you've set yourself to solve. Four men have been murdered, and Chandler says he'll admit to killing all of them."

Atticus held his eye. "I know it's not a joke. Four girls were murdered, too, and I never felt we got to the bottom of that, including whether there are more. I think there *are* more, and I'd like to find them. You don't have to worry about me—I want the answers as much as you do."

"Good."

Mack looked at him. "Is there anything you want to say now?"

"About Jack? Don't underestimate him. He's clever. He's already manipulated you by making you bring me here. And he's played me for months. We should break at regular intervals so that we can compare notes. I might see something you've missed."

"We'll break every thirty minutes," Murphy said.

"And you're welcome."

"What?"

"You're welcome—I was enjoying a walk with the dog. I've changed my plans to help you out."

Murphy stared at him. "Thank you *very* much," he said. He straightened out his jacket and cleared his throat. "Right—shall we try again?"

CHAPTER 86

Atticus followed Murphy down the corridor and into the interview room. Chandler—it was difficult for Atticus to think of him as anything other than Jack—smiled at him as he took the empty seat next to him.

"Thank you for coming."

"No problem."

"I'm pleased you could. I want you to hear this."

Murphy resumed his seat on the other side of the table and ran through the preliminaries for the second time.

"We've been joined by Mr. Atticus Priest," he said once he had repeated the caution. "Mr. Chandler has indicated that he would like Mr. Priest to be here as his appropriate adult." He turned to Atticus. "Mr. Priest—you are not here to act simply as an observer. Your role here is to advise Mr. Chandler, facilitate communication and ensure that the interview is conducted fairly."

It was the rote wording for when an appropriate adult was requested by a suspect, but Atticus could only just hide his satisfaction that Murphy was forced to recite it.

Murphy turned to a fresh page in his notebook and picked up his pen. "You're still sure you don't want a lawyer, Tom?"

"I told you—I don't need one."

"And you know you're being investigated for very serious crimes?"

"I do. And I already explained why I don't want one—I want to confess."

"To what?"

"That I killed four men."

"Four?"

He nodded. "Summers and the other three."

"Mr. Summers isn't dead."

Chandler showed the first flicker of emotion. "Shame." He paused as his irritation became resignation. "Doesn't matter. I'll make sure you've got everything you need to prosecute him for what he's done. Not even the CPS will be able to mess it up." He looked over at Atticus. "Not like they did with Alf Burns—right?"

Atticus nodded but held his tongue.

Murphy drummed his fingers on the table. "Shall we start?"

"Who should I tell you about first?"

"Let's start with Mr. Miller."

"Can I go back a little before that? The context will be useful."

"Of course."

Chandler turned so that he was addressing Atticus. "It's relevant to you, actually. I know we've chatted, on and off, but I've never really given you all the story. I started paying attention to you when you first investigated Burns. You knew that he was guilty of a lot more than he was being charged with.

And you were frustrated when he went to Thailand. That's why I messaged you—*lots* in common." He paused, arranging his thoughts, and then started again. "Burns and York and Miller were working together. You know that, and you know York killed Burns when Burns blackmailed them. You know *some* of what the three of them were doing, but not all of it. I tried to tell you when we spoke, but I don't think you were really listening. I was disappointed about that. I thought you would've worked it all out."

"Why don't you tell us now," Murphy suggested.

"Miller and I had a long chat," Chandler said, still looking at Atticus. "Before I cut his throat. Burns and York met him when they were in the army, and they got into business together. They started in Northern Ireland with robberies and moved into prostitution. They made money and carried it on when they got back home. He said it was normal to start with—they were pimps, basically, found women who wanted extra cash and set them up in properties they owned where they could entertain clients. But they got requests for illegal stuff—kids—and saw there was more to be made. Miller said he and York didn't want to do it at first, but Burns showed how they could make a packet and told them about a way they could do it without being found out."

"How was that?"

"Burns was working at Grosvenor House youth club in the city. He'd find vulnerable kids, groom them, and then he'd bring them out to the old Manor House at Imber. He'd worked out there for the MOD after leaving the army. He had the keys for all the properties and knew it'd be quiet. There was never anyone there aside from when the army were doing exercises, and those were always posted in advance. They set up in this big old room and then brought the customers out there. They did videos, too. Made to order. They did that exclusively when they moved out of Imber. Less risk, I suppose."

"And that's when you got involved? You were one of the children?"

"Yes," he said. "They took me there more times than I can remember—I tried to black it out. I was perfect for them. I was fourteen, and I'd had a shitty childhood. My dad died when I was a baby, and I was just a pain in the arse for my mum. I was with her until I was three; then they put me in care when she got wasted one too many times; then I was back with her again when she cleaned up and promised it'd all be different." He chuckled bitterly. "It was never different, though. She'd make a promise and then break it, over and over again. I had a friend from school, and she took me to Grosvenor House. She said it'd be a laugh. She said one of the helpers there would give the kids booze and fags."

"Burns?" Murphy asked.

Chandler nodded. "I was easy pickings. He had a bottle of vodka in his office, and he'd pour me drinks. He had weed, too, and he'd roll joints, and we'd smoke them together out the back. He made me think I was his friend, and then, once he was sure I could be trusted, he offered me money if I'd do things for him." He swallowed and was silent for a moment. "They took me out there a lot. Alf used to pay me a tenner every time. He told me I could never tell anyone, and I said I wouldn't. He must've believed me because, well… I'm still here, aren't I? The ones they killed must've given them trouble."

Atticus was rapt. "These are the girls we dug up?"

"Yes."

"Did you know any of them?"

"There was one girl, one time—the customer paid extra for the two of us. We got talking afterwards, when they drove us back."

"Do you know her name?"

He shook his head. "Can't remember. She said she was going to tell the police what they were doing. I never saw her again after that. A man who said he was her dad turned up at the club and asked if anyone knew where she was. I didn't make the connection at the time, but it's obvious what happened—they saw she was trouble and got rid of her. Killed her and dumped her like the others."

"Do you think there were more?"

"Than the ones you found?" He chuckled bitterly. "I was involved with them more than twenty years ago, and they never stopped. You saw what Summers had set up in the chapel. What do *you* think? You could dig the whole bloody village up and you still wouldn't find them all."

"What happened to you?" Murphy said.

"The council sent me to a family in Warminster who actually cared about me. I never went back after that. I tried to forget about it, but I never could. I've had nightmares about what they did all my life. I can't form relationships. Can't trust anyone. I get nightmares, every night, always the same. They ruined my life."

"What about the men this week?" Murphy asked. "Campbell and the others. They were all customers?"

Chandler nodded.

"How did you find out about them?"

"You know Alf ran out of money and that he blackmailed Miller and York for cash. Miller told me that Alf had a hidden camera in Imber, and he filmed everyone who went there. Alf told them unless they paid him, he wouldn't have any choice but to go to the punters and squeeze it out of *them*. So they killed him and went looking for the tapes he said he had. Miller told me they broke into his place in Andover."

"They did," Atticus said, thinking about the night that Summers's goon had knocked him out.

"But they didn't find the tapes. Derek Burns had them."

"Derek was Alf's brother," Atticus explained for Murphy's benefit.

"They went after him," Chandler continued, "but he got the drop on them and ran. He wasn't as clever as Alf, though, and it didn't take me long to find him. He told me where he'd hidden the tapes, and I picked them up. You've seen what they're like—all labelled, nice and neat, plus Alf had a ledger, too, with details of the customers. It was easy to match one to the other. I had a plan—Burns and York and Miller first, then I'd work through the list. I killed them and sent their tapes to the papers so that everyone knows what they did."

"Why?" Murphy asked.

"Why?" He looked surprised at his question. "Why'd I send them to the papers? Seriously? Have you watched them? It's the only way men like them are ever going to be held to account."

CHAPTER 87

Chandler spoke with an expansiveness that suggested that he was intent on making good on his promise to confess. Murphy would guide him to a topic and then had nothing more to do than occasionally nudge him back on track. Chandler would answer the question and then expand upon it, offering the additional information with an ease that was enough to convince Atticus that he was being truthful.

"Let's move on to Miller," Murphy said. "What happened?"

"I waited outside his house after he was released," he said. "I got him into the back of his car and drove him away."

"He didn't struggle?"

"I came up behind him and hit him with a hammer. Knocked him out. I drove him out to Downton. There's a road up by the leisure centre—you can get right into the countryside. There's never anyone there, not at that time of night. We had a talk. He told me everything."

"And then?"

"I cut his throat, drove him back into town and left him outside Atticus's office."

Atticus looked over at Mack. It was obvious from her raised eyebrows that she shared his opinion that Chandler was telling the truth. He was giving them everything they would need to bring charges against him and for those charges to lead to a conviction.

"What about Campbell?" Murphy said. "Why him?"

"I know why," Atticus said. "He was one of the men who abused you."

Chandler nodded with a smile. "How'd you work that out?"

"You have an appendectomy scar," Atticus said, pointing down to Chandler's belly. "I noticed it when you were struggling with Summers's man. The boy on the tape with Campbell has the same scar."

He nodded. "That was a good spot. I looked through the videos to see if I could find myself, and I did—in the video with him. He went right to the top on my list. I didn't want to take the chance that I'd get caught if I went after someone else before him. He was easy to find. His name was on the video, and he's got a decent online footprint—that blog he's been doing, the photos he was taking at the cathedral—I just had to Google him, and there he was. I watched him for a week and scouted for the best place to do it. I went up the tower on one of the tours to get a look around." He looked to Atticus. "There are several ways to get to the stairs—you knew that?"

"I did."

"They've got cameras that'll show anyone going through the door they use to get the tourists up, but that's it—once you're on the stairs, there's nothing. They did this special tour last month where they'd take people to look in the attics that the masons and glaziers used. I could see that it was perfect—

there's a way through the attic above the nave onto the tower stairs."

"When did you take the tour?" Murphy asked him.

"A week or two before."

"Because we can check."

"Then check. Why would I lie about something like that?"

"What next?" Atticus pressed.

"Campbell had been taking photos at the same time every day for months. I knew he'd be up there. I climbed up the scaffolding early in the morning, used the attic to get to the tower and waited for him."

"What happened?"

"I drugged him."

"Why?" Murphy said.

"Takes the fight right out of you. I wanted to have a chat with him before I threw him over the side."

"With what?" Atticus asked.

"Ketamine."

"How'd you get hold of that?" Murphy asked.

"It's not that hard to find. You go down to the Friary and ask around."

"The Friary?" Murphy said.

"Not the best part of the city," Atticus explained.

Chandler made a fist and thumped it against his thigh. "I injected him in the leg, just enough to make him woozy—not enough to knock him out completely. I wanted him to know who I was and why I was there. And I wanted him to know that I was going to ruin his good name *after* I'd killed him."

"Did he remember you?"

"He said that he didn't. But he admitted he'd been at Imber. I got him over the side and waited in the attic until the evening—it wasn't hard to get away without anyone seeing me."

"Why do it there?" Murphy said.

"You mean why be so dramatic?"

Murphy nodded.

"He *wants* to be dramatic," Atticus answered for him. "He wanted everyone to know."

Chandler tapped his nose and then pointed at Atticus. "*Exactly*. I doubted I'd get through all the tapes, even if I was lucky. You would've caught me eventually. And, besides that, what about the men who'd been at Imber who Alf *didn't* record? Or all the ones who bought their videos afterwards? There must be dozens of customers I don't know about, but that doesn't mean I can't make them *think* I know. I can scare the shit out of them, scare them that they'll be next. The only way to do that was to make as much noise as possible. Think about it—you open a newspaper and you see a photograph of *that* room. It's distinctive. You'd remember you were there or that you watched something shot there. It's not the sort of thing you'd forget. I knew that if I could make it lurid enough, it'd get attention. And then, if I sent the tapes… every newspaper and TV station is going to run a story like that. It'll be all over social media. Facebook, Twitter, TikTok—and it all happened that way, just like I knew it would. You'd see that room on the TV and you'd shit yourself. Every time you hugged your kids, you'd think it might be the last time. Every time you kissed your wife, you'd be terrified that you'd be next."

Atticus nodded. "Is that why you included the Bible verses with the tapes? To be lurid?"

"That's exactly why."

Mack scribbled notes on the pad in front of her. Murphy took a moment to compose his thoughts.

Chandler shuffled in his seat. "Shall I move onto Kajetan?"

"Please," Murphy said.

"Harder to find. I asked around, and one of his homeless friends told me he was living in the sluice house on the river. I found him there, but it didn't go as smoothly as Campbell. I tried to inject him, but he saw me coming. There was a scuffle. He was pissed, and I was able to get him into the water. I held him down until he drowned."

"And Hartnett?"

Chandler took a sip from his water. "More challenging, obviously, because he was an MP. I followed him after he left Parliament, broke into his flat and killed him there."

"Ketamine?"

He nodded. "I messed up with him—used too much. He overdosed."

"What about Summers?"

"Miller told me about him when we had our chat. I don't know exactly when he got involved, but it was early on. As far as I can make out, they had a close call at Imber and decided that they needed to move. He'd just sold his company and bought the big house. He suggested they could use the chapel. They made it look like Imber and started again, but, this time, everything was online. They'd film scenes and distribute them to everyone who paid whatever it was they were asking. More professional all around—dark web servers so they couldn't be tracked and cryptocurrency for payment."

"That's strange," Atticus said.

Chandler cocked an eyebrow. "What is?"

"The timing. I only made the connection between Summers and the tapes yesterday. And you went out there yesterday evening."

He shrugged.

"You don't think it's unusual?" Atticus said.

"I think it's one of those things."

"Francine didn't know anything about it," Atticus said. "She couldn't have told you."

"Miller did—he told me."

"Really?"

"Yes, Atticus. *Really*. I'm telling you everything. Look— I'm *confessing*. Why would I lie about something like that?"

Atticus watched Chandler as he spoke and, for the first time that afternoon, he didn't believe him.

CHAPTER 88

Atticus tried to take the stick from Bandit's mouth so that he could throw it again, but the dog was having none of it.

"Give," Atticus said.

Bandit tightened his jaws around the stick and growled playfully, jerking his head from side to side as he tried to loosen Atticus's grip.

"*Give.*"

The dog bit down harder until the wood splintered, and then let go, tail wagging frantically as he waited for Atticus to throw it again.

"Ready." He drew back his arm. "Go!"

The stick looped end over end and landed in the water, with Bandit racing after it at full speed.

"He looks happy," Mack said.

"He'd be up for doing this all day if he could. He never gets tired."

She slipped her hand into his as they followed the path around the park. The interview with Chandler had lasted for seven hours, and when it finally finished, Atticus saw it was nearly eight o'clock. They had the right to hold him for twenty-four hours before they needed to charge him, apply for an extension, or let him go. Murphy sought—and received—an extension for a further forty-eight hours, but they all knew they wouldn't need it.

Chandler had been returned to the custody sergeant and taken to a cell where he would be held until the CPS had decided whether there was enough evidence to charge him. It would be automatic; Chandler had provided a full confession and been credible throughout, and there was no question as to his capacity. The suggestion of a concussion was an obvious excuse to have Atticus present to witness the denouement to the investigation. The police doctor had confirmed that he was fit to be interviewed, and there was nothing to show any kind of impairment. Chandler had given consent for his fingerprints and DNA to be taken and had not complained when he was told that he would be held until a charging decision had been made.

Chandler had stopped in the doorway as he was being taken out of the interview room, and turned back to look at Atticus. He said that he hoped Atticus would be at the trial. Atticus had said that he would, and Chandler nodded in satisfaction and smiled as he was led away.

It had been gloomy when Atticus had returned to the office, and Bandit had leapt on him as soon as he opened the door. Atticus had struggled to fit the excited dog into his harness, clipped on the lead, and met Mack in the park.

"What do you think?" she said.

"I'm still trying to work it all out."

"Murphy seemed pleased."

"Of course he is. He gets to go back to London and claim the credit for solving the case." They walked on, watching as Bandit splashed off in pursuit of a startled duck. He turned to her. "Did you believe him?"

"I think he told us the truth, or he's a world-class liar. What do you think?"

"Most of it is true. Fyfe should be able to find ketamine when he does the bloodwork for Campbell. It'll last thirty days in urine. Four months in hair. He might even find bruising from where the needle went in, assuming he's able to do his job properly."

"That might be unfair," she said. "His body was a mess."

"Maybe," Atticus conceded, "but it'll still be in his blood. It'll be the same for Hartnett, and there shouldn't be any problem in finding where the needle went in with him. No one else can say they know about that—the ketamine. It'll be powerful evidence to back the confession."

She stopped, his hand still in hers. "So what's bothering you?"

Atticus exhaled. "He was at Summers's house just *hours* after us. I didn't tell anyone about that. You say you didn't tell anyone—"

"I didn't."

"Not Francine?"

"No one, Atticus. I didn't tell anyone."

"So either he's been following me, or it's a coincidence. I don't think I was followed, and you know my view on coincidences. It's lazy thinking. It's what we say when we can't see the levers and pulleys that connect everything. So no—it's not that."

"What is it, then?"

"I don't know."

Bandit returned with the stick in his mouth.

Mack let go of Atticus's hand and knelt in front of the dog. "Drop."

Bandit stared at her, his tail wagging with frantic enthusiasm. Mack took hold of the stick and braced herself as Bandit tried to wrench it free.

"*Drop*," Atticus said.

Bandit opened his mouth to release the stick and sat expectantly as Mack straightened, drew her arm back, and then threw it as far as she could. The dog spun around and sprinted after it, spray flying as he leapt into the water again.

"What about the cigarette I found on the roof of the car park? Has it been tested yet?"

"I sent it to the lab," she said. "But you know what it's like—they're not always the fastest."

"Can you expedite it?"

"Why?"

"I just want it confirmed that it was him."

Mack turned to stand in front of Atticus, put her hands on his shoulders and reached up to kiss him.

"Can I say something?"

He nodded.

"You've been preoccupied with this for months. It's normal to have doubts, but they might be misplaced. Chandler gave us a credible explanation for what happened—I know you'll keep picking away at it, but it could be just as simple as he said."

"Maybe."

They walked on.

She took his hand again. "Do you want to come back to mine?"

"I would, but…"

"But you want to work on the case?"

"I want to check a couple of things." He glanced over at her. "Sorry. I could come over afterwards?"

"Come over when you like," she said, squeezing his hand again. "Just promise me you won't obsess over this. It's not good for you."

"I know. I'll try."

CHAPTER 89

Max Mason looked out of the Bentley as his chauffeur flicked the indicator and turned onto the long private drive through the forest that would finally bring him home. The drive rose gently between an avenue of lime and cherry trees, passed the ponds and then reached the circular driveway at the southern end of the house. Mason felt the same flutter of pride that he always felt when he returned home. This was his favourite view of all: the huge Jacobean manor, lights shining out from the windows to welcome him home, a shimmering jewel that nestled in the green forests and fields that protected it, and its owner, from the intrusions of the world beyond.

Steve rolled up to the front of the house and brought the Bentley to a stop. The evening was cold and wet, and Mason waited inside the car as Ross hurried out of the house with an umbrella. He opened the door and held the umbrella up so that Mason could shelter beneath it.

"Evening, sir. Good drive?"

"Traffic on the 303," he grumbled. "Crash near Andover."

Steve went to the rear of the car, took out Mason's small suitcase and followed Mason and Ross to the house.

"Do you need me tomorrow, sir?"

"No. I'm going to be here until the weekend."

Ross stepped aside so that Mason could make his way into the entrance hall. Mason took off his coat and the indigo-coloured suit jacket that he had been wearing at filming today. Ross took both, hanging up the coat in the cupboard beneath the stairs and keeping the jacket so that he could have it dry-cleaned.

"Shall I ask Claude to prepare a light dinner for you?"

"I'm tired. I'm going to bed."

Mason went up to the first-floor landing and walked through to his bedroom. A fresh set of pyjamas had been laid out for him, but he decided to take a quick shower to warm up before changing into them. He undressed, stood in front of the gilt mirror and examined his reflection. He had put his body through all manner of surgical interventions through the years: blepharoplasty on his eyelids, a rhytidectomy to tighten the skin on his forehead, dermal fillers to add fullness to his cheeks and lips. He had Botox injections every three months, and as he prodded his forehead, he could see that he might have to increase the frequency. His body was harder to maintain. His skin was withered and wrinkled, and the flesh beneath his arms hung loose. His hands were gnarled, the skin thin and translucent. That didn't matter so much as his face, though. He could cover everything else up beneath his bright suits.

He stood under the warm water and scrubbed shampoo through his hair. His mind wandered. He had watched the news on his phone while Steve had driven him home. There had been a second murder in Salisbury, and the *Journal* had been sent a video that, once again, featured the red-lit room that looked so similar to the one that he remembered from twenty years ago.

He thought of how Summers had been adamant that there was no tape with him on it, but how could he be sure? What else could Summers have said? Mason had fretted at it all day and had reached the vaguely reassuring conclusion that, if there *was* evidence that he had been there, then it would have been released first given his fame. Whoever was responsible for the murders was looking for as much publicity as possible; a video showing Mason's involvement would have made for a huge story, and the fact that there had been nothing about him was encouraging.

Encouraging, but not a reason for complacency. He would ask Ross about looking into additional security until the police had caught whoever was behind the murders.

He changed into his pyjamas, tracing his finger over the monogram of his initials on the breast. He was tired, and he needed to get to sleep. A full-time security guard at the house. Another camera. Floodlights in the gardens. He would mention it to Ross at breakfast tomorrow.

PART 6

Saturday

CHAPTER 90

Mason woke with a start.

He sat up and blinked until his eyes had adjusted to the darkness, the gloom lightened only by the faint silver moonlight that shone through curtains he had forgotten to close. His breathing was rapid, and he closed his eyes until he was able to slow it down. He opened his eyes again and tried to work out what had woken him. The house was quiet, with just the ticking of the grandfather clock in the hall and a regular dripping from the tap in his en suite; he had asked Ross to see that it was fixed and was annoyed that it hadn't been done.

There it was again: the creaking of a floorboard.

"Ross?" he called out.

He swung his legs out of bed and padded across the thick rug to the hook where his dressing gown was hung. He put it on, slid his feet into his slippers and went to the door. He opened it and stepped out into the corridor. The curtains were drawn, and it was too dark to see anything.

"Ross?"

THE RED ROOM

He took a step, and the infrared motion detector lit up, bathing the corridor with a flash of soft blue light. He stopped, and the light flicked off.

He heard the creak again.

"Ross? Is that you?"

The blue light flicked on again and, this time, it wasn't because of him.

CHAPTER 91

Atticus worked until five and then tried to sleep. He managed a couple of hours before he woke, and, as he opened his eyes, his mind was still buzzing with the same doubts and questions that he had been unable to shut out when he had lain down. He got out of bed, washed his face with cold water and dressed. Bandit opened a single eye as he stepped around the bed and then buried his head beneath the duvet and went back to sleep. Atticus envied him his peace of mind.

He went into the other room, cleared the pages of notes from his desk and dumped them on the sofa. He had tried to work in a more organised fashion, but it hadn't worked. The case was finished now, and, thinking of what his cleaner would say when she visited, he tried to put it back into the professional state that she had left it in.

He picked up a textbook on evidence and put it back on the shelf, then binned the two cans of Diet Coke and the paper bag that had held the cheese straws that had sufficed as his dinner. He used his hands to corral the crumbs of the cheese straws onto one of the sheets of paper, then binned that and the others.

THE RED ROOM

He was left with the report that he had written for Nina Parsons on Robin Wintringham. He had forgotten all about that; he had emailed her the report with his invoice, but, at least as far as he could remember, she hadn't acknowledged receipt or paid. He tossed the report into the bin and tapped the keyboard to wake his computer. He navigated to his email and saw, with a sinking feeling, that his failure to attend to his inbox in a prompt manner had seen more than a hundred unanswered messages pile up.

He confirmed that Nina hadn't replied and then checked to see if the email had bounced; it hadn't.

He dialled her number, but the call went straight to voicemail. He rang off rather than leaving a message.

He opened the first email that she had sent him. There was nothing remotely unusual about it: it had been sent from a nondescript Gmail account—ninaparsons2918—with a signature strip at the bottom that had a link to her Facebook and Instagram.

He drummed his fingers on the desk and chewed his lip. Something was wrong. He took his mouse, maximised the email from Nina and clicked on the icon with three dots at the top of the screen, selecting the option to show the original format of the message. The screen broke down the email into its constituent parts—message ID, creation date, sending account and receiving account, SPF and DKIM data—and then, in a large window below, a plaintext version of the full header. Atticus opened the search box and typed in 'received,' looking for the numeric IP address that would give him the geographical location from which the email had been sent.

He found it: 84.66.44.160.

He opened an IP lookup tool, pasted in the IP address and waited for the results: the email had been sent from Boston Tea Party, the large café in the middle of the city.

That struck him as odd. Nina *might* have composed and sent the email while she was out and about, but surely it was more likely to have been something that she would have done at home. Emailing a private investigator about a sensitive matter was not something that one would do on a whim over coffee and cake.

And, in his experience, people tended to use public Wi-Fi when they wanted to prevent someone from finding their real address.

Why would Nina have done something like that?

He pushed his chair away from his desk, stood up and grabbed his jacket. Bandit looked up in hope that he was about to get a walk.

"When I get back," Atticus said, scratching the dog behind the ears. "There's someone I have to see first."

CHAPTER 92

Atticus got into his car and drove to the address in Laverstock that belonged to Robin Wintringham. He recalled the details of the file and knew that the conversation that he was going to have to have might be difficult. That wasn't what was making him uneasy; he knew it was necessary. Rather, it was what he suspected he might discover.

His phone rang: it was Mack.

He answered it. "Hi."

"Hello, stranger," she said. "Are you okay?"

"I'm fine. Why?"

"You were going to come over last night."

He winced. He'd forgotten. "I fell asleep at my desk. By the time I woke up, it was too late. Sorry."

"It's all right," she said, then paused. "Are you sure you're okay?"

"Absolutely."

"Where are you?"

"Taking the dog out for a walk."

The lie came easily enough. He wanted to tell her his fears and what they might mean, but it would have to wait.

He knew she would be busy with Chandler, and the theory he couldn't get out of his head was based on nothing more than guesses and conjecture. Mack would tell him to stop, and he wasn't about to do that. He had to follow his thoughts to their conclusion for good or ill.

"I just thought you'd want to know that the CPS has agreed that there's enough evidence to charge Chandler. We'll have him in front of the magistrates this afternoon."

"He still says he's going to plead guilty?"

"Yes."

"What time's the hearing?"

"Two. Why? Want to come?"

"Do you think that'd be okay?"

"Probably. Murphy's in a good mood. He's been crowing about solving this all morning."

"I'll see you there, then."

"One other thing," she said. "We heard from the hospital this morning about Summers. He took a turn for the worse last night."

"How bad?"

"Bad as in they don't think he's going to make it."

"Shit. I wanted to speak to him."

"Doesn't look as if that's going to happen."

"What about the DNA test on the cigarette?"

"Nothing yet," she said. "I'll chase the lab."

Atticus arrived at the address. He glanced over at the house as he went by, then turned around and found a space to park.

"Where are you?"

"Figsbury Ring," Atticus said. "Bandit's excited. I'd better go."

"I'll speak to you later," she said, and rang off.

CHAPTER 93

Atticus climbed the hill to the house, walked up to the door and pressed the doorbell. He heard the ring from somewhere inside, and then saw the shape of a person coming to the door through the frosted-glass panel.

The door was opened by Laura Wintringham. "Hello?"

"Hello. Sorry to disturb you."

"Can I help you?"

"Could I have a word with your husband?"

"He's with the kids—I'm sorry, who are you?"

"I'm a private investigator."

She frowned in confusion and then concern. "Why do you want to speak to my husband?"

"It's probably best if I speak to him about that. I'm sorry to be so vague. It's nothing to be concerned about."

Robin Wintringham appeared in the hallway behind his wife. He had a child's rucksack in his hand. "Who is it?"

"Says he's a private investigator, and he wants to talk to you."

"I'm sorry—*what?*"

"It won't take long, Mr. Wintringham."

"Go on, then."

"Might be better if we spoke in private."

"Say whatever you've come to say—the kids are just eating their breakfast, and then I've got to get them to their clubs. You'll have to be quick."

Atticus had done his best to be discreet; Wintringham was about to be put in a difficult position that he could have been spared if he had only taken the hint.

"This is a little delicate, but… never mind. Do you know a woman called Nina Parsons?"

He frowned. "Who? No, I don't think so."

"She's about thirty years old, about the same height as your wife, slender, dark brown hair and brown eyes."

"I don't know anyone like that."

Laura folded her arms. "Why are you asking?" She turned to her husband. "Robin—why is he asking?"

"A woman with that name hired me because she said that your husband was in a relationship with her. She wanted me to carry out what we'd call a background check. She wanted me to confirm that everything he'd told her was true."

Atticus watched Wintringham for a reaction. An accusation like that would elicit confusion in the innocent as a first response; on the other hand, someone with something to hide might react with indignation or an overcompensation that would signal that there was truth to what had been said. Wintringham's mouth fell open, and his brow creased with a perplexed frown before—perhaps remembering that his wife was standing next to him—the angry denunciation followed.

"That's bullshit."

His wife was watching for his reaction, too, and Atticus guessed that there had been something in their relationship in the past that gave her grounds to think that a transgression was possible.

Wintringham noticed the stiffening of her posture and made a quarter-turn so that he was facing her. "It's bullshit. *Complete* bullshit."

"For what it's worth," Atticus said, "I believe you. I've been concerned that my client was lying to me, and now I'm sure of it."

"*Thank* you," Wintringham said with a mixture of sarcasm and relief.

His wife wasn't quite ready to let it go, though. "That doesn't make any sense. Why would someone ask you to investigate something that wasn't true?"

"That's something I need to work out. I'm sorry for bothering you."

He turned and walked down the middle of the road back to his car, keen to put some distance between himself and the domestic spat that he had just caused. He thought of what had happened over the last week and of what had happened at Harry Summers's house, and how Chandler had been there just hours after Atticus and Mack.

Mack's suggestion was wrong: he *hadn't* been followed.

It was something else.

He was still in the road when a car approached and had to stop abruptly. The driver pressed the horn. Atticus was hardly aware of it. A realisation struck him like a hammer. He put his hands to his head and, with an incredulity that grew as he made one connection and then another and then the next, he started to trot and then run back to the car.

He needed to get back to the office.

CHAPTER 94

Atticus double-parked, sprinted to the door, fumbled his key into the lock and opened it, taking the stairs two at a time. He was out of breath when he reached the door to the office and stopped himself just in time from opening up and going inside. He went to the bathroom, ran the cold tap and rolled up his sleeves. He held his right wrist under the flow and concentrated on how it felt, closing his eyes and willing his pulse to slacken. He switched wrists, opened his eyes and stared at his reflection in the dirty mirror. His eyes were wide, and there was a sheen of sweat on his skin. He cupped his hands, filled them with water and then dunked his face. He did it again, wiped himself dry and took another moment until his breathing was under control.

He couldn't be agitated.

He needed to be himself.

To be normal.

Atticus took another deep breath, and, finally calm, he went to the door and opened it. Bandit bounded out and leapt up at him, planting his front legs against his hips so that his head was in range for a scratch. Atticus obliged him and looked around; the office felt different—less trustworthy—and it made him feel uncomfortable.

"Okay, boy. Let's get you some lunch."

Atticus went into the hallway again, opened a can of wet food and scooped it into the dog's empty bowl. He took it back, set it down and looked around again.

He knew he was right, but he didn't know where to start.

He took out his phone, connected it to the Bluetooth speaker, opened Nick Cave's *Push the Sky Away* and pressed play. 'Jubilee Street' started, and he turned it up enough so that it would—he hoped—mask the sound of what he had to do.

He reached up for the spotlights that were fitted to a track on the ceiling, unscrewed the first, examined it in minute detail, then set it aside and unscrewed the second. There were four on the first track and another four on the second. He removed them all, one by one, and found nothing. He screwed them back into the holders, stood with his hands on his hips and looked around the room.

They've made a fool of me.

The song picked up pace, matching Atticus's heartbeat. He stared left and right and then moved the sofa in the bay window out of the way. He knelt and examined the router and cable that connected it to the socket. There was nothing out of place.

Where is it?

He pushed the sofa back into place and went to the large set of drawers that he used to store his papers. The speaker was on top of it, flanked by two large wooden lamps.

It's here. I know it's here.

Atticus slid his fingers between the back of the drawers and the wall and pulled, moving it out enough to get to the dual socket. The lamps and the speaker were connected to a power strip, leaving the second socket free.

But it wasn't.

A USB plug had been pushed into it. It looked just like a standard Apple product: white, with a port at the bottom into which a charging cable could be inserted. It looked normal and innocuous and might have escaped detection save for the fact that Atticus knew that he was looking for something like this, and he knew the device had not been there last week.

The song raced to its crescendo.

Atticus stared at the plug for a long minute, wondering what he should do. He reached down for it and then pulled his hand back again; he decided that he would speak to Mack and then changed his mind. He knew his options, and that one of them—regardless of however long he thought about it—would always be the course that he chose.

He set his phone down on the desk in front of him and switched off the music. He found a piece of paper and a pen and noted down the things that he wanted to say. He ran through them, point by point, until he was confident that he could deliver the message convincingly.

He drew in a breath, exhaled, and started to speak.

CHAPTER 95

Atticus walked across town to the magistrates' court. A jumble of thoughts cluttered his mind, and he tried listening to music as a distraction; it didn't work. He took the earbuds out, put them back into their case and dropped them into his pocket. He thought about what he had discovered: the client who had disappeared into thin air and the device that looked like a plug but almost certainly wasn't.

He thought about the gamble that he had taken and wondered if it had any chance of paying off.

He turned the corner on Wilton Road and saw that the press had arrived at the court before him. Newspaper and TV journalists jostled for the best position, armed with microphones, cameras, and notebooks. The atmosphere was charged with excitement. He saw Mack speaking to a reporter beneath the stencilled letters on the wall that read SALISBURY LAW COURTS. She noticed him, held up a hand to indicate that he should wait, finished the conversation and came over to him.

"Everything okay?" he asked.

"It's bedlam," she said, indicating the crowd.

"Feels like we've been here before," he said. He gestured to the reporter. "What did he want?"

"The usual—what could I tell him about Chandler, did I think he did it, why didn't we catch him more quickly than we did?"

Mack led the way through the main door. They queued to go through security, emptying their pockets into plastic trays and then passing through the scanner.

"Should all be straightforward," Mack said. "He says he'll plead guilty. The case will be allocated to the Crown Court, and that'll be that. In and out."

Atticus looked up at the screen on the wall and saw that *Crown v Chandler* was being heard in court number two. Atticus slid between two reporters and followed Mack to the door that led into the area of the court that was reserved for the prosecution.

"Anything else about Summers?" he asked her.

"Nothing more than I told you this morning," she said. "They don't think he's got long. He's been in a coma ever since they brought him in. They gave him a transfusion, but the damage was already done. His heart wouldn't have been able to pump the blood he had left. His organs would've shut down, and he's probably got brain damage. That's what they said."

"No one's told Chandler?"

"Not as far as I know." She nodded to the corridor beyond the door. "You'd better stay here. Let's not push it."

Atticus would have protested, but, before he could speak, he was interrupted by Murphy. He pushed the door open, saw

Mack and Atticus and gave a nod that was somewhere between satisfaction and irritation.

"Good," he said. "You're here."

"What's up?" Mack asked him.

"Chandler's being difficult again." Murphy pointed a finger at Atticus. "He wants to have a word with you before he goes up and pleads. I've no idea why—he wouldn't say. I'd have no trouble sending a couple of brawny lads down there to drag him up, but it'll probably be a lot less of a headache if you just go and see what he wants."

CHAPTER 96

The cells were in the building's basement. Murphy led Atticus down the stairs and along a corridor with four cells, two to the right and two to the left. There were no doors, just wide spaces blocked by bars painted a bright shade of blue. Blue-rimmed white squares had been painted on the floor with markings that identified them as 'search areas.' There were cameras on the walls, and a panic strip had been fitted at waist height. The building in Salisbury was more modern than many that Atticus had visited, and, as a result, the cells were in better condition. That didn't mean that they were pristine; the walls of all of them had been marked with graffiti by the prisoners who had been held here.

"Where is he?"

"Last on the right," Murphy said. "There's five minutes before they take him up. I'll be at the end of the corridor."

Atticus walked along the corridor. The cell had a bench that had been fitted to two walls in the shape of an L. There was a window just beneath the ceiling, through which an oblong of dim light fell across the vinyl floor. Chandler was sitting on the bench. His back was against the wall, his knees were drawn up, and his chin rested on them. He had always looked confident before, but now, at the start of a chute that would deposit him in the bowels of the legal justice system for the rest of his life, he looked vulnerable and alone.

Atticus cleared his throat.

He looked up. "You came."

"You wanted to see me?"

"I thought this might be the last chance we get to speak before the trial."

"Probably," Atticus said. "How are you?"

He shrugged. "Just wrapping my head around it. I knew it'd come, eventually—getting caught—but that doesn't make it any easier to deal with."

"You got a lawyer?"

"Scrape the barrel for a brief on Legal Aid? No thanks."

"You know what they say about a man who is his own lawyer?"

"He has a fool for a client. It's fine—I don't need one."

"You're pleading guilty?"

He got up and nodded. "I'm not interested in fighting. You were right—it's over. I've done as much as I could. I'd like to have done more, but it is what it is."

He came over to the bars, and Atticus took a corresponding step back.

"I'm glad you're here," Chandler said. "It's good to have a proper talk. I'm sorry about all the deception from before."

The vulnerability disappeared as he spoke, and now Chandler's voice had the confidence that was at odds with what might have been expected from him, given his circumstances.

He had been insouciant about his legal situation when they had interviewed him yesterday, and the indifference had continued despite his imminent first appearance before the bench. Atticus had noted it before, and it was even more obvious now; Chandler had expected to be caught and had approached the prospect without concern.

"Can I ask you a couple of questions?" Atticus asked.

"If I can ask you one after."

"Okay."

"Go on," Chandler said. "What do you want to know?"

Atticus paused, focusing on the graffiti that had been scratched into the wall. "I'm curious about the videos."

"What about them?"

"The first one—Campbell. How did you get that to the *Journal*?"

"I dropped it off."

"When?"

"I don't know exactly."

"Campbell was killed in the morning."

"You know he was."

"But you stayed in the attic until the evening."

"And?"

"There's a camera outside the office. No one put anything through the letterbox from lunchtime onwards. But you were in the attic until the evening."

"Yes."

"How did you do it?"

"I went over there as soon as I got out of the cathedral."

"But you didn't—the camera doesn't see you."

"I don't know what you want me to say."

THE RED ROOM

Atticus paid attention to his body language. Chandler hardly blinked, a sign that he was struggling with a heavy cognitive load and needed to give careful thought to everything he was saying. He was staring at Atticus, as if to reassure himself that his explanation had had the desired effect.

"Okay," Atticus said. "The night when you attacked Summers—how did you get out there?"

He frowned. "Why is that important?"

"It's twelve miles from Salisbury."

"I know. What's your point?"

"Did you drive?"

Chandler didn't answer.

"That's rhetorical. I know you didn't—I've been out there, Thomas. I've been up and down the roads, and, when I found nothing, I walked every single track I could find. There's nothing there. No car, no motorbike, not even a bicycle. Nothing."

"I walked."

"Really? Twelve miles."

"Prove I didn't."

Atticus took a moment. Chandler was becoming uncomfortable, and he wondered whether he might work the carapace loose a little if he kept prodding. His assurance—so uncanny in his interviews—looked as if it might be failing.

"Is that it?" he asked.

"What about the video that was sent to the *Sun*. Was that you?"

"Yes."

"Why send it?"

"Because the story wasn't spreading quickly enough. I decided that using the *Journal* was a mistake."

"Why didn't you go straight to the *Sun* from the start?"

He closed his eyes and breathed out. "I didn't think I'd need to. The *Journal* did a good job with Imber, and I knew the story would get picked up if they wrote it first. I didn't really think much beyond that."

Atticus kept watching and noticed the way he closed his eyes and how the timing of his sentences was slightly off; he was trying to give the impression that he was frustrated, but it was unconvincing.

"How did you send it?"

"Email."

"But you'd sent the tape to the *Journal*."

"Not before I digitised it. I needed to keep a copy for myself."

His eyes darted left to right, and Atticus was left with the impression that, for the first time, he wasn't sure what to say. He was confident that Chandler had told the truth in his confession, but now he wondered what he had left out.

"Is that it?" Chandler said.

"I still don't understand why you felt you had to do this all yourself," Atticus said. "You knew you'd be caught. And you knew what the cost would be when you were caught. Your life—you've thrown it away."

He laughed bitterly. "What life? They took it from me."

"You could have sent the tapes to the police. You could've sent them to me."

"That would never have led to anything. Men like Summers and Miller and Hartnett have resources. They have money, or influence, or both. They get to act with impunity. What happened to them is *justice*. They got what they deserved."

"Justice or vengeance?"

"Are we doing this again? Spare me the semantics."

"I'd rather make a case and then let a judge and jury decide."

"Your faith in the system is quaint."

"I know it's not perfect."

"That's an understatement. It failed you before."

"With Burns? Yes. You're right—it did. But it doesn't mean that I've given up on it."

Chandler chuckled. "Hypocrite. You broke into Burns's flat. And what about last night? Trespassing on Summers's property. You've never followed the rules, and you've always been frustrated with those who do—that's why you left the police."

"I left the police because—"

"—because you did drugs?" Chandler shook his head. "No, you didn't. You'd given up on your career by then. You'd seen enough, so you gave them an excuse to get rid of you."

Atticus was unnerved. It was unusual for him to find someone he considered his equal. He was the one who was able to get into the heads of others, yet, resting against the bars of his cell with an enigmatic smile playing on his lips, here was Chandler, getting into *his* head.

"Think about the men who were running their dirty little scheme," Chandler said. "Maybe Burns *would've* been caught and jailed, but he was a nobody—he cheated justice for years, and *he* didn't have *their* resources." He waved a hand dismissively. "York would never have been caught were it not for what happened with his daughter. But Miller? A decorated soldier and serving MP? *No.*" He rapped his knuckles against the bar. "He would've been given a slap on the wrist.

And Summers? A *general*? No. *Never*." He hit the bars again. "Men like them never answer for their crimes. You know it as well as I do. And you know there are others. All those customers I'll never be able to punish. This week will have put the fear of God into them, but once they see I've been caught and put away, they'll relax. And men like that, with those perversions. Do you think they'll just stop?" He shook his head. "No. They won't stop. Other kids will suffer. I don't blame you for what you did, but me being in here will let those men—and there are *dozens* of them—it'll let them get right back to what they were doing as if nothing happened."

"So give me the videos. Tell me where they are, and let me figure it out."

"How are you going to do that?"

"DCI Jones will go after them."

"She's one officer. One *woman*—not that I mean to sound chauvinistic, but we both know her face doesn't fit. It's an Old Boys' Club, and she'll always be on the outside looking in. Look at Murphy—he's not even from Wiltshire and they parachute him in to save the day. How long do you think it'd take for someone above her who's either implicated or bought to shut her down?"

"'Implicated'?"

"You don't think the police are involved? Paid to turn a blind eye?"

"Can you prove that?"

"No, they're too careful. But I know."

"There are other ways you could go after them," Atticus pressed. "The tapes could still be used. Give them to a reporter.

It'd be a scandal. And the police would *have* to investigate then."

"I don't share your optimism. My way was best. You won't be able to persuade me otherwise."

Murphy cleared his throat at the end of the corridor. "Time's up."

"You said I could ask you a question," Chandler said.

"Go on."

"Why were you so interested in Burns?"

"Because I knew he was guilty, and I didn't like the idea of him being out on the streets."

"No. It was more than that. You were obsessed. I mean, it was why I was drawn to you in the first place, but then I started wondering why."

Atticus shuffled. "I wasn't any more interested in him than with any other case."

The roles had been reversed: before, Atticus had watched Chandler for evidence of mistruth; now Chandler was looking at him.

Chandler shook his head. "No. *No.* I don't believe you."

"There's nothing I can do about that."

Chandler stared at him. "Did you know him from before?"

Atticus felt a moment of nausea. "No."

"Did you go to Grosvenor House?"

Atticus shook his head. "No."

"Are you sure?"

"Completely sure. I didn't go to Grosvenor House."

Atticus was distracted and didn't notice Chandler sliding his arm through the gap in the bars. He reached out and grabbed Atticus by the wrist.

"Who was it then? Your dad? An uncle? A friend of the family."

Atticus tried to free himself, but Chandler held on with a firm grip.

Murphy hurried over. "Hey!"

"A little fiddling late at night. What did they say? It'll be a secret—just them and you?"

Atticus tried to shake his arm loose, but Chandler held on.

"I told you before—you and I are alike. More alike than you're prepared to admit."

He let go.

Atticus stepped back.

"Are you okay?" Murphy said.

Atticus felt blood in his cheeks and the hammering of his heart.

"Atticus?"

"I'm fine."

Chandler held onto the bars. "You can't kid a kidder. Come and see me after the trial. You can tell me all about it."

"I don't think so."

Atticus turned on his heel and hurried back to the stairs.

CHAPTER 97

Atticus went to the bathroom and took a moment to compose himself again. He ran the cold tap, cupped his hands and filled them, lowering his head so that he could dunk his face in the water. It ran between his fingers, so he did it again, clenching his fists and using his knuckles to rub his eyes. The nausea had passed, but his heart was pumping hard, and he took deep breaths—in and *hold* and out, in and *hold* and out—until it stopped racing.

He had been very close to losing it; it would have been bad enough if it were just Chandler, but Murphy had been there, too. What if Murphy said something to Mack? Atticus would have to think of a response, something that he could say—something glib and throwaway, something she would expect of him—so that he was able to change the subject.

He looked up into the mirror and stared into his own eyes. He had panicked. *Panicked*. Chandler had caught him by surprise, and he had only just been able to maintain his equanimity. Atticus already knew that Chandler was perceptive, but his acuity—his instincts—looked as if they might be the match of his own. Atticus found that he was relieved he was in the basement cell and not on the street. It was unheard of for him to be daunted by someone else, yet Chandler had managed it with just one facile observation.

And that moment of intuition had brought a torrent of memories back. It had been all he could manage to staunch the flow. He had managed it—just—but now he found himself with doubt to contend with, too.

Atticus closed his eyes again. He took another deep breath, held it, and exhaled.

There was an irritated knock on the door.

"Wait!"

Atticus yanked a paper towel from the dispenser and patted his face dry. He balled up the towel, dropped it in the bin and—with a final look at his reflection—he unlocked the door and went outside.

Murphy was waiting with his arms crossed.

"You took your time. What were you *doing* in there?"

"I felt a bit sick."

"You don't look great."

"I think I'm coming down with something."

It was the closest that the two of them had come to a normal conversation, and it was obvious Murphy felt awkward. "I'll see you inside."

Atticus stepped aside, then turned back before Murphy had closed the door. "Can I ask you a question?"

"I need a piss—be quick."

"Does Chandler smoke?"

He looked puzzled. "What?"

THE RED ROOM

"He didn't ask for a cigarette break during the interview when I was there. What about afterwards?"

"No," Murphy said. "Not as far as I know. Why?"

"It's nothing," Atticus said.

Atticus turned away.

"Priest? Why's that relevant?"

Atticus didn't answer and made his way down the corridor before Murphy could ask him anything else.

CHAPTER 98

The courtroom was full. Atticus came inside and stepped carefully along the row to the seat that Mack had reserved for him. He sat down.

"How was he?" she asked.

"No change. Full of himself."

"And still pleading guilty?"

"He says he is."

"So what did he want with you?"

"I told you—he thinks we have a common cause. A connection."

"You know you don't have to humour him."

"It's worth the aggravation if it means locking him up is easier."

"Not if he gets under your skin."

"That'll be the last time. They can send guards down with rubber truncheons if he kicks up a fuss again. I'm finished with him."

Atticus looked dead ahead. He saw Murphy, another officer from his team and Robbie Best. The small public gallery was taken up by members of the press, their notepads ready. The usher, a large bald man whom Atticus recalled from the Mallender proceedings, looked more anxious than he remembered. The atmosphere was tense and expectant.

He knew that Mack was looking at him, but he didn't want to catch her eye. He needed to repair the façade that Chandler had nearly knocked down.

She reached for his hand. "Are you sure you're okay?"

"I'm fine."

"You look like you've seen a ghost."

He could feel a bead of sweat rolling down from his scalp, and the small of his back was damp. "I'm *fine*."

The usher caught the eye of another member of staff and cleared his throat. "All rise."

"Here we go," Mack murmured.

The proceedings were before three magistrates, two of whom were familiar to Atticus and one—the chief magistrate—who was not. They came into the court, nodded to the others in the room, and sat. The legal advisor to the justices stood and spoke to them; they listened and, when he sat back down, they frowned with a solemnity that spoke to the unusual gravity of the afternoon's work. The solicitor from the Crown Prosecution Service was sitting to Atticus's left, but the desk to the right—usually accommodating the solicitor for the defence—was empty.

The chair looked to the usher. "Bring the defendant up, please."

Mack squeezed Atticus's hand.

Chandler emerged from the doors at the side of the court and was led into the dock. There were two guards with him;

one of the men removed his handcuffs and took up position with his colleague directly behind Chandler. They looked alert and on edge; Atticus couldn't see any prospect of Chandler being able to escape. He looked around the room until he found Atticus; he gave a nod and a smile. Atticus might have disturbed his sangfroid before, but the façade had been put back in place. Atticus looked away and ignored him.

The legal advisor glanced at his papers and then at Chandler. "You don't want legal representation, Mr. Chandler?"

"That's right."

"And you *do* understand the charges against you are serious?"

"I do—and I still don't need a lawyer. Can we get on with it, please?"

"What's your name?"

"Thomas Chandler."

"You are charged with murder. How do you plead?"

"Guilty."

"To all of the charges that have been laid against you?"

"Yes," he said. "To all of them. I killed them all."

The advisor conferred with the justices. The chief justice nodded his understanding and leaned in close to his microphone. "Thank you, Mr. Chandler. As you know, sentencing for charges *this* serious can only be dealt with at the Crown Court. Your case will be sent up to Winchester Crown Court, and the matter will be dealt with there as quickly as possible. We can adjourn now." He turned to the security guards. "Take the defendant down again."

Mack leaned back and sighed. "Done. Thank God for that."

Atticus was glad that she was still holding his hand. It stopped it from shaking.

* * *

Mack and Atticus shuffled out of the courtroom into the lobby outside.

"There are drinks tonight," she said.

"First I've heard about it," he said.

"Just a chance to let off steam. Everyone's been on edge. You should come."

Atticus shook his head. "I'm knackered. I haven't been sleeping well—you know what I'm like when I get my teeth into something."

"Sure?"

"I'm fine. I'll go home and get an early night."

"Want me to come over?"

"When you're pissed, like last time?" He smiled at her. "No thanks. Go home. I'll see you tomorrow."

CHAPTER 99

Atticus waited in the queue to get outside. The lobby was busy as the courtroom emptied, the flow not helped by the journalists who were clustered around on the pavement outside the entrance. Outside broadcasts were being prepared, with reporters recording pieces to camera explaining what had just taken place inside. Passing cars slowed down as the drivers gawped at the scene and, as Atticus slipped through the door, a delivery van braked just in time to stop it from ploughing into the back of a Volvo that was at the end of a queue waiting to get onto the roundabout.

Atticus saw a man he recognised. It was Ian Bird, the reporter from the *Sun* who had broken the story about the Campbell video. Atticus remembered him from the Imber investigation, too; he was a typical hack, single-minded and ruthless and with a questionable interpretation of ethics.

Atticus was about to go over to him when he saw Eddie Thorpe heading in the same direction. He waited and watched as the two men shook hands. Thorpe said something to him, Bird replied and, after shaking hands again, Thorpe moved away.

Atticus squeezed through the crowd to intercept Bird.

"Mr. Bird? Could I have a moment?"

Bird turned to meet him with a smile. "I remember you."

"We spoke during the Imber enquiry."

"Atticus, isn't it? Like in the book."

"That's right—Atticus Priest."

"What can I do for you?"

"It's about the case. I need to know who sent the video to you."

He frowned. "I assume it was Chandler. I can't be sure, but who else would it have been?"

"I don't think it was."

"Why?"

"You know I've been involved with this investigation?"

"Yes," he said. "The word I heard used was 'peripheral.'"

"Who told you that? Murphy?"

"Maybe."

"He would say that."

Bird grinned at him. "Looks like he's hurt your feelings."

Atticus was tempted to tell Bird what Murphy was like, but he realised there was no profit in it. "Let's just say it's in the DCS's best interests to minimise my involvement and maximise his."

Bird chuckled. "Fine. Indulge me, then—why don't you think it was Chandler who sent it?"

"I spoke to him before they brought him up for the hearing, and I asked him. He said that it was, but I think he was lying."

"Why would he lie about something like that?"

"I don't know. That's why I'm asking. How was it sent?"

"Email. We sent it to the nerds at the office. They poked around, but they couldn't get anything useful. They said it was sent through a VPN—the IP address would've been masked." Bird took a beat. "Who do you think sent it if it wasn't him? Who else has even seen it?"

"The police and the *Journal*."

"Can't be the paper. Why would they scoop themselves?"

"I don't know. Maybe someone got paid."

"Not by us."

"What about the police?"

"No. We didn't pay, and we'd *never* pay a police officer."

"Of course not," Atticus said.

Bird gave a shrug. "It's true. Maybe a few years ago, but not now. It's not worth the hassle."

"What about Eddie Thorpe? You were just talking to him."

"Eddie? I used to work with him. We were just catching up."

"You didn't pay him?"

"You're like a dog with a bone," Bird said. "No. It wasn't him, and we did not." He reached into his pocket and took out a business card. "You'll let me know if you ever have anything useful? I scratch your back, you scratch mine?"

Atticus took the card. "You'll be the first person I call."

CHAPTER 100

Atticus went back to the office, sat down at his desk and turned so that he could look at the plug; he stared at it for what felt like an age and knew that his gambit was both uncertain and reckless. He knew he was right about what he had found but had no guarantee that the bait he had laid would be taken. Atticus also knew that if it was taken, then he would be on his own to deal with the consequences.

It was too early to head out to Hawthorne Manor, so he took the dog for a walk in the hope it might help him clear his mind. He started toward the cathedral and then, realising that seeing the spire would have him questioning what had happened on the tower again, he changed course and went to Churchill Gardens instead. Bandit raced across the sodden turf, collected a branch, and then tried to persuade Atticus to wrestle it out of his mouth. He did, eventually, and tossed it as far away as he could manage. The dog sprinted after it, his tail held high.

A discarded page from this week's *Journal* had blown out of a bin and into the river.

Atticus stared at it as it went by.

"You all right, mate?"

It was an old man on a mobility scooter. Atticus was blocking the path.

"Sorry. Million miles away."

Atticus stepped aside so that the man could continue on his way. The newspaper was out of sight now, but he couldn't stop thinking about the idea it had triggered.

He called the dog back to him, attached his lead and set off back to the office.

He dried Bandit's paws, changed his water and biscuits, and went over to his desk. He woke his computer and navigated to the *Journal*'s website. Things were already getting back to normal, with the headlines that usually filled the front page: 'Mini smashes into Pret window in Salisbury'; 'Man breaks arm after challenging burglars'; 'Cat stuck in tree rescued by fire service.'

Atticus wasn't interested in any of those; he clicked to the day of Campbell's death and then went through the headlines and articles, hoping to find something that might lend credence to the idea that was too tantalising to dismiss.

CHAPTER 101

Atticus drove out to Hawthorne Manor and parked his car in the same lay-by as before. The rain had picked up on the drive south, and now, at just after eight in the evening, it was a deluge that hammered against the road and thrummed against the roof of the car; the wipers struggled to keep the windscreen clear.

He switched off the engine and reached back to the rear seat for his waterproofs. He put on the jacket and cursed that he had left the trousers in the office; it didn't matter, he would just have to get wet. He reached back again for his binoculars, taking them out of their case and hanging them around his neck. It was dark, and the rain made it difficult to see too far ahead, but it would be better to have them than not.

Atticus opened the glovebox and took out his torch and lock picks. He had a second phone in the glovebox, too, one with a disposable SIM that he kept in the eventuality that he might need to make a call that wouldn't be traced back to him. He took the phone and put it into his pocket with the picks and the torch.

Atticus took a moment to compose himself.

Atticus felt lonely and exposed, but he was caught up in the mania of the hunt and knew himself well enough to know that it would be impossible for him to walk away without knowing if he was right.

He took a breath, then another, then opened the door and stepped outside. The wind lashed at him, and the rain quickly soaked through his trousers. He ignored both, closing the door behind him and looking for a gap in the hedge so that he could approach the house away from the track and without being seen.

PART 7

Sunday

CHAPTER 102

Atticus raised the binoculars to his eyes and scanned the house again. The windows were all dark, and the door that had been damaged when Chandler had forced his way inside had been protected with sheets of plywood. The place looked empty.

He took a moment to choose the best approach and, after checking that there was no one who might see him, he hurried to the French doors that gave access to the garden from the drawing room. The doors were enormous—nearly three metres tall—with leaded windows. The curtains were drawn, so Atticus couldn't see inside, but, like the rest of the house, there was no suggestion that anyone was there. Atticus knelt and examined the lock: it was an old mortise with a brass doorknob above the keyhole. He put on his gloves and quickly picked it. He turned the handle, opened the door and, after pausing for a moment to listen, slipped between the curtains and into the drawing room.

Everything was dark. He could remember the layout of the house from his previous visit and, using his torch to light the way, he passed through the entrance hall and the library and then the dining hall. He took the stairs to the first floor and went to the master bedroom. The bloodstain on the carpet was still there, and the dishevelled bed had not been made. The curtains had been closed. Atticus opened them an inch and then went over to the bedside table and switched on the lamp. He went back outside to the corridor and switched on the lights there, too. He looked around for another minute, turned on a third light—this one in the family bathroom—and then went back down the stairs.

His phone buzzed with a message as he was halfway down. He stopped and saw it was from Mack.

>> *Summers died tonight. Thought you should know.*

He stared at the message, imagining for a moment how she would react if he had told her how apt it was that she had sent that message now, given where he was.

He typed a reply.

>> *Anything from the lab?*

The phone indicated she was typing.

>> *Nothing. Sorry. I'll chase tomorrow.*

There was a pause, then another message.

>> *Come over?*

Atticus stared at the screen. She had likely just returned home after the celebratory drinks. She was probably the worse for drink and would—probably—collapse into bed. He replied he was tired, he needed to sleep, and that he would see her tomorrow. He switched the phone off and dropped it back into his pocket.

He went to the drawing room, switched off the torch and let himself out, closing the doors behind him and using his picks to secure the lock. He waited by the wall, allowing his eyes to adjust to the darkness, and then ran back into the shelter of the trees. He settled back into place, and shivering in his sodden clothes, he watched.

CHAPTER 103

It was four in the morning, and Atticus had been sheltering in the cover of the trees for hours. The rain was coming down harder than ever, and, although the stout boughs overhead offered some protection, their leaves were gone, and Atticus had quickly been soaked through. He shivered, trying hard to ignore the impulse to go home and have a shower. Or, he thought, he could go and have a shower at Mack's. Either option would be a vast improvement on staying out here on what was increasingly looking like a waste of time.

He had started to doubt himself. Perhaps his ruse had been transparent? The voicemail to Mack that he had pretended to leave had tested his acting ability to its limits: he had spoken of his outrage that Summers was being discharged and his frustration that the evidence they had found in the chapel had been deemed inadmissible due to his flouting of the law. He had reported back the news that he *said* he had received: Summers was returning home tonight, and the fear was that he would be leaving the country before a more successful case could be made against him.

THE RED ROOM

It wasn't true, of course, but he knew that it would be tempting.

But now he wondered: had he gone too far?

He looked up at the lights in the upstairs windows and doubted that strategy, too. They would've been switched off by now. Surely anyone watching would have realised that they had been left on to foster the impression that someone was home.

Lightning crackled across the sky, and thunder boomed a moment later. Atticus looked at his watch and started to entertain the thought of leaving. The prospect of warmth—a warm shower and a warm bed—was attractive. It was only his stubborn refusal to accept that he was wrong that had kept him here, but the wasted hours that had passed had eroded that.

The storm grew stronger, and the crash of the rain hammering down ever harder almost—but not quite—obscured the noise of footsteps on gravel.

Atticus held his breath and froze.

He reached for the binoculars but left them where they were; he could see the person on the way to the door with his naked eyes. Visibility was limited by the rain, but he could see that the figure was dressed in black with a black backpack and a black cap pulled all the way down over the face so that the brim offered cover from the rain. Atticus reached up slowly and wiped the water from his eyes with the back of his hand. He blinked, trying—and failing—to make out anything else that might be useful.

He had given thought to what he would do if he was fortunate enough to find himself in this position and, despite the urge to step out and stop whoever it was, he decided that it made better sense to stick to his plan. He wanted more than just a confrontation; he wanted answers to all his questions.

The person went to the damaged door, ignored it and continued to the main door that led into the entrance hall. They stopped at an uncovered window, cupped a hand against the glass and peered into the darkened room inside. They moved on, edging around the building until they reached the door. Atticus was still holding his breath; the figure, facing away from him, tried the handle with a gloved hand. It was locked. They moved on, continuing around the house until they reached the French doors that Atticus had used. He had to change position a little to be able to watch, and, as he lowered himself behind a rhododendron bush, Atticus heard breaking glass.

Lightning crackled overhead; the flash showed the newly opened door and a glimpse of the figure passing inside. A torch was switched on. Atticus could see the glow of the beam against the thin curtains, the light moving into the entrance hall and leaking out through the single uncovered window next to the cloakroom.

Atticus crept forward, looking for a better place to hide where he could be closer to the open door. He risked stepping out of cover and, keeping low, he went to another collection of well-kept shrubs. There was less cover here, and he knew there was a chance that he would be seen when the person emerged outside again; on the other hand, he was close enough now that he ought to be able to get a better look at them.

Atticus looked at his watch: the person had been inside for five minutes. It must have been obvious: the house was empty.

Why were they taking so long?

Thunder rolled over the countryside again.

THE RED ROOM

The door was pushed open, and the person stepped outside.
Veins of lightning lit up the sky.
The person turned and looked up.
The flash was brief, but enough.
Atticus got a good look at her face.
He had been right.
It was Nina Parsons.

CHAPTER 104

Nina put up her hood, rested her torch on the ground and closed the door. She paused for a moment, looking—and listening—for anything that might suggest that she was not alone. Atticus held his breath. She turned her head so that she was looking right at the bushes behind which he was hiding, then glanced away again; she picked up the torch and walked away.

Atticus waited for thirty seconds, ensuring that there was enough distance between them that he would be able to hide his pursuit. Nina went north, past the chapel and into the fields behind it, then continued in that direction until she reached the tree line that separated the first field from the even larger field behind it. The ground was treacherous from the days of steady rain; it was muddy in most places, occasionally deepening to a quagmire that had to be skirted for fear of getting stuck in the middle. Atticus stayed well back, grateful that Nina was herself staying close to the boundaries of the fields. It would have been difficult to stay hidden if she had gone directly across the field; even with the rain, a glimpse back would have meant that his pursuit would have been obvious. But here, close to the boundary, there was enough vegetation to break up the line of his silhouette.

Nina passed through the trees and continued to follow the southern boundary of the next field. The going was tough and the route challenging; it took Nina twenty minutes to reach a large tract of trees, another twenty to circumvent it, and another fifteen to cross a final field to the road that ran north to south. This final field was the most open yet, and Atticus had no choice but to wait by the hedge that divided the previous field from this one, which gave Nina the chance to stretch out her lead a little more. He dared not wait too long, though, and, fearing that she might well have left a vehicle in the road, he hurried after her.

He saw the lights of a car glowing through the hedge when he still had a quarter of the distance to cover. He picked up speed, ignoring his sodden feet and his wet, mud-splattered legs, trying to plot a course across the field that combined the soundest footing and shortest distance. He slipped and fell, slapping into the mud face first, but, desperate with the fear that the car would leave and he would lose his chance to test his hypothesis, he plunged his hands into the slop all the way up to his wrists, shoved himself upright, found his footing again and staggered on.

He reached the hedge and found a spot that was low enough for him to look over. There was a one-lane track road beyond, and a passing space opposite with a metal five-bar gate behind it. A car—an old Volvo Estate—was pulling away.

Atticus wiped the rain from his eyes and stared at the back of the car.

The numberplate was muddied, too, but he thought he could make it out.

YKN 207X.

The car picked up speed, turned into the gentle right-hand bend and disappeared. He saw the glow of the taillights for a moment longer until, they, too, passed out of sight.

He took out his phone, opened his notes and found the details of the officers at the nick that he had noted down before he left. He found the number of the PNC Bureau and called it. The operator picked up on the second ring.

"This is Sergeant Neil Blyford," Atticus said. "Oscar November nine-two-three-four from Bourne Hill in Salisbury. Could you PNC a vehicle for me, please?"

"Go ahead, nine-two-three-four."

"Yankee Kilo November two-zero-seven X-Ray. Code two."

"Reason for request?"

"Erratic driving. I'm going to pull it over."

Code two indicated a moving vehicle that had not yet been stopped. Atticus knew that the operator had asked for his reason for making his request so that the right box could be ticked. He didn't expect any follow-up questions, and none came.

"Reading back, nine-two-three-four: Yankee Kilo November two-zero-seven X-Ray. That right?"

"That's it."

"One minute, please."

Atticus walked along the raised verge until he found the gap in the hedge that Nina had used to get onto the road.

"Nine-two-three-four, I have your details for you. The car is registered to an Elizabeth Chandler."

"Address?"

"Priory Farmhouse, Priory Lane, Britford."

"Thank you."

Atticus ended the call and opened his map. It was twelve miles to Britford from here, but the pursuit across the fields had left him two miles away from the spot where he had left his car. He ought to be able to get to it in thirty minutes if he walked briskly, and then it would be another thirty to drive to Britford.

He turned to the south and started walking.

CHAPTER 105

It was early in the morning, and the roads were empty. Atticus followed the A354 back toward Salisbury, continuing through Coombe Bissett until he could see the red warning light at the tip of the cathedral's spire shining out over the fields. The road was long and straight for the mile before it reached the city, and Atticus had to fight back the urge to speed up. He was tense with nervous energy and the anticipation of what the next hour might bring, and there was no point in risking an accident or the attention of the police when there was still so much to learn.

He turned off toward the hospital, continued onto the A338 and then took the left turn and drove into the tiny village of Britford. He stopped and checked his map: Priory Lane was an unadopted dirt track that ran down to the Avon. He located the opening of the track—just off the village green—switched off the engine and got out of the car. He grabbed his phone and continued on foot, checking the map as he negotiated the deep puddles of water that stretched across the surface of the road. The track continued into the countryside before it split at a junction: the branch to the right ended at a trout fishery, and the branch to the left headed north to the farm at which the Volvo was registered. The track terminated at those two points; the Avon cut around them as it looped from east to south, forming a border with no obvious way to get across the water to Alderbury on the opposite bank.

There were two mailboxes attached to a post that had been driven into the ground at the junction. One of them was labelled TROUT FARM and the other CHANDLER. Atticus opened the second one, reached a hand inside and withdrew a collection of letters. He shone the light of his torch down on the envelopes and flipped through them: most of them were marketing circulars, but there was one that looked official. He opened it and took out a letter from British Gas. He read it: the letter confirmed that the account held in the name of Elizabeth Chandler had been closed by reason of the account holder's death and that there was nothing left to pay.

He put the letter in his pocket, replaced the circulars in the mailbox and switched off the torch. He put it in his pocket and continued along the right-hand track. It cut through fields that were used to graze cattle and sheep, dotted with poles carrying telephone lines and fibre to the farm buildings. A chalk stream ran to the right, and the water bubbled and burbled as it poured over and around stones and branches that disturbed the flow. He heard the scream of a fox and saw a flash of movement as the animal burst out from the hedgerow behind him and scurried away; a cow lowed; somewhere overhead an owl screeched.

It took him five minutes to reach the farm. He stopped and, shielding his phone behind the trunk of an old tree, checked the map. The farm was arranged on either side of the track. There was a series of seven large outbuildings to the left and the farmhouse itself on the right. The farm was bracketed by fields with the Avon at its eastern boundary, a hundred yards away.

The map made it worryingly clear: Atticus was alone, more than a mile away from the nearest property.

It didn't matter.

He wasn't about to turn back now.

CHAPTER 106

Atticus edged around the side of the first barn and saw that a space had been formed between the buildings. The track continued to the river with the farmhouse to the left. The space itself was empty save for a mud-spattered Volvo Estate.

He crept over to it and used it to shelter from anyone who might be approaching from the nearby buildings. He could hear a ticking from the exhaust; the hot gas had made the metal expand and, now that it was cooling again, it was contracting.

Atticus didn't need to check the numberplate to know that the car was the one that Nina had used to leave Hawthorne Manor.

He slipped around to the side and tried the door. It was unlocked. The backpack that Nina had been wearing at the house had been left on the passenger seat. Atticus reached in, undid the clasps, opened it and looked inside. There was a large knife with a serrated blade and, beneath that, a small plastic container. He opened the lid and looked inside: there were three syringes—their points sheathed in plastic nipples—and a glass bottle with a silicone sleeve. He took out his phone and, hiding behind the car, switched on his flashlight. The label on the bottle identified the contents as Anesketin, and, below that, 'Solution for injection for dogs, cats and horses.'

Atticus heard a sound—a door squeaking on rusty hinges—somewhere to his right, most likely from the farmhouse. He switched off the light and stayed behind the Volvo. He heard footsteps and saw the beam of a torch, the yellow light shining through the windows of the vehicle. Atticus shuffled around the vehicle so that he could glimpse around it. Nina had crossed into the yard and was walking toward the brick shed that was between the two largest barns. Atticus watched as she turned a key in the lock and opened the door.

Atticus took out the burner phone, powered it up and dialled 999.

"Hello, 999. Which service do you need?"

"Police," he whispered.

"I'll connect you now."

The call was transferred.

"Police," the handler said. "What's your emergency?"

He kept his voice low. "I'm being burgled."

"Okay—just confirming, you say you're being burgled now?"

"*Right* now. A man just forced his way into my house."

"What's your address?"

"Priory Farm, Priory Lane, Britford."

"I've dispatched a car now. Are you in immediate danger?"

Atticus killed the call and powered the phone down. He closed his eyes and, sweating despite the frigid weather, left his hiding spot and walked toward the brick shed.

CHAPTER 107

The building appeared to be some sort of storage shed. Atticus edged up to the corner and peeped around it: the door was open, and light from inside was spilling out, glistening in the puddles that had gathered in the yard. Atticus turned around the corner of the shed and stepped over to the open door. He looked inside. The shed had been equipped with racks of metal shelving along the two long walls. Each rack had three shelves, and the shelves were filled with videotapes. There was a table in the middle of the shed with a pile of empty Jiffy bags on it.

Nina stood at the table with her back to him. She was sealing a cassette into a Jiffy bag.

"Nina."

She turned, saw him and swore.

"Take it easy."

She chuckled bitterly. "You clever, *clever* bastard. You tricked me."

"I was hoping I might be wrong."

She finished sealing the bag and set it down on the table, then turned fully to face him. "You found it, then?"

"Yesterday. You left it the second time you came to the office—right? When you asked me to make you a coffee? The first visit was to scope it all out, find somewhere to leave it, and the second visit was to fit it."

"I was going to come back and take it away, but I had to wait—I told you I was going abroad."

"You did, and I checked that out. I don't know why I called you Nina—it's Zoë, isn't it? Lieutenant Zoë Chandler. You're seconded to the Royal Welsh from the Royal Army Veterinary Corps, just rotated back from Estonia, won't be sent out again for another six months."

"Didn't think you'd go to the trouble of checking."

"They said they didn't have a Nina Parsons. I sent them a still from the security camera in the alley beneath my office, and they found you from that."

"How did you work it out? What gave it away?"

"Your brother's attack on Summers. If you'd waited a month, I doubt it would've caught my attention. But you went after him the *same day* I worked out that he had something to do with the tape. And the thing is, I didn't tell anyone apart from DCI Jones, and I know she kept it to herself. I couldn't understand how you got to him so soon. I'd almost persuaded myself it was just one of those things. *Almost.* There was something that stuck in the back of my mind about you, and then, when you ghosted me… well, I checked. I spoke to Wintringham. I told him what you'd said, and he nearly had a heart attack."

She chuckled. "Must have been uncomfortable."

"It was in front of his wife, so yes… it was. I knew you'd used me then; I just had to find out how you'd done it. I went back to the office and found the bug and..." He shrugged. "I thought it was worth a try to see if I could get you to break cover."

She clapped her hands in sardonic applause. "I'm *actually* impressed this time. I shouldn't have made fun of you. That was clever—using it against me. I fell for it. Summers was the worst of them. I thought tonight was the only chance I'd have to get to him."

"If it's any consolation, it doesn't matter. He's dead."

"Really?"

"He died tonight."

She gave a brief nod. "Whatever. I hope he suffered."

Atticus looked around the room for any sign of a weapon that Zoë could use against him. There was a tape dispenser with a serrated edge on the table, but, save that, there wasn't anything obvious.

"Who knows about your little trap?" she asked him. "Your girlfriend?"

"She doesn't know I'm here. No one does."

"That's risky."

"I wanted us to talk. There're a few things I'd like to understand."

"About me and Thomas?"

"That'd be a good place to start. He's older than you?"

She nodded. "A year."

"He told us he didn't have any relations."

She shrugged. "You didn't think he'd be honest about everything, did you?"

"Is that what you decided—if either of you got caught, that person would confess to everything to protect the other?"

"Something like that. What did he tell you?"

"That he had a tough childhood. That he was in care."

"*That's* true. We both were. Dad was a thug, and Mum was a prostitute. She died—overdose—and we were taken away when it was obvious that he didn't give a shit about us. They sent us to a family in Salisbury."

"And how was that?"

"Better. They cared for us. Gave us a chance to make a fresh start. Excellent school, nice holidays on the coast. Didn't last, though. My stepmum and stepdad split up, and Mum had to work two jobs just to keep food on the table. She sent us to Grosvenor House in the evenings so we had something to do, and that's when we met Burns. And you know what happened after that."

He gestured to the tapes. "Are you on any of them?"

"With Kajetan and Hartnett and a handful of others."

"And your brother was on the tape with Campbell."

She nodded. "Why'd you think we started with those three?"

"Who killed them?"

"What did Thomas say?"

"He said he did."

She nodded. "There you go, then."

"But you were involved, too. I saw the ketamine in your bag. Is that from work?"

She nodded. "We were a team. I did the planning, and he went after them."

"I'm sorry about your stepmum," Atticus said. "When did she die?"

"How do you know that?"

Atticus reached into his pocket and took out the letter. He held it up.

"Last year," she said. "I've been slow to shut the accounts down."

"And this was her place?"

"Yes," she said. "How did you find it? You didn't follow tonight."

"I saw you leave in the car and checked the numberplate. It's still registered to her at this address."

"Shit," she said. "DVLA. I forgot."

"You and your brother were abused at the same time?"

She shook her head. "He was first—I was a year after. We didn't know it had happened to us both until we saw Alf Burns in the papers. Thomas told me first, and then I told him."

"And you did nothing until your mum died?"

"Didn't want her to know. She would have been distraught. It would've been pointless and cruel."

Atticus noticed she looked over his shoulder and to the left, back in the house's direction.

"Is that your dad?"

She clenched her fists.

"Eddie?" Atticus called out. "Come inside—you'll get soaked."

He took a quarter-turn so that he could look back as Eddie Thorpe stepped into view.

He had a large kitchen knife in his right hand.

CHAPTER 108

Atticus's mouth was bone dry, but he did his best to ignore it. "I'm right, then—you're Zoë's stepdad?"

"Well done."

Atticus looked to Zoë. "And Chandler is your stepmother's name."

She nodded. "Thomas and I took it when they divorced."

Thorpe stepped closer, the knife held in a steady grip. "How'd you find us?"

"He tricked me," Zoë said. "He found the bug and set a trap. We walked right into it, and he followed us here."

Atticus looked back to Thorpe, trying to ignore the knife. "Were you driving tonight?"

He didn't answer.

"And you drove Thomas that night, too? Actually, you don't need to answer—I know you did. I spoke to him earlier, and he tried to persuade me that he walked. He obviously didn't do that."

Thorpe glanced over at Zoë. "I *told* you we should never have involved him, and *now* look where we are."

"It's happened," Zoë said. "No point worrying about it now."

"Come on, Eddie," Atticus said. "Don't blame them. You made mistakes, too. Look at how you delivered the Campbell tape. There's a camera over the road from the *Journal*. Carly said someone must've dropped it off by hand, but, when we checked it, no one went into the office in the only times it could've been left. No one apart from you, her and Alice, and it obviously wasn't either of them."

Thorpe held up the knife. "You talk a good game for someone neck deep in shit."

Atticus was frightened, but he found that talking—and his usual showboating—helped. "Who decided that going to the *Sun* was a good idea?"

Thorpe glared at him.

"Well, it wasn't. You worked at the *Sun*—I checked your LinkedIn profile. Did you know Ian Bird endorsed you?"

Thorpe didn't answer.

"You sent it so he'd think it was from Jack."

"Things were going too slowly," Thorpe muttered. "I wanted to run the still from the video, but my boss said I couldn't. He was so *timid*. I tried and tried, but it was like banging my head against the wall—'we can't prejudice the police enquiry,' 'we need to run it by the police first,' 'we don't want to do anything that puts them under pressure.' It was bullshit."

"But the *Sun* would print it?"

"Yes, they'd see how important it was, and they'd have the balls to run it. We needed to make it as big a story as we could as fast as we could so we could put the fear of God into those bastards that they might be next."

"I spoke to Alice," Atticus said. "She told me you were pushing for the picture to be run. You take that, add the fact that it had to be one of the three of you who left the video at the office, and it all points to you. And there was another thing, too. Getting up to the tower through the attic would have taken some planning. I knew the cathedral was offering tours, so I had the police check out who was on them. There was no one interesting, but then I wondered if it might have been the kind of local interest piece that the *Journal* would've run. And it was. You wrote it. David Campbell took you up there himself."

Thorpe brandished the knife. "I didn't know it'd be him who showed me. It was all I could manage not to do him there and then."

"But you didn't. You've been cleverer than that."

"Why did you come out here if you knew all that?"

"I had to be sure I was right. Curiosity is one of my many weaknesses."

Thorpe turned to his stepdaughter. "Can you go and put the kettle on?"

"No, Dad."

"Please—I don't want you to have to watch this."

"We're not going to hurt him."

"What choice do we have?" Thorpe stabbed the knife in Atticus's direction. "Haven't you been listening? He knows *everything*."

She breathed out. "So maybe it's over. We knew they'd figure it out eventually."

"*No*, Zoë," he snapped. "You've got the rest of your life ahead of you. I'm not having you spend it in prison like Thomas. Not after what you've been through."

Eddie took a step toward Atticus.

"*Dad.*"

Atticus held up a hand. "One more thing you need to think about. You smoke, don't you? Your fingers are stained with nicotine, and the office stank of it."

"So?"

"You were careless when you called me from the car park. You dropped a cigarette. The police are testing it for DNA. You ever done anything that'd mean your DNA is on file?" Thorpe clenched his teeth, and Atticus knew that he had. "What are you going to do when there's a match?"

It was a gamble. Atticus hadn't had the results from the lab yet and, if he was wrong about it being Eddie who made the call, there was a chance that Thorpe would call his bluff. The tapes on the racks behind Zoë were all the evidence that Atticus needed to know that they weren't finished with the work that they had started. Thorpe might decide that Atticus's murder would be balanced out by the additional justice that they would be able to mete out.

Atticus heard a siren from outside. Thorpe and Zoë heard it, too.

"I called the police fifteen minutes ago," Atticus said.

Thorpe clenched his jaw.

"I didn't have a choice—this is the only way. We agree on everything apart from what justice means. Murdering those men makes you as bad as them." He nodded at the shelves. "I'll make sure they're punished, but it'll be done the right way. There'll be an enquiry; they'll be prosecuted; they'll be sent to prison."

Zoë grabbed Thorpe's arm. "Dad," she urged, "let's go. It's done." She held up the Jiffy bag that she had just sealed. "We've just got this one left."

He nodded, and the two of them went into the yard and headed left, following the track east toward the river. Atticus watched them as they were absorbed by the rain and the dark and wondered if he had done the right thing.

The siren was louder now and, as he turned in the direction that he had arrived from, he could see red and blue pulsing through the branches of the trees that lined the track. He left the door to the shed open and the light on, making sure that it was impossible that the officers who were on their way to the farm could miss it. They would investigate and see the tapes inside. The enquiry was a *cause célèbre*, and it was unthinkable that they wouldn't understand the significance of their find. They would see that the owner of the property had been the wife of Eddie Thorpe, and from there, it would be easy to join the dots.

Atticus made his way between the shed and the barn and clambered over the post-and-rail fence that formed the boundary of the paddock that he had seen on his way to the farm. He crouched down behind the hedge as the patrol car bumped and splashed through the potholes, waiting until it was out of sight behind the outbuildings before picking a way through the mud and heading back to the spot where he had left his car.

EPILOGUE

Francine Patterson woke up with the absolute certainty that she was about to be sick. She slid out of bed, stumbled to the bathroom and sank to her knees, holding her hair out of her face as she vomited into the toilet. She got unsteadily back to her feet, flushed, rinsed her mouth at the sink, turned to go back into the bedroom and stopped in the doorway. Someone else was in her bed. He was face down, but the glow from the streetlamp outside the window fell through a crack in the curtains and washed over his face. It was Robbie Best. The sheets had fallen to reveal a Celtic band tattooed around his bicep, and he was snoring loudly.

Francine bit her lip as she recalled the night's festivities. They had started in the Royal George and then crossed town for a lock-in at the Huntsman. They had gone somewhere after that, too, she thought, although she couldn't put her finger on the details for the life of her. She remembered Robbie walking her back and inviting him to come inside.

It had been a raucous night. They had all been wired tight during the investigation, and all that pressure and stress had been released now that it had come to an end. Francine had kept herself busy to help stop her thinking about Chandler and how he had involved her in his scheme. She had spent time with the girl they had found beneath the cottage in Summers's property, gently extracting her story from her. Maria had explained over the course of several gentle sessions that she had fled to Poland after the invasion started and had been offered a room in a house in Salisbury by a man she later identified as Doyle. She had been taken to Summers's house and told that, unless she took part in the films that they produced there, she would be hurt. Her compliance had been won with fear and then drugs, and the doctor had found evidence of barbiturates in her blood. Social Services were involved now, and she had been found a safe place to live while efforts were made with the Ukrainian embassy in London to find her brother.

Francine crept back around the bed and lowered herself onto the mattress, keen not to wake Robbie. She didn't know what she would say to him and, although there would be no way of avoiding it, she would rather do it in the morning when her head wasn't pounding quite so much.

She looked over at the bedside clock, saw that it was just after four, and closed her eyes again. She tried to work out how she felt about what had happened. Robbie was senior to her— a DI to a DC—and ten years older, too. But she knew he had always fancied her and, if she was honest, she had found him attractive, too. She knew she had had too much to drink last night, but the alcohol had only made it easier to do something that she would have liked to have done anyway. Her friend Jules had texted her last night with the ribald advice that 'the best way to get over someone is to get under someone.' Robbie had been flirting with her all night, was a consenting adult able to make his own choices, and, as some of the memories emerged from the fog that the drink had left behind, Francine remembered they had both had fun.

Where was the harm in that?

She held her breath as Robbie stopped snoring. He turned over, grunted, and reached out an arm and draped it over her. She snuggled into him, enjoying his warmth, and allowed herself to fall into sleep once again.

* * *

Atticus went back to the office, collected the dog and walked across the city to Mack's place in Harnham. It was an hour before dawn, and the streets were quiet. Atticus tried not to think about what had happened that night, but it was impossible. He didn't know how long it would take the police to work out what had happened at the farm and start to look for Thorpe. It wouldn't be long. There would be plenty of forensic evidence to confirm that both stepfather and daughter—and, presumably, stepson—had been at the property. Atticus doubted that they would need his help, but, if they did, he would be able to provide judicious and anonymous hints to nudge them in the right direction.

It was coming up to five when they arrived at the house. Atticus opened the lockbox, took out the key and unlocked the door. Bandit would normally have barrelled straight up the stairs in search of Mack, but, perhaps aware that it was early, he went into the front room and curled up on the sofa. Atticus took the blanket that Mack used to keep warm when she was watching television and covered the dog with it.

He climbed the stairs, undressed in the bathroom and left his clothes on the floor. They were damp and dirty, but he was bone-tired, and they could wait until tomorrow. He went through into the bedroom and sat down on the edge of the bed.

Mack stirred. "Hello," she mumbled, her voice thick with sleep.

"Do you remember what you asked me when we had lunch in the square?"

"Mmm."

"About why I haven't been able to let this go? About Burns and what happened at Imber?"

She started to reply, then drew in a breath, rolled over and exhaled. Atticus waited a moment, listening as her breathing slowed and became more rhythmic, the soft sound of the air passing through her slightly parted lips.

"Don't worry," he whispered. "We can talk about it another time."

He lay down beside her and closed his eyes. He heard a car driving by as he waited for sleep to come.

* * *

Mack awoke to the buzzing of her phone's alarm. She had left it on the bedstand next to her glass of water, and, as she blearily reached out for it, she nudged the glass and sent it tumbling onto the floor. She cursed under her breath, sat up and carefully slid her feet down onto the now-soaked carpet. Atticus was on the other side of the bed, the sound of his breathing a quiet murmur that was audible over the engine of a car as it ran along the street outside the house. She looked at the clock: it was seven.

THE RED ROOM

She felt a weight at the end of the bed and, when she looked down, saw that Bandit was curled up between their feet. He opened a single eye and glanced up at her, then closed it and, with a sigh of contentment, went back to sleep. Mack remembered: Atticus had come around earlier that morning and must have brought the dog with him. She had been asleep and had probably still been drunk after the drinks to celebrate the end of the enquiry had become raucous. She had a headache now and needed to wash down a couple of Nurofen with a pint of cold water.

Mack got up and went into the bathroom, switched on the light above the mirror and stared at her reflection. She felt as if she had aged over the course of the last year, but it wasn't evident in her face. Her skin was still good, and save the odd wrinkle here and there, she was confident that she could pass for a woman a good few years younger than she really was. She thought of Atticus and was reminded of the age difference between them. She had been his boss, and she had always wondered how much of that had led to his initial attraction to her. She had joked about it with him, hoping to prompt him into explaining why he wanted to be with her, but he'd always been obtuse when it came to identifying personal feelings and emotions or those of the people close to him. Mack had come to accept the fact that he wanted to be with her and that she, despite the damage that it had done to her family, wanted to be with him.

She showered, dried herself off and put on her dressing gown.

Atticus had left his clothes in a pile on the floor. She picked them up and noticed that they were filthy: his trousers, in particular, were damp and caked in dried mud.

She bundled the clothes up, dumped them into her washing bin and took it and her phone downstairs. She opened the washing machine and checked the pockets of the trousers before putting them in. His wallet was there, together with two items that she hadn't expected: a mobile phone that she didn't recognise and a leather roll-up pouch, that, when she undid the clasp and opened it, revealed a set of lock picks. She put the phone on the counter and ran her finger over the picks. The phone was curious enough, but she wasn't worried about it; some might see a second phone as proof of a cheating partner, but Atticus was a bad liar, and Mack knew that she would have seen infidelity in him without needing evidence.

It was the picks that she wasn't sure about.

She rolled the pouch up again and weighed it in her hand. She didn't think he kept it with him all the time; it was bulky, and she would have noticed.

So why was it in his pocket last night?

She put it on the counter next to the phone, tipped washing powder and fabric softener into the machine's tray and started the program. She knew that there were things that he didn't tell her about, and that was fine. There were things in *her* life that she kept to *herself*, and she knew that that was usual in any relationship. The difficulty she had was when Atticus ignored her clear instructions about matters that could have an impact on her professionally. She knew that he had only a passing relationship with the rules of procedure that governed the police and had seen more than once how he was prepared to break the law when he thought it would bring him closer to answering a question that had been vexing him. She had tried to knock sense into his head, warning him that he would eventually find himself in trouble that he couldn't talk his way out of, and that, when that happened, he might end up dragging her down with him.

She tapped a finger on the pouch and then turned her back to it and went into the kitchen, where she took the kettle and filled it at the sink. She wondered whether she should take the picks upstairs and confront him about it but decided to leave it where it was and give him a chance to volunteer an explanation.

Her own phone rang as the kettle boiled. It was Mike Lewis.

"Morning, boss."

"Morning, Mike. What's up?"

"We had something weird last night, and I thought you ought to know before you got into the nick."

She took a mug from the cupboard and reached for the coffee. "Go on."

"Two things, really. Dave and Phil responded to a 999 about a burglary in the early hours. It was in Britford, this empty farmhouse at the end of the track. Thing is, when they got there, it looked like a crank call."

"Right. So?"

"They had a look around. One of the barns was open, and a light had been left on. They went inside and found videos. *Lots* of them."

Mack's stomach fell. "Like…"

"Like the same as the ones we've been looking at."

Mack leaned back against the counter. "Shit."

"That's not all of it. We had a walk-in at the nick in Andover an hour ago. You remember Eddie Thorpe."

"Eddie Thorpe from the *Journal*?"

"Yes. He turns up and says that he wants to speak to an officer and, when he does, he says that Thomas Chandler is his stepson and that the two of them were working together."

"*What?*"

"I know. He says the place in Britford belonged to his ex-wife before she died, and they'd been using it. Thorpe said he decided to hand himself in after we got Chandler."

"And he did it the same night we find the videos?"

"I know. It's weird. Maybe he called about the burglary himself?"

She looked at the burner phone and the lock picks and thought about Atticus's filthy clothes and shook her head.

"Boss?"

"We'll find out when we speak to him. Where's Murphy?"

"Went to London yesterday. Should I let him know?"

"Tell Beckton. He can do it."

"What about you, boss?"

"Call Andover and tell them to bring Thorpe back to Bourne Hill. I'll get dressed and get over there. Give me thirty minutes."

* * *

Alice had been in the office since six. The murders had shaken the city, and the revelation that Thomas Chandler had been charged had acted as a balm to frayed nerves. It had also generated a huge amount of interest, and, with connections to the local police and criminal justice community that national reporters couldn't match, she had found herself in high demand. She had been interviewed for half a dozen different newspapers, and her profile had been included on websites with traffic that made the *Journal*'s look puny by comparison. It was the fulfilment of her childhood ambitions, but there had been no time to sit down and savour any of it. She had been working twelve hours a day all week, and now, with the case closed and the media circus moving on to the next sensation, she had her work to consider. Eddie had cleared ten pages of the new edition for the story, and Alice had agreed to take on most of the writing herself.

She went into the kitchen, filled the kettle, and set it to boil.

"I'll have one if you're brewing up."

She turned: it was James Ward, the freelance photographer they used when they needed something for the paper. "You're early."

"I took a million snaps last week, and I need to go through them. Thought I might as well come and get started. Have you seen your email?"

"Not yet. Why?"

"There's one from Andy at Storyville. He sounds pleased—says we've had the best week of revenue for years."

Storyville was the publishing company that owned the *Journal*. They all knew that they had been one of the worst-performing papers on the roster and had been living in fear that they would be merged with another local and then downsized.

"And remember that Eddie's been asking for the cash for me to go full time? Andy says he's going to okay it."

"That's great."

"It's good timing," Ward said. "Suzy's pregnant again."

"Congratulations."

Ward opened the cupboard, took out two mugs and a jar of instant coffee. He unscrewed the lid and spooned two scoops into each mug. "What are you doing?"

"Finishing the profile on Chandler."

"Can't be easy."

"Why?"

"Because he's so *average*."

"*So* average. And you know what's weird? The banality of it all. You wouldn't look twice at him if he went by on the street, but he killed four people, and he would've kept killing if he hadn't been caught."

Alice heard footsteps coming up the staircase from the ground floor and, as she poured water into the first mug, Carly burst through the door. Her eyes were wide, and the blood had drained from her face.

Ward turned to her. "Are you all right?"

Carly held up her hands as she tried to regain her breath. "You will not believe this. I went out to my car this morning, and this was on the bonnet."

She held up a package.

Alice put on a pair of disposable gloves that she had bought from Boots and took the package from Carly. She took the end of the flap and peeled it back, careful to make sure that nothing was ripped, then tipped the package up so that the cassette box inside could slide out onto the desk. She picked up the box and turned it over so that they could see the label that had been slipped down the spine.

Mason, Max / 3 February

Ward swore.

Alice stared at the box with an open mouth.

GET EXCLUSIVE MARK DAWSON MATERIAL

Building a relationship with my readers is the very best thing about writing. Join my Reader Club for information on new Atticus Priest books and deals plus occasional free content from all of my series.

Sign up at my website: **www.markjdawson.com**

"Max *Mason*?" Carly said.

"That's what it says."

"No way. I mean—*no* way. Not him. It can't be."

"Jesus," Ward said. "What are you going to do with that?"

Alice put the box on the desk. "Where's Eddie? I need to speak to him."